LANDSMAN

Peter Charles Melman

LANDSMAN

a novel

COUNTERPOINT
A Member of the Perseus Books Group
New York

AUTHOR'S NOTE

Landsman is a work of fiction. Although many of its characters and events are based in historical fact, liberties have been taken for the sake of narrative.

Portions of this book appeared previously in *Jeopardy Magazine, Connecticut Review, and Mississippi Review*

Copyright 2007 by Peter Charles Melman
Published by Counterpoint Press,
A Member of the Perseus Books Group

Books published by Counterpoint are available at special discounts for bulk purchases in the United States by corporations, institutions, and other organizations. For more information, please contact the Special Markets Department at the Perseus Books Group, 11 Cambridge Center, Cambridge MA 02142, or call (617) 252–5298 or (800) 255–1514, or e-mail special.markets@perseusbooks.com.

Designed by Brent Wilcox

Library of Congress Cataloging-in-Publication Data
Melman, Peter Charles, 1971–
    Landsman : a novel / Peter Charles Melman.
        p.   cm.
    ISBN-13: 978-1-58243-367-7 (alk. paper)
    ISBN-10: 1-58243-367-4 (alk. paper)
    [1. Louisiana—History—Civil War, 1861–1865—Fiction.   2. Jews—United States—Fiction.]   I. Title.
PS3613.E4486L36 2006
813'.6—dc22

                                                                                          2006033305

10 9 8 7 6 5 4 3 2 1

landsman. (lăndz′men) –n. One who lives and works on land.

landsman. (länts′mən) –n. A fellow Jew who comes from the same district or town, especially in Eastern Europe.

—*The American Heritage Dictionary of the English Language, 4th ed.*

ONE

1

Beyond the walls of the Vieux Carré where his mother sells her greens, beyond the deep fetid stink of Gallatin Street's brothels and the crotches of its whores, its swindlers and inebriates and roving gangs of violent footpads, Elias Abrams fears for the first time that he might lose himself to the sky above. This prospect frightens him because although he suffers from no lack of courage, unlike the other ragtag immigrant sons with whom he runs, young Elias rarely dreams of flight. The hours of labor in his mother's small garden plot have trained him to trust the soiling of one's hands above all else. She has instilled in him the belief that land provides life, and as with land, life is meant to be hard-tilled. Thus, for a boy of such industry, the sky is not to be trusted. That he has on too many occasions seen Muscovy ducks dangling by their necks from market beams, their feet suspended aloft, air their only purchase, does nothing to diminish this distrust.

So the immensity of the outdoors terrifies him. He has heard rumors of square miles where sugarcane roots fast in clay dirt and cotton fields reach in all directions, ranging broader even than the width of his outspread arms. Presented the truth of things here in Napoleonville, however, he sees that the rumors do no justice.

The sun is high, quivering white. There are no clouds. The dry road crunches beneath his feet. Crickets in the ditchweeds whir for a spell, and then cease. The air is heavy and still. It is a wilting heat, in which shade offers little reprieve.

Back in Lafayette City, the New Orleans faubourg where he and his mother live, Elias is known as a boy who stands his ground in the face of anyone who lifts a chin against him. Among the gutters, his aim with brick chunks is truer than most. He swings hickory shafts at whichever skull he thinks earns it, his defense of his mother's small garden plot from which she grows an unfathomable yield, devout. Yet out in the emptiness of Assumption Parish, with few hard sights to keep him staked to the ground, he feels his weight slowly easing, his head lightening with dread, like linens caught in the augur breezes of a hurricane slow-riding up the Gulf. He moves closer to his mother as she limps along. Then, catching himself, he resumes his own course.

Gerta Abrams stops in the dust, shielding her eyes from the sun. Her son halts beside her. "Got a ways yet," she says.

The plantation home rises in the distance. Not far from the immigrant waterfront where they live, Elias has challenged the gates of such homes, his fists at iron bars, the St. Charles Avenue and Prytania Street homes where wealthy merchants spare no expense. Corinthian columns, plastered facades, artists imported from Europe. Magnificent flower gardens rich with the treacly scents of jasmine and honeysuckle and the odd gardenia transplant, the vibrant blooms of yellow jonquils, red roses, blue flag irises, the variegated petals of rain and spider lilies, the height of hackberry and magnolia trees topping each third story. Always, a Negro houseboy in some threadbare waistcoat pruning away, whistling his favorite Congo Square dance tune as he clips one leaf, then another, content to spend his days perfecting the African notion of beauty. *Ain't never a vegetable,* thinks Elias at these gates with equal measures of envy and disdain. *Ain't never a need.*

Here in Napoleonville, however, the plantation home stands unflanked by neighbors or commerce, silhouetted by the very horizon he now finds unnerving. He has never seen a structure so unto itself.

That a single man lives in all that space, shy of white company, astounds the boy.

"Twenty-four rooms, that house," Gerta tells her son flatly, suggesting the plantation with a nod. She limps on, disgusted by the thought of the man within, of his hands, before suddenly veering from the road toward one of the fields that lines it. The crickets in the weeds cut silent. A straight blade nimble in her fingers, she slices through a stalk of sugarcane low at its base and limps back toward her son, stripping it clean along the way. "Here."

He accepts the stalk but makes no move to eat.

"Go on," she says. The honesty of her smile assures him that it is allowed.

Throughout his eleven years, Elias has seen sugarcane bundled and sold beside corked clay jugs of molasses and syrup, and has filched it from unsuspecting vendors too many times to count. He has watched slave women buying it, their heads wrapped in ruby kerchiefs, their lips pursed and eyes narrowed skeptically at the scales, guarding their masters' money against the vendors' thumbs. And so, beneath the sun of that hot August noon on his first trip to the country, he gnaws until the stalk becomes pulp, his mouth glistens, and his hand drips with resin. Something in that flavor, more than just the raw sugar but perhaps the dirt, too, the actual earth, relieves him of his worry. At once he loosens in the face of the man in the mansion before him, of the reasons behind their heading there, and of the overwhelming expanse that frames them all. Under that sun, beside his mother, he cannot remember ever tasting anything so sweet.

Gerta places her hand to his back and prods him gently forward. "Might as well get on with it then."

2

That was 1852. Nine years later to the day, at the Battle of Oak Hills, Missouri, Elias Abrams will again taste the land, though its flavor will differ altogether. There, his face caked with a mortar of grime and sweat, Union canister and rifle shot shrieking everywhere he turns, men beside him slaughtered into the earth, he will taste the metal of the mire and of his own blood, the bile of his belly and the acrid smoke of battle so thick that it will have all but devoured the sun above.

The dawn before the fight—the last of peace the men of the Third Louisiana Infantry will know for years—has brought with it the chance for gallantry they have long been awaiting. Most did not sleep during the night. Some played poker, others euchre, while still others pawed the ground expectantly, dancing, as if horses hungry to move. They cursed and laughed and punched one another's arms in an attempt to prove themselves worthy of such a noble cause. Many drafted letters home, their handwriting an illegible scrawl from the thrill of history upon them and a near total lack of learning. Murmurs of Biblical passages, weapons oiled and re-oiled. More than a few sat listless, staring, wondering whether, when the Minié balls began to fly, with cannon shot exploding overhead and their comrades slumping next to them like fallen sacks of meal, they would flee in cowardice as they had dreamed so fitfully in nights past. "Should I be shot," they prayed in earnest, "dear

Jesus, may it be through my front. That's all I ask, Lord, let 'em pierce me through my front." Manhood, the more contemplative ones understood, emerges when the person you wish to be meets precise accord with the person you must be. They understood, too, that this uncertainty was never so at stake. They looked into themselves and found few assurances. All eyes flickered in the night fires.

Yet when the battle finally comes, it comes first as sound. With surgeons' quarters perched along the hillside ridge anticipating a stream of bloody charges, the litter bearers and ambulances anxiously in wait, the assembly of Louisianans, troops from Arkansas and South Kansas-Texas, and Missouri State Guardsmen, over 15,000 strong, are all awakened by the early morning roar of Union artillery. The puffs of cannonade through the trees to the northwest, the screams of shot approaching, and the subsequent explosions quake the Confederates' teeth in their heads as the shells thunder into the earth beside them. Hearts pound in chests, eyes widen, tongues swell with a sudden, implausible thirst. Whereas in the days before the men have been hobbled by the thinning soles of their shoes, they now skip like goats over their hillside footing. General Benjamin McCulloch is a fury, his horse rearing and mauling the air, as he bellows at the disorganization he has spent so many months attempting to drill out of his regiment's acquaintance. Officers on horseback have commenced their commands, the sergeants in turn ordering the troops to attention. A drum rolls; a fife sounds. The regimental colors appear, instilling a whiff of pride in those who witness the flag's unfurling, though it proves only a brief distraction before they return their focus to the gun barrels that lie across the valley.

Elias Abrams, newest member of Lieutenant Colonel Samuel Myers Hyams' Company G, Pelican Rangers, No. 1, redoubles his grip on his rifle. Only nine days in gray, his collar abrades his neck, his new leather brogans causing his feet to ache with stiffness, though they are the envy of those around him. Unlike those around him, however, this is not at all where he wishes to be. A shrewd twenty-year-old, his profile strong, his waist lean, a scar jaggedly cleaving his upper lip, Abrams would rather be elsewhere. Drawing cards in some gamblers' hall, entwined in the arms of some night's soft comfort. Fleecing the Creole dandies who stroll the riverfront, sleeping past noon from an evening eased too uninhibitedly into morn. But circumstances have necessitated that he leave the warmth of these dens and women's arms behind, the cigar smoke and plush cushions, and escape into the embrace of a peril only slightly less immediate than the one New Orleans suddenly proposes. A visible, unified enemy he can fight. One that creeps among the shadows to bash a cudgel into his brain or slip a blade between his ribs he knows to be much more lethal. Understanding this, he has enlisted. And so, at daybreak on August 10, he steels himself.

Beside him stands a man in his early thirties wearing wire-rimmed spectacles and a fine straw Panama. He reeks of stale pipe tobacco, perspiration, and to Abrams' surprise, the trickle of warm urine slow-staining his trousers front. The man looks down at his own soaked crotch, at the very caricature of a man afraid, and his studious appearance aside, laughs at the fear that has so wholly seized him. He removes his Panama to run a hand anxiously through hair the color of wheat chaff. He is embarrassed but concedes to himself that this is no time for shame. Afterward, perhaps, but not now.

Abrams says nothing, concentrating instead on the terrain ahead. He surveys the miles of hills and fields before him, the bisecting thoroughfare of Telegraph Road that runs from Springfield all the way to Fayetteville. He studies a modest farmhouse, nearly centered, a second to the south of it. To the northwest is Bald Knob, with two more farmhouses to the east and north, respectively. Skirting the corn and stubble fields below, Abrams discerns thick undergrowth of blackjack and hazel, an impasse of brambles if confronted head-on. In an instant he has taken the course of Wilson's Creek, recognizes the alluvial soil along its banks, the rocky sediment of the ravine off to his left. The years of running Gallatin Street have not been able to undo his mother's teachings.

In spite of the cards and quick scams, Abrams still possesses a nose for the land. He immediately grasps the ground before him, which footing will give, which will hold firm. The line of fence behind which the enemy waits is Missouri sweet pine, a wood too soft when green, too brittle when aged, to provide a hardy defense for long. He does not need battle experience to tell him this. This Abrams knows, implicitly.

The rain of the night before has collected in the cornrows—he can smell it—and will turn the earthen aisles between them into utter pitch should he need one as an avenue of advance or escape. The corn itself, neck high, will provide valuable cover but will likewise shred any exposed flesh if met with too much haste. Between the nettles of the undergrowth and the fields of cutting corn, the rifles and cavalry and cannons in wait ahead, Abrams knows he will not end this day unscathed.

—

The battle has opened on all sides now. Artillery is dueling with such thunder that leaves quiver on dogwood trees up to a quarter mile away, the valley reverberating each boom along its length until a new shot replenishes the one diminishing before it. Around Abrams men are assembling, some calm, others visibly shaken, and yet all flooded with excitement. They are gnawing on their lips nervously, mopping their foreheads with handkerchiefs embroidered by lovers back home, coddling their weapons like newborn babes. Down the quickly forming line, one, a cross-eyed trapper from Houma still in his buckskins, kisses the walnut stock of his daddy's 10-gauge shotgun, beseeching its blue steel barrels for accuracy, for which he will in turn treat the gun more fondly than all the women of his past. "Promise," he whispers. "More'n that handsome Miss Sheila, from Mechanikham. More'n Miss Eugenia even, swear it."

The man in the fine straw Panama meets Abrams' eye and nods. "John Lee Carlson," he says soberly.

"Elias Abrams."

A Classics professor at the College of the Immaculate Conception, as a disciple of his texts, Carlson still finds glory in war, though in just a few hours his faith will be shaken. "'O would to Jove,'" he suddenly quotes aloud, his eyes fully alight as the bugles begin to sound, "'thou Pallas, and thou Sun, that only we two, escaping death, might have the thundering down of every stone stuck in the walls of this so sacred town!'" He has been waiting to recite these words for weeks.

Abrams pauses at this: "If you say so, mister."

"Together," states Carlson, his hand now on Abrams' shoulder, "we shall prove ourselves worthy today."

"Just don't shoot me by mistake. That's about all the worthy I'm askin' out of you."

The orders come quickly. On Lieutenant Colonel Hyams' command, Abrams and Carlson have fallen in with the others, the boys in ill-fitting uniforms who have lied about their ages, the grandfathers who have awakened stiff-jointed each winter morn for decades. They are marching double-time as one, their middle-aged lieutenant colonel dismounted among them, advancing through the dense blackjack and hazel that concerned Abrams moments earlier, toward the corn and stubble fields on valley's plain. Their gun barrels entangle in the brambles; their uniforms catch on every thorn. They grunt and strain, slogging themselves through, as though their ankles and legs are being seized by a host of fiendish limbs clutching upward from the pit below. In such blind exertion, the men crash into one another's backs and offer quick looks of fear and apology. "What I wouldn't give for a cane knife and some kerosene!" shouts one. "Steady now, boys!" shouts another, an officer, for at that instant a dreadful and scathing enemy fire is loosed upon them from Brigadier General Nathaniel Lyon's U.S. Regulars. The balls whistle viciously through the air, cutting all they confront, vine and bramble, flesh and bone. Screams of the struck arise from the undergrowth, as does a lone officer's exhortation for action.

In a frantic burst of effort, the men are through. Already fewer in number than when they set out just minutes ago, they take their position on the captain's orders. Abrams turns and glimpses the dead fallen into the thicket, their arms and legs suspended akimbo in the sinister manner of marionettes left to dangle. Necks bent at awkward angles, arms and wrists discordant with the sockets that join them. Though young, Abrams has seen ghastly things in his life, far too many to count. Bloated corpses face down in the Mississippi, lone knife handles stemming from their backs, their tragedy's main mast. Winners' heads cleaved in two by the city's sorest losers. Negroes hanged from tree limbs, their tongues lolling fat in their mouths, for looks indelicately cast toward the wrong race of woman. Rapine. Thuggery. Once, in a Basin Street bordello, a public castration by a pimp unimpressed with another's claim of seminal largesse. But nothing, he now knows as he gulps down his terror, has prepared him for the events of the morning as they are unfolding, for the massive scale of violence. A man of imagination, already Abrams admits that he could have never conceived such magnitude.

His strong-featured face is scarified from thorns, while Carlson's fine straw Panama, above his right ear, has been pierced in the brim by a sharpshooter's aim. At the moment Carlson does not know how close he has come to death, though later, by the campfire, he will stick his studious index finger through it and remain so for almost an hour in silence. Rather than Achilles, it will be Hector he contemplates.

The air is heavy with spent sulfur, the noise absolutely deafening, many of the officers' shouts dying unheard amid the din. Cannons roar, rifled muskets crack in such a series of firing and reloading that it seems one long deadly announcement. Union soldiers snipe from behind that Missouri sweet pine fence, while the remaining undergrowth behind which the Pelican Rangers jostle one another for cover obscures the view of the enemy ahead. Still, in the midst of the booming percussion, men on both sides concentrate foremost on steadying themselves. With rifle shot whizzing by, with cannonballs carving out alleys of air filled by men and horses just instants before, their job now is to retain enough of a head so that they might return the punishment being sent their way.

And so, for the first time in his life, Abrams draws a bead on a man he has never met. He has wielded a sap on innumerable occasions, found the base of men's skulls with a sudden blow, rummaged through their pockets and relieved them of their billfolds and watches. He has held knives to throats, flung his fists at jaws, fish-hooked cheeks in assault, but he has never killed another man, nor has killing ever been his intent. When a gambler risks Gallatin Street, he knows what awaits him: the prospect of a wager's riches, the prospect of then losing those riches to a greed more profound than his own. Abrams knows this, too, and respects it. Yet he has made another pact, one bound solely to himself, that while he will connive, threaten, and strike a blow for money, he will never kill for it. That his involvement in another man's murder has forced his escape into the madness in which he is now embroiled suggests an irony not lost on him. When he laughs about it in quieter moments, he laughs bitterly.

In spite of the battlefield noise, the bugles, the screams of the dying, and howitzers launching their twelve-pound rounds of iron, Abrams aims down the barrel's length precisely as he was instructed during his few days of training. Perched behind the fence railing, the Yankee in his sights sports a heavy black beard. His chest is thick, his blue kepi pulled down low over his bushy eyebrows. He is reloading his rifle, staring hard at some unsuspecting mark of his own. Abrams steadies his breath despite the tumult of the world, the calamity of this intimate apocalypse, then narrows his eyes, exhales evenly again, and just as evenly pulls the trigger to a tremendous roar, the sudden kick of the Mississippi rifle against his shoulder nearly knocking him to the ground. Yet perversely eager to see whether he has broken his own pact, with the smoke slowly clearing, he searches to see if his man has fallen. Seconds pass without answer when a lieutenant, a gangly, raw-faced youth, bellows into his ear, "Quit your gawkin', you damned fool, and fire, fire, *FIRE!*"

Now planted less than a hundred yards apart, the two armies pour lead into each other as quickly as their martial abilities allow. Already a furious exchange, it has amplified into an outright frenzy. They fire with individual accuracies, but all reload by tearing the end off a paper cartridge, pouring the powder down the bore, and with a couple *jam-jam* motions, ramrodding the ball down onto the powder bed at the barrel's base. With the hammer cocked, a cap placed on the nipple, the weapon is again ready to shoot. During the heat of action, the profane education of past drill sergeants—"listen up, you scabrous cunts, BITE, BALL, ROD, COCK, NIPPLE!"—becomes an urgency in their ears. Gun barrels have become scorching to the touch, thousands of shoulders bruised from the repeated impact of their weapons' recoil. Faces are blackened by spent powder, mouths withered with a thirst so severe that later, once slaked, survivors will swear they would rather spoon down measures of rock salt than ever again endure such dehydration.

An hour has passed. Two hours.

The sun has been eclipsed, so darkened has the hot morning become by the sulfurous discharge of cannons and rifled musket smoke. The scene gives those battleground poets the image of a day suddenly regressed toward night, as if the dawn has quailed in the face of such abomination and receded into the safety of the horizon from which it was conceived. Cavalry horses litter the countryside, Virginia-bred bays and Ohioan chestnuts, their riders thrown broken-boned or shot dead into the dust just beyond the animals' corpses. Scores of infantrymen are slain. All along the lines they have fallen, some deprived of heads or hearts, some torn meatily in two, while others clutch their bellies in agony from slow-leaking wounds. Here a father of nine from Arkadelphia, demolished by a loose pattern of grapeshot; there, a Lowell abolitionist's only grandson breathes his last from a Minié ball aimed true. Here lies a lone Confederate private who owned no slaves; there, a Federal lieutenant whose family owns a multitude. The land is stained with blood. Wilson's Creek is awash in it. Abrams stands in awe, too shocked to judge that which envelopes him, even though his vision has become a hawk's, his smell and hearing like the most well-bred hound's. Everything is slowed. The world about him stirs with clarity. Sounds arrive shriller; the sights and smells of mid-morning appear intolerably sharp. He is neither coward nor hero, but simply this, a series of impressions leading to a series of actions. He is beyond himself. For the time being, he is no longer Elias Abrams at all.

At once Colonel James McIntosh of the Second Arkansas Mounted Rifles comes sprinting astride his horse through the heavy air, demanding an attack. "Y'all get the hell at it already!" he orders. "Jesus *fuck*!"

So bolstered by the officer's bid, the men promptly charge, making that Missouri sweet pine fence in seconds, the one now abandoned by the Federal regulars who have taken to their heels in flight. Positioned behind the very cover that protected their enemy moments before, the Confederates fire mercilessly into Northern backs, killing and wounding dozens, compelling each unfortunate to pitch violently forward into a graceless and final collapse.

With powder and ball quickly back in place, the Pelican Rangers begin to hop the fence in pursuit. In doing so, however, Abrams is forced abruptly to a halt, nearly landing atop the burly Union soldier at whom he had earlier aimed, a third of his jaw—and thus a third of his heavy black beard—gone, a toothless, gurgling mash, destroyed by musketry. The soldier's eyes have already filmed over, his hands frozen in two hard clutches. One leg is bent awkwardly beneath him, the other foot inexplicably shoeless, its gray toes curled into the mud. His blood-soaked kepi has been dislodged from what remains of his head.

True, Abrams has witnessed a dozen killings in his life, but never has he found a killing so immediately strange. He can find no angle to it. There is no material gain for anyone here, no promise of winnings or affection at the end of a long night. The absurdity of this fact does little more than stump him. While the war continues to rage, Abrams' confusion stands him upright, his head tilting as he leans forward to examine the contours of the soldier's half-face, the blood slowly cooling, the flies descending without the least obeisance paid. He discovers a bruise yellowing the man's left eye. It is days old. This strikes Abrams as especially queer, that his enemy was ever alive enough to receive such slight injury in the first place. He only breaks off his scrutiny to wonder if he is responsible for the death now before him, though he chooses, for the moment, to think he is not. When Abrams first kills, he will need certainty.

Quickly he joins the Confederates giving chase, most of whom offer loud huzzahs as they race across the fields, overjoyed chiefly by their continued ability to do so. Their joy meets a swift dissolution, however, when they come up fast on a battery of howitzers behind which the Federal regulars have taken refuge. The Louisianans spin about in retreat, falling to their hands so that the trails of white-hot metal will sail overhead each time the cannons roar behind them. After every barrage, the men spring to their feet and run until they dive at last behind a hill toward the rear of Sharp's cornfield. There, panting on their backs and without warning, a sudden battle weariness settles on them all. In an instant it has blanketed their muscles and bones, shrouding their minds so thoroughly that those with the most burdensome consciences begin to doubt they will ever again muster an untainted thought.

The fight is three hours old, and Abrams is fatigued beyond all measure. He has never been so exhausted, not even after the three-day binges of cards, whores, and liquor. He rolls over with great effort and spots Carlson in the dust not far away. He whistles. They make eye contact. Abrams tips his now-dusty bowler. Carlson smiles weakly in reply, and then returns his attention to the sky.

Lying behind that hill while the howitzers continue to boom, Abrams, as are all his comrades, is in desperate need of water. He bleeds from a number of minor wounds received from where and when he does not know. His blouse is shredded, his trousers, too. The milky eyes of the dead man back at the fence will not quit him. They gaze blankly into his own, bearing the aspect of a gambler's most stone-faced play. Only now, a half-hour later, Abrams begins to grasp that though experience has trained him to hold the stare of any man who sits across from him, this is one bluff he cannot call.

He spits bleakly into the dust, wishing for neither home nor peace but for a steadying pinch of Piedmont tobacco, dreaming of a bluer, earthier smoke than the one now filling his lungs: *Just to kick up my fuckin' boots and smoke, goddamnit. That's it, that's all it'd take to make me a happy man.* But before he can continue his lament, up rides Mc-Culloch to confer with Hyams and McIntosh. The stallion beneath him wild-eyed and darkened with lather, chomping at its bit, the general turns to his beleaguered soldiers and implores them to join him in one last attack.

Along the valley, around the hill's base, the worn-out men thus resign themselves to the rhythmic sway of the great steed's rump before them, one haunch then another, as they march toward the battery the general has in mind for them. In approaching Wilson's Creek, the first water the men have seen in hours, many break formation and fly to its banks, ignoring their commander's call for restraint and the bloody filth that has flowed from bodies all along the stream's course. They dunk their heads, gulping down mouthfuls to cool the fires within, paying no heed to the soft flotsam they consume from the countless injuries that have polluted the water for miles in each direction. It makes no difference. Most are oblivious to the dead, to the charred human remains and grisly burns being soothed mere feet from where the rest of the regiment is swallowing it all down. Indeed, though these men drink gulp after gulp of the detestable swill, its silted blood and shards of bone, those damned few still attuned to the horrors about them simply cannot, for all their purifying attempt, successfully wash their mouths free of the first taste of war.

3

_____

Later that night, Abrams is propped on an elbow by a campfire, his body a seamless ache as he stares into the embers, watching the logs crackle and send sparks swirling aloft into the darkness above. He groans with each movement. He has tended to his wounds, winced at the poultice mixed from mashed blackberry leaf and water, an astringent concocted from a recipe long ago passed down from his mother. He has barely finished his tin plate of panada, though his extra ration of rye he sips with a slow, even pacing. When an itch develops along his calf, he does not shift to address it.

Unlike the men around him who through food and drink have regained spirits enough to celebrate their victory, the only superfluous motion Abrams makes is to inhale some of that Piedmont earth he so longed for earlier. His teeth clench his briarwood pipe firmly in place. His nostrils fume with smoke. In his canvas knapsack, he has secured the day's spoils. While the men of the Third Louisiana had hotly pursued the remaining Union forces through the cornfields, Abrams, realizing the day won, lagged behind to collect a few of what he would later refer to as "memorables." Plucked from the cooling bodies of Yankee corpses, he finished his first day of war richer by a gold watch and fob, two rings—one Masonic, the other ruby—a bone-handled penknife, a pouch of Caswell County gold leaf, and a walnut-butted derringer found tucked in the small of a slain Union major's back. *What kind of ignoramus brings a fuckin' peashooter to war, anyhow?* Abrams had wondered grimly as he palmed it. Now, hours later, he does not consider himself a plunderer but a man in step with opportunity. Gallatin Street, that brief stretch of thoroughfare extending but two blocks from Ursulines Avenue to Barracks, lectures long into a man's soul.

"You mind?" It is Carlson, standing above him.

"Suit yourself."

"Quite a day," sighs the professor as he settles beside Abrams. "Few more like it and this war'll be over in no time flat."

Abrams cannot contain his laughter. He claims he hopes Carlson is right.

"Got a pinch you feel like sharing?" As he asks this, Carlson is tamping his chindangler into his palm. It is a fine but empty pipe, its bowl carved of cherry heartwood, its stem of the blackest ebony branch. He looks at Abrams. Abrams looks back, spotting the hole of busted cane through the brim of the Panama hat. Seconds pass between them.

"Sorry," sighs Abrams at last, "had to beg some myself." He tosses his bowler over a knee and then rolls over to consider the night sky, fingers entwined behind his thick black hair. His pipe works low to the side of his chin, a fiery little furnace.

"'Abrams,' was it?" asks Carlson as he dusts himself off in standing. His own pipe has already been stowed. He stamps a heel in the dirt. "Unusual name, I'd say. Don't hear it called out much in the church registry."

"Reckon not."

"Reckon not," Carlson agrees, and then trudges off.

Of the day earlier, it had not taken long to capture that final Union battery. Under McCulloch's cool leadership and tactician's eyes, his soldiers had called upon their last stores of energy and crested the hill. To the astonishment of the Federal artillery crew, together they arrived at the mount's summit. As before, the Yankees quickly abandoned their posts and fled into the cornfields below, followed by the Pelican Rangers in pursuit. Between the cornrows Lyon's men endured horrific casualties, while in the rear the Confederates seized three 12-pounder howitzers and two 6-pounder field guns. The day, they would soon learn, was theirs.

But back at the campfire later that night, Elias Abrams feels no elation at his side's triumph. His pleasure, faint as it is, lies elsewhere. With his eyes closed, pipe smoke curling, he imagines he can hear his new watch marking off each moment, and this forces a tight smile. He is comforted by his supply of tobacco. The rings he will pawn as needed; the penknife he will keep. The derringer, to be secreted away in preparation for his first trip back to New Orleans.

All throughout the camp he hears men bragging of their exploits on the battlefield. One proud fellow, his thumbs hitched into his armpits as he flaps and squawks around the campfire, calls himself, "The damnedest bantam that ever lived, I am!" Another staggers to his feet, jug of whiskey in hand, claiming to be the marksman who slew General Lyon: "Sorry, boys!" he shouts at the riotous contention of his neighbors, smacking his dusty haunch, "but that red-bearded Connecticut cocksucker took my ball harder'n I ever gave it to his wife, and trust me, fellers, I've gave it to her *hard!*"

Some are drunk, some are proselytizing, some are both. A preacher stands above a small fire, his weathered Bible open, his congregants listening in rapt attention. They nod and puff on their pipes or cigars. He speaks to them of God's will. "Y'all know," intones the preacher, his hair and beard as long and white as an egret's plume, "that the Lord Jesus Christ died for y'all's sins. Corinthians 15:3 tells y'all so, and y'all, as men of God, have little trouble acceptin' this as truth. Y'all see His beauty in the smiles of y'all's children, in the light of their eyes, y'all hear it in their laughter. Y'all see and feel this, and y'all *know* there is a God. Y'all see this, and y'all *know* His only son paid for our transgressions." The preacher pauses here, and then leans in. "But that's the easy part, my brothers, the believin'. Oh yes, my brothers, I said it and I'll say it again, faith's the *easy* part. 'Cause any man with a plug nickel's worth of sense—well, he just knows God's rich in the world 'round him, don't he?"

"Yes, Lord," he sighs to the night sky, answering his own call. "The world's just *full* of Christ-love, as full of love as I am for y'all here tonight." Suddenly his face falls serious. "But let's not be vain, brothers—oh no, let us not be vain—we may revel in Christ's love, we may love in the ways He would ask of us, but it takes more than love to be a good Christian—it takes the will to fight. It takes *work*. See, a man don't need ordination to be a minister of the Lord, so long as he works hard—hard as can be now—at praisin' Christ's sacrifice. Just as y'all must, this night, work hard at praisin' the sacrifice of them men of the field—*our* men of the field, them dead boys still out there tonight—who gave their lives so everything we hold dear'll be protected from them God-forsaken, blue-bellied heathens who now dare threaten all we stand for." He stops. "Oh sure, they'll say it's about the nigger. But let me tell y'all, it ain't hardly about the nigger. Nossir, the nigger's just fine where he is, doin' what he's been doin' since the birth of Creation—I know it, y'all know it, and that 'cursed Mr. Lincoln knows it. But even the Devil needs an excuse, my brothers, to show off the rapaciousness of his own black, black heart. Go ask our boys about rapaciousness, them boys out there on that field—they'll tell y'all—just as black as a nigger's skin, so, too, is Mr. Lincoln's own rapacious heart."

One man spits into the fire. Another stands and then sits.

"And so, just as we govern our vengeance upon these invaders, these miscreant sons-of-Satan, like we done this very day out there on Bloody Hill, our wrath righteous, our purpose true, I say let us praise these fine, dead men, these soldiers of the Lord, once so full of love and spirit, so full of the noblest cause. Let us praise *each* of them, every one, as if they was Jesus Christ himself, 'for if we have been planted together in the likeness of His death, we shall be also in the likeness of His resurrection,' Romans 6:5." The preacher stops once again. "Now I ain't blasphemin' here, boys—I'm speakin' of the Southern man. Bow y'all's heads. Let's pray."

Though he is no Christian, Abrams obeys the call for prayer. Life is a cheapness; he is not deluded. He knows how easily it could be him out there on that field. A moment of silence passes. Stars dot the firmament above.

Soon, Abrams turns his attention to those who have chosen a different path, those slamming down cards on barrelheads, roaring at pots either won or lost. Still others sport dice, throwing them hard into empty wooden ammo boxes in games of craps or sweet cloth. Although Abrams rarely passes up a chance to take a twist at the tiger, he has no heart for gaming this night. This night, Abrams thinks of the stars and in part due to the sermon he has just overheard, the milky eyes of the dead man, his enemy, back on that field. He thinks of him still out there, uncollected, untended by loved ones or ceremony, dew condensing in his bushy hair and beard as the rest of him slowly decomposes. Abrams thinks of this man, of the profession he will no longer practice, the fields he will no longer till, wonders whether there was a woman in his life, or children, if the timbre of his voice complemented his bearishness. He wonders about the bruise that rimmed his left eye, about its origin, whether it was the result of an accident or the fist of another man with whom he may have earlier quarreled. A man who, at that instant, perhaps bears a bruise of his own, providing he, too, is not slowly decomposing somewhere along the banks of Wilson's Creek.

Abrams understands this type of thinking does him no good. War, he is learning, like cards, treats the merciful no better than the unyielding. In this he also understands that had he and this now-slain Yankee met in life, they would have assuredly ignored each other as men are wont to do with those they do not know. Annoyed by his own hypocrisy, Abrams exhales in frustration, realizing that only in an instance as peculiar as this would he ever give a stranger so much concern. Breathing men, he confesses, tend to have little bearing on him.

In that glimpse of death, his thoughts flit like flies on a corpse to the murdered gentleman back in New Orleans, the very cause for his enlistment into the disaster now overwhelming him. Stuck in Missouri beside a field of a thousand rotting souls, Abrams again feels the blow he struck to the base of that man's head, the solid impact of leather-encased lead meeting cranial bone. Pulling mournfully on his pipe, he imagines that bruised skull lain at his feet before him, hears the man's faltering breaths, watches the tendons in his shoulders slacken. Abrams sighs. He does not wish to reflect on this man at all, though for the time being, governed as he is by such affairs of his conscience, he has no choice.

Like the flitting of these thoughts, so, too, has Abrams' guilt at his complicity in this crime been flitting, settling upon him unpredictably and at awkward moments. When the guilt does settle upon him, it forces his stomach to meet his spine, his innards to go hollow. In these times, he stares at the sky. He does not blink. He falls deeper into himself. The weight he bears is insistent.

Abrams takes another sip of whiskey, shaking his head to clear it of these memories, his mind instead falling to a gang of men still living and, in their living, far more dangerous. Though they are seven hundred miles away, he sees them all plainly. They are Placide Arceneaux, the Creole knifeman; Jurgen "Goliath" Mueller, the brutish keelboat brawler; Tasker Gundy, the whoremonger; Jimmy Byrne, the Irish fop; and, of course, Silas Wolfe, the Smile. Back when Abrams could still run rowdy among them—a time as recently as only ten days before—together they comprised the Cypress Stump Boys, so called because their namesake they figured to be an improbable wood: tough as it comes, eternally thirsty, impervious to attack by bug or decay, resistant to splitting and cracking, and as a matter of particular pride, one that never bleeds.

On a lazy noon a few years prior to that night out in Oak Hills, the name had been Abrams' suggestion, although once agreed upon, with perfect sincerity Wolfe had claimed it as his own. Abrams had laughed in his friend's face, believing him to be joking. Wolfe's mouth, known the length of Gallatin Street for its devastating smile, immediately drew tight. He sniffed. "Ask them," Wolfe said gravely, nodding toward the crew. "They'll tell you. My idea." None of the others dared match Abrams' disbelief. They just kicked the dust instead, picked their nails with knives, and mulled deeply over whom they would next rob, which bordello they would next frequent, or where they might buck their next gamble.

Abrams recalls everything he shared with them in the years since. The elaborate cons and bouts of drunkenness, the melees at one another's backs, the countless women passed between them. The days loafing on wharf-side cotton bales, smoking, drowsing, and playing cards, their nights devoted to drinking, carousing, and still more cards. On occasion, whenever Mueller felt particularly pugnacious or Wolfe sly, whenever Arceneaux perceived a slight, any slight—for as a Creole, his vaunted *Code Duello* dictated his every movement—or Gundy's blood was roiled by a rival pimp, after some cowboy tough had scoffed at Byrne's Asiatic cravat or Abrams knew he had been dealt to from the bottom of the deck, the six of them would band together to take on the world. In these marvelous times, they came crashing into dancehalls or gin mills, their fists and bludgeons raised aloft, screaming giddily as the bouncers and bartenders, the jakes and prostitutes, all fled out the back door, scrambling over one another like starved puppies to a teat. As a pack, the six would smell out the night's offender and then descend on him as one. Fists, leaden pipes, knives, bottles, saps, oaken chairs—all of them rising and falling on their target with ruinous speed. Whoever he was, he would never again think of cypress in anything but the most punishing terms.

Abrams' thoughts drift back to that night only ten days before, the night that changed everything. Visions of the older man, their mark, slumped onto a fine parlor Oriental, resurface to haunt him, that skull bruised by the one clout Abrams cannot now forget. Byrne dances a jig around the body, yanking from the mantel an ivory-faced clock, two silver candelabras, and a series of Austrian porcelain miniatures, while Arceneaux balances the weight of an antique *colichemarde*, a Creole dueling sword, with the pride of one whose lineage alone knows the nobility of such arms. Gundy hoots in delight at the growing heft of his carpetbag and at the tinkling within it. Wolfe directs his men to those few valuables they have missed. He wants the oil landscapes off the walls, the tailored suits from armoires upstairs, the flatware, that bottle of Madeira, the leather-bound volumes off the bookshelves—everything. The room revels with theft, Abrams is filling his own satchel with silver and crystal, and yet for a thief, he moves too deliberately. He has dreamed of this moment for weeks, schemed for a night precisely like this one, but now, confronted by his dream's fruition, he knows something is not right. The act itself is wrong, he cannot help but know this, and his principles do not fear telling him so. He cuts short his thieving to look down at Wolfe—the slick, pomaded hair, the handsome Hebraic nose, the full lips and penetrating eyes—who is now crouching beside the man on the floor. Abrams watches him stroke the man's head lovingly, while whispering to him perverse indulgences. "Aw honey, hush," Wolfe is whispering. "Everything's fine, just as fine as can be. You'll see." He quits his fussing to meet Abrams' gaze, where far more than silence is exchanged between them. The entirety of their lives together inhabits that stare: their introduction at the Jewish Widows and Orphans Home five years before, the shared months there, their dreams of wealth and wine, their first drunks, first fights, and first fucks, their joint decision to tempt New Orleans' streets. Everything fraternity implies—all of it, inhabiting that instant.

Wolfe's eyes narrow as he brandishes a slender knife, its blade stropped to a lethally cold gleam. Then, without breaking their stare, he calmly shoves it into the unconscious man's ribcage through his back, to the hilt, piercing all the way into the hind of his heart. The man gasps once, his back suddenly arching in a wretched bow, and then deflates in a long and conclusive wheeze. Blood pools black and thick on the parlor Oriental. Abrams is stunned. He cannot move. "Hush now," Wolfe whispers into Abrams' eyes, still stroking the older man's head. "You just go on and hush."

In recalling all this seven hundred miles from the scene of the crime, the Cypress Stump Boys and the New Orleans law each doubtlessly on the hunt for him, with the entire Union army aiming for his death, before finally drifting off to sleep after his first day of war, Elias Abrams is forced to digest the hard truth that every circumstance of his life now conspires to kill him.

4

The day after the Battle of Oak Hills, the Third Louisiana packs up its bivouac and tramps three miles closer to the town of Springfield, Missouri. Not for love of municipality or populace, but to escape the effluvia that has begun to rise in putrefying waves off the bodies out in the fields. The faces of the dead have blackened and swollen in the night, their eyes bulging amphibiously. Bellies have burst asunder from the pressure of the death vapors billowing tumultuously inside them. The morning air reeks of decay as the sky fills with bluebottle flies, buzzards, and crows. And so, to maintain morale, the commanders have decided to move their men onward.

From that second campground, a day later they move to a third, one located near the source of Wilson's Creek, miles upstream. Here they stay for two weeks, most sleeping in the open air without blankets or tents, beneath an intermittency of thundering downpours. The sick list lengthens. The men smell like death themselves, their feet and scrotums and breath all stinking of mold and rancid cheese and shit. The nights fill with the sounds of coughs and muted curses. Dysentery is commonplace. Everything they own is soiled and sodden, their uniforms in tatters. The soles of their brogans worn through, many damp soldiers now stumble barefoot as they pick their paths daintily over the hard-cutting personality of the Missouri terrain. The innovative have learned to track down scraps of rawhide from the butchers, and after swaddling their feet in filthy rags, sew up the leather around them. Lice begin to rampage in the millions, teeming over bodies in such numbers that the men rant and swear and rend their grimy flesh, raking bloody trails across their bellies and backs, from which these vermin then sup gaily. The men are thankful only that Union ranks do not swell with such an inviolable bloodlust.

They now scavenge their meals from wherever they can find them. Rations have been reduced to three ears of green corn a day, which forces their guts to quake and later erupt disgustingly. Their unwashed rectums have become red and sore. Stout men have grown lean. Lean men, into rails. This is not what they had envisioned of war.

Abrams is as ragged as the others. Alone, he pines for a long hot bath drawn into a claw-footed tub, poured of scalding jasmine water, steam rising in perfumed billows. He dreams of talc, of a clean flannel for his face, of more tooth powder, of dry woolen socks, of a hat brush for his bowler, of any clothes but those he is wearing. He wishes for trowels laden with his mother's pennyroyal salve with which to smear the length of his body, hoping to repel the clouds of mosquitoes that fume ceaselessly in the night. They pester him without mercy, as they do every other hot-lunged creature in camp, until, in this nightly battle of attrition, their swarms erode fully the resolve of those they would devour, hands and tails that once slapped and swatted now fallen limply by hips and haunches in an utter breakage of will. Aloud, Abrams gripes to no one. But unlike the others with whom he silently commiserates, in exchange for the Masonic ring filched from the battlefield, he has secured from one of the sutlers a fair measure of salt pork, a sack of seed potatoes, two Jenny Lind melons, and a Winnigstadt cabbage. At first the sutler, a hard-bargaining Scotchman from Monroe, had balked at the idea of throwing in the cabbage, but Abrams swore the deal would queer unless he did so. After a requisite show of quibbling, the Scotchman finally yielded, claiming through a wry grin, "I'll admit to ye, it's a rare dey, I git jewed by'an enlisted mahn."

The fact remains, once he sees it, Abrams must have the cabbage. That evening he studies the vegetable's firm, pointed head and tight, ruffled leaves. He closes his eyes and smells it deeply. He draws in its scent of greenery and soil, but dares not yet cook it for fear of piquing the hungrier stomachs around him. Oh, what memories those scents bring. They spring at him relentlessly, jumbled madly atop one another like cards fluttering forth from a deck. That delectable stench of boiled greens so often filling the home of his youth, Gerta bent over the kettle dropping in pinches of salt, pepper, and caraway seeds, then slathering the leaves in bacon and sweet butter afterward. Her turning to him as he sat at their butcherwood table, his feet dangling, her smile warm and inevitable. He thinks of her small garden's abundance, the hours they shared working together, her lessons to him on irrigation and aeration, on the merits of the earthworm versus the sins of the weevil, the talk of silica and clay and calcareous soils. "A man's a man," she used to say as she weeded, the sweat run away from her brow by the back of her wrist, "but I'll be damned if he ain't more of one, he got himself a plot. Back in Alsace, our kind couldn't own a fistful of nothin', 'specially not land, that's why your granddaddy went ahead and redemptioned us, to get us on over." Here she would stand and survey the garden around her, her hands on hips. "Sure, I got this little parcel, it ain't bad far as dirt goes, but it's up to you, Elias, to really stake that claim now."

Even these years later, while he admits Gerta to have been less striking than the whores of Corduroy Alley who tempt with their bent knees or the Irish maidservants who trudged alongside her daily into the Vieux Carré from their shared upriver district, with its steamboat landings and slaughterhouses, its sewerage and clattering immigrant accents, Abrams still believes his mother to have been the most beautiful woman in the world. It was not her hazel, almond-shaped eyes or the faint remnant of her native Alsatian tongue commingled with a heavy Southern drawl. Nor was it the fullness of her Semitic hair or lips or chest or the strength

27

of her nose. These are the attributes other males admired, the drunks and swaggering keelmen, attributes that forced her to lift her pagoda skirts above the muck when crossing the street in avoidance as they staggered toward her up the city's plank walkways. On occasion, these men forced her to avoid some parts of New Orleans completely, especially after dusk.

Sometimes events proved inevitable. When this was so, when cornered by men with their fat, grubby fingers, Gerta chose to quietly endure the petty molestations, the foul noses at her neck. She endured them because once, thirteen years after her arrival from the Alsatian village of Eguisheim, on the eve of her eighteenth birthday, she had borne the brunt of much, much worse.

But while she endured these affronts, she would endure them only to a limit. In prayerful anticipation of a day that exceeded this limit, she carried with her a mother-of-pearl-handled straight razor. It was a gift from Brona Kincade, a neighboring washerwoman who had likewise suffered such ill treatment, though from a different pair of hands. "Oh aye," Brona had said, clucking her tongue in sympathy, "I've known such a walk, I have. Here, m'dove, take m'blade—you'll never have to walk so again." Silently ashamed, grateful for a kindness, young, bruised Gerta accepted the gift. And many times over the ensuing years, she stropped its blade wistfully, dreaming of exposed male necks.

No, it is not for this that Abrams remembers his mother as beautiful. He remembers her as beautiful because despite her uneasy gait and the gaps of two lost teeth—keepsakes each from that fateful birthday eve— Gerta was incurably kind to her son. Her smile meant more to him than racing the wharves with his friends, than the catfishing or pipe smoking or the nights slipped into keno halls where he earned tips for running grog to the slow losers. To him, Gerta's smile was worth more than all of it.

Abrams chuckles at this remembrance. The idea of his mother's love of the land makes him happy even still, even after the years of cobblestone and wood plank, the winding alleys and leather-flap windows, after that one but hard-killing day at Oak Hills. Land. Rows of crops alternated by years—cotton, then maybe sweet sorghum or sugarcane—the blistering summer sun, the winter rains, the scent of manure and fresh air and workaday sweat. The exhaustion of a day well-worked, of a night's sleep well-earned. A life left to do what a man is supposed to. Abrams has never told anyone this before, but he would like that, to own some land. He sighs contentedly at the thought.

Yet in the midst of his reverie, he hears a man a campfire away break the rhythm of his snores, and in such interruption, Abrams comes crashing back into himself. He checks the pocket watch snatched from the battlefield. It approaches three o'clock. He surveys the hundreds who lay sleeping in the early morning beside him. He has heard too many boys wishing for the same, the talk of the acres they have coming to them, the crops they will sow and bounties they will reap once the war is done. He spits in the night. Disgusted by his lack of imagination, Abrams knows that while he is alone in his dreams, he is not exceptional for it. Hard knowledge for a man just turned twenty.

His thoughts veer darker.

They veer to the yellow fever that first stole the blush from Gerta's cheek before then taking her life, along with the almost 10,000 other poor souls in the epidemic that ravaged New Orleans during the summer of '53. Streets at the time were choked with evacuees and death mongers, those who pulled wagons behind them and bellowed at the surviving inhabitants of each home to haul out their dead. Once managed, bodies were thrown haphazardly atop one another into the wooden carts, arms and legs dangling over the sides, mouths frozen aghast. Thousands of coffins floated below sea level in the city's shallowest graves. The air of summertime New Orleans, already cloying with heat and humidity and the fecund scent of the river, for an entire season became filthier with flies, the burning of purifying tar barrels, and the pestilential stink of human rot.

Abrams remembers his mother's jaundice before the fever killed her, her flesh grown waxen and yellow, her eyes like yolk drops. The sweat and chills, the febrile screams, her collapsing weakness. On her deathbed in their cramped Lafayette City two-room, he remembers her lips like withered leaves on his ear. "Read me that passage again," she had whispered in a rare moment of lucidity, her eyes smiling weakly. "Go on, practice that French."

Young Elias, his own eyes swollen from tears, exhausted from grief, dutifully opened his copy of Jacques-Felix Lelièvre's *Nouveau Jardinier de la Louisiane* and read in broken fluency the passage his mother so dearly loved. "There is no need," he began softly, "to reject a plant when it does not succeed during the first years of its introduction to a particular climate. One must realize fully that culture more or less modifies the nature of vegetation, and that, through well-understood care, one can succeed in naturalizing plants to which the climate once seemed completely adverse."

Although neither of them understood the French completely, as immigrant stock arrived to foreign shores themselves, from the context they had each gained plenty. She thanked him. He closed the book, put his head on the bed beside her, and in deep, heaving sobs, began to dampen her mattress with tears.

She begged her son not to cry. She touched the crown of his head. "Just when you've been pulled apart at the seams for good," she whispered tenderly, "right when you've lost yourself entire, the love I've got for you now, that's the love I'd like you to fall back on, keep you whole."

His reply was to fill the room with the sounds of a misery that would outweigh any the war could ever marshal. He would carry it with him forever.

Embittered, refusing to submit to his sadness, Abrams has come to grasp the lengths that men will go to in order to survive. Even now he stashes his food in an artilleryman's valise, and defends it vigilantly. He eats alone, sheltered by trees or wagons. When others beg for a plateful, he asks what they have to offer in return. He has been unimpressed thus far; if anything arouses his interest, he simply waits to sit with them at cards. Before the night is through, whatever he aimed to own is his, and no food has been spared.

The men of the Third Louisiana begin to speak about him. "Slicker'n pelican shit, that one," they say, looking over their shoulders. "About as charitable, too." Abrams has proven that he will fight beside these men in arms, but he makes no pretense: he will not fight by them in spirit.

Only once in these first weeks of war does he open his heart. On a warm evening almost a month after Oak Hills, John Lee Carlson of the fine straw Panama returned to offer a pinch of tobacco he had finally been able muster for himself. Strangely moved by the gesture, despite his better judgment Abrams dropped his ladle into the skillet with a sigh, and invited his guest to a plate of beans and sowbelly. Carlson's eyes immediately flashed, but he showed restraint by adding, "Providing you've enough for yourself, mind you."

"It ain't no seven-course, if that's what you're askin'—but I got enough."

"You sure?"

"Look, you want to pussy-foot, that's fine, but me, I'm eatin'."

Together they ate, sighing heavily between bites. They spoke in low tones about small things. Carlson, Abrams learned, was thirty-four and had a wife named Imogene and twin daughters, Ella and Marguerite, back home in New Orleans. He was the second son of a wealthy Levee Street textile merchant, but unlike his elder brother, from an early age he showed no interest in joining the family trade. He had chosen instead a curriculum in the Classics at Centenary College, where he learned to revel in the immortal imaginings of Homer and Sophocles, Horace and Seneca. For pleasure he turned to Shakespeare's comedies, justified by the homage paid to Plautus and Terence therein. That night beside Abrams he referred to Louisiana—to the Confederacy as a whole, actually—as his own little

31

Peloponnesus, meant to be protected from the invasion of Persian forces, or Troy, from Menelaus' jilted wrath. He saw a fair analogy between the secessionist South and past civilizations grappling for self-sovereignty in a world that would have otherwise. "Since the dawn of time," Carlson said, "all politics of the governing have been about one man's hand making sure another's remains empty and without. Well, Elias, I'm here today, a proud rebellionist, to stem that tide of denial. Yes sir, I'm here to offer my own two hands, so that liberty may be guaranteed for those future generations of Southerners I love, though may not as yet be born." True, he admitted to a "slightly loquacious manner" but made no apology for it. Only one of a handful of faculty members who was not a Jesuit priest, he now taught his passion at the College of the Immaculate Conception to students whose faith in Christ differed greatly from his own.

Of Abrams in return, Carlson learned almost nothing save that his new companion was laconic, without family or lover, and in the hardness of his eyes, the guardian of what appeared to be a crushing secret.

After dinner they smoked Carlson's tobacco, their legs kicked out long and leisurely. They stared into the campfire, content to think of nothing but what they had just learned of each other and the coals slowly dying. "So," groaned Carlson at last, rubbing both hands down his belly, "an Israelite then, are we?"

Abrams quit pulling on his pipe in mid-draw. On New Orleans' rowdier streets, any mention of his faith had invariably caused his hackles to raise, the least insult leading to a swift and furious reprisal. Oftentimes, before some unsuspecting fool's derision could be fully discharged, Abrams would flurry on his chin, nose, cheeks, and eyes—four, five, six times, *pow, pow, pow*—with such precise punishment that his fists' recipient frequently hit the ground before the offense could be completed. Even among the Cypress Stump Boys, Abrams was known and prized for his lightning hand speed. When it came to pugilism, none of the others remotely approached his natural talent. That night, however, Abrams found no contempt in Carlson's tone.

He agreed that it was so.

"I've long admired your people," nodded Carlson, loosing a stream of smoke. "Understand there're quite a few of y'all fighting for the Cause these days."

"I ain't no census taker, John Lee."

But Carlson was already tabulating. "Let's see, first off you got old Senator Benjamin up there in Richmond, just appointed Secretary of War by Jeff Davis himself. Then there's Yulee, the Floridian, and that Luria fellow, hero of Sewell's Point. Of course, Hyams's here with us, with his son pulling second lieutenant in Company D—"

"That don't mean they're kin to me," Abrams broke in. "I run my own flag, case you were wonderin'."

"Ho now," calmed Carlson, "rein yourself in, son, save it for the boys in blue. I'm merely recognizing that you've an old, proud faith there. A strong faith. Smart."

"Some proud, some smart," granted Abrams. "But plenty scrawny and foolish, too."

"Shit," laughed Carlson, rolling onto his shoulder to nudge a bed into the earth. "I'm Methodist-born, teaching at a Catholic college. Believe me, Elias, I've an intimate acquaintance with both scrawny and foolish."

5

Following drill one afternoon, the men of the Third Louisiana are left to their own devices. Some doze under nearby trees, others flip lazily through their copies of *Hardee's Tactics* or draft letters home, lamenting their condition and the stultifying boredom that has settled over the camp. More weeks have passed. They have returned to Camp Jackson but found no succor there. In that time, Abrams and Carlson have begun to share night fires, playing cards at which Abrams almost always wins, though without the merciless manner he is known for back home. When among a larger game, a group of haggard swamp rats their opponents, he has even steered a pot or two Carlson's way. For much to his surprise, he has come to view these evenings as almost pleasurable, something to take his mind off the skulking sense of remorse, Wolfe, the New Orleans law he assumes to be on his trail, and the Union army that is said to strike any day now. He confesses none of this to Carlson, of course. Rather, he simply nods grimly at most of what the professor has to say, bites his smile when he finds something amusing, and offers another ladle of old beans and grizzled fatback whenever he has one to spare. Least of all does he question why his new companion, evidently a man of high birth, refuses to exploit his family's position to keep his own larder stocked. Carlson, he has come to understand, prefers life beyond his father's influence.

Carlson himself sees no contradiction of character when requesting a helping or two from Abrams. In doing so, he once claimed, he was graciously enabling his young comrade-in-arms to perform the time-honored ritual, once so prevalent in Classical Greece, of *xenia*, or hospitality. "For one never knows," Carlson belched contentedly that night with a wink, "when the gods might come a-calling in disguise."

During these times together, the professor speaks at length on many subjects, his daughters' precocity and his wife's beauty not the least among them. Between puffs on their pipes, late at night beneath the stars, he rambles on about Greek heroes and divine lechery, Roman poets and eternal punishments, about such grand abstractions as victory and peace. Given Carlson's chatty nature, Abrams is content to mostly listen, divulging almost nothing of his own past. It does not matter; this one-sidedness is a dynamic they both condone. Indeed, his eyes absent toward the heavens, Abrams can scarcely believe how much he enjoys hearing the paternal, lulling tone of Carlson's voice. He is unaccustomed to another man's words being anything but false or threatening.

"Happy Kippur," says the professor one evening with a polite nod. "I'd ask whether you were fasting, but attesting the current state of our rations, you've not much of a choice. Seems we're all of us a bit Hebrew tonight."

Abrams had no idea the Day of Atonement was upon him. Though he has no religion, he broods deeply on those sins committed past and present. On a thick pine log by the campfire, wrenched by his thoughts, he cannot sit still. He shifts his position, spits into the fire, purses his lips, and frowns. He sucks pensively on his pipe. He mutters to himself. Furiously, he stokes the coals. Asleep, he tosses and turns, calling out in terrified bursts to the night as he dreams of bloody teeth falling from his head like hail raining down from a rufescent sky. Come morning, he eats all the cold and coagulated pork he can stomach.

The war continues. Reports arrive from places like Dry Woods Creek, Carnifax Ferry, Cheat Mountain Summit, Lexington, Blue Mills, and Barbourville, of clashes colorfully named, like the Battle of the Mules and the Battle of the Hemp Bales. The men of the Third Louisiana feast on rumors of Confederate victory outstripping the Union's threefold. This, while filling their bellies on unripe apples, only to groan and shit violently for it afterward. For many, the surgeon's ministrations have been replaced by the priest's. For those more fortunate, fervor has become listlessness. In this sedentary and unprovided-for life, most of the surviving men pick apart their purpose, and what purpose awaits them. Such time for reflection ill-suits the fighting man. In it, he regresses toward individuality, the moth hole of any blanketing ideal. Yet in the two who now loom above a squatting Abrams on this late September afternoon, a joy lives still, grounded in their pickled and fat-chunked livers and the desire to play some draw.

"Heard you was handy with a deck," says one.

Abrams squints up, shielding his eyes. The man is small and dark. He has the look of the rat about him. His beady eyes neighbor too tightly in his narrow face, his nose twitching upturned and sharp. He possesses a tilt to one side, his bony shoulders set askew, as though his frame were a balance, but weighted unjustly. Atop his splayed ears sits a brown flop hat, its felt brim ragged with use.

Beside him is an oaf, a man whose head is so big he has taken to banding it with a soiled cloth and leather strap rather than track down a hat that will fit him. His face is made of dirt and beard. Strands of long hair freed from their binding mat greasily to his forehead and cheeks. Together, their odor is nearly overwhelming.

"I've been known to play a hand or two," Abrams replies at last.

The men are on the ground beside him, shuffling. Abrams interrupts, asking whether he might have the honor of first deal. With a begrudging smile, the smaller man passes him the deck.

He goes by Petitgout, the larger of the two by Cobb, both from Company K, the Pelican Rifles under Captain James Viglini. They are distant cousins from across the river in Algiers but have spent most of the previous year in New Orleans proper, running the same track as Abrams. In fact, Abrams recognizes them from Quinn's, a syphilitic flophouse and gamblers' den on Chartres where more than one man, once entering in buoyant spirits, exits lifeless, slumped over a meaty shoulder. Although he has never gambled against them directly, from several tables away Abrams remembers these two to be a shifty and dangerous pair. He need only ask the ill-fated gent against whom they played the night they first caught Abrams' attention. The gent who now feels his way through the world with flailing hands and a cane, his eyes thumbed out like rotten plums by Cobb, at Petitgout's drunken demand. He had apparently possessed an uncontrollable fluttering of the eyes, which, in conjunction with too much whiskey and a great deal of loss, proved a distraction for his rather short-fused competitor.

Initially Abrams is concerned they will recognize him in return, for with recognition will no doubt come a stream of questions he does not wish to field. After a tense moment, however, he eases, confident that drunk as they were on those few occasions they shared time at Quinn's, they do not know him at all. Still, he is glad Carlson is nowhere to be found. This, he fears, will be no game for the weak.

"Listen here," declares Petitgout, "come my turn, I'll deal you square. 'Gainst these country corks, I'll lay the bottom stock as sure as the day's long, but 'gainst a feller such as yourself, I won't play no brace."

Abrams has already run the dimensions of the deck with his nimble fingers, felt the slightly longer cut of the four aces and two kings, and despite the menacing history of the men before him, withdrawn and fanned in one hand these six cards for Petitgout's inspection, all in an instant. "That's the case," he responds flatly, "then what say we play a deck that ain't met the stripper plate." His eyebrows arch and stay there.

Petitgout's face goes red at his cheat's discovery. Cobb gawks from his cousin to Abrams and then back to his cousin. His fingers creep for the Bowie knife latched to his hip. It is a long, hard moment. But before any violence erupts, Petitgout explodes into a guffaw of laughter so loud it belies the small diaphragm from which it has emanated. "You keep a looky-look on this one here, Cobb!" he roars, wiping a tear from his eye. "This fucker's got sand, by golly!"

Truer cards appear. Already identified as a serious player, Abrams does not try to sharp them with clumsy card work. Instead he shuffles the deck magnificently, a quick bridging *thrip, thrip*, then a cut and shuffle again. His hands flow like rippled silk, like quicksilver, they are masterly in their element. His cool eyes betray no pride at this talent, but simply the placidity of a man performing what he has grown to know best.

They are hands born of training. Not long after his mother's death, Abrams started as a capper for Jules Bouchard, a small-time monte man who needed a shill to step up and show the crowd how easy winning could be. In return, Bouchard staked the boy to meals of gumbo and raw oysters and beer, a pallet to sleep on whenever he needed it, and most valuably, lessons in manual dexterity. Before long, Abrams was running his own sport not far from the Presbytère, sliding and cupping and switching the tickets—two aces and a queen—with impossible speed. Once a mark placed his dollar down, the boy's hands would begin their flight, stopping only to flip the old lady over once or twice to show her placement before the cards resumed their swiftly winding route. Up and down, round and round his hands blurred, until, ready to move in for the kill, he palmed the queen imperceptibly into his sleighted hand, where a third ace was waiting to be shunted into her stead. In his months running the scam, he was never once caught.

He attempted to teach this skill to Wolfe, who labored at it day and night with a tongue lodged into the corner of his beautiful mouth. It was during these practice sessions of monte, still early on at the Jewish Widows and Orphans Home, when the boys sensed that theirs would harden into a firm brotherhood. For Abrams, his talent at conning established that he, like all youths in search of friends and fathers, actually had something to contribute to a life other than his own, something irrefutable were his new companion ever asked to speak of his strengths to another. This provided Abrams a feeling of self-importance that, as an orphan, he was unaccustomed to experiencing but to which he was quickly and wholly seduced. Wolfe's genius for arrogance and cruelty to almost every other living being only added to the allure.

Wolfe, in turn, admired the serpentine beauty of Abrams' hands in motion, so graceful, so clean, but loved above all their brutal efficacy. He

admired them so much that on occasion he even volunteered to act as a shill in the crowd himself, just as Abrams had once done. "Goddamn if you ain't a thoroughbred talent, Elias," he would say affectionately afterward, tousling his friend's hair as they split the winnings between them. "Whoreson or no, you do have your qualities."

These rare instances at monte would prove to be the only times Wolfe willingly assumed the role of minion to anyone. Ultimately, though, he had no knack for such illusion. His gifts, they would soon realize, were suited to a different method.

—

Over the first hands of pot-limit five-card draw, each player studies the other nonchalantly, searching for tells. Where do the eyes go? Do they linger on face cards? Do pupils constrict? Dilate? Does the jaw tighten? Does it go slack? Who holds his breath? Whose jugular pulses? What are the betting patterns? Is strong played weak? Weak strong? During these first hands, Petitgout blathers on easily while Abrams and Cobb just listen, their minds, however, all three of them, calculating with the ruthlessness of popes and kings. They ante. They call. They raise or fold. Cobb's ignorant air is difficult to read, though Abrams knows he will require but a few more rounds before the large man's defenses begin to reveal themselves. Petitgout is simpler. His silence behind strong hands is obvious; when he receives a card he needs, his mouth clamps shut and his eyes flicker directly to his cash pile and hold, as if making sure his funds will stand by him on his march toward triumph. Abrams also notices how when the small man bluffs, his talking intensifies, the kind of chatter to suggest he has not a care in the world. Abrams understands this behavior because he does not practice it himself. Nothing shows a man's worry more than false cheer.

Meanwhile, his own erratic style of peck-and-bet, then drop-a-bomb, has frustrated his opponents. He can see how angry Petitgout is becoming, his rat-face twisting each time Abrams shows his kings. Vitriol escapes his filthy mouth in steam-pipe bursts. It is one thing to lose.

No man likes it. But a select breed of bastard soul finds it especially hateful to watch others win. And Petitgout's soul takes source from the latter pool, there is no question. Disgust for any joy but his own hangs smothering above him, black and indecent.

Abrams shrewdly decides to dump a couple hands. He is tough, but he is no fool; he knows a devil when he sees one. He has watched men of New Orleans stagger out into the night through swinging doors, faces stricken, hands bloodied over punctured guts, all because their cards proved consistently sharper than their opponents'. Too often he has heard shouts of victory ratchet hideously upward into shrieks of death. If he can help it, his fate will be otherwise.

Petitgout's second win becomes a third. He cackles, slaps his thigh, and spits, drawing a dirty sleeve across his cankered bottom lip. His smile is stained with tobacco and years of neglect as he rakes these pots toward him across the bare earth. Giddily, he informs Abrams that his luck is turning hot. "Hotter'n a red-hot poker," he grins, "one I'm liable to ram up your bung, you step back in my way, now." Finally, then, granted a small taste of success, Petitgout relents enough to ask Abrams his reasons for fighting, the question all combatants eventually ask one another.

Abrams thinks on it. He does not mention running for his life as a motive. Instead, he lies. "For God and country, suppose. Like the rest of us."

"Oh nossir," laughs Petitgout derisively, "don't stir me into that pot. Them ain't the reasons that I'm out here. Not on your fuckin' tintype, they ain't. Not hardly."

When Abrams does not respond, Petitgout asks whether he would like further explanation. Appreciating that with such men it is best to express interest, Abrams agrees.

"Well, I'll tell you," says Petitgout with a nod, "I'm out here fightin' 'cause there ain't no rhyme to it." He gestures vaguely to the camp around him, the trees and fields, the clouds and sun, the very day itself. "No fuckin' rhyme t'all."

Abrams waits for more.

Petitgout leans in. "See, sooner you realize that old cunny upstairs don't give two shits about you, sooner you start realizin' all them folk who tithe and kneel and what-not ain't got no more of a say in how things get played out than sinnin' motherfucks like you and Cobb and me." He winks.

Abrams broods on this. After a moment, he says, "Pretty grim aspect you got there."

"Well, hold on now, there's peaches in that cream, too, you know." He shifts his position. "Look, good don't mean shit, bad don't mean shit, 'cause in the end it's *all* shit. But seein' as such, least out here I get to watch my so-called betters, them pillars of the fuckin' community, well, I get to watch them cocksuckers die moanin' for their mommas, right there in the mud. And when they do, boy, I'm tellin' you, I just stand there pissin' all over their moral fuckin' fiber. Fuckin' hi-larious. Love it."

Abrams stares. He cannot help himself.

"God ain't tendin' us, Abrams. No use thinkin' contrariwise." With that Petitgout spits into the dirt and then returns to his cards. "Now it don't hurt much neither, them payin' me. I'll take old Jeff Davis' eleven dollars a month, every goddamned time."

Hands come and hands go. Day eases into night. Pipes have been smoked and spent and repacked. Tobacco has been chewed. Cobb, though nearly mute, proves to be a surprisingly skilled player, while Petitgout continues to play his hands alternately hushed or brazenly, depending on their strength. He is either total silence or bullying bluff that rides too stridently above any levelheaded play. In one game, he roils his chaw from one corner of his mouth to the other and asks Abrams where the pot stands. In observing this, Abrams folds at once. That tell, Abrams realizes from experience, means Petitgout has a powerful hand: any decent player knows exactly how much each pot is worth, at any given time. Petitgout's chin falls to his chest. He spits an oath. He flips a full house, knaves high. He had hoped to take Abrams for more than two dollars. He collects the money but is fuming. More hands are dealt. Twilight settles.

The strain between them deepens.

6

———

Somewhere off in the distance, the pale moon rising above them, a soldier's voice soon breaks mournfully into song, a lament Abrams recognizes straightaway from his time spent loitering on the steps of Christ Church Cathedral, smoking stolen, rum-cured tobacco on Sunday mornings while waiting for the fine-eyed Episcopalian girls to skip outside once the last of their psalms were sung. It is beautifully resonant, this soldier's voice, and Abrams cannot quell the great stirring in his breast he feels for it:

> There is a fountain filled with blood
> Drawn from Emmanuel's veins,
> And sinners plunged beneath that flood
> Lose all their guilty stains.
> Lose all their guilty stains,
> Lose all their guilty stains,
> And sinners plunged beneath that flood
> Lose all their guilty stains.

Abrams' first instinct is to hum along with the tune, but he knows, too, that music, in its very ability to calm, betrays a man's disquiet like little else in the world. He thus deals silently, flicking each player his card with the solemnity of a mortician distributing hymnals among the anguished.

Moments later, gnawing on a grimy hangnail and musing on his hand, Petitgout heels up onto a haunch and looses a fart so appallingly rank that even Cobb wrinkles his nose in disgust. "So," the small man begins casually, complementing his flatulence with an easing groan, "how's the Smile and them, anyway?"

Abrams pretends not to hear this.

"Silas Wolfe," continues Petitgout. "Cypress Stump Boys. Your fellers back home. I'll take two. How they doin'?"

The abruptness of these questions has caught Abrams off guard. His belly drops out from under him and then flops over sickeningly as blood rushes thundering to his ears. He was right to be concerned. If he is found to be a liar, falsehood will beg far more suspicion than truth. He swallows back his dread, suddenly aware that Petitgout is savvy enough to grasp that no one simply leaves a gang like the Cypress Stump Boys. Falling outs, Petitgout must know, tend to end in very bloody ways. Yet the idea of admission paralyzes Abrams even more. He is exposed. He has nowhere to run. In the language of cards, he has been put on tilt. After a brief pause, he decides his final play. "They're awright, guess. Been a while, though." He passes Petitgout two cards, hoping this will satisfy.

It does not. "Strange thing," says Petitgout with a sniff, organizing his new hand. "You up here. Alone. Can't quite figure it." His eyes rest dully on Abrams' own.

Abrams has underestimated his opponent. It has happened before, in games of greater stakes but of far less consequence, and each time the self-loathing he suffers afterward turns his saliva caustic in his mouth. It is a perilous illiteracy, the failure to read the motives of men. Desperate to conceal any anxiety for it, he involuntarily shifts his gaze away. A clumsy play. His years of gambling have come to this, and his years have let him down. Already the small, dark man has made up his mind about something, this is evident, and before their time is through, Abrams now knows he must learn precisely what that something is. His life will depend on it.

"What," adds Petitgout, "you feelin' poorly?"

"'Course not. Just here we are, playin' cards, when all of a sudden I got a goddamned inquisition on my hands."

Petitgout's eyes fall to half-lids. "You don't wanna draw my ire, boy."

The silence between them is fraught with violence, the hostility made plain. Abrams' mind is racing. He longs for his old deerskin gambler's boots, those in which he kept a blade sheathed along his right calf. At the moment he has no weapon handy, the derringer and penknife stowed in his haversack, his Mississippi rifle too unwieldy for such close quarters. Providing he lives through this, he will never go unarmed again. "Well, if you must know," he begins, the blood rising to his face as he decides it will be Cobb he jumps first, "Silas felt it wouldn't be proper, us Cypress Stumps gone unrepresented in this imbroglio here. Said wherever there's a scrape, that's where we'll be. And me—lucky me—I drew short straw."

Petitgout rolls his tobacco and narrows his eyes further. He spits. "Naw," he says softly.

Abrams licks his lips, bracing himself for the attack he must now launch. Already he has foreseen how it will go—with his left hand he will hurl a fistful of campfire ash into Cobb's face, with his right he will smash the large man's jaw, before swinging to his feet and kicking Petitgout full force in his teeth. *Five,* he breathes, *four, three, two—*

It has come down to this, the calm before a thunderclap.

Suddenly, in the split-second before events prove irrevocable, Petitgout erupts into another roar of laughter, this time slapping his knee gaily, sending a small cloud of dust into the evening air. "Go'on and fuck yerself!" he roars, throwing a lighthearted palm at Abrams, "I ain't no goddamned confessional!" Here he turns and hoots to his companion, "You saw him, though, huh, Earl?"

"I saw him, Skip."

"Shut the fuck up, Earl," laughs Petitgout. "Naw, c'mon, we're just funnin' you," he says to Abrams amiably, placing a hand on his knee. "But your face, goddamn. Like you was a nigger child caught stealin' pies from the sill, I'd swear to it."

Abrams laughs weakly in reply. The moment of challenge has passed, for now. Still, he does not unwind.

"Like to piss myself entire," chuckles Petitgout. "Say now, got me thinkin'," he goes on, cheerily changing the subject once again, "you've ever heard about old Grampin, feller who ran that little roulette table on Tchoupitoulas back in the day?"

Quietly deliberating the new jeopardy of which he knows he is not yet absolved, Abrams says no, never.

"Look, sure you have, only square game in town, that fuckin' Grampin. Just so happens, had himself a regular, went by the name of"—here he turns to Cobb again—"what that fuckin' guy's name was?"

Cobb answers with a shrug.

"Brains of a shit sack, this one here," says Petitgout to Abrams, nodding toward his cousin. "Well, for the sake of gossip, we'll call this feller, 'Lucky Fuck.' Man's a flatboat captain, Lucky Fuck is, old cunt who comes in every time his boat's tied up. Now this Lucky Fuck's stingy as a whore with her pussy on Sabbath morn, always has been. Comes in, places twenty-five cents—never more'n twenty-five fuckin' cents—on red, every time. One night, puts that bit down on red, same as ever, same as always. Only this night Lucky Fuck's tired, see, so he rests his fuckin' beard in his hand and closes his eyes, catch him a nap."

As Abrams listens, he cannot help but feel appalled by his miscalculation: he is confronting in Cobb and Petitgout something born sinister, he feels this in his gut, everything wrong with an already wrong world. He sees in them a lesson once learned from his mother's *Nouveau Jardinier de la Louisiane*. There, as a boy, he had read that when one's garden suffers from rodents, two rats must be trapped alive and imprisoned together in a jar, wherein they are then to be starved for days. When a third rat is added on the fourth day, the ravenous pair will attack him with singular purpose, squealing with delight as they tear him to pieces, their necks thick with descending meat as they gorge on their hapless kin until nothing remains but its whiskers. After eight or ten days of this process' renewal, within that jar will remain two pure cannibals who, when loosed upon the world, will prey solely on their own kind, and thus devour, with great relish, a whole host of innocents.

In these cousins Abrams witnesses those very rats. Yet he admits, too, that this kind of judgment means nothing. Of the many he has known, despicable men mostly live very fruitful lives.

"Now would you believe it," says Petitgout, "but Lucky Fuck wins that first round. Only he's so fuckin' sleepy, cocksucker don't move to collect, so Grampin just spins that wheel. And what do you suppose happens, but Lucky Fuck wins again. And wins, and wins, and wins. But he's so fuckin' tired, see, he keeps right on sleepin'. Poor fuckin' Grampin's pullin' out his goddamned hair, that's what he's doin', he's going broke as balls, 'cause that captain cocksucker's doublin' his goddamned winnings every single time." Petitgout coughs wetly into his fist. "Well, swear to holy Christ, Abrams, sixteen rounds come and sixteen rounds go, and every one—every goddamned one now—lands on red. Grampin's goddamned at this point, can't hardly take it no more, so at long last he throws the man's winnings at him—eight thousand dollars all told now—and screams to 'get the fuck out, you!' 'Get the fuck out, you!' he screams, but that captain's so goddamned tired, he don't move a stitch. Well fuck, what's a man to do? Grampin pokes him some, and would you believe it, cocksucker rolls hard from his chair, goes crashin' to the floor like a slab of dead cunt. Deader than my dear sweet momma, that captain was."

Petitgout's story concludes here. Silence falls. His beady eyes become slits, and he offers an especially contemptuous little grin. There is meaning in that grin. All levity has vanished, at once replaced by the purest air of malevolence Abrams has breathed since the night of the murder from which he has fled. "Funny thing, ain't it?" sneers Petitgout. "Gambling 'gainst a dead man."

The game ends not long thereafter.

As the two stand to leave, Petitgout hoists up his britches. He looks down at Abrams. In that look flashes something beyond the animal; it is the look of a beast that enjoys its brutish station in life. "I'll make sure to give Wolfe your best, I see him next, huh?" he says wickedly.

An hour later, alone in the dark, Abrams debates whether these cousins from Algiers have been expressly sent from New Orleans or if, by chance, they are merely obeying the laws of Gallatin Street and are therefore distrustful of what they have just met in him. He can draw no conclusion. He knows only that sleep, from here on in, will be one-eyed and light.

7

Abrams awakes one early October morning with a toe nudging his ribs. With the speed of a snake strike he grabs the offending ankle, brandishes in his right hand the knife with which he has taken to sleeping nightly. He has crossed paths with neither Cobb nor Petitgout since, but knows enough about the laws of predation to understand the patience required before a kill is made. In his haste that morning, he nearly severs an Achilles tendon, his eyes focusing to discover he is clutching an officer's boot, there is no question, its leather too fine and tall, its toe too tapered, to be an infantryman's. Samuel Myers Hyams, the company commander, stands above him. In each hand Hyams holds a tin cup that steams in the early morning air. His hair is rumpled steel; his eyes are crisply intelligent. His double-breasted frock coat of cadet gray is no less soiled than those of the sleeping men over whom he has stepped to reach the spot where he now rests. His saber dangles low on his left hip, below a scarlet belly sash. He is unbothered by the near-knifing: "You make me spill my coffee, son, and you'll be hauling wood for the rest of your natural born days. Now, kindly put up the blade."

Born in South Carolina, moved to New Orleans in the manner of many Sephardic families following the cotton trade westward, Hyams eventually settled in Natchitoches, Louisiana. There, he began a successful and varied career: U.S. deputy surveyor, clerk of the district court, decorated captain in the Mexican War, six-year veteran as sheriff, U.S. marshal of the Western District of Louisiana, and register of the Land Office. His sense of public service temporarily fulfilled, he then joined the ranks of the landed gentry. He founded a plantation, Lac des Mures, on the Red River above Grand Ecore and Natchitoches. When the War Between the States began, he was forty-eight years old, brother to Louisiana's lieutenant governor, Henry Hyams, in command of his own large family, and one of the state's most thriving agriculturalists.

The men of the Pelican Rangers Nos. 1 and 2, over two hundred and thirty strong—the company he raised himself and the largest in the state—love him as a concerned father is loved by his sons. "You Abrams?" he asks bluntly.

His blanket thrown off, his knife stowed, Abrams is pulling on a brogan, hopping up and down to catch his balance. Though he usually defers to no one, something in Hyams' demeanor demands it. "Yessir," he says, finally standing at attention.

The officer sips from one of the cups. The other he offers to Abrams, who accepts it with a nod. The younger man is shocked and then pleased to discover a fine, strong coffee dosed liberally with Kentucky mash. It is a far cry from the poor substitutes of peanut husk, boiled pea, dried apple, okra seed, potato peel, and other seed-tick brews he has been forced to swallow in the past weeks. Until that time, his gambling had been able to maintain a fairly regular supply of coffee. Professor Carlson, offering his services as tutor to some of the regiment's most ignorant, if earnest, men, had also been contributing the odd tablespoon of grounds to their pooled reserve. At present, however, coffee has become among the camp's most prized commodities.

Hyams takes a good long look at his private. "You make it through Oak Hills all right?"

"Better than those I killed, reckon."

Hyams grunts. "You put off by Fremont's proclamation, one about all those taking up arms against the Union now subject to execution?"

Abrams shrugs. "Figured they wasn't offerin' up no twirl at the cotillion to begin with."

The lieutenant colonel laughs at this. "I saw your name on the company roster. Joined up not that long ago, seems."

Abrams nods. "Couple months."

"From New Orleans?"

"Yessir."

Hyams continues to size up the young man before him. "Who's your father?" he asks.

At his father's mention, Abrams' jaw hardens. Despite his better judgment, he does not lie. "I. J. Lieber," he says at length.

"I. J. Lieber?" Hyams is astonished. "The planter?"

After a pause, Abrams nods again.

Hyams narrows his eyes. Following a few seconds' hard appraisal, his face broadens with recognition. "Oh sure," he exclaims, "there you go, I see it now. It's in the eyes. Same challenge. Thing is, I didn't even know he had a son."

Abrams sniffs. "Him neither."

"I see." Hyams takes a judicious sip. He winces as he arches his back. He stretches his neck to one side. "Toughest son-of-a-bitch I've ever had to negotiate against, I'll tell you that much. But boy, talk about *smart*. He still own that plantation out in Napoleonville?"

Abrams has known someone would eventually ask these questions of him, and yet, despite the preparation, he finds the answers difficult to manage. "Nossir."

"War hit him hard, has it?"

"Man's dead, sir."

Hyams goes disconsolate. "Sorry to hear it. When?"

"Fairly recent."

"Surprised I haven't heard," mutters Hyams. He takes a sip. "Then again, never did possess much of a congregational air about him, your daddy."

Abrams does not explain just how recent. Instead, at the mention of Lieber's land, his thoughts flash inescapably back nine years to that hot August day in 1852, to the time and place they were first introduced. It is a cruel memory that comes flooding through him, and though Abrams now stands older by nearly a decade, a man of his own fists and wit, in this sudden recollection he clenches his teeth, immediately discomfited by the remembrance of the pain that first day caused.

A week before their meeting, Isaiah Joshua Lieber, Esq., owner of city and country dwellings, had apparently decided it was time to meet the fruit of his loins. Through a message dispatched to Gerta by Tartuffe, his most conscientious house slave, Lieber had requested "in most emphatic terms" that they visit him at Beau Rivage, his Assumption parish estate.

At first Gerta had blinked at the note in disbelief. When its gist finally sank in, the boy watched her eyes set into a wrath he had never before seen. The note crumpled in her grip. Her other hand found, as if of its own accord, a porcelain pitcher that she then hurled violently against a wall, shattering it into a dozen pieces.

"Bastard ain't gettin' his hands on you unsupervised," she hissed. "Lord, you can be sure of that."

And so they spent the day together, father and son, mother seething a few paces behind, white-knuckling her straight blade, while man quizzed boy on all matters. I. J. Lieber was of slight build, a thin, gray-haired man with a hawk's nose, sunken cheeks, and sharp jaw behind hoary old sideburns. Gold-rimmed bifocals perched at the tip of that nose, fronting an intense pair of eyes. With those eyes he checked his pocket watch, often.

They walked the land thoroughly. Bordering nearby Bayou Lafourche, the plantation was only sixty-five miles from Lieber's resplendent Toulouse Street townhouse, yet according to him, a full world away. "Now I don't mind the city," he told the boy early on, "but I'd gladly stay out here forever."

At the evaporating barn, Elias learned about the new process of re-fining sugar by way of Rillieux's multiple-effect evaporator rather than the antiquated open-kettle system still used by so many of Lieber's neighbors. The boy heard terms like "latent heat" and "condensing coils" and "vacuum chambers." He merely nodded in reply, detesting himself for his ignorance.

Noticing his son's distress, Lieber asked whether he had had much schooling.

The boy kicked the dirt. Again, he said nothing.

Lieber turned to Gerta: "Well, has he?"

She gritted her teeth. "He knows a jackass from an Arab, if that's what you're askin'."

His face went stern. He took a step toward her. "No, Gerta, that's decidedly *not* what I'm asking. I'm asking whether he's being officially educated."

She, in turn, stepped challengingly toward him. "Well frankly, *Isaiah*, we ain't had a whole lot of time for inkwells and slate—or can't you do your own goddamned sums?"

In the entrance of the evaporating barn they stood, silence descending between them. Elias picked at the wooden doorframe. With hands on her hips, Gerta followed I. J. Lieber's eyes wherever they went, refusing to let him escape her distaste. A consummate man of business, in this showdown he then did something rare: he balked in the face of a stare-down. "You there, nigger," he called to one of his slaves, a behemoth in the midst of stripping sugarcane for treatment. "Come see."

With the docility of a well-heeled dog, the large man dropped what he was doing, lowered his eyes, and lumbered barefooted outside to meet his master's request. "Take off that blouse," he was ordered. "Turn around."

The slave complied, exposing a broad musculature that forced Lieber to inhale proudly at the thought of past deals shrewdly struck. Woven across the slave's back was a coarse latticework of whipping scars, each thread raised thick and white in the noonday sun. "See Lucius here?" Lieber asked his son. "How scarred his back is? How strong?"

The boy said he did.

"Well, the next time you think that life's treated you unkind, I want you to remember Lucius and this back here."

In heading for the great house, Gerta limping a few paces behind, boiling with rage, Elias noticed how the laneside live oaks met over him at the very tips of their limbs, the sun piercing through in gaps of geometry, leaf to leaf, angle to angle. Walking on, limbs welcoming above, the scene struck the boy as a soldier's processional, with him charging slowly beneath a hall of outstretched sabers meant as protection against a series of astonishing new hazards. It was by far the happiest notion of the day.

For lunch they ate shrimp rémoulade and drank cellar-cooled sweet tea with sprigs of fresh mint. Around five o'clock, Lieber formally consulted his watch, turned to his son, and declared, "Young man, it's been a pleasure." The meeting, Elias discovered, had ended. He then received a pat on the head and a gold coin that glinted like a thick slab of sunlight in his childish palm. And with that rather slight purchase, I. J. Lieber, Esq., had dusted his hands clean of progeny forever.

Lieutenant Colonel Hyams takes another sip of his coffee. When he finishes, he flicks the remainder into the coals of the spent fire. "So, how about you, then? You Dispersed of Judah? Or one of the Teutonics maybe. Gates of Mercy? Gates of Prayer?"

"Sir?"

"Your synagogue back home—which one?"

"Not much of a prayin' man, actually."

"Such are the heirlooms we bequeath our sons," says Hyams, chuckling humorlessly into the bottom of his cup. "Few more skirmishes, though, and look out Jerusalem, here comes company." He studies the back of his knuckles with vague interest. "You got any other family?"

"Nossir."

"Got a girl?"

"Not as such."

Hyams looks up hard into Abrams' eyes. "Then you won't mind if I hand this over." In his grip appears a letter, sealed in red wax across the flap, with the words "To a Most Brave Soul, Company G, Pelican Rangers, Third Louisiana Infantry," written flowingly across the face. "Reverend Gutheim," explains Hyams, "rabbi over there at Dispersed of Judah, started a little letter-writing campaign to help with morale. He wrote me a while ago, asking if I had any fellow *Yehudim* in my outfit who might benefit from some encouragement. Said he was orchestrating to have a group of his congregants show their appreciation. Well, I've had a stack of letters like this one here setting on my table for some time now. Saw your name the other morning, figured you as a coreligionist. Hope you don't mind."

Abrams is slightly stunned by the prospect of something nice in his life. Quietly, he says he does not mind at all.

"Good. I know the girl, around seventeen or so, comes from fine stock. Her father's a friend of mine, serving as a sutler in the Eastern Campa—" Here Hyams' face suddenly grimaces, and though he does not drop his cup, his knees nearly buckle. "Apologies," he gasps, clutching the young man's shoulder for support, "rheumatism, comes in spells." He carefully stretches his back. His eyes refocus; the pain has subsided. "If you decide to send her a reply, I'll run it officer's post, make sure she gets it in a timely fashion. If not, that's fine, too. Up to you."

Abrams scratches the back of his head uneasily. "I ain't much for penmanship, is all."

Hyams breaks into a grin. "When it comes to sharing thoughts, Private, been my experience that cursive's just about the *last* thing to concern a woman, long as you've got the soul of a poet scripting them." He claps his hand on Abrams' shoulder, this time affectionately. "Keep up the good fight." And with that, Lieutenant Colonel Samuel Myers Hyams wanders off, leaving his subordinate to stand awkwardly alone, a strange woman's greetings in his dirty hands.

8

Abrams quickly drops to the earth, his legs crossed beneath him. Ever so carefully, he breaks the waxen seal. He does not wish to admit that his hands are trembling. In unfolding the letter, he is met by the powdered scent of femininity, a dainty gust of rosehips and lavender talc, which forces from him a small groan of pleasure. He licks his lips and, squinting his eyes to focus, begins to read intently:

September 12, 1861

Dearest Kind Sir,

Allow me first to impress upon you how delighted I am to have this opportunity to offer my support in the cause for which you are fighting, blindly offered though my endorsement may be. Such a proud and wonderful thing, the service you do us. We at home hold you in nothing but the highest regard, though you are as yet a stranger. In this, permit me to make myself clearly understood. Reverend Gutheim, our blessed rabbi, assured me that no offense would be taken were I to send you this missive unsolicited. I hope for your sake and mine that he is correct in his estimation, as he is correct in so many other arenas of life.

I further ask that you pardon my poor chirography, and that you forgive any foolishness you may perceive henceforth. Yet who is this silly girl, you are no doubt wondering, who so shamelessly writes to you this day? In answer, I will tell you. My name is Nora Bloom, second of four daughters born to Solomon and Rosa Bloom, each arrived of South Carolina. I was born in New Orleans and reared to enviable advantage on Hercules Street. I am currently a student at the Louisiana Normal School, where I train to become a teacher, though find with ever growing dismay I possess little capacity for my intended profession. I shall not endeavor to describe my physical aspect, for that would be too forward indeed. Let us say then that I am merely a vessel of admiration for anyone who willingly risks his life so that we at home may remain true to our customs and beliefs.

We are a wandering people, or so it is said of we Hebrews, but we lucky four thousand have found a home here in New Orleans, have we not? Have we not been welcomed in matters of business, society, and government with far more open arms than so many of our unfortunate coreligionists to the North? Do we not abide by the laws of the land, trust in the sanctity of education and tradesmanship, and wish above all to be deemed, not as mere occupiers of Southern soil, but as honest Southerners ourselves? I ask you, is it not a fine time to be among our people? Is this not a fine time for pride? I therefore see no reason why we should not fight with the greatest imaginable zeal to protect that which we have not possessed in centuries: namely, a fatherland we may rightly call our own.

I do not wish to bore you, gentle Sir, but my heart is near to bursting, and it must find recourse. I have tortured my sisters enough with my prattling on about our faith's achievements, both on the battlefield and off. I sincerely hope you find my enthusiasm for your actions a vindication and not, as my sister Alice once so indelicately phrased it, "an enslavement of banter."

Of course, this is to say nothing of your regiment's majestic triumph at Oak Hills. Lieutenant Colonel Hyams no doubt led

admirably, as his person is one of the noblest in my acquaintance. I hope and trust that you acquitted yourself beyond all expected measure as well. I confess that I should have liked to have seen you, Sir, even though I do not know you. Bravery needs no introduction other than its barest witness, and my eyes have been called the barest witnesses of all. My sisters say I see far more than what G~d intends me. To this, I must protest. But there may be some truth to the notion that I see beyond the corporeal, for in terms of sentiment, I am certainly one to feel matters deeply. As much as this certainty makes my life a marvelous exaggeration, it, too, has its moments of cursedness, I assure you.

We have never met, good Sir, this is incontrovertible. Yet I write to you because in now knowing even abstractly of your existence, I feel most acutely for you, for any man capable of a selfless action such as yours. I am so sincerely grateful. Please, do know this.

Allow me but few more words before I close. Allow me to say that I hope you are well and protected from harm. That gentle rain greets you in times of aridity, that the sun warms your bones when they are most chilled. That you forever keep love enough in your heart to sustain you through even the most hateful hours. And finally, from this point onward, that you spend a moment each day remembering that though you may not know her face, a young woman lives who prays for your sake nightly.

Respectfully yours in G~d's love,
Nora Bloom

Again, Abrams hastily reads the letter.

He explores it for irony with narrowed eyes, holding it both far and near, hunting through it for any mockery, for any lie, but after a thorough investigation, can find none. He fidgets uncomfortably. His neck leaks heat, forcing him to tug on his collar. He looks about him, stranded by the unaccustomed feeling of such warmth in his hands.

A third time he reads it.

Then, warily, Abrams draws it to his face. He inhales as deeply as his lungs allow, wherein they collect the letter's every spare essence. Its scent of rosehips and lavender talc, the faintest trace of India ink on pulp, even the oily hint of her fingertips—everything his imagination can muster. They are pure and wonderful, the smells he imbibes. He detects in them an innocence unlike any he has smelled in years, so flooded have his daily affairs become by the cynical stenches of sweat and shit and death.

Despite his skepticism, something in that letter's fragrance provides Abrams momentary freedom from Wolfe and the New Orleans law he figures to be after him, from Cobb and Petitgout and the Union army, from the burden of a conscience he cannot relieve, paroling him instead into an odorous realm of compassion unknown since he last drew in the air of his mother's sweet embrace. He is, in fact, astonished by how joyous these smells make him, leaving him to smile disbelievingly at the thought of this young woman he has never met, yet who has somehow, in the matter of mere minutes, pried as if with a miraculous lever his soul open to the dimmest prospect of love.

Still, he is not fool enough to think her discriminating when it comes to affection bestowed. She is a girl, he quickly tells himself, a naïf. Idealism is a currency spent by the rich, and this proud Jewess, an evident profligate. So, too, is he a young man alone among men, and in this he cannot quell the images suddenly arisen of his mouth on hers, of his fingers moistened, his cock sheathed in flesh and heat. In his mind, he already sees her stripped bare, without bruise or callus. She smells of fresh Savannah peaches, her chestnut hair made silky with buttermilk washes, her flesh approximating the finest Chinese silks. Naked, he hears her whispers. She traces the jagged scar above his lip. She admires his circumcised penis with a warm, curious grip. She does not laugh or think it exotic. She asks for no apologies. She does not judge him for what he has done in this life, ever.

At these last images, he shakes his head, chuckling grimly. Decency, so often accompanied by a cheat in his life, lies unexpectedly within his grasp for the first time in memory. Out there in the wilds of early autumn Missouri, thinking these thoughts, try as he might Abrams cannot restrain his smile, for these girlish smells have filled his chest with a quiet resuscitation that he was simply unaware, until that point, he had been so lacking.

Certainly, he has known the scent of women before. The countless whores reeking of Florida Water and cigar smoke, their sex of something else, an inward something, not woody, not musky, not fungal, but something ripe and inarticulate, as if each woman presents nature a confusion reconcilable only in her particularity of sex and person. Raised with Gerta as the guiding force in his life, Abrams tends to prefer the character of women to men. Women fail, they know this, and he finds them beautiful in their admission of it. It is the casual resilience born of this admission that men do not share. The male spirit is brittle—Abrams has seen far too many men break throughout the course of his life—while the women he has known have been supple not only in form but also in temperament. Women are destined to outlive his kind by centuries.

Perhaps because of this, too, he has done French on the cleanest of them and enjoys it immensely. With the avidity of a penitent breaking his fast on a most extraordinary gruel, Abrams searches for the flavor of each, detecting within them an ability to yield gracefully toward a survival that he, as with all men, so relishes yet finds so incapable of living himself. He can explain none of this, and yet tastes the mettle of every woman who has ever allowed him.

He was fourteen, his first time. Her name was Angeline, a sixteen-year-old redhead whose strong thighs and freckled rosebud breasts had men howling and banging tables whenever she danced at Madame Godeaux's of Corduroy Alley, Abrams frequently among them. He arrived one night for her alone, a fistful of money fleeced from his many monte scams in hand. Before he knew it, her show was over and, emboldened by several jars of corn whiskey, he was drunk as hell and naked on her stinking mattress, gasping, propped onto his elbows as she pushed him back. She rose and fell on his cock with her mouth and grip, rose and fell—"damn, boy, you got one of 'em Jew-cut links, don't you?"—and together they reached and grabbed and groped. "Ohh," he moaned, disbelieving his good fortune, "if this ain't about the finest feelin', Angeline." But soon, sighing to realize that full experience requires as much give as it does take, he pushed her off an instant before climax.

Sliding to his stomach, he parted Angeline's legs with the vigor of a criminal, kissing each crease of her pelvis. Her ammonium tang curdled pleasantly in his nostrils as she ground herself into his jaw. He slid further onto his belly and drove her up into the bedframe in one forceful motion, buttressing her buttocks with his shoulders, his arms wrapped under and around her thighs, wrists bent in. He looked up to her looking down upon him, her breasts as focal interruptions, nervous and expectant, and he smiled as he tongued her delicately, an exploration, labia parted with his right thumb and forefinger as he had heard it done by men of greater practice. "Goddamn," he whispered, pushing through, "a man could make a meal down here."

"Well," she sighed, "dig in, cowboy."

And he did. He devoured her whole, his hunger seeking the depth of her, her softness, her soul. She was salt and she was sweet and his erection strained against the confines of skin, begging for the smooth slide of pleasures only imagined. He tasted in Angeline that sturdy femininity that would enamor him for the rest of his days. She groaned and slapped the top of Abrams' head, while he held her firmly vised, lapped and lapped, left and right and circular, until his jaw tired and tongue went numb.

Quickly, she grabbed him by his armpits and pulled him up into her. "Get on it," she breathed.

So with a fluid stroke he was in, and in the shared surprise that life actually affords such delight, the two of them gasped, stilling all motion. They simply lay there, silent but for their panting, in awe of their respective abilities to enjoy something as common as flesh. "Oh, dear *Lord*," said Abrams with a quiver, "goddamn, you just feel *so* good, Angie."

She moaned, eyes closing, her feet arching taut.

"Oh," he moaned in answer, as he began to pump more and more furiously, "oh dear Lord."

"Slow it down now," she warned, "you don't wan—"

When he ejaculated a second later, Abrams immediately felt as if everything in his life, its every severity and challenge, was but, for that instant, absolutely worth enduring.

Now, these six years later, he has spent time among the whores who roam among the men of the Third Louisiana, hunting out their salaries amid business so far from home. Like a wolf pack drafting a wounded deer, the prostitutes of rural Missouri follow the bloody trail of soldiers with hungry, determined smiles. They arrive under false pretext or none at all, for at this early stage of the war, regulations are loose as to accepted companionship. It is not uncommon for prostitutes to situate themselves a hundred yards from camp beneath gaudy parasols and painted faces, their cerulean eyelids aflutter. "Sirens," Carlson once proclaimed of their smiles. "Fetching, true. Women, undoubtedly." He rubbed his mouth eagerly. "But S-I-R-E-N-S."

When the loneliness deafens him, when their calls prove too sweet, Abrams counts out a measure from his billfold, safeguards the rest from their pickpocketing, and arrives to a few minutes pleasure. He is not charming with them. He does not ask their names. He fucks them, pays them, and then leaves them. His respect for woman is as real as it has ever been, but of late he has had no desire to outwardly esteem anyone. Since that fateful night among the Cypress Stump Boys, he has been in no mood for nicety.

Yet now, without warning, something in him has changed.

He stands. Stowing Miss Bloom's letter in his soiled breast pocket, he pats it twice, takes a deep breath, adjusts his bowler, and wonders against whom he might next play some poker. Though it has been years, he is suddenly in need of pen and ink.

9

Within hours of first receiving the letter and shortly after several well-played hands against a trio of wealthy lieutenants, Abrams has won a plentiful supply of writing material, another growing rarity in camp. At present, he is seated with a plankwood desk drawn across his knees, a Gorham dip pen nibbled between his teeth, his gaze trained upward in thought. Eyes aloft, he soon notices an enormous mass of dark clouds gathering to the northwest. The pressure of the atmosphere has dropped sharply, the sounds of camp appearing a hollow, tinnier echo of a life usually steeped in richer air. Few seconds pass before the first brilliant flash of lightning strikes, followed by a deep rumble of thunder. Eager to beat the advancing storm, Abrams writes faster, more haphazardly, blunting his nib, but three lines in, he knows the race is lost. He gets as far as *Deer Miss Bloom I seet Myself now to saye my thanks to You for ever thing you have rote in that letter of yours it was nice to here that People like yourself are lookin out for People like Myself i can onely hope that* before the storm comes down hard upon him. Soldiers scurry about as if the enemy has caught them unawares, sledge-hammering what few tent pegs remain, shouting nervously as they tighten ropes in the vain hope of staying dry while canvas flaps in the wind. Trees creak and quiver. The rain arrives an instant later, first in large splattering drops, then in cords, in torrents, in absolute sheets of water. Atop the unremitting boom, the call of a world in quake, huge bolts of lightning fork in the sky, trailed by terrifying crash upon crash of thunder. For those of a Biblical turn, the din's quick and violent renewal suggests pagan gods come to destroy themselves with wrath. Not a permanent destruction, however, but one swiftly lost to clamorous rebirth so that they might again render themselves destroyed.

And again, and again, continuing with this, some perverse game of rage and riotous resurrection, until such a thing admits itself tedious, which in the course of mankind's damnation, it never once will.

It is the most powerful storm Abrams has ever experienced. Recoiling from the driven rain, hand clamped down on his bowler, he scuttles for refuge under a large poplar along with several men he has never met. He is sopping wet. In his grip, his letter he has been composing now drenched beyond repair. The others look about them slack-jawed, their eyes worried, muttering of Noah, of Horsemen, of plagues and pestilence. In the squall's intensity and in their fear, Abrams, too, interprets a harbinger for which he has no words but feels in his bones. Silas Wolfe, if scheming to kill him, has taken his time about it. Although unsure whether the New Orleans law is seeking him, Abrams trusts that Wolfe has somehow conspired to lay the blame at his feet. The threat of Cobb and Petitgout has thus far proven empty. For the moment, the Union army slumbers. Yet of plagues and pestilence, Abrams is familiar with the ways of the locust. He knows they may sleep for months on end, often years, lying dormant beneath the earth. Crops grow lush above them. Lovers wed, houses are built, babies get born. Ignorant life is lived. But when the rains inevitably come as they must, their waters awaken, like seedlings grown of Satan, a multitudinous ruin whose single-minded purpose is the destruction of everything in its path.

And so, Abrams' eyes clamp shut with each thunderclap. The storm has wrought in him an irrational fear, one that constricts the soaked, clammy flesh over his ribs with each burst above. While the tempest rages, he dwells on the murder from which he cannot flee. He sees the back of the dead man's head on that fine parlor Oriental, the black blood slowly cooling, the stab wound administered by Wolfe perfectly lethal. It lingers with him. The vision of this death has proven inescapable, embittering his thoughts and spittle. It has begun to haunt his dreams. It oppresses his days. Guilt remains with him, and grows.

In such awareness, one fist whitens around the letter in panic, the other clutching the poplar's black bark. He has been seized with dread, there is no explaining it. Wet and cold, his teeth chattering, he cannot stop the knocking of his knees. He is a bad child, awaiting the one, true rebuke.

It is simply a matter of time.

—

A week passes. The earth has dried, the sun has resumed its position above, and Abrams has calmed. Alone, he now chuckles at the foreboding he assigned the storm. *Fool,* he chastises himself. *Damned, damned fool.* Rather, those drier days later, he shifts his thoughts back to a more immediate and frustrating concern, namely the letter he cannot seem to finish. After a half-dozen fruitless attempts, his stock of paper has dwindled, his inkwell run dry. He has taken himself in hand on several occasions between drafts, late at night, deep in the woods away from the other men committing the same sin of Onan. His cock hardened in his callused grip, his eyes closed, he takes a lover's time in constructing this Nora Bloom whose face he has never seen but with whose mind he feels intimately acquainted. He forms her from a composite of every woman he has known. The long legs of Nance, the full, brooding lips of Belinda, Ruth's ample bottom. The plump Latin breasts of Frederica, Marie's brunette, Gallic mane. Henrietta's favorite postures and Eudora's blessed talents. Out in those woods, Abrams feels the heat of these women-as-one on his neck, their sweet breath on his belly, their tongues teasing. He groans, and so quickens the pace of his tugs. He now tastes this imaginary Nora, he licks her from foot to crown, buries his face in her soft-thistled hair. He cannot satisfy the craving within him, he grinds his teeth as he tugs, for he feels the wetness of her tight, virgin sex on his, of his slow, glistening slide inward. Her hot gasps intermingle with his own, her moans, her whimpers of joy—he cannot stop himself—he pulls and pulls like a driven fool, his breaths rasping, until, like the heavens' eruption of only a week before, the lightning behind his eyes explodes madly, his temples boom with thunder, his jaw clenches as his body arches in an orgasm of pleasure and abandoned procreation.

Afterward, he sighs, deflated by the release and the disappointment of having come to, once again, the shuddering reality of war.

His problem, he knows, is the uncertainty. For what does he expect of her, anyway? That she continue to write him, a nameless stranger? That she sit before an artist in her Sabbath finest, holding her pose long enough so that her image might be indelibly made for his eventual adoration? Or that she, after the war has at last ended and they have met breathlessly face-to-face, one day dare to love him for the person he is, transgressions and all? Preposterous. As a result, everything he wishes to say logjams in an exasperating muddle somewhere between his cluttered mind and crimped right hand, forcing him to curse and ball up the paper fiercely. After his seventh failure in as many days, he stands with a last obscenity and seeks out Carlson.

He finds the professor puffing on his cherry heartwood pipe and thumbing through a copy of the *Illustrated Manual of Operative Surgery and Surgical Anatomy*. Beside his knee, a chapbook of Shakespeare's sonnets. "Ah, Abrams," Carlson grins, "do sit. I've been learning all about the meat behind the soul. Seems our blood boils as much in truth as it does in metaphor."

"I ain't got time," Abrams replies soberly. "We got cards to pitch, you and me."

Carlson's smile widens as he gently puts his book down. "The hell we do."

Abrams shifts his weight. "I mean it. I'm wantin' for paper." His stare says he is not kidding.

"My, my, but you're a starchy son-of-a-bitch." Carlson is already rummaging through his haversack for some stationery. "Sit, smoke with me."

Together by Carlson's fire pit, over mugs of a repellent brew of corn bran and potato scrapings, Abrams soon confesses the root of his needs. Carlson has noticed how guarded his companion is when it comes to speaking about himself to others, and therefore does not embarrass him for it. The teacher within takes dominion, becomes Socratic in the manner of past masters, asks Abrams what he wants the letter to say, what tone he would like to adopt, what he would like the ultimate aim of the correspondence to be. Abrams replies by furrowing his brow, fuming on his pipe, doffing his bowler, replacing it, digressing about card games recently won or lost—whatever he can do to show his discomfort at the current topic without admitting to it outright. Carlson, in turn, broods over each response, and with fingers bridged, comes to a hard conclusion: this young man is ignorant of almost all things tender.

"I got ten dollars," offers Abrams at last, "says you can write my mind better'n me."

Though he needs the money, money he would like to send home along with the Confederate pay no soldier has yet received, Carlson has been an exceptional teacher for too long. "Can't do it," he sniffs, aligning his spectacles. "Plagiarism's nothing short of the Devil's own epistle."

Abrams bursts into laughter. "Then your Devil's got a helluva lot more time for writing'n mine." He spits. "Plagiarism, shit."

"Man's got to have his standards, Elias. Without them we'd be *homo vulgaris*, content to kill, thieve, spread vice and perniciousness without a scintilla of homage paid to human integrity. Without standards, we'd be lost."

Abrams stops. He smiles. He begins a slow, steady applause.

"Don't mock me, son. It shows a palpable disregard."

"Out here, you speak to me of standards." Abrams looks wide-eyed about them. "Out here?"

"One's beliefs should never be contingent upon geography, I've found."

"Hell's bells, John Lee, this whole goddamned war's about geography."

"Be that as it may." Carlson folds his arms; he will not budge. "Now understand," he continues agreeably, "I'll gladly render whatever council's requested of me. But the letter, my boy, is yours."

Abrams sees that he has met in Carlson someone stalwart, something indefatigably true. He usually finds this type of absolutism amusing, meant for spoiled children in short pants, but in Carlson, Abrams admits to finding a stirring conviction. He has met few in his day who stand firm in the face of something larger than their own need. Appreciating this, his head falls into a nod. He spits into his hand, holding it aloft. "She writes me back impressed," he says, "I got a plug of tobacco, name of John Lee Carlson all over it."

Carlson, reluctantly, spits into his own. They shake and set to work. With permission, the teacher studies her letter, something Abrams has done countless times since its receipt. Over the past week, he has read and reread it, nibbling on mealy apples, wearing its paper thin at the creases, soiling it where his thumbs have held it fast. He can already recite much of the text by memory, and while he dismisses her pride in their faith as little more than youthful fancy, he admires her for it as he now does Carlson's principles on plagiarism. That she possesses pride at all, in anything, he finds refreshing.

He delights in the letter's every word, but it is the concluding lines that move him most: *Allow me to say that I hope you are well and protected from harm. That gentle rain greets you in times of aridity, that the sun warms your bones when they are most chilled. That you forever keep love enough in your heart to sustain you through even the most hateful hours. And finally, from this point onward, that you spend a moment each day remembering that though you may not know her face, a young woman lives who prays for your sake nightly.* Abrams is not a soft man. He understands this. Nevertheless, in the kindness of such words so rarely met, even from those so vaguely intended as these, he is having a difficult time contextualizing what they actually mean. For lack of a better word, the letter's closing makes him feel oddly human.

When Carlson concludes his reading, he issues forth a long whistle of praise. "Fine hand, this girl has." Without further preamble, he adjusts his glasses, dips his pen, and smoothes the paper. "We'll commence whenever you see fit."

And so, with Carlson as scrivener, Abrams dictates the letter in halting, frustrated bursts. When he grows stymied, Carlson gently prods him through. The professor speaks of lubricating the cogs of the human heart, of its genteel vocabulary, of loves like Baucis and Philomen's, of Pyramus and Thisbe's, then that of the later-adapted Romeo and Juliet. He mines slowly, attempting to unearth the softness beneath the hardened exterior of a young man who, despite their differences, Carlson would like to believe is evolving into a friend.

An hour goes by before Abrams finally stamps his foot in exasperation, declaring, "And that's all that needs sayin', goddamnit." Carlson passes him what they have drafted. With a stained index finger, he alerts Abrams to the more difficult spellings. Stylistically, the professor knows the letter is puerile, but he also knows that the girl, should they ever make acquaintance, will meet the honest Elias Abrams and not some polished likeness thereof. Its sentiment, though, Carlson finds unexpectedly beautiful.

He stands with a groan, placing the Panama upon his head. "I'll be off for my evening perambulation then." And with his hands tucked collegially behind his back, he walks away into the night.

In his own untrained hand, with fresh paper, pen, and ink, Abrams is thus left alone to labor through the first and only letter of affection and thanks he has written in his lifetime:

Dear Miss Bloom,

It is with great pleasure that I write you this afternoon. Your letter to me was most satisfactory. I shall now go as far as to admit it was a joy and privilege to read. Please tell Reverend Gutheim thank you for thinking of us. He must be a good man. I am not too much for religion myself, but I believe I know what is good. I do not wish to sound so boastful, but I think that is true. Then allow me to be so bold as to say that what you have done for me is good, too. You say in your letter that you do not think you are too good at teaching. Here I must beg to differ. We do not know each other, as you say. But as you have taught me how to think of people I do not know in a better way, I must say that you have taught me something very special indeed.

I have not had much need in my life to write. I am without much talent for it. I see how my thoughts on paper do not show that I am capable of much intelligence off of it. For now, this makes no difference to me. It is plenty enough that I have the excuse to write at all.

It has also been a long time since I have been allowed to say what I am thinking. I therefore want you to know that I am thinking about your life and your happiness, like you said you are of me. I am thinking about your hands and I am thinking about the quantity of your smiles, hoping they are many. I am also thinking with great hope that you will write to me again. It has been a balm for my flagging spirit. Though faith comes to me in short supply, I hope you do not mind me closing by saying that you are the angel God has sent to one who is most in need.

Faithfully yours,
Pt. Elias Abrams, Company G, Pelican Rangers

"You tell anyone about this," Abrams demands of Carlson after he returns from his walk, "and I'll lop off your goddamned tongue, use it as a canteen stopper."

Carlson laughs, holding his palms innocently aloft. "Fear not," he says. "I've long believed a man's correspondence falls well within his personal province, one to be staked by him alone."

"Christ," sighs Abrams, "the trap you got on you." He folds the paper in thirds and, with borrowed wax and seal, binds it fast. He copies her address onto the face, dries the ink with a few shakes in the air, and then slides the letter delicately into the canvas haversack he has slung over his shoulder. Done, he wipes his hands along his chest and exhales proudly.

"You've got reason to be satisfied," affirms Carlson. "It's a fine letter."

To this Abrams simply glowers and stomps off, leaving the professor to chuckle softly behind him and poke at the pit's ashes with a gnarled, fire-hardened stick. Sitting alone in the early night, Carlson soon hears the muffled, resonant, six-noted hoot of a great horned owl in the distance. Then, moments later, a faint response. Ever the man for leitmotif, his mood lightens all the more, for somewhere out in those Missouri pines he knows two souls now yearn for each other amid the advancing darkness.

10

Abrams arrives at Hyams' tent almost twenty minutes later. The weakening autumnal sun has set in the meantime, the day's thrushes nestled with beaks beneath their wings, the night's nocturnals waking with gentle calls and flutters. The temperature has begun to chill those Louisianan bones more accustomed to fairer climates. Men shift uneasily on log benches, shoulders hunching. Famished, they blow morosely into tin cups of weak teas brewed of birch and pine bark. They rub and hold their hands over stoked fires. They burn log after log like a gathering of industrialists. Asleep, they now jackknife into one another, arms draped and huddled tight.

Standing before his commander's tent, Abrams repositions his hat. He exhales sharply, bracing himself. Though Hyams' tent is but a few hundred yards from Carlson's fire pit, Abrams requires three circuitous attempts before finally summoning the courage to consign his letter to the post. He removes his bowler, runs a hand through his thick black hair, and tells the adjutant outside that he would like to have a word with the lieutenant colonel. The adjutant—a ginger-haired blueblood from Baton Rouge—gives Abrams a thorough appraisal. He does not mask his disdain. "Matters regardin'?" he asks coldly, stroking his Vandyke.

"Matters regarding my own particulars."

The adjutant clucks his tongue in disapproval. He folds his arms.

Abrams meets his eyes. "Sorry, friend, it's gonna have to do."

The adjutant smiles and steps forward.

"Look, goddamnit," sighs Abrams, "all's I want's a parley. Everything in this world ain't have to end in a dance." But here his voice hardens; he takes his own step forward. "'Course, if you reckon otherwise, believe I know a waltz from a minuet."

"Is that right?" asks the adjutant, his eyes widened with amusement. "A waltz from a minuet, you say?"

"Believe so."

"Then your mother must've been one of those Congo Square dance niggras I've heard so talked about, just—"

The adjutant does not know what hits him. All at once he is on the ground, sucking for air. As much as he is startled by the pain, he is doubly perplexed, for his ribs and sternum, left eye and bottom lip have all been struck by jabs whose issuance of speed he simply does not believe possible. It is inconceivable that anyone could have gotten off so many blows so swiftly. His face soiled in the dirt, through his swelling eye Holcomb peers up to Abrams looking down upon him. "That's what we call the Tchoupitoulas Street Clogger," explains Abrams calmly, straightening himself. "Now I got me a whole repertoire, you care to learn it."

The adjutant has a decision to make. He can continue down this path of derision, no doubt receiving future penalty for it, or he can convalesce with what remains of his dignity. Above even the call for honor, the gentlemanly class to which he has been bred prizes the state of preservation. Ways of life, codes of conduct, societal standing—all delights of the status quo, currently threatened by Lincoln's assailants from the North. Of the threat now standing before him, the adjutant knows that should he protract this line of insult, the preservationist state he so reveres will be nothing if not additionally disturbed.

He decides against further provocation.

He does not think this cowardly. Too many years of indulgence have taught him to believe that in him flows the kingly blood of Christ, and to risk shedding it unnecessarily would, in the adjutant's eyes, be an affront to all things divine. With two fingers, he dabs the shiner developing above his eye. He coughs once and rolls to a seat. "I could have you brought up on charges for that, you know."

"Believe you'd be within your rights to do it, too," admits Abrams. He has nothing more to say on the matter.

Adjutant Holcomb moans as he gets to his feet. He dusts himself off. He tames his ginger hair and takes a deep breath. "The lieutenant colonel's resting," he informs Abrams with a wincing adjustment to his uniform. "If you want to risk his displeasure, it's on you. Hold here."

The adjutant steps past Abrams, easing the tent-flap doorway aside. Seconds later, he returns with a stiff nod.

Once inside the tent, Abrams takes an immediate review of the quarters. A four-sided canvas wall tent, it is fairly luxurious by an infantryman's standards, standing a full seven feet in height, running almost twelve in length and eleven in width. In his quick inspection, Abrams' eyes rest for an instant on Hyams, who lies atop a virgin wool blanket, which is itself atop a thin army cot. On the table, maps of the Western theater, reams of field reports, volumes of officer's tactics, a pair of wire-rimmed spectacles, a bronze spyglass, various writing supplies, and a tin plate of broken hardtack, half-eaten. The tent is brightly lit by one of the few hanging oil lamps in camp. Other than a tintype of a severe-looking matriarch amid the tabletop clutter, and a large, leather-hinged pinewood chest overflowing with the commander's personals, the tent is austere in aspect.

It is only when Abrams perceives himself in a looking-glass that his eyes fix for any length of time. His Adam's apple bobs at the sight. He is no man. Since he has last seen his reflection, his face has drained of all vigor, growing instead wan and cadaverous, assuming the ashen color of boiled horsemeat. His cheeks are gaunt. A constellation of grease pits his large, aquiline nose. His strong chin, traditionally clean-shaven, is now thatched with a sparse black beard suggesting the foulest back-alley Chinaman's.

He is indecent in his filth. His bowler is soiled beyond saving, his uniform draped on his slight shoulders long torn and muddied. But it is his eyes that alarm him most. Once as crisp and hazel as his mother's, they have dulled inexplicably into a kind of sullen pewter, the bruised half-moons beneath them offsetting the flatness therein. He has seen such eyes sunken within the skulls of sated opium eaters, in the oft-raped, in the murderous who have killed more men than they have lived years, and most recently in the burly Union soldier slain almost two months before at the Battle of Oak Hills, a man Abrams has endeavored, though failed, to forget. As a matter of policy, throughout his life he has done his best to avoid being the focus of such eyes, yet in his commander's looking-glass that night, he is left no alternative.

"What's the trouble here?" Hyams croaks from his cot. The lieutenant colonel clears his throat. "What's the trouble here?" he repeats more firmly.

Abrams shifts his attention from his own shameful state to his commander's, finding him old and tired. His uniform is unbuttoned down to his navel, exposing a belly that was once prodigious but now, after months of shrinking portions, has, too, diminished. His eyes are red and bleary, his steely hair unkempt. Hyams winces as he moves on his cot, his back seizing. There is no glamour in war.

Embarrassed as much by Hyams' condition as he is by his own, Abrams averts his gaze. "Private Abrams, sir, wishin' for a minute."

"Private who?"

"Abrams, sir. From New Orleans. Of late, Miss Nora Bloom's correspondent."

"Abrams," says Hyams with growing recognition, "yes, yes, of course, the Hebrew. Wasn't certain I'd be seeing you again."

"Yessir." Abrams kneads the brim of his bowler, and looks down at the bare ground beneath him. "Well sir, providin' your offer still stands, I'd be thankful if you sent what bit of chicken scratch I was able to muster down New Orleans way." He withdraws the letter from his haversack and holds it waist high.

74

"Leave it on the table," orders Hyams without hesitation. "I'll see to it as promised."

Abrams' heart leaps as he does what he is told. He is afraid, however, that disorganized as the tabletop is, the letter will be lost. He therefore places it atop a leather-bound volume of John Ordronaux's *Hints on the Preservation of Health in Armies*, its address side up, and flattens it gently. He gives the letter a last lingering look before returning to Hyams.

"I should tell you, son," says the lieutenant colonel with a careful stretch, "it's damned serendipitous, you showing up just now." He has risen to his seat on his cot. "I've had a thorn in my side the past few days, perhaps you can help me dislodge."

"If I'm able."

Hyams nods his appreciation. "Now," he says, clapping his hands once, "you're a Jew, are you not?"

"Much as anyone's born to a notion, yessir, guess I am."

With a scarcely audible groan, Hyams is up and hobbling to the table where he begins leafing through the piles of paper. When his letter slides from the book to the ground, Abrams quickly picks it up and secures it between the volume's pages, jutting it out halfway so that it will not be misplaced in the future. Meanwhile, after a scattered search, Hyams dons his spectacles and retrieves a tattered tract that he holds up for Abrams' inspection. "Seems there's a certain congregation in Philadelphia," he begins, "*Keneseth Israel* or some such, that's got a particularly opinionated rabbi name of Einhorn in charge. Seems these opinions of his lean toward an abolitionist view of things. Now as I'm sure you can imagine, with such a leaning, this Einhorn's got a bone to pick with folks like you and me fighting for our due and proper."

Abrams chews his cheek, but says nothing.

"And I quote: 'The root of my concern,' he says, 'is that our fellow Israelites to the South, born of a minority, prone to bouts of ethnic alienation and fits of religious deprivation, are fighting, indeed killing, so that another breed of misfortunate may remain just so. They may brandish

Rabbi Raphall's malignant contention that the Bible actually condones slavery, what with the Abrahams, the Isaacs, the Jacobs, and the Jobs all once wielding the mantle of slaveholder, and yet, is this not the same book that demands we 'break the bonds of oppression, let the oppressed go free, and tear every yoke?' To follow the letter of every Biblical law as Rabbi Raphall, that deluded New Yorker, would have of us, should we not then restore the practices of stoning our women, polygamy, blood vengeance, and royalty, simply because they, too, were sanctioned in days of yore? Do our Southern brethren not see how their struggle to suppress the liberty of the Negro soul is irreconcilable to the plight we Israelites have been forced to endure for millennia ourselves? Have they never read Exodus? In the Egyptian principles they practice, do they not see the hypocrisy of their manner? In the physical subjugation of one, is there not the moral subjugation of all?'" With that, Hyams tosses the pamphlet onto the tabletop and removes his spectacles slowly, pinching and rubbing the bridge of his nose. "Evidently, we should be suffering a sympathy with the Negro that precludes any participation in a cause that seeks to enforce his bondage." He stares hard at Abrams. "What say you then, Private? Is this Einhorn correct? Are you no better than a Negro?"

Abrams shrugs evasively. "I ain't too sociable with old John Brown, if that's what you're askin'."

"Come now, speak to the point. We're discussing human nature, no more."

Abrams pauses. "Put up to it as I am at the moment," he offers at last, "I'll admit I've had reason to ponder this some in the past."

"And?"

"And nossir, don't find I'm a whole lot better'n a nigger at all." He thinks only fleetingly of his father's words on that hot August day in 1852 and of Lucius' whip-scarred back. There is more behind his reasoning.

Hyams is shocked by the private's admission. He demands explanation.

"See, sir," says Abrams, "me, I'm a redemptioner's baby. My granddaddy bought my momma and them passage from Alsace on a promise, back in '28. Didn't have a penny in his pocket, not a lick of English, no relatives here to speak of, he got linked with a charter who'd stake them their fare and board, so long as someone'd purchase the family off his hands once they all arrived. Then, they'd work off the shippin' fee for that feller afterward."

"You're speaking of indentured servitude."

"You might could call it that," allows Abrams. He shifts his weight, unaccustomed to speaking at length on any subject, let alone one quite so personal. And yet, perhaps due to the cleansing sentiment of the letter he has just posted, he feels as though a bit of rust has been chipped clean of his reticent soul, and therefore grows increasingly brave in his disclosure. "When my granddaddy and grandmomma died from the typhus not long after arrivin', my momma and auntie was stuck workin' off the whole payment themselves. Only, auntie herself died a year later, leavin' momma to finish it off all alone. She wasn't more'n five years old at the time. Till she was eighteen, never had a free day in her life. Even after, quality of a poor woman's freedom's open to some hard questionin'."

Hyams tightens his lips and nods.

"Then there's me, her boy. Sure, I got me papers *sayin'* I was born free, but you can bet I've been more'n one man's dog in my lifetime." Here Abrams looks directly into his commander's eyes, confirming the insubordinate tone of his words. In truth, little irks Abrams more than talk of freedom. In Miss Bloom's hand, he finds it quaint. In Carlson, he has made an exception. From the grizzly mouths of soldiers around the campfires, however, he has heard his fill. He has witnessed too much atrocity and deceit to believe in such absolutes: there is no freedom, only the dogged march between yokes. Northern rule or Southern, rule is rule. But before he delves into too much defiance, Abrams resumes the original course of conversation, for now that he has begun to speak, he is finding it difficult to stop. Framed in this unexpected need to reveal himself is Carlson's story of the Gordian knot, told just hours before while they composed the letter together. How he who solved the knot was prophesized to rule all of Asia, and how rather than pull apart its Phrygian intricacy, Alexander the Great merely cleaved it in two with a single stroke of his sword. "Because sometimes," Carlson had explained, "the human heart gets so wrapped up in itself, it can't be unraveled unless you give it a few good whacks. Now I want you to think of that pen there, Elias, as your sword, giving that knotted heart of yours a whack or two. May not be pretty, but it'll sure cut through some of that bailing twine you've got fettering your spirit."

Abrams thus continues his tale, his voice gaining strength and purpose. "More'n that, though," he says, "after I come along, years after Momma finally got her so-called liberty, she bought herself a garden plot up in Lafayette City. Aside from a bit of corn, grew some of the fattest heads you ever saw, too, all kinds of leaf. Yorks, Sugarloafs, Quintals, Batterseas, you name it, she grew it.

"Problem is, murder of crows took perch nearby, like they're liable to. Now I couldn't been but eight or nine myself, but I did damned near everything I could to get rid of them. Didn't make no difference. Come morning, that garden was ate up, plain and simple, and them birds just laughin', laughin'."

Hyams smirks at this.

"Local neighbors, Kincades, advised we fix us up a scarecrow. 'Make 'im a nigger,' says Miss Kincade. 'Scares the bejesus out of beast and man alike, the nigger does.' So that's what I done, too. Took me a couple beams, made the crossbones, then some burlap, painted it black with pitch. Left two big old lips, two big old eyes. Nappy head of hair made of cotton dipped in that self-same pitch. Overalls, raggedy gloves for hands. When I was done, had me the biggest, scariest coon you ever saw, I'm tellin' you."

"I imagine he was quite the sight."

"Indeed he was," agrees Abrams. "Now what d'you suppose happens, I stuck him up there?"

Charmed by the story, Hyams shrugs.

"Not a thing," declares Abrams flatly. "Birds came through like always, tore up that garden, makin' a mockery of the whole damned world."

Hyams chuckles at the thought.

"So I set myself to thinkin', if a nigger won't scare 'em, I got to take me another tack. 'Course, by that time I'd heard mention about us bein' the chosen people and all, so, prideful nip that I was, decided I'd make me a Jew scarecrow, figurin' it'd do the trick better'n ever. And I made one, too, boy, let me tell you. Big old cob nose, skullcap for his pate, couple danglin' horsehair locks, beard down to here, the whole basket of apples. Arms spread wide, looked the picture of Moses himself partin' the Red Sea. That scarecrow'd put the fear of God into the staunchest sinner, no lie."

Hyams says that it must have been so.

"Next day, I come runnin' out into that garden all hell-fire, and what d'you think I find?"

"I've no idea, Private."

"Them bastard crows, same as before, perched on that old stuffed Jew, not a care in the world. No better'n that first nigger, that old Jew couldn't scare off nothin'." Here Abrams leans in. "So nossir, in answer to your question, I ain't better'n a nigger." He pauses. "Come to find in my life, ain't none of us are. Fact is, most folks're ignored equally, by all."

Hyams grunts at the saliency of this point.

"In the end, only thing to scatter them crows was my momma's aim, her .410 shotgun, and a rockin' chair for waitin'. Like she'd say from that day forth, 'When a murder sets its sights on you, can't hardly be stopped 'less you got a mind to defendin' your own.'"

Hyams pulls on his bottom lip judiciously. "A wise woman, your mother."

"She knew her way around a plant, that's for sure. Speakin' of which," says Abrams, digging into his haversack and bringing forth a battered tin cup and a leather draw-string pouch, "I got your mug here, one you loaned me last week. And if you got a nip of brandy for soakin' these fresh swamp laurel cones and seeds in, you can make you a tincture should stave off that rheumatism. My momma's recipe, swore to it."

Hyams is caught slightly off guard by the non sequitur, but accepts the pouch without protest.

"Now it'll rouse you up some," warns Abrams, "but no more than a few stiff cups of coffee'll. It'll make you sweat some, too, but steep them cones and seeds in brandy, drink it down, and you should be fixed up right in no time."

"I must say, Private," says Hyams with arched eyebrows, "I'm deeply, deeply appreciative."

"Ain't nothin'," says Abrams with a wave of his hand. "Swamp laurel's all over these parts."

"I'm not only thankful for your proposed remedy here, mind you, but for your opinion on the matter discussed."

"*Bah*," says Abrams, kicking the earth. "And the letter?"

"She'll be reading it by week's end."

"Much obliged for it."

"Well, then, good night, Private."

"G'night, sir."

11

Outside his commander's tent, Abrams meets the battered Adjutant Holcomb, who immediately stands nervously firm. Abrams shoots him a wink and walks off into the night. He is relieved to have the letter attended to, pleased at the smiles he hopes to bring this Nora Bloom, a woman with whom he has so little in common but so peculiarly wishes to impress. He cannot explain it. It is not jealousy of her pleasant world from which he suffers, or bitterness, but rather the joy that such a world exists at all. There is redemption in the depth of her feeling, he can sense this, and although he remains unconvinced that these feelings are specific to him alone, he hopes his letter will distinguish him as a man in his own right. Carlson was correct: to have replied in any other hand would have perpetrated a fraud that, pitted against the innocence he now finds so charming, would have glared all the more deviously. Indeed, while he knows his writing is crude, for the moment he has forgiven himself for his ignorance. For the moment, the attempt is enough.

He walks on in the night.

In considering his tale to Hyams, however, the thought of those scarecrows suddenly clears like a small patch of sky in Abrams' gut, leaving him with an oddly hollow sensation. It is not disagreeable, this feeling, but merely foreign to him, for it has been years since he has spoken about his upbringing. Abrams is having a difficult time digesting what it means. He has heard bespectacled men speak of the restorative powers of speech, but in the past he has always scoffed at them as gossips and fools. Yet on this night he soon concludes that the empty feeling in his stomach is actually attributable to one of unburdening. It both puzzles and pleases him.

He has been so quiet on the subject of his past because the last time he spoke about it in any detail literally scarred him for life. In treading back to his fire through Camp Jackson, the notes of a lone banjo thus begin to pluck at the sharp and melancholy turn of Abrams' mind, causing him at once to remember the brutal splitting of his upper lip and all that led up to it. He scratches the length of his jaw. They are not pleasant memories now flooding him, but surely among his strongest.

His father, that noble absence, had laid no claim to him after Gerta's death. Administrators of the Jewish Widows and Orphans Home, founded on Jackson Avenue and Chippewa Street by members of the Hebrew Benevolent Association for those who had lost loved ones to the epidemic, had failed to successfully enlist I. J. Lieber's sense of paternity. As a result, young Elias had been forced to move between the gutter and neighborhood families, Jules Bouchard the monte man and brief stints at the home. He enjoyed the clean sheets there, the steady meals, even the local Jewish matrons who clucked like hens as they licked their thumbs, attempting to tame his cowlicks and scour the smudges from his face.

It was at the Jewish Widows and Orphans Home where he met Silas Wolfe, a boy older by several months, though by Abrams' estimation, far older than that. Like an emperor deigning to walk among the masses, in striding through the orphanage Wolfe would hold his nose high, offering the back of his fingers to those younger children from whom he demanded genuflection. His smile—a wickedly confident smile—whipped women and men of all ages into submission, his portions at mealtime always doubled, his pillow fluffed daily. Admitting to no mistake, he was seldom blamed for one.

Like Abrams, he, too, had lost his family to the fever. His parents had emigrated as redemptioners from Ribeauville, an Alsatian town not far from Gerta Abrams' Eguisheim. In this shared history, together the boys soon agreed without words that their paths would be inexorably bound, though there was never a question as to who would blaze those paths and who would follow. Physically, they bore the same Semitic form, their noses strong and eyes sharp, their jet hair thick, their bodies taut and lean. They cuffed one another like cubs, fought the same bullies, dodged all religious instruction, perfected their poker and sweet cloth skills. Although the work ethic Gerta had instilled in her son by and large remained intact, the moral integrity she had strived to cultivate soon began to wither under Wolfe's tutelage, desiccating into a dry-heartedness that would serve Abrams well on the streets. It was this same dry-heartedness that helped him manage his father's indifference. He often skulked by the man's Toulouse Street townhouse, shooting its balcony dirty glances, but by the time Abrams turned fourteen, he rarely entertained the idea of reunion.

Months passed in this way. With Wolfe as his prompt and companion, by his fifteenth birthday Abrams had fled the orphanage for good, choosing instead the city's lowest rungs of life. On the night of their first real drunk together, they pilfered a bag of oysters from one of the local fishmongers and staggered up the Mississippi levee, where they intended to slurp them down one after the other, Abrams imagining the salty, wet meat within that of Angeline at her most warm and welcoming.

It was well into evening before he hoisted the burlap sack over his shoulder, staining his back with the stink of detritus and Vermilion Bay water, Wolfe walking gaily beside him. Up one side of the levee they walked, one burdened, the other free, and down the other to the water's edge below. Wharf-side crickets filled the silence between them, while from several blocks away dance hall barkers were heard shouting their lies as they escorted lechers and lonely men by the elbows into their candlelit establishments. Water lapped at the levee's shore. A calliope rang out in the distance. Whores sucked cock after cock in the dankest alleyways, their customers' moans echoing low into the twilight. On most summer evenings in New Orleans, when the air was thick and the sky burnt orange and the Mississippi viscous with all that swirling mud, these were the sounds of nightfall itself.

"Goddamnit, Elias, you *should*, though," Wolfe was urging. Abrams had never seen him so earnest.

Abrams shrugged and once more removed the cork stopper from the jug of sugarcane brew they had pinched, taking a mighty swig. The boys, supine and well on their way to drunk, had been discussing his father. Since that hot August day in 1852, Abrams had spoken about I. J. Lieber to those who asked but did not otherwise volunteer him as a subject of discussion. Now, however, drunk and knocking back oyster after oyster in the serious manner of men, he felt that he might open up some without revealing the years of pain behind it. "Cocksucker of the highest order, that's for sure," he admitted. "Don't know what my momma ever saw in him. Mistake of youth, guess. Must've been his money." He slurped down another oyster. "All's I know's he left me simmerin' in her belly like some damned stew chicken boilin' in a pot."

"But that's what I'm sayin', Elias," pleaded Wolfe. "Feller like that deserves some hurt, don't he? I'm talkin' curl-your-toes kind of hurt."

"Then, for that matter," Abrams went on, nodding vaguely at Wolfe's suggestion, "one day, outta the blue, decides he wants to meet me, calls us all the way out to Napoleonville, three days hence, three days back, and when we do, day's as hot as blazes, I won't never forget it. Thing is, afterward, hasn't offered so much as a 'How d'you do' never again. Never! Now what kind of man's that, anyway? I'm askin' you, Sy—what kind of man?"

Here Wolfe's mouth twisted sourly. "One who wouldn't know how close he was to dead, he was my pa."

Drunk and disgusted, obviously anguished, Abrams scowled and reached for another swig.

Wolfe rose slowly to his feet. "All's I'm sayin', could be beautiful, most beautiful thing in the world, pain gifted to a man like that." His eyes were ablaze, gleaming in the light off the river's surface. "Sure as that water'll wet you, together you and me could get arty with that son-of-a-bitch's sufferin'. You need just say the word now, and we're on it."

"Believe we could, too," approved Abrams. But he had lost all conviction in his voice, and both boys knew it. A few moments passed and still Abrams did not stand to join his friend's call for vengeance, so in the darkness, Wolfe's shoulders fell discouraged. He stomped his heel into the thick riverbank. Soon, visibly dejected, he bent down and picked up a large oyster half-shell. Abrams watched with curiosity as Wolfe bounced it on the flat of his hand twice, measuring its weight, its shape and heft that of a shingling hatchet head. Then, in the side-armed delivery of the best skipped stones, Wolfe hurled the jaggedly honed shell directly into his friend's face.

Until that moment, Elias Abrams had never truly felt physical pain. Yet in a flash he was doubled over, his flesh rent completely between his nose and upper lip, blood suddenly gushing as he pounded the earth with one fist while attempting to stem the flow with the other. "God-damnit all, Silas!" he screamed, running his tongue over his teeth to make sure they were undamaged. "The fuck'd you go'n and do that for?"

"You got a problem," replied Wolfe evenly, that infamous smile now breaking across his face, "you're more'n welcome to stand up and tell me so." He shifted his stance to gain solid footing, his eyes glinting malevolently in the moonlight. "C'mon, honey—stand up and tell me your problems."

When after several seconds Abrams continued to refuse the challenge, when instead his fury had dimmed to a low keening, Wolfe eased and knelt down beside him. Abrams was rocking back and forth on the levee bank, moaning and spitting blood, cupping his mouth and fighting back the tears. The hatred he felt for Wolfe right then was pure, and yet, in the purity of its emotion, Abrams also felt for the first time since his mother's death a feeling approximating love. For what Wolfe had done in the searing intensity of that pain's administration was to jolt him awake from the slow deadening he had long begun to suffer since her loss. Later, this would be the event Wolfe proclaimed as Abrams' rebirth.

Wolfe placed a hand delicately on his friend's shoulder. Without violence, without threat, as gentle as a lover, he met Abrams' eye, drew a finger over his friend's shredded lip, and then brought that bloodied finger to his own mouth. Silently, he licked his finger clean. "My own momma used to say a woman bleeds, Elias," he said softly, "means she ain't no longer a virgin. She ain't a virgin, means she can handle the mess of living with her fists raised high. Now, you want to raise them fists to all who done you wrong, that's fine. But if you don't, if them fists're too heavy for you to hold, you'd better just quit that fuckin' whinin'."

—

Like the humiliation and pain he endured following that night with Wolfe, at Camp Jackson years later, something in his telling of the scarecrow story seems to soil Abrams at his core. He cannot put his finger on it. His eyebrows furrow and his lips draw tight. It is not the weakness of admission he fears, though in the past he would have. He does not think Hyams will judge him poorly for professing to an immigrant ancestry or for his views on the Negro. Rather, it is the unsettling realization that the essence of Wolfe's words—*You want to raise them fists to all who done you wrong, that's fine. But if you don't, if them fists're too heavy for you to hold, you'd better just quit that fuckin' whinin'*—echoes strongly his mother's warning issued years earlier—*When a murder sets its sights on you, can't hardly be stopped 'less you got a mind to defendin' your own*—each providing him the wisdom to deal with his current dilemma, yet each gone unheeded. There is a right way to live, one met head-on, and Abrams is now struck by the fact that he has been dismissing it completely. True, he doubts cheap epiphanies. He has seen too many hustlers give up the gambit for the cloth, only to lose their newfound faith when the call of liquor and cards eventually out-shouts the divine voice of abstinence. Some lessons, he knows, are to be ignored.

Others are not.

12

Lying on the ground by his campfire, flames flickering in the evening sky, Abrams absently polishes his teeth with a splay-bristled tooth-brush as he stares off into the woods. Since leaving his commander's tent almost three weeks prior, he has concentrated solely on plotting his next move. In that stretch, he has confronted truths he can no longer deny. His enlistment was an act of cowardice. He has had enough of flight. He is now deciding whether to desert the army. If he does, he will forage his way back to New Orleans, where he will face Wolfe. He will ease his conscience. He will atone for his sins, or he will die trying.

In the passing of those weeks, the weather has worsened. The end of October in southwestern Missouri is Louisiana's rawest winter dawn. Abrams' big toe peeks at the chilling world through a hole in his left shoe, the stinking sock beneath long worn bare. At night, he wakes to stamp his feet for warmth. He has taken to walking bent over, his hands jammed beneath his armpits. He can count his ribs with ease, his abdomen etched into muscular segments that women once traced languidly with their fingertips but would now cause them to gasp with alarm. His ragged trousers require a hemp rope belt tied tightly over his hips. He is hungry and he is tired and he is disturbed by what he has become. The idea of returning to New Orleans grows increasingly appealing, for a variety of reasons.

Certainly, he realizes his is a fool's errand. He has been among the Cypress Stumps when one of its members is cornered, and knows it to be a very bloody affair. Once, when Tasker Gundy convinced a fledgling whore that she would be best served by serving him, the slighted pimp—a large, meat-fisted brute named Blackwell—let his aim for retribution be known throughout the Quarter. Wherever he stomped, he bellowed about miserable daughters of man and those who would lead them astray. His oaths tore up and down the Vieux Carré, how when he caught up with him, he'd carve out that cocksucker Gundy's heart and cram it down his gullet before it stopped its goddamned thumping, hers too.

The confrontation occurred at last in Truett's Saloon, a damp hole-in-the-wall off Gallatin Street with only a handful of rickety tables and a plankwood bar to recommend itself as a genuine place of leisure. The whiskey was rudely concocted of neutral spirits with a half-pint of creosote poured into them, the ale typically as warm and flat as piss. The air reeked of stale tobacco, skunked beer, and cheap pig-fat candles that blackened the mirror behind the bar with soot. Above the makeshift mantel hung a set of steer longhorns, the left prong stained four inches deep with the blood of some failed swindler. Gundy was sitting with his back to the swing doors, young Delia, subject of the tension, curled on his lap. She was daintily feeding him bits of pickled okra with fingers that he licked clean. He was chuckling and telling her lies, for Gundy was a masterful liar, while she believed his every unctuous word. All was right in the world.

Until the moment Blackwell stormed in chasing an anonymous tip, that is, an enormous cane knife in his grip and a mad killing in his eyes. The room cleared straight away, the other gamers and drunks seeking refuge from the pimp's wrath with the expediency of rats fleeing a sinking ship. Yet peculiarly, neither Gundy nor Delia moved, continuing instead their lovers' delight, blissfully ignoring the behemoth now seething just paces away. His breast heaving in rage, Blackwell stood hulking in the doorway as he swept the room with his gaze. When he spotted them,

he lowered his head, his eyes steadfast on their backs. Quickly then he launched a murderous route, wordlessly raising the blade aloft.

In the split second before he felled them both, from behind the bar and barrels the remaining Cypress Stump Boys materialized as if out of thin air, bounding over stools and tables with knives and saps held high. From one corner roared Goliath Mueller, who, an instant before Blackwell's blade completed its arc, caved in the fat man's right knee with a leaden pipe in a tremendous, double-fisted swing. From another corner darted Abrams with a bludgeon to the base of his skull. Downed, stunned beyond belief, Blackwell began groping dumbly about him. But the Cypress Stumps had only just begun. Arceneaux flashed swiftly with his Creole blade, sending rips of cheek and facial blood across the floor in grotesque spurts. Byrne, ever the dapper aggressor, joined in with his silver-tipped boots to ribs and head and groin, kick after bloody kick.

The ensuing melee was relentlessly one-sided.

All the while, Gundy and the girl carried on with their pleasantries, tickling each other beneath their chins, the brutality behind them seemingly to do little but stoke the flames of their courtship. Finally, once Blackwell was reduced to a bloodied hump, face down and begging, Wolfe appeared like a soundless apparition and sauntered up with that smile, stopping only to shake his head in pity over the pathetic heap at his feet. He knelt down gently. No one heard what he whispered into that thick rind of an ear. It did not matter, for within hours, despite a jag of bloody coughs that would not cease for weeks, Blackwell limped out of New Orleans forever.

As fate would have it, Gundy abandoned the girl four days later. Aggrieved beyond measure, mournful of an innocence lost, in her despair Delia soon plunged into the Mississippi, only to wash up dead on its banks the following eve, feasted on by every living beast that would have her.

With twilight settling, Abrams recalls several such instances, his lips pursing gravely with each recollection—the blood, the laughter, the raucous celebrations of victory at other men's expense. Recently, he has felt an unanticipated shift within him, as though the axis on which his disposition revolves has, in the months since his flight from New Orleans, been somehow disengaged from its moorings. Dawn continues to spin freely into dusk, dusk back to dawn, and yet with each new day a friction now grows, abrading the turn of his conscience. This, from a nature long characterized by a well-oiled indifference to all matters beyond its own concern. Perhaps his change has come from living beneath the oppressive thumb of Wolfe's and the law's likely search for him, the carnage witnessed at Oak Hills, the near starvation, the creeping risk of Cobb and Petitgout, or the realization that, despite himself, he is as much subject to the caprices of guilt as the weakest men he has known. Perhaps Miss Bloom's letter has something to do with it. He does not know. He is twenty years old and faces the doubts of that age. Regardless of the reasons, unlike the Elias Abrams of only a couple of months prior, he is now questioning whether his soul should be freighted by these cruelties of his past. He thinks of the countless blows he has administered over the years, the revelry and destruction. He is unsure. He is beginning to suspect that maybe he has been wrong all along.

His thoughts naturally wend to the New Orleans murder that will not leave him be. Admitting this to no one, in the darkest hours of the night he frequently awakens with a gasp, bolt upright, a cheap sweat gathered around his collar. In such times, he hugs himself for warmth, his breath registering in the night air, wishing like a shamefaced boy to confess all his wrongdoings to Carlson, to Hyams, to whomever might listen, but by morning inevitably changing his mind. Lying there by his fire, twirling that toothbrush soberly between his fingers, he pits his involvement in the New Orleans murder against the minor aggressions he has so often perpetrated in his life. The past beatings of Blackwell and those like him, the boxed ears and bruised ribs of those adversaries to come. Are there lines to be drawn, he wonders? Can a man expect justice from a world in which he is uncertain whether he lives justly himself?

After a long, contemplative pause, Abrams shakes his head. No, he spits bitterly, he has no regrets about harming men like Blackwell. In that, he is without remorse. He owes them nothing, for in the very filth of their lives, he acknowledges that they, like he, are complicit in their own demise—

"Abrams?"

Abrams blinks twice, snapped from his reverie, and looks up to Adjutant Holcomb. In the weeks since its infliction, the bruise above Holcomb's eye has gone from hideously mottled to healed, his split lip from creased and swollen back to plump and pink.

"Lieutenant Colonel Hyams requested I deliver this." A letter trembles in his deerskin-gloved hand. The official business notwithstanding, Holcomb is mortified by the menial task he is now performing. Little is more demoralizing than serving the fellow who has thrashed you. "I'm also to offer his gratitude for the tonic you prescribed. Apparently, he hasn't felt this spry in quite some time."

But Abrams hears not a word of it. Wrenched from one deep reflection, he has been immediately delivered into another, that born of a familiar penmanship. Pondering how to best vindicate himself from his past while navigating the future only moments before, suddenly, at the sight of the letter's face, his heart has begun to pound in his chest, his eyes gone wide, his mind drawn blank. He sits upright. He tucks the toothbrush into his lapel. He licks his lips. He tries to calm himself. He reaches for the letter, scarcely managing a word of thanks.

"Think nothing of it," sniffs Holcomb. "Please." And with that, he spins on his heels and heads off in the direction from which he came.

Abrams retains poise enough to unfasten the letter slowly. He loses himself, however, when, with the waxen seal broken, he is greeted by the same explosive bouquet that has nearly driven him mad since he unsealed that first letter those weeks before. All lingering thoughts of the Cypress Stumps and his violence among them are instantly usurped by the pleasures of that fragrance. Much as he did the first time, he draws these fresh pages to his nose and inhales long and deeply, detecting in that lungful of air identical hints of rosehips and lavender talc. He thinks of this Nora Bloom he has never met, tries to imagine her laugh, her toes, her taste, and discovers that he has never felt so strongly or foolish about anyone, ever.

His heart is driving hard; his palms are perspiring despite the frosty air. He prays the news is good, for in spite of his every hard-hearted defense, he is falling in love with a woman he has never met. This is absurd, he tells himself. She's a flirt and I'm a fool. He runs a hand through his hair. He is swallowing down the lump in his throat. He takes another deep draw of the paper. Afterward, he sighs and looks up to the sky. Following a last, bolstering breath, he begins to read:

October 19, 1861

Dearest Mr. Abrams,

Even as Union forces gather to deprive us of our liberties, I fear I may be committing an offense of my own by expressing to you just how marvelously thrilled I am to have received your response. A woman of profounder wisdom might oblige herself to a primmer sense of enthusiasm. Alas, I am no such woman. I am instead a silly girl, impetuous, ever one to express her joys while forgoing occasion's propriety. In such an admission and with your continued patience, I shall henceforth draft my letters to you with such purpose as to imagine they are intended for G~d's very eyes. Truly, I am most pleased to make your epistolary acquaintance.

And yet, were I to be wholly truthful with you, Mr. Abrams, I believe I would have persisted in my writings regardless, even were you or the comrade into whose hands my first letter might have fallen to have proved an unresponsive audience. Why so, you may ask? To this, I must confess that in these letters I find a most

92

purgative release. For although I possess a journal, my Polyhymnia, in her I feel as though I am merely packing my thoughts into a valise, to be bound, clasped, and tucked away forever. With the very idea that someone like you might read these petty reflections of mine, however, I feel my thoughts suddenly liberated, sent out wide into the world beyond my simple girlish scope. In the anonymity we share, I have thus found a boon companion. If you have found instead an annoyance, I shall know soon enough by the spleen of your next response or in its protracted absence.

It is approaching late October here in New Orleans, Mr. Abrams, and the city's horticulturalists shall soon bed down their gardens for winter. How much I prefer late spring and early summer and the myriad flowers in bloom. With autumn comes the grayness of an impending solstice, and with it, a gloom settles over my soul. I fear a terrible chill this winter.

Along this vein of despair, the Federal naval blockade has begun to take its toll on us here. I dare not speak too petulantly of our deprivation, for I have heard tell of the dire straits field soldiers are now forced to endure, but it is indeed noticeable, the goods so hard come by. Each day we send our girl Violet, a fine, sharp-minded slave, to the market, and each day she returns with less and less in hand. Truly, I carp in a manner most foolish, but in the eyes of many a home front mother, concern now lingers with regards to filling the squalling mouths of her children.

Were I more callous to your plight, Mr. Abrams, I would catalogue with great lament all that we may no longer purchase in the markets. Instead I choose to speak of that which remains abundant, and freely so, namely my continued admiration for you. How can this be, you are no doubt wondering? Admiration for one never met? Perhaps you perceive me as a girl who lacks judgment, and in this, I would wholeheartedly support your perception. I am indeed foolish. But do not suppose me foolish for admiring you merely because we are strangers. You may be of poor integrity, Mr. Abrams, though your fine letter to me certainly argues contrariwise. Verily, you may be the basest sort of man. And yet, in your enlistment to the cause for which you are now fighting, according to the sage Reverend Gutheim with whom I emphatically agree, these imagined defects of character are forthwith reconciled, and your soul magnificently cleansed.

Whether you agree with these audacious suppositions or not, I am well-comforted by my decision to admire your bravery nonetheless. Of course I trust that you are a man of high moral standing, faithful and true. Your letter alludes to a nature most worthy in its own right. Even so, how much I would prefer to discover these truths for myself. I tempt insolent grounds here, I know it, and in this I am emboldened by our shared anonymity, but I would very much like to hear you purport yourself to me in person. I do not know if this shall ever be, and I sigh for it. However, until such time as we might meet, please do know that I continue to offer you the completeness of my attention, my every affectionate prayer, and in closing, a most impertinent and gentle kiss to your brow.

Respectfully yours in G~d's love,
Nora Bloom

"Goddamn this woman," Abrams whispers, biting his bottom lip as he clutches the pages tightly to his breast. He shakes his head. "Goddamn, goddamn, goddamn."

13

—

"I got some things need takin' care of here in camp 'fore I head out," states Abrams, "but I just wanted to show you it ain't wholly foolish, what I'm proposin'."

Carlson removes his spectacles as he hands the letter back over. "Surely, though, you'll agree that while it's one thing to write a stranger, it's something else entirely for that stranger to come knocking on your door, I don't care what she's suggesting there. Think about it for a moment, Elias, please."

Abrams dismisses this with the bravado of one who, young as he is, has already brought his share of women to orgasm. "Look, John Lee, you're right, could be oil'n water, no denyin' it. Only way we'll know is if this girl and me actually get to meetin'. 'Sides, I've never been much about the Stars 'n Bars, you know that. And if we *are* as close to winnin' this war as you keep sayin', what's the difference, I cut out a few weeks early, take my chances runnin' the guard? Hell, you think old McCulloch's going to miss me?"

"Oh Elias, don't," scoffs Carlson with a wave of his hand. "Obtuseness ill suits you." He nibbles on a spectacle stem. "What troubles me here is the manner and timing with which you're planning this meeting, that's all. She's an intelligent and evidently highly sensitive person, fine. I'm doubly glad you two appear to be developing a relationship, impersonally begun though it may be. Certainly, there's a romanticism to epistolary affairs. Yet one need only consult Abelard and Heloise or *Les Liaisons Dangereuses* to learn there's great potential for tragedy bred into them as well. That being said, whether you're apathetic to the Cause or no, if you're caught deserting ranks, the authorities will hang you first, ask questions later." Carlson lets his reasoning sink in. "Now if that's not enough to dissuade you, all right then, you're a damned fool and I'm perfectly willing to accept that. But personally, I happen to be averse to watching men with whom I've shared my fill of tobacco dangle freely in the wind."

Abrams is frustrated. He had not expected such argument from Carlson, nor the quality of his points. Rather, he had believed that the man with whom he composed his first love letter would endorse his mission unconditionally. "You're talkin', John Lee," he says defensively, "and honest to God I hear your words, I do, but my leaving's about more than just cozyin' up to this Miss Bloom. She's a draw, that's a hard fact, but there's something else." He pauses, choosing his words wisely. "I got some matters in New Orleans need attendin', first and foremost."

Carlson is merely exasperated further. "Dear Lord, Elias, we've *all* got matters back in New Orleans that need attending. That's hardly a justifiable excuse."

"Not like mine, y'all don't."

From their time spent together, Carlson knows that Abrams, despite his youth, is not one to overstate his concerns. He therefore grunts at his young friend's words, and pulls at his nose in contemplation. "Well then," he sighs, "maybe I can help. I'm only slightly ashamed to admit that my family, in certain circles, exerts a fair degree of influence."

"I appreciate it," says Abrams with a sober nod, "but this here's mine."

In the ensuing silence, each man takes a moment to study the other. Carlson finds in the beleaguered young cardsharp a mind that, born to different conditions, trained with a pedagogue's rigor, would have been a force to reckon with, of this he has no doubt. In Abrams he has discerned an alchemical blend of brashness and budding compassion, street smarts and skepticism that suggests the kind of golden potential found in only the rarest student. In this sudden decision to desert, however, Carlson must now mourn a failed fruition, realizing that the boy, once he leaves Camp Jackson under the cover of night and is caught for it, will be executed before these base elements within him ever have a chance to develop their worth.

Abrams, too, takes some time to reflect. He has spent many hours with Carlson over the past months, quietly listening to the didacticism and the Grecian odes, to the tales of his twins' theatricality and his wife's baked hams, but until that instant he had seen in Carlson little more than a caricature of the Southern intellect. Now, though, their parting imminent, Abrams thinks back to the first day they met, to the battlefield at Oak Hills and the warm trickle of urine that soaked the professor's trousers front. He has not mentioned this since, not even in jest, although on occasion Carlson himself has laughingly brought it up. "A man's got to wonder whether Perseus pissed himself when confronted by Medusa. Or Hercules, by Cerberus." Here Carlson would take a meditative puff on his pipe. "Odds are against it, I'd wager."

Standing there, Abrams considers the professor's individual parts: the filthy, broken-caned Panama atop his long, wheat chaff hair, the round spectacles, the watery blue eyes, his Confederate frock now held as one by a patchwork of stitches and scraps, his beard, formerly a pair of well-tended muttonchops, grown full and red. Yet in spite of everything, for the very first time on this, their last night together, Abrams also conceives Carlson as an entirety: dedicated husband, loving father, gifted teacher, generous spirit. Months before, back among the Cypress Stumps at tables of cards and whiskey, lounging amid whores and their venereal decay, he would have clearly mocked such a man. But no longer. Indeed, Abrams is surprised by the emotions welling inside him. Should one have faltered on the next field of battle, the other would have lifted him by his elbow and wrenched him forward. Should one have fallen in death, the other would have borne his memory back to the camp and beyond. Formed through neither legacy nor loving choice in the manner of other relationships, the bond between Abrams and Carlson has been rooted instead in the will to live, the most primal of all truths. Therein lies the cohesion, because in unguarded moments as they lay by their campfires, each has witnessed in the other's eyes the same dogged, panicky survival instinct that he himself shares. They have not requested heroics of one another. Heroes possess a venerable but alienating presence. They needed only to find survivors. Survival is reassuring, sane, worthy of respect; it ratifies their own instincts. It lets them know they are neither foolish nor alone. And so in recognizing this during their brief time together, they have formed a bond unlike any either has ever known.

Abrams is somewhat stunned. He had not expected to feel anything but a stock sense of departure.

"John Lee," he says curtly, tipping his bowler, "been a real pleasure. Now if you'll excuse me, I got some matters needin' attention 'fore I head out." Without another word, he slides the letter into his breast pocket next to the first and pats it per custom. He then heads off determinedly to tackle his final obligation before abandoning the Army of the Confederate States of America altogether.

14

"C'mon, you fuckin' whore, you fuckin' nag, fess up—ain't I about the goddamnedest gator in rut you ever saw?"

Her reply is gritted teeth. She will not give this revolting little man the satisfaction of a scream any more than she did his dumb, massive friend who now slumbers, his appetites spent. Still, the pain of Petit-gout's violent thrusts forces her to think back to pleasanter times. To times before the war, before her man, an enlistee in the Missouri militia, was blown to pieces by Yankee thunder. She thinks back to the meaning of his sighs and of his strength and of their wedding day down at the chapel by Bull Shoals Lake, the water gentle on her ankles as they strolled hand in hand. She remembers his tender kiss to the nape of her neck, and his promises. She remembers the first cornhusk doll she ever owned, crafted by her father when she was six. "For my Molly," her father had said. She remembers his large, flat hands delicately teasing the husks and the twine. She remembers him giving it to her one Michaelmas Day, and his booming laughter as her hands clasped with delight. She had named that doll Junie Mae. Now, as this disgusting little Louisianan pays to rape her, as he does his best to pierce her innards with his tiny prick, she is whispering that doll's name, *Junie Mae, Junie Mae, Junie Mae . . .*

"That's it," Petitgout croons, "oh, you dear sweet bitch, take that stinkin' root. Oh mercy me, take it, take it, take it—"

"Mostly, you wouldn't get the benefit of my voice, I was creepin' you," interrupts Abrams, tapping Petitgout hard on the shoulder. "But there's things you and me need to discuss." He has tracked them down by a small fire out in the woods, a hundred yards from the nearest bustle of camp. In his hand, Abrams brandishes the derringer.

Petitgout withdraws instantly from Molly with a slight puckering sound, causing a gasp of appreciation from the farmer's-wife-turned-prostitute. Stringing together a litany of furious oaths, Petitgout is erect, though unimpressive, as he struggles to pull up his trousers. "Cobb!" he bellows, his eyes yellow with hatred. "Git up, you fuckin' louse!"

At this Cobb snorts, awakens, and quickly construing the situation, just as fast has his Bowie gleaming in the moonlight.

"Whoa, now," says Abrams evenly, showing the small pistol to them both, "y'all just calm it. And you," he orders Cobb, "you'll be wantin' to use that sheath there."

"I got 'im, Skip," growls Cobb from his seat. "I swear to fuck, I can git him."

Petitgout thinks hard for a moment, staring down that short barrel. He is pondering his cousin's blade's speed against the speed of Abrams' bullet. The derringer holds two .22-caliber slugs; they may not always kill, but their ability to maim is certain. Meanwhile, Molly is working madly to draw up her pantaloons and stow between her breasts the greasy bills she has been given. She stands and huffs, running a hand gently over her hair. Her face is flushed, her vagina sore and oozing. If any dignity remains in her, she is having a difficult time rallying it.

After a tense few seconds, Petitgout tells Cobb to stow his blade. When Cobb obeys, Abrams offers a nod and lowers the gun only slightly.

"A gun ain't nothin' but a hunk of metal, boy," seethes Petitgout with a long, dirty spit. "It's who's holdin' that gun, it's *him* whose mettle matters most." Here his eyes narrow. "How 'bout it then, Abrams? How's your mettle?" He takes a small step forward. Molly moves in the other direction an equal pace, but does not yet break away. She figures her sex is incongruous in the battle between men and thus moves a second step. "Stay where you at, cunt," snaps Petitgout, holding out his hand.

Abrams ignores this harshness; he is not here for chivalry. Rather, he is here to learn the nature of the relationship between these two and Silas Wolfe. He is here to take the initiative for the first time in months. He trades his weight between his feet. "I aim to find out what y'all're about," he says plainly.

"Oh, well then," replies Petitgout, his hands on his hips. "You heard that, Earl? Feller here wants to know what we all 'bout."

"Hell, I can school him but quick." Cobb's eyes are murderous. "Lemme school him, Skip. Go on, lemme school him."

Petitgout takes no notice of his cousin's plea. "Now you fine at cards," he tells Abrams, "means you got some sand. But what happens, that game turns harder?" He takes another small step forward.

"Stay yourself, Petitgout. I mean it."

"What, we just chattin', ain't we?" His eyes have grown big with innocence, his hands wide open. "That's what you wanted, huh? Chat a bit? Find out what we all 'bout?"

Only now does Abrams realize his mistake. His ego has gotten the better of him, once again. Had he simply left the camp quietly and without confrontation, there would have been fewer questions asked of him, fewer answers to give, less blood to shed. But his desire to stand firm in the face of his threats—perceived or otherwise—has forced him into an unnecessary peril. His brow begins to bead with sweat. Fear creeps up his spine. Then, with all the gravity he can muster, he says, "You brung up the Smile, last we spoke. I'm lookin' to find out who y'all are to him, is all."

Petitgout stops at this, his head tilting in amusement. "The Smile?"

"Whether y'all're in league together or no."

"And if we was, pray tell me, you shit-stain, you darlin' little cunt rag, what difference'd that make to you?"

Abrams cannot stop himself from speaking the next words: "Just that him and me had ourselves a fallin' out, as y'all likely guessed."

Petitgout leans in. "And so you thinkin' Cobb and me mighta been sent word to stick you? That it?"

"Something like that."

"Listen, you fuck, we was meant to stick you, you can be damned sure you wouldn't be standin' here to ask it of us later." Petitgout takes another step forward. "See, me," he says, scratching a cheek absently, "I was willin' to let things go, that poker game we played. What I said 'bout Wolfe back then, you ask all them who know me, they'll say old Skip Petitgout likes throwin' scares into people—ain't that right, whore?" Molly holds her chin high, but she is doing all she can to keep from crying. She does not know it yet, but this will be her last night as a prostitute. She will take her polluted womb and her three hungry children and move farther south to her aunt's, where she will eventually fall in love with a crippled shopkeeper from Tupelo. "Truth is, Abrams, I'd all but forgotten 'bout you." Petitgout takes another ominous step forward. "Till this moment, 'course."

Cobb is standing now. He cracks his knuckles. He shifts his hulking weight.

This has been an enormous blunder. Abrams' decision to challenge these men without facts, with his gun drawn, comes crashing to him now as both childish and petulant. No grown man, he suddenly realizes, makes this kind of assumption and lives very long for the telling. Should he survive the night, he will take this lesson hard indeed. "Awright now," he says falteringly, taking a step backward, "awright."

But Petitgout is not done. "Any soul vexed about such things got to have a price on its head worth collectin', eh, Earl?"

Cobb nods imperceptibly, his gaze unbroken from Abrams. With one hand, he rubs his mouth hungrily while the other moves back to the knife on his hip. He, too, takes a step forward. Molly, realizing Petitgout's preoccupation, quickly bolts off into the night. In an hour, she will have begun packing. In three, she will have hitched her horse and wagon. By midnight, her children groggy with sleep, she will be hunched bleakly over the reins and heading southward. By morning, her life will have changed forever.

"Y'all hold it," Abrams warns them both, lifting the derringer and aiming it at the center of Cobb's chest. "If you think I won't fire, y'all're just flat-out wrong."

"Shit," sneers Petitgout, "Cobb here's taken heavier stings than that fuckin' skeeter's got to give."

Abrams then swings his arm toward Petitgout, drawing aim directly at his face. "How 'bout you, Skip? How heavy a sting can *you* take?"

"Boy, oh boy," laughs Petitgout, "last time a man aimed at my head, got his ball sack cut off, dried to a leathery grain over the knob of a hickory bough, and used as a walkin' cane grip, helpin' me high-step it all up and *down* the street."

"Then I'd say that cane grip's in need of immediate disinfection." From out of the darkness, up walks Professor John Lee Carlson, his rifle waist high but trained on Cobb, his Panama pulled low. "We wouldn't want to give that man's poor scrotum, dead and leathery though it may be, the chlamydia, now would we? Because given your evident hygiene, dear sir, that'd appear a distinct possibility." He pauses, nods, and takes a strengthening breath. "Hello, Elias. Gentlemen."

At Carlson's arrival, Abrams' stomach instantly flops, as much from relief as from worry. Relief at now having a comrade to fight beside, worry at the danger into which that comrade has followed him. He has had few honest friends over the course of his lifetime. He has neither brother nor father. In the jeopardy he and Carlson now share, however, Abrams realizes he risks losing the one man who has grown to embody all three. "John Lee," he says sternly, "this ain't no place for you."

"According to my wife," replies the professor, "tragically few places are."

"I ain't messin'," says Abrams. "Scat."

"After tracking you all the way out here? Elias, please, you wouldn't begrudge an old man his respite, would you?"

Petitgout can stand this banter no longer. "Hey!" he barks to Carlson, "don't know who the fuck you are, and honest, don't much care. But you want to continue livin' peaceful, I'd take your lover's words to heart. You go on and get out now, 'fore you get in too deep."

Carlson licks his lips and redoubles his grip on his Mississippi. "I appreciate the concern," he says, "but I know where I'm standing."

"Maybe so, maybe no."

"Believe I do."

"All right then," shrugs Petitgout, "if that's the way y'all want to play it. Just remember, y'all got the guns, but we got the guts. So way I see it, together we got us an impasse."

"Impasse, hell," murmurs Cobb as he lowers his head and begins a slow, steady march toward Carlson, his blade out, his eyes fast and mean.

"Hold it now," stammers Carlson, realizing for the first time just how dire the circumstances truly are, "stop right there, mister."

"Shoot 'im!" cries Abrams. "Dear Jesus, Carlson, you got to shoot 'im—"and here, seizing his chance at the distraction, Petitgout shrieks and lunges at Abrams himself, grabbing at the hand that clutches the derringer. Suddenly, while Abrams and Petitgout begin to grapple over the gun, several paces away Carlson is quaking as he pulls his hammer back. But before he is able to fire, the large man has stampeded upon him, the Bowie's blade carving the air toward his throat. Miraculously, Carlson brings the length of his Mississippi up to block the thrust precisely as he was trained at Camp Walker those months ago, just before his jugular is sliced apart, locking the two of them in a violent stalemate. Heightened as his senses are, however, as aware as he has become of the peril, Carlson is unprepared for the knee that Cobb drives up into his stomach with a grunting, full-forced delivery. Gasping, the professor doubles over without air but knows that if he loses himself, he will be lost entirely, his wife widowed, his twins left fatherless, so he takes a few biting, measured breaths and works to regain his footing. His rifle wrenched from his grasp, he only just succeeds in scrambling away from

Cobb, who is circling him, crouched, his blade aloft, tossing the knife from hand to hand. "Cold as these days is," says Cobb grimly, "I'm gonna stuff my hands inside you, you fuckin' catamite, bathe them in the warmth of your belly blood."

Meanwhile, the battle between Petitgout and Abrams rages. The smaller man is frothing at the mouth, screaming and spitting in Abrams' face—"You're as good as killed, you maggot, you ragged fuck!"—as he tries his best to stomp a toe and gnaw at the hand that controls the gun with his sharp, yellow-stained teeth. He is tearing at Abrams' chest, at his lapel, at his face and throat. He has gone berserk, wild, become a beast without government or caution; his only focus is the destruction of that which endangers him. Abrams, in turn, for the first seconds of the scuffle is at great disadvantage. Although he is masterful with his fists, wrestling in close quarters suits him poorly. And even though he is tough, he understands that those like Petitgout actually delight in the forfeiture of their membership to mankind. They seldom look at other men as men at all, but as tools to satisfy their most depraved whims. A man with money, they see as a means of enhancing their own wealth. A woman with hips, they see as a means of pleasure. A trinket, soon theirs. A desire, soon met. A threat, soon dispatched by any means necessary.

Abrams has confronted such men on rare occasion, and when he does, he knows that if he is to survive, a portion of his soul must temporarily die. It is never a cognizant decision, of course, but one pondered after the fact, even more so since the murder in New Orleans. For until the fight is over, he must take aside whatever social decency he possesses and place it delicately on a shelf, away from the primitive fury he keeps caged inside him until such conditions require its parole. This is one of those times. As a result, realizing that his fists will do him no good, instead he pulls the smaller man closer to him, hugging him tightly while attempting to fend off blow and tooth in their tussle over the derringer. Something in him snaps; he can feel this discernibly. All at once he is standing outside himself and marveling at the purity of his anger, its enveloping warmth, the liberating sense that whatever happens next, he is no longer accountable for it. It is blissful, the violence coursing through his veins. He has been freed from all constraint but that obliged to survival. "I'm stronger'n you," he sputters, throwing the smaller man this way and that, then again, louder, "I'm stronger'n you." A third time he says it, only this time he is shouting. "I'm stronger'n you!" he yells, "I'm stronger'n you!" In this abandonment, Abrams is shaking his head fiercely to clear it of its bowler. He then ratchets his head back, holds it for a second, and bashes his forehead violently forward into Petitgout's left temple. The resulting head butt shoots stars into Abrams' eyes, but again his head rears back for another blow, and another. He is ramming the top and sides of Petitgout's head mercilessly now, deadening the flesh there, bloodying his own, the hair and dirt and blood matting, clotting into a pulp. Together they are grunting like stuck boars as Abrams rears back for the fifth time, crashing his head into Petitgout's until, at last, he feels the smaller man's grip begin to weaken on the gun. And again he rams, his neck tendons taut, then slack, and again, his neck aching, his head pounding, but he no longer has any control over himself because as long as he can continue to punish the wickedness he now embraces, he will hold it to his breast forever. Finally, with a ninth and closing blow, drunk on the bloody taste in his mouth, Abrams feels his foe go unconscious. Only when he is sure Petitgout has been beaten senseless, does he loosen his grip. Once done, the smaller man sinks like ballast to the earth.

Thus bloodied, his chest heaving, Abrams takes a last raging look to confirm that Petitgout is indeed out cold before whirling about to come to Carlson's defense. He finds his friend on the ground now, fifteen yards away, struggling mightily as he and Cobb wrestle over control of the rifle. The larger man above is laughing, dropping thick yellow sputum into Carlson's face, one viscous globule after another. He is toying with the weaker man like a well-fed tomcat plays with vermin, wounding it, damaging its will, easing just enough to let its prey believe in the chance of escape, only to pull it back toward greater abuse. Cobb is so engaged in this death game that he does not see Abrams staggering toward him, a thick length of birch in his grasp, its tip dragging in the dirt behind him. He sees neither Abrams' windup with that length of birch nor its whizzing arc as it comes crashing down on his head. After that, save for a split-second brilliance upon the limb's impact, Cobb quickly sees nothing at all.

"Ho there, John Lee," gasps Abrams, bending down to pat his friend's knee. "You awright?"

Carlson gulps and blinks. He does not know.

15

The next morning, before stepping away from the remains of their campfire, Carlson demands Abrams stay exactly where he is. He has scrubbed his face over and over again during the night but still feels the slow trickle of that thick yellow sputum coursing into his eyes and nostrils. Memory of the sensation will disgust him for as long as he lives. His clothing is torn. The bruises on his face are pronounced. "Don't you dare move," he orders Abrams. "I'll be back."

Abrams, his own head knotted with lumps, his body sore in every muscle, grimaces but does not argue.

Together, they had taken turns dozing until dawn, on guard against the cousins' stewing vengeance. Between them they spoke little, each morosely consumed in his thoughts. Though nearly killed by that Union sharpshooter at Oak Hills, until his encounter with Cobb, it had never occurred to Carlson that he might die by ignoble hands. None of his ancient texts prepared him for such an end. In them he had learned quite plainly that heroes are slain by other heroes, principle defeats villainy, good inevitably triumphs over evil. And even though he had long been aware of his own naiveté, actually growing to revel in it as his wife giggled behind her fingertips whenever he pronounced to their twin girls, with open text and the dramatic air of Thespis, the merits of Truth and Honor and Beauty, it had simply never dawned on John Lee Carlson that these absolutes, at long last, were not truthful indeed.

Abrams' turn of mind was different. Initially worried about Carlson's welfare, by first light, he had regressed completely toward the callous character of his youth. He needed but hours to return to these mercenary ways. Now, checking his pocket watch over a mug of nettle tea, he has decided that his botched affair with Cobb and Petitgout will not deter him from his course back down South, regardless of the danger suddenly confronting Carlson. *Shit,* he reasons, spitting a fragment of leaf. *I told him to clear off, didn't I? Ain't my fault that stubborn jackass can't heed a warnin'.*

Carlson soon returns. "Pack up your kit," he insists, kicking Abrams in the ankle. When a surprised Abrams does not budge, Carlson kicks him again. "Let's go, get moving."

"Now hold on there—"

This is the spark of contention Carlson was hoping for. "No, Elias," he snaps, "*you* hold on. See, I'm not asking about last night, because when you finally get around to opening your goddamned mouth, I'm sure I'll have story enough for years. But here's what I won't brook: I won't brook watching you run off into the woods to get yourself hanged for desertion. Not after what I went through, no sir." Carlson is on his knees, stuffing his gear furiously into his haversack. "I'm not blaming you, mind you. I take full responsibility for my own, absolutely. But because of it, you're not dying anytime soon, nor am I, certainly not at that vile son-of-a-bitch's hands, not by a long shot. So whatever you've got to tell me about the how and why, you can say it later. For now, I don't want to hear it."

"John Lee, wait—"

"Go on, test me." Carlson sniffs. "See if I'm in jest." The glare in his eyes tells Abrams that the professor has never been more serious. "I told you my family has some influence," he continues, angrily rolling up his bedroll. "I've just had to use it, something I'm loathe to do. How're your riding skills?"

"My what?"

"Horseback, you damned fool. Can you ride?"

"I ain't cavalry material, if that's what you're askin'."

Carlson shoots him a look and waits.

"I've ridden some," confesses Abrams. "But I wouldn't call myself downright horsey."

Carlson shakes his head and chuckles, marveling at the madness of the world. "Well, I hope you're a quick study then," he says, buckling his haversack. "We'll be riding hard. As of today."

"John Lee, look, I appreciate your—"

"I'll have none of it, Elias, so save your breath. Bruslé's heading to the Indian Territory, mustering a regiment of Creek and Seminole. Man's a family friend. I asked. He agreed to let us join. Both Hébert and Hyams signed off on it, a miracle. We leave in an hour."

"Yeah, well, I wouldn't be so certain."

Carlson stops again. "Right now I'd say you're in no position to judge the certainty of anything."

"But you can't just expect me to—"

"Hold it right there," interrupts Carlson with an annoyed flick of his hand, "just hold it." He takes a consternated breath. "Here's *precisely* what I expect you to do: I expect you to shut your fucking mouth and pack up that fucking beehive already. *That's* what I expect of you, Elias."

Abrams is dumbstruck. He is unaccustomed to being spoken to in this way, especially not by the likes of Carlson. He is unsure how to proceed. After a long pause, he manages, "Well, what about New Orleans then? And the girl?" He is doubly surprised by the bleating tone of his voice. Usually in command of such matters, he suddenly feels very much like a child.

Carlson laughs bitterly. "Lord, son, problems don't just go *away*. They age, grow a bit of nuance, like an old Louisville Bourbon. So whatever predicament's awaiting you back home, I promise it'll be there upon your rightful return, don't you worry. Hell, it'll have a finer distinction even." Here Carlson removes his glasses and wipes them on his shirt-sleeve. "And as to the girl, I hate to be so brusque, but considering the circumstances, I can ill afford falsehoods—forget her."

"C'mon, forget her. You're cracked."

Carlson shrugs. "Cracked or not, there's something called a romantic ideal in this world, Elias, and y'all two appear to be perfecting it into an art. As flesh and blood, you're no more real to her than she is to you. Sorry."

Abrams feels the sting of Carlson's words. Deep down, he has known from the first that what Carlson says is true, though he has worked hard to lock these doubts away so he might, at least for a short while, imagine a life rich with love and ease and splendor. For weeks now one fantasy in particular has consumed him. They are in a rowboat together on a beautiful spring day, Nora beneath a white Chinese parasol, him at the oars, floating aimlessly around the shores of Lake Pontchartrain. They feast on chilled grapes and drink champagne from heirloom crystal. Lazily, they scoop the warm lake water into their hands. They splash and smile. They kiss, delicately. He pushes her gently backward into the prow of the small boat. She resists. He whispers into her ear. She relents. He unbuttons her corset. She stares unblinkingly at the clouds above. He places a grape in her quivering navel. She bites her lips. He circles the grape slowly with his tongue. She whimpers. He devours it. Her eyes go wide. He raises the crinoline and petticoat, parts her split-crotch drawers, and moves to his knees. She gasps at the cool champagne he pours between her thighs. He nuzzles his nose in her soaked vagina. She grips the boat's sides for support. He drinks from deeply within her, relishes the commingling of flavors and warmth and sweet wetness, before deftly unbuttoning himself to slide softly in and out of her for hours and hours on end. And when the day is done, as Abrams escorts his weak-kneed Nora by her hand onto the dock, the boat inevitably bobs, forcing her to lose her balance and fall into his arms for what he imagines will be the rest of their lives. Now, though, confronted by the absurdity of these thoughts, Abrams becomes all the more protective of what they have come to mean to him. "That's plain horseshit, right there," he tells Carlson defiantly.

"Fine." Carlson replaces his spectacles by looping them behind his ears. "Let's suppose I'm wrong. You're not a whole lot of use to that girl dead, and that's exactly what you'll be if they catch you taking French leave. But let's take it even further. For the sake of argument, let's pretend by some grace of God you evade your pursuers and make it all the way back down to her very doorstep. Do you honestly believe from the sentiment of the letters she's written, she'd allow a deserter into her life?" Carlson does not give Abrams time to answer. "No, certainly not. And why wouldn't she? Because it's your *valor* she worships, Elias, nothing more. Surely not you as an individual. So you show up while the war's yet to be won, as a deserter, and you'll have reduced to rubble any chance you may have had, you can bank on it. Now, if that doesn't register, you've got an even thicker skull than the one that did all that damage last night. But if it does, if you can possibly grasp what the fuck I'm saying here, then you'll quit your goddamned arguing, open that haversack, and begin packing. Do it, Elias. Now."

Abrams has nothing left to say. He is without foundation, and he knows it. Quietly, he obeys.

16

Headquarters, McCulloch's Brigade
Camp Stephens, Ark.

Capt.—You will proceed without delay to the Creek Agency in the Indian Territory, and there muster a regiment of Creek Indians. It appears from treaty stipulations made by Captain Pike, Commissioner, that this regiment is to be composed of eight companies of Creeks and two of Seminoles.

It will be proper for you, as soon as you reach the Indian Territory, to make Captain Pike, the Commissioner, aware of your mission, who will, no doubt, give you valuable information in regard to this regiment. As soon as the regiment is organized and mustered into service, an election will be held for a colonel and other field officers, whom you will also muster into service.

Major Clark, Quartermaster at Fort Smith, will be directed to send to you an agent of the Quartermaster and Commissary Departments, to furnish the necessary supplies. Beef and flour can be furnished in the country, or certainly from Texas. It will therefore only be necessary to furnish the regiment with coffee, sugar, and salt from Fort Smith, and direction will be given to that effect.

A quantity of powder and lead will also be sent from Fort Smith to the regiment.

I have the honor to be, Captain,
Your obedient servant,
James McIntosh, Capt. C.S.A. and Adjt.-Gen.

Captain Charles A. Bruslé, of Company A, the Iberville Greys, finishes reading aloud the order to the small band he has assembled to accompany him on the trail. He is a tall man, of noble bearing. At thirty-six, he looks younger by a decade. He waxes his thick brown mustache each morning, brushes his shoulder-length hair each night with the assiduity of an aspiring debutante. His boots, unlike almost every other pair in the Confederacy, shine brilliantly, thanks to the keen-eyed attention of his Negro houseboy attendant from home. Those who do not know Bruslé well call him vain. They are wrong. His actions do not reflect vanity. Rather, to look or act anything but gallantly, regardless of circumstance, he has long felt would disrespect those forefathers who labored so hard to grant him the lifestyle into which he was born. In maintaining a dignified appearance, Bruslé believes he is expressing thanks for every advantage he has been given.

He is thus not only a well-kempt man but a fabulously wealthy one. Like so many of Louisiana's richest natives, he, too, has earned his fortune through inheritance and sugar. His plantation is located in Plaquemine, Iberville Parish, just ten miles downriver from Baton Rouge and north of I. J. Lieber's Napoleonville by twenty-five. Since 1857, he has served as a member of the state House of Representatives. After the war, he will be elected Iberville Parish tax collector, sheriff, and eventually state senator. But for now, he has left his farmland and politics behind him, having first received his commission as captain, then advancing quickly to the rank of aide-de-camp to Colonel Louis Hébert. That he has been chosen to lead a mission of such great tactical importance is testament to the high regard in which he is held. He does not take such obligations lightly. His carriage is formidable, his spine erect. His voice is capable of great volume, but he rarely uses it so. He is the very model of the Confederate Cause.

He and John Lee Carlson have known each other for decades. Their fathers—one mercantile, of New Orleans, the other agricultural, of Plaquemine—met as youths themselves, on an exquisitely rendered duck-hunting trip to the Atchafalaya Basin, hosted by the lieutenant governor of the day. One lazy afternoon, after lopping off the necks of three bottles of Bordeaux and passing them back and forth, they staggered drunkenly into the swamp to hunt the only game they soon realized they were truly interested in—each other. When they returned empty-handed hours later, the remaining members of the hunting party had laughed and whooped, calling them poor shots indeed, unaware of the sport the two had in mind. The young lovers laughed in reply, their hair mussed, but in their mirthful winks knew each had hit his mark perfectly.

Years later, at the outbreak of the War Between the States, John Lee Carlson intentionally avoided enlisting in the Iberville Greys under the command of his father's paramour's son. Not because he knew of the illicit and lengthy affair—neither of the sons did, or ever would—or because he thought Charles A. Bruslé anything but intelligent and sophisticated company, but because he wished to avoid any appearance of nepotism. Man is provided a broad palate of phobias from which he may tint his life, and for John Lee Carlson, accusation of preferential treatment is chief among those fears. He has no time now to honor such fear, however. At the risk of wounding his pride, he will do what is necessary to keep him and his young friend alive.

There are seven members of the party in all. Aside from Carlson and Abrams, Bruslé has recruited Jean-Baptiste, his fifteen-year-old Negro house slave from Plaquemine, Corporals Hank and Lionel Jeffers, of La Place, brothers gifted in the art of long-range marksmanship, and Private Obediah Todd, a half-breed Creek trained as diligently in the language and scouting techniques of his mother's people as he is in the devout Christian faith of his father's. It is past noon, and the men quickly make one another's acquaintance. They transfer their gear from their haversacks to saddlebags, then tie their bedrolls behind the saddles of the horses they have been detailed. Abrams and Carlson leave their unwieldy rifles behind in camp. In return, each has been loaned a .52-caliber Sharp's carbine, stocked cap and cartridge boxes, and a .40-caliber, nine-shot LeMat revolver, dubbed the grapeshot pistol because of its lower, 18-gauge single-shotgun barrel. With almost four pounds of metal now holstered to his hip, Abrams will need some time to adjust his balance. Bruslé holds his gloved hand up to the weak autumn sun. Without further ceremony, he orders them to mount up.

Abrams takes a deep breath, hitches his left foot into the stirrup, and hoists himself over his pony's back. He has been assigned Small Bill, a hardy little pinto chosen for him because of his steady gait, sure footing, and even disposition. "John Lee says it's been a while," Bruslé had informed him earlier. "He also says you might need a bit of a refresher. Well, we both know we've no time for that, don't we?"

"Yessir, guess we do."

"Small Bill's a good animal," said Bruslé, clapping the horse affectionately on the neck. "Grab ahold of the pommel if you need to, no shame in it." But here his voice fell. "Because remember, Private, we've no time for dawdling. This is war."

Abrams agreed.

"Good," said Bruslé with a prudent nod. He withdrew a hand from his glove and held it out for Abrams' grip. "Welcome aboard. Pope himself offers no better voucher than John Lee Carlson. The fact you got Hyams' vote to boot—well, that's all the confidence a man could ever need. Just keep up and keep alert. We've got some time in the saddle ahead of us." Bruslé replaced his glove. "And Private?"

"Sir?"

"I couldn't care less how you and John Lee got those bruises. But I *will* care, and I will care *greatly*, if their source proves an interference with my mission. Do I make myself clear?"

17

With almost one hundred and fifty miles between them and Fort Smith, the men ride with purpose, driving their horses hard each day. During slower moments, Abrams watches Small Bill's breaths frost in the late autumn air, feels the beast's exhalations between his legs with every plodding step. The sky is gray. The trees are bare and black. Each biting gust tightens the men's faces. Noon chills them to their bones. Together, they ride in dour silence from Missouri's Osage Plain, a flat region rich in corn and grain in warmer months, southward to the Ozark Plateau. The sweet, seasoned scents of sweat, cracked leather, and horseshit fill their nostrils for hours on end. Only occasionally do they speak. Atop Gaston, his massive black charger, Bruslé explains to the men their mission. "We will be diplomats," he says resolutely. "Ideally, Captain Pike of the Territory will have organized whatever full-bloods he's been able to rally. Regardless, we will return with the promise of far more guns than when we set out."

Some time later, Jean-Baptiste, rocking gently in his saddle, looks up to the stark heavens and begins to sing quietly, sonorously, to himself:

There's a balm in Gilead
To make the wounded whole
There's a balm in Gilead
To heal the sin-sick soul

Sometimes I feel discouraged
And think my work's in vain
But then the Holy Spirit
Revives my soul again

Don't ever feel discouraged
For Jesus is your friend
And if you lack of knowledge
He'll ne'er refuse to lend

If you can't preach like Peter
If you can't pray like Paul
You can tell the love of Jesus
And say, "He died for all."

Save for Bruslé, who has heard the boy sing since he was three, the men of the small company are shocked by Jean-Baptiste's tonal purity, the resonance and depth of his voice. Carlson has heard strong voices before, especially in his college's choir, but never one so agile, so rich with adoration for Christ. But profounder still, he has never heard a voice so peacefully reconciled to a life lived beyond its vocalist's own control. It is a divine acquiescence, Carlson decides, one arisen from faith alone. He does not attribute it to the bondage into which the boy was conceived. He has met too many slaves whose eyes burn with hatred, whose hands clench murderously at the thought of their master's throats. He has heard them singing in the fields and known in their songs that a weapon exists. He will own no man because of it. Not because he is afraid of their rebellion, but because as a student of antiquity, John Lee Carlson has learned that weapons born of art and endurance prove to be the most righteously wielded. He is not now fighting to preserve slavery—rather, he finds it an odious institution—but for other reasons altogether.

The Jeffers brothers, two burly, flaxen-headed youths with only ten months' age difference between them, by late afternoon of the second day have begun to squabble continuously, about everything: "Please, you ain't never shot no garfish at no three hundred yards, Lionel," or "Shit, I had Polly Anne first, Hank, and she was as sweet as glacé peaches in the springtime," or "Momma told me 'fore we left she loved *me* best, not you, so quit your crowin', fool." They are children, and quickly becoming a source of both nuisance and amusement for the others. For Carlson and Bruslé in particular, the oldest men in the company by years, the brothers are a pleasing reminder that some conflicts, innocent as they are, may still fall beyond the province of nations.

Private Obediah Todd, half-breed Creek scout and pastor's son, rides ahead of them all. He lifts his strong nose to the air. Dismounting, he crouches and runs his fingers over muddy trails. He makes the sign of the cross whenever he sees a raven on the wing. His hair is as black as flint. He whispers the Lord's Prayer to the threatening sky.

At night, they pass tin plates between them, ladle out scoops of hot, steaming meat and beans, throw fistfuls of sugar into one another's coffee. Thus far, however, they have not felt the urge to explore the true character of the men with whom they ride. Quick tales, tobacco, and jokes are exchanged, but that is all. Intimacies are not. "Young soldier leaves home to join the army," begins Lionel Jeffers at supper on the second evening. "Tells his old gal he'll write her every day. And he does, too, regular as rain. After 'bout six months, gets a letter from her. Trollop's fixin' to marry someone else. Sakes alive, he's pained, but he writes home to his family, find out who she's marryin'." Lionel waits a beat. "Son-of-a-bitchin' postman, 'course."

Most of the party laughs. Abrams does not.

He is unbothered that these men remain strangers. Instead he turns away from them, toward the terrain of the surrounding world. He has not thought of the land in quite some time. It quickly proves an awesome distraction. As they trudge onto the high tableland famed for its gardening loam, with mountains looming in the distance, Abrams cannot help but recall the filthy crescents of his mother's fingernails, the hardened, brown knobs of her knees from so many years spent there. "A man's a man," she used to say, "but I'll be damned if he ain't more of one, he got himself a plot." With so much time in the saddle, Abrams' mind strays from all that has befouled what, as a child, he believed would have been an admirable life. Working his own parcel of earth, sturdy stalks of cane sweeping as far as the eye can see, a clean cypress plank homestead, a faithful woman by his side—these are the hopes Abrams once foresaw for himself and, in the quiet hours of the night, confessing this to no one, still wishes to see fulfilled. Only now, unlike months before, he is unfazed that other people wish for the same. Man, he is slowly learning, is not defined by the originality of his dreams but by his commitment to those dreams' fruition.

It occurs to Abrams only vaguely that the tenacity of what he has envisioned for himself is rare. After a decade wedged between the walls of Gallatin Street, stuffed into its close rooms and locked behind its doors, that his heart and mind persevere in their joint quest for the openness of land hardly strikes Abrams as unusual at all. It does, however, lead him to wonder, dangerously, he knows, what his life would have been like had his mother survived. Had she been able to conclude her life's lessons to him, shown him how to cultivate with love and diligence all he might seek to raise. He wonders about the man he might have been. Whether he would now be fighting for a cause he truly believed in, and not for one that merely provides him escape from the morass in which he has so long been mired.

Abrams then thinks of his father, of *his* dedication to the land, but cannot stomach such notions for long. He quickly goes awash in shame and disgust at these very thoughts. It has, in fact, been years since he allowed himself the gratuitous idea of family, and now, circumstances being what they are, he can only laugh cynically and spit for it.

Had his mother lived or his father shown him the least concern, Abrams realizes, too, that he would have never set foot in the Jewish Widows and Orphans Home. And had he never set foot in the orphanage, he never would have met Silas Wolfe. Just who, then, would Elias Abrams even be? How much happier a person? How much simpler a soul would he possess? How much purer?

"Goddamnit all," he sighs at last. Try as he might, he cannot convince himself to wish for a life without having met Wolfe. Because even as he fears and detests his old friend, condemns him as a murderer and villain, neither can Abrams yet be persuaded to wholly regret him. "Cocksucker's got a clutch on me stickier'n pitch."

—

The world soon steepens. On their trek, they spot gaping mouths of caves delving deeply into the hills. Down in New Orleans, where even graves must be built above ground, the idea that men may burrow like Nebraska badgers into the land would have caused a younger Abrams to squint sideways in disbelief. Now faced by such truths, he concedes that this countryside is the most marvelous he has ever seen. Creaking in his saddle, he twists and turns, awed by the beauty of the surrounding black pine–forested hills and low mountains. Clouds thickly blanket a hundred summits. Green mosses carpet countless boulders and trunks. Dead leaves litter the ground, fallen from trees taller than any Abrams had believed possible. The terrain of southern Louisiana, while rich in alluvial wealth, is level and uninspiring. Its brown waterways are slow-moving. Out on the border between Missouri and Arkansas, though, the rugged mountains and raging rivers thrill Abrams to no end, such a raw and pristine world, one so ignorant of the appetites of human empire. Given the choice, he would remain out there forever.

There is a god of some sort encompassing him, he feels it, though for Abrams, a man unversed in the language of divinity, it is a nameless god.

Gerta offered her son devotionals on soil, not text, and his time at the orphanage was spent shirking whatever Hebraic instruction it offered. On the streets of the Vieux Carré, Abrams embraced instead a life of secular mischief, with Wolfe decreeing which page they would turn to for the day's iniquitous sermon. These years later, however, plodding over this vast and unfamiliar temple of earth, Abrams takes a moment to reflect upon the divine, and consequently, upon Reverend Gutheim's initiative, upon Nora Bloom's faith, upon the hours they and others like them must spend indoors, their eyes closed, muttering an archaic language Abrams had long believed to be a tongue spoken most articulately by eunuchs and the deluded. Six months ago, he would have laughed at the idea of such piety. He is not laughing now.

—

On the eve of that third day, the men bathe their aching bodies in a natural hot spring, groaning with pleasure and passing bars of lye soap from hand to hand. It is the first real enjoyment they have shared together. Their smiles grow genuine, their questions sincere. They cut one another's hair with straight blades and shears. They scrape penknives across their bodies and the soles of their feet, scouring the layers of grime that have accumulated over the months since their last thorough washing. The lice and shaven dead flesh float in swirls around them like the slow boiling of a gumbo composed of their own filth.

Afterward, they swab their cracked heels with tallow, admiring one another's blisters and jabbing them with knives. The remaining lice they pop between their hardened nails, persisting in a battle of hygiene they will keep fighting, if lucky, in the months and years to come. Lucky because lice, they have come to learn, feast only on the living.

The men cannot remember such a fine feeling.

Still, while Carlson and Abrams continue to sleep beside each other, their conversations have grown terse. They politely ask for coffee to be passed, for any tobacco that might be spared, but unlike the other men

with whom they are becoming familiar, they no longer speak as com-
panions. They limp in the same manner after dismounting, use the same
method to hobble their horses, moan as they sit by campfires in the
same way, but something ineffable now stands between them.

In this strain, Abrams does not mention his most recent and terrifying concern. On the fourth day, well into the mountains, he lagged a few
horse lengths behind to reread one of his letters. With Lionel Jeffers' joke
of the postman lingering in his ears, Abrams wished more than anything
to find in Nora Bloom's words something to disprove Carlson's opinion
of their relationship. Some little hint that she, despite their being
strangers, understood him as Elias Abrams, the individual, the man.

To his alarm, he discovered her second letter to be missing. Hours
later, he has come to a single-minded and devastating conclusion as to
its whereabouts. If he is correct, he fears it will be among the gravest
mistakes of his life.

When the men bed down on that fourth night, Abrams decides the
dread he bears is too heavy for him to shoulder alone. He has rebuked
himself for his negligence since the late afternoon, spitting curses that
forced Small Bill's ears to quirk back each time. For most of his adulthood,
he has kept such things bottled within him and dealt with them accordingly. In this new loosening of his soul, however, the emotions whirling inside him have begun to require an outlet. Finally, after hours of
self-reproach, he can stand it no longer. He is twenty years old and needs
a friend. "John Lee," says Abrams bluntly, "I might've got me a problem."

Carlson purses his lips and nods. He clears off a space on his horse
blanket. "Sit," he says.

Abrams sits. He removes his bowler and runs a hand anxiously
through his hair. "Can't find one of her letters."

"Pardon?"

"One of her letters, John Lee. The personal one. Nora's. It's gone."

"Yes, well," says Carlson, clearing his throat, "regardless of what rub-
bish I may have uttered the other day"—and here Carlson's face reddens

with a shame of his own—"I'm sure she'll be more than happy to send you another. She quite likes you. I wouldn't worry."

"You ain't gettin' me." Abrams pauses. "I think those bastards might've gotten their hands on it, in the scrape. I got pawed at pretty good." Abrams has grown certain that the letter was ripped from his inner breast pocket during his struggle with Petitgout. He can think of no other reason for its disappearance. Now, the vision of Nora Bloom's address fallen into Petitgout's possession not only disgusts Abrams but frightens him terribly.

"You haven't seen it since?"

"Wish I had." Abrams' imagination has been running wild all day, for he has witnessed firsthand Petitgout's treatment of women. As a result, in his saddle that afternoon he envisioned the cousins back in New Orleans at dusk, lying in wait for Nora to stroll past the mouth of an alley on her way home from school. He saw them licking their lips and elbowing each other's ribs as she approached. He saw their lunge, heard their cackles and her screams. He watched her legs flail as they dragged her deeper into the alley. Her screams became shrieks, and then, to Abrams' anguish, he imagined her shrieks becoming silence. He shook his head to rid it of these images. More than simply fearing for her safety, he has grown furious at himself that not only Carlson but now Nora, too, may have become imperiled because of their acquaintanceship with him. Already burdened, his conscience can scarcely take this new weight.

Carlson's face clouds. He takes a contemplative sip of his coffee. Brooding quietly in the night, he realizes why Abrams has come to him. Although this young man is tough, Abrams, like all battered young things, is only now cautiously learning the power of trust. Considering how ashamed he, too, has been since the morning following the fight, the professor is therefore more than happy to oblige him. After a moment, he scoffs amiably and says, "First off, it's not likely this Petitgout fellow got anything from you that night but a terrific headache. Truly, her letter could be anywhere. Secondly, you're a gambling man, correct?

Supposing he did find it, you tell me, what're the odds on him actually acting on it? Lesser still. And even if he does, what's he going to do? Think about it, Elias. She's almost a thousand miles away, safe in the arms of her family."

Abrams appreciates his friend's optimism. "Reckon you're right."

"Of course I am," says Carlson. In truth, he is relieved that Abrams has come seeking his advice. His atrocious honesty of those days before has haunted him since it first left his lips. An instructor who prides himself on his compassion, that he vented his own fears and frustrations on this young man, especially about something as harmless as an epistolary courtship, causes him humiliation like he has not felt in years. Some lessons, he knows, need no teacher but time. But here, given the chance to atone for these sins, Carlson will not fail his companion again. "Anyhow," he says easily, clapping Abrams on the shoulder, "there's nothing to be done about it now. Come, let's sit down to some of that venison. Those Jeffers' boys' recipe for backstrap, if they're to be believed, sounds to be nothing short of gastronomically miraculous. Not to mention what Jean-Baptiste, God bless his little soul, can do with cornpone. What say you? Shall we?"

Abrams grits his teeth and nods. "Sorry I dragged you into this mess, John Lee," he wants to say. "Sorry I ain't been able to tell you all's been preyin' on me, that I ain't been able to ask for forgiveness neither. Of you, nor nobody. 'Cause Lord knows, I could sure as shit use some relief right about now." Elias Abrams thinks these things but says none of them. Instead, he stands stiffly and without a word, follows his friend to the bubbling stewpot.

Suddenly, he is ravenous.

18

After supper, their bellies full of chunks of hot deer meat and gravy-smothered cornpone, the men stretch their tired legs by the campfire and break out their tobacco. They swap pouches, each proclaiming the strengths of his leaf. Soon, puffing on their pipes, Carlson, Bruslé, and the Jeffers brothers begin to trade stories of wives and lovers, of eight-point bucks and fifty-pound catfish. "My wife," sighs Carlson. "Petals of asphodel, graceful as droplets of morning dew, born of Cordelia's integrity and Cleopatra's good looks." They speak of rising sugar prices and blockade runners, of the venerable President Davis and the indomitable Southern spirit. They grimly recall Oak Hills and those they lost. They hope and pray that the French and British come down on the Confederate side of the war. Bruslé suspects that they will, particularly the British, as he finds them "an honorable people, given to honorable ways."

One after the other, the men talk and argue and do their best to incorporate Abrams and Obediah Todd—the band's two naturally reticent soldiers—into the conversation. "So Obediah," says Carlson, "what brings you to our current straits, anyway?"

"Jesus." He will be pushed no further.

Bruslé asks Abrams the same question. Abrams quits idly shuffling his cards and meets Carlson's eye. Like Private Obediah Todd, he will offer no details. "Got a thing for saddle sores, is all."

The men laugh heartily.

"Personally," says their captain, contentedly twirling his mustache, "I'm more than happy to be among the lot of y'all. And Lionel? Hank? Jean-Baptiste? The meal, damned fine."

Mention of their supper forces several satisfied groans of agreement. Jean-Baptiste begins to brew another pot of coffee. Though the night will get colder, the warmth of the fire and their full stomachs cause them to chuckle with pity at the thought of their compatriots back at Camp Jackson. The past months have been hard. Already scarce supplies have grown scarcer. Thousands of thin men now spend their days on their backs beneath whatever threadbare blankets they can find, shivering and dreaming of the meals they will eat once home, piling imaginary plates high with all their favorite foods. In awed, hushed tones, they speak like lovers of their wives' big cast-iron pots of jambalaya cooking over hardwood fires. They bite their hands at thoughts of heaping bowls of thick Monday red beans and rice, of the salted Sunday ham hock within, of spiced beef tips and gravy, of steaming hunks of fresh-baked breads, of plump, savory links of andouille bursting over fire pits, of roasted meats dripping fat from slow-rolled spits, of cauldrons gurgling with okra gumbos, of sweet butter and sweet cream and fresh morning biscuits trowelled with layers of rich, gooey honeycomb. They stare off into the woods and up into the night skies, sighing, licking their lips as the hunger in their bellies gnaws at them ceaselessly. There is no avoiding it. Starvation, they are realizing, has become as despised an enemy as any Union army.

"Poor sons-of-bitches," says Hank Jeffers of them, "nothin' but hardtack and shoe leather tonight, starvin' to the leanness of an ashwood scythe. And even if they're lucky enough to get their hands on some sowbelly, what then? Black as a rind of pitch on the outside, yellow and wet as snot on the inner." He wrinkles his nose in distaste. "Like to make a man give up eatin' altogether."

"The hell you say," argues his brother. "Ain't *nothin'* could make me give up my meat. Rancid or no, I could chomp a whole beef, given the chance. Two beeves, maybe." Lionel arches his eyebrows for emphasis. "I come out the other side of this war with my guts intact, trust me, y'all, I'm grabbin' a knife and spoon, tuckin' in my napkin just so, and eatin' through the whole godforsaken world, one bite at a time."

"Already been done," says Carlson, pulling deeply on his pipe. "And, son, if history's any account of things, nothing but heartache follows that kind of gluttony."

Lionel narrows his eyes skeptically. The others wait for more.

Carlson repositions himself by the fire. He dusts off his knees and stares into the spent coals of his pipe bowl. When he understands that his offer of a story has been accepted, he looks to the constellation of Perseus above, its double cluster riding high. "Ever hear of an old fellow named Ovid?" he asks absently, tamping his pipe onto his heel.

"Our momma's cousin had a slave named such," answers Hank Jeffers. "Oldest, gummiest nigger you ever saw, too, but could play that Jew harp like nobody's business. Different fellow, I'm supposin'."

"Different fellow indeed," agrees Carlson with a smile. "The one I'm talking about was a Roman poet back in the day, wrote hundreds of fables, wove them into one long narrative he liked to call a *carmen perpetuum*, everlasting song. One in particular was about a king named Erysichthon."

"Boner of a name, that."

Carlson grins. "Even more impressive than his name is his tale. You all got a minute?"

The men move closer now, preparing themselves for Carlson's story. Though they would prefer to be back home, sleeping beside the woman of their choosing every day for the remainder of their lives, for the moment, a full belly, a warm fire, and the prospect of a well-told yarn provides satisfaction enough. They quiet and crane their ears. Carlson, in turn, knows his audience. He will alter his speaking style because of it, for he does not wish to alienate these men. He does not disappoint.

"Now this Erysichthon was an ancient king," he begins casually, "a real arrogant son-of-a-bitch. But what separates him from all the other arrogant sons-of-bitches this world's seen was his distinctive brand of greed. Seems one day he came upon a sacred grove of oaks owned by Ceres, goddess of the harvest, a real powerful goddess back in the day. Importantly now, said grove was inhabited by these nymphs of hers. Fairies, if you will, actually living inside the trees. Well, when one of this son-of-a-bitch's servants tells him he won't chop down those oaks because of what's living inside them, despite his orders to do so, what do you suppose happens but the bastard king grabs an axe and cuts that poor servant in two, just like that, *whoosh*."

Lionel whistles.

"Next thing you know, old Erysichthon turns that axe loose on those oaks himself, starts chopping them down one after the other, *whack, whack, whack*. But remember now, like I said, there're these nymphs living inside them—dryads, they're called—so they're getting the axe as well. It's horrific, a slaughter, they're crying out for him to stop, but that old king keeps right on hacking.

"Soon enough, the task's done and he heads for home." Carlson leans toward the men. "But little does he know, he's fixing to get it good. Because boys, let me tell you, those old gods were creative sons-of-bitches in the most scolding sort of way. I say this because Ceres, furious as all get out, decides to enlist Famine in the cause—"

"Hold on there," interrupts Hank, "just hold it. Decides to enlist *who* now?"

"Famine, the entity. Back then, things like famine had actual bodies, Hank. They could walk, talk, do everything you can." Carlson refills his pipe and lights it with a branch from the fire, then takes a deep draw. "But see," he says, exhaling, "Ceres can't meet with Famine directly— threatens her fertility—so she sends over a minion with a message: 'Punish this king.'" Carlson smiles and shakes his head. "Now y'all can't imagine how horrid Famine was to look at, y'all just can't. Hair like a mop of muddy ropes, sunken eyes, gaunt cheeks, crone's nose all covered with warts, teeth like a broken fence. Gray flesh pocked with boils, dugs dangling from her bony chest like flaps of leather. Her back—dear Lord, her back—y'all could see her spine come poking through like a ridge of broken gravel, like neighbors in dispute. Each rib was plain as day, hips jutting out from her pelvis like shovelheads. Tiny little thing for a waist. Beneath whatever belly she *did* have, her skin was wrapped so close around it, you'd see her entrails snaking and crawling about in there. Horrible, just horrible."

Hank wipes his mouth uneasily. Jean-Baptiste's eyes have gone wide.

"So now that y'all know who we're dealing with," continues the professor, "Famine, ever obliging, agrees to help Ceres. One night she enters the king's chambers, straddles him where he sleeps. She bends her withered old self over his sleeping body and breathes her very essence into him, filling his lungs and soul with a hunger such as no man has ever endured, before or since. Not even you, Lionel. The king's sleeping through all this, mind you, even as she's leaving through the window again, even as his appetite's about to overwhelm him forever." Carlson stops. "Essentially," he says quietly, "when he woke, he was famished in ways nobody's ever known. Imagine the panic of waking to that kind of hunger. Before he knew what he was doing, he began eating everything he could get his hands on, every morsel in sight. But nothing, not a damned thing, could sate that appetite of his. He became tormented, insatiable. He devoured entire herds, flocks of sheep, caught and ate every school of fish in the sea, drank rivers dry, ransacked towns, sold all his possessions to feed himself, including his daughter, but still, nothing could fill that craving inside him. The more he ate, the hungrier he became, because here's where the punishment really works its genius: he actually grew *emptier* after each bite, not fuller." He pauses once more. "In the end, his avarice was such that he wound up devouring himself entirely. Poor fellow gorged on his own shredded flesh and bone, gulped down his toes and drank up every ounce of his blood—much to his very lasting destruction."

A silence falls over the small company.

Soon, to the surprise of each man there, Jean-Baptiste offers a meek declaration. "Men's like dat," he says softly. "Just gobblin' up any old thing in they path, don't care what it is—God hisself, could be—so long as it somehow gits in they belly. But come sundown, at the end of it all, with preacher man leanin' over, come to find it's they own heavenly soul they been eatin' at, nothin' mo'." His words said, Jean-Baptiste looks up guiltily from the fire, ashamed at having spoken beyond his place. Hoping to divert this new attention, he quickly asks the men if they would like more coffee. "Ain't got no mo' cornbread," he adds innocently, "otherwise I'd sugar it up for y'all good."

19

They arrive at Fort Smith the following evening. Weary from several days in the saddle, Abrams slips from Small Bill's back, places his hands on his knees, and huffs once before standing to stretch his spine. His body is sore in ways that he had not known possible. Only after a last grimace does he take in the fort around him. Built at the confluence of the Arkansas and Poteau Rivers, the garrison encompasses over seventy muddy acres, most of which are enclosed by a serrated pine-log wall. Now within its gates, Abrams catches sight of a gallows craned ominously in the courtyard center. To his left, the jail where the incarcerated await their verdicts. He has heard rumors of harsh frontier justice. In his time since enlisting, drunkenness, fighting, petty theft, malingering, and insubordination have become the oft-seen offenses of military life. Still, he can only imagine the form of sin committed out here, so far from pen-and-ink authority. Although the chain of command calls for due process, at a place like Fort Smith, on the farthest reaches of white society, there is neither time nor manpower to waste on an organized judiciary. Instead, frontier sentences are reputedly off the cuff and, oftentimes, sadistically inspired. Beyond extra work, fines, skipped rations, reductions in rank, and jail time, there is mention of the dreaded buck-and-gag, or bucking, where the offending soldier is gagged and kicked to the ground after his hands and feet have been bound. His knees then drawn up between his arms, he is further incapacitated when an iron rod is slipped snugly behind them and into the crook of each elbow. Abrams has heard, too, of men hanged by their thumbs, an excruciating torture, or those forced to "ride the wooden mule" and thus sit for hours on end atop a narrow beam set high enough so their feet dangle inches above the ground. After his days on Small Bill, he has particular sympathy for those to whom this punishment is meted. The more serious crimes of mutiny, murder, cowardice, treason, or—as Carlson has informed him repeatedly—desertion, merit execution by either firing squad or hanging. For those damned and fortunate few capital offenders whose lives are spared, red-hot brands are scalded into their cheeks or hips, followed by merciless drubbings out of camp. The resulting scars, like death, are permanent.

Abrams understands the need for this kind of discipline. Outside Fort Smith's walls lies a westward expanse that has staged the slaughter of thousands over the course of the past half-century. From his experience with Gallatin Street, a frontier in its own right, he knows that leniency has no place in the face of such a great and ceaseless brutality.

Over twenty years in its construction, less than half of Fort Smith's buildings have been completed. Now, with that kind of unresolved feel lingering about it, Abrams senses a strange pall surrounding him. Time and again, he has heard Gallatin Street referred to as infernal. Those lucky enough to survive their first visit typically describe it as hell itself, a claim Abrams accepts without argument. But here, at the very edge of the world, he recognizes in Fort Smith an element not hellish but purgatorial. The handful of soldiers in view seem more wraiths than men, appearing dedicated to no cause whatsoever, neither life nor death. Their stares are vacant, their voices mute. When called to, they pay no heed. Their feet, not their minds, lead them aimlessly toward their destinations. Save for the incessant barking of a large black dog, all is silent. If there is a war at hand, it has not been initiated by mankind.

"I've got to meet with Major Clark, quartermaster here, about furnishing the regiment with supplies," Bruslé informs his crew. "Private Todd, you're with me. Jeffers boys, you head over to the commissary, see what you can arrange for our ride come morning. Be firm and demanding, cite my name alone. John Lee and Private Abrams, find the stables, have the groom tend to the mounts. Tell him for liniment, we'll take warm peppermint oil, no lye or ammonia bases. Alfalfa, if his stores allow it. Gaston's right fetlock needs a bitterroot poultice, please remember. And get the farrier on each hoof, sparing no rasp." He claps Obediah Todd on his shoulder. He nods to each man. "Providing all goes according to schedule, we'll dine here tonight and head out for the Creek Agency at dawn. These chores completed, you're at liberty until then."

With that, the men disband.

After Carlson and Abrams have boarded the horses with the stable buck, they walk with difficulty to the canteen. There, over plates of beans and black bread, they meet a mangy corporal named Dooling who immediately takes them for the outsiders they are. He smells of purest rot, as though, bearing witness to his own decomposition, he has just climbed from the earth to rise like Lazarus, only to find the world above of comparable demise. In a foul whisper he offers them a jug of bust-head for no less than ten dollars. Abrams does not need to be asked twice. He is more than willing to risk reprimand for the burn of rough whiskey. He digs out the money from his billfold and, once it has been exchanged, deftly hides the jug in the saddlebag slung over his shoulder. He will share the whiskey with the other men, he has decided, but only after he and Carlson sample it first.

"Here we are, in relative civility," Carlson says, his hands wide on the table. "It's grown chill and drab outside, but we've a flagon of home-still about to invigorate us well. Tonight, we'll sleep with ticking beneath us and a roof over our heads for the first time in months. But perhaps best of all, not two hundred yards away, we've access to a mail dispatch." At this point, together with a letter to his wife, he withdraws from his small canvas rucksack a few blank sheets of paper, a traveler's inkwell, and a pen. He pushes the pile toward Abrams. "Which brings me to my next topic." He grasps his young friend's wrist. "She's waiting, Elias."

Abrams quits shoveling the spoonfuls of beans into his mouth and looks up. "Reckon I'd be leavin' that one alone, I was you."

Carlson inclines forward. "Listen, I spoke of ideals the other day, nothing more. And were I wrong, you'd be proving me so by continuing with your attentions, regardless of what I may have said. But as you indeed appear to be giving up on this Miss Bloom, my point has been proven exactly. Maturely as you tend to acquit yourself, sometimes I forget that you're still subject to the caprices of your age." Carlson leans back and folds his arms. "You obviously don't care about her in the least."

Abrams tosses his spoon hard into his plate. "I ain't above smackin' you, John Lee. Know that."

Carlson removes his glasses and sighs, pinching the notch between his eyes. "For the first months of our courtship, before we were married, my wife's parents detested the very sight of me. That I existed at all was anathema to them. I was a young student then, who, while from a reputable family, showed few prospects. Yet I persisted. My point is this: had I lent their opinion of our relationship any credence, I wouldn't be the fortunate fellow that I am today." He replaces his glasses. "Now, for posterity's sake, I apologize wholeheartedly for what I said. It was uncalled for, there's no disputing it. Nonetheless, I'll assume no responsibility for your cowardice from here on in. How you negotiate your future with this girl is entirely up to you."

"If you're aimin' to rile me," says Abrams, "I ain't givin' you the satisfaction." He resumes eating with a shrug. "'Sides, she don't know me. Said so yourself."

"Christ, Elias, here's your chance, though. Come, we'll work on it together. What's the worst that can happen? You've won hands before, in poker, playing straight up? So, you'll show her your best cards. As long as you're forthright about who you are, you've absolutely nothing to lose. Truly now, what've you to lose?"

Abrams stops eating. He thinks hard. He has no reply.

"If she doesn't write you back, so be it. But at least you'll have salvaged your dignity, and in the long run, you'll have saved yourself a great deal of heartache. Deny me that much, I dare you."

Try as he might, Abrams cannot. He begins sucking on an inner cheek.

"The more important question is *this*, though: just how ready are you to get your hair wet? By which I mean all-the-way wet? Because if you send this letter off and she responds and y'all *do* establish a real intimacy, you'll have committed yourself to the matter of this young lady's feelings. And commitment to a young lady's feelings, dear sir, once done, is a pact written with the Devil, I assure you."

But in his mind, Abrams has already begun the letter's composition.

An hour later, a quarter of the jug of whiskey gone, he passes Carlson the third draft of the second love letter he has ever written. After a number of spelling corrections and the odd grammatical issue addressed, the professor returns it. "For allowing me a brief window into your past, Elias Abrams, I humbly thank you," says Carlson with a small bow and toast of the whiskey jug. From it, he takes a long pull, and then scowls at the flames riding down his throat. With those parting words, Carlson heads off to join the others, jug in hand, with its owner's consent. Abrams will follow shortly. First, he must amend the letter one last time:

Dear Miss Bloom,

I am writing to you today to say thank you for the second letter you sent to me. I am glad that you received the first one I sent to you. I must be clear here. You say you are worried that I might not care for your letters. Nothing could be further from the truth.

They are the only reason I have any joy left at all. Without them, I do not think I would be capable of it. So with all honesty, I am saying that your letters are very dear to me. I have been called blunt by men and I cannot be blunter than to say to you right now that I cherish your letters like they are pearls dropped from Heaven.

I will spend some time writing about my life, because I think it is important that you know of it. I am from upriver in Lafayette City, born of a redemptioner's background. My mother was a fine woman. She taught me that to grow something is to grow love itself. My father is dead. I am twenty years old. I have black hair and am not tall but I am not short either. I have never told anybody this before but I would like to own a great plantation and grow crops for the rest of my life. I do not mean to be a poor farmer, of course, but a landsman rich in prospects and admiration.

I must ask three things of you before I close. Number one is to please be careful. Some people are mean and desperate. Though New Orleans is far from enemy lines, you never can tell. Like you say, times are growing difficult. In difficult times, men will do terrible things. You are obviously a beautiful person, so you will be attractive to them. This is bold to say, I know it, but like you said in your last letter, we have the freedom to say such things because of how far apart we are and have never met. So please watch for men looking to do you wrong. I could never forgive myself if something bad happened to you. Number two is for you to please keep sending me your letters. I have no words to tell how much joy they give me, though I have been trying in this letter to let you know it. Number three is to say that I would very much like to meet you also. But I do not wish to deceive you in the man that I am. I have not the education or grace that you do, or the people that you know must have. I have been no angel in my life. But even though that is the truth, you should also know that the thought of meeting you arises my soul in the morning and beds me to sleep at night when I lay my head on the cold, hard earth. You are my morning lark, Miss Nora Bloom, and you are my pillow.

With greatest devotion,
Pt. Elias Abrams

Abrams straightens himself, takes a deep breath, and contentedly dusts his hands clean. He folds the finished letter into thirds and prepares to join the others. The sun has set in the meantime, the night grown cold. Walking a little unsteadily from the whiskey in his system, he locates the mail dispatch and offers a few awkward words of prayer. "Lord above," he whispers to the moon, "if you got a set of ears on you, I'd appreciate you listenin' up for a spell. See, I know you favor them who favor you first, and I can respect that, honest I can, but seein' as that girl's been so devoted to you—and come to find I ain't entirely above the notion myself now, neither—I'm here askin' you to do right by her, let her get this letter. Go on'n reward her, Lord, show her how thankful you are for her faith. Guess what I'm sayin' is this: I'm volunteerin' to be that gift. 'Cause she ain't never gonna be happier'n what I can give her, nossir, nor find herself another love like mine. Never, never, never. And that's all I got to say. Amen."

With that, he posts the letter.

20

In heading toward the barracks from the dispatch, in the darkness of night Abrams almost fails to notice the garrison soldier standing in the courtyard center, leaning on his rifle and staring up at the gallows. Like most Confederate soldiers, the man is thin, but his presence is thinner still, one hardly corporeal at all. "Evenin'," says Abrams, tipping his bowler.

The gaunt soldier ignores this, his gaze still fixed on the gallows. "You reckon Jesus, livin' today, would've built one of 'em things there?"

"Pardon?"

"Jesus Christ. Heard tell, man was a carpenter." The soldier nods his head up toward the wooden scaffold. "You reckon he would've built one of 'em there, if'n he was ordered to?"

Abrams frowns. "Don't know, actually."

"Damn." The soldier spits, scratches his grimy head, and then turns to Abrams. His eyes are insane. "I can sure as shit tell you this, though," he says, "man's greatest invention ain't fire, nor steampower, nor gunpowder, nor the Devil even, nor nothin' else. It's wood. Think on it, now."

Abrams takes a step backward.

"You don't know the ways of wood, its properties," the soldier rambles on, "you ain't got fire. No fire means no cookin', neither of food nor metal. No wood means no pickax handles means no gold or coal. No wood for looms means you got no clothes for wearin'. You got no buildings. You got no wood tools for farmin' means you got no crops. No wood, no wheels, no movin'. No ships, no explorin'. No wood, no paper, means no settin' yer knowledge down." The garrison soldier has worked himself into a fury. "Damnation, man, that's why them Bible-scribblers must've writ up Christ as a carpenter in the first place, I figure, show the rest of us ten-thumbed folk how to be all civilized." He pauses, seemingly run into a wall of confusion. "But goddamn if them gallows there don't confound things."

Cautiously admitting the merits of the soldier's reasoning, Abrams bids him goodnight and steps away, giving a wide berth.

He soon pushes the door of the barracks open. It is a large, windowless cell, lit by several candles. The floor is worn plankwood, the walls raw pine. Bunks stretch into the darkness of its farthest corners. While it can house thirty men, Bruslé's are the barracks' only inhabitants; where the garrison soldiers reside has been a source of heated discussion among them. Now, save for Obediah Todd, who is concentrating on a small Bible, the men appear greatly pleased to see Abrams. Hank Jeffers, already bleary-eyed, holds up the jug in his honor. "Cheers and hurrah to you, you picklin' bastard!" he shouts. "Cheers and hurrah!"

Abrams smiles. "Keep your cheers to yourself, Hank. I'd rather a swig of the popskull."

"While you're at it," says Hank with a wink, passing over what remains of the whiskey, "go on'n hoist one in the name of that fine-soundin' schoolmarm you got waitin' for you." His mirth is plain.

"John Lee Carlson," sighs Abrams, "in all my days, I ain't never met a whore with looser lips'n yours, I swear it."

To this, the professor merely doffs his filthy Panama and laughs.

"Aw now, Elias, don't," pleads Hank. "Sounds to be sweeter than cherry goddamned pie, the two of y'all together."

"Hank!" It is Obediah Todd, looking up from his Corinthians across the room. "I'll not tell you again."

"Sorry, Obediah. Didn't mean no disrespect by it."

"What's goin' on here?" Abrams asks.

"Seems old Todd there ain't partial to blasphemin'," answers Lionel Jeffers. His face is flushed from alcohol. He totters to his feet. "But like I said earlier, he don't like the way my brother talks, he can pick his Injun ass up and move it on outside where'n his kind belongs anyhow, have himself a grand old time. While he's at it, he can take that little nigger with him, too." Lionel Jeffers is grinning as he weaves, his eyes twinkling and unfocused. An otherwise agreeable youth, whenever he drinks too much, the worst of him surfaces. On Gallatin Street, Abrams has witnessed this in many men, the slurs and aggression born of an inability to handle liquor. He has witnessed almost as many throats slit because of it.

Private Obediah Todd, half-breed Creek and pastor's son, quietly closes his book.

"Now Lionel," interrupts Carlson, bolting from his bed, "I recommend you dig deep and find a way to control that idiot mouth of yours. And Obediah, with all due respect, you may want to pay particular heed to the Sermon on the Mount here, turn that other cheek." The professor then spins to Jean-Baptiste, who is watching all this in frightful silence from several bunks away. "Boy, we might benefit from your master's presence right about now."

Jean-Baptiste dashes from the barracks without delay.

Carlson's importuning has no impact on either man; the room is fraught with tension. Abrams decides it will be Obediah with whom he sides, if it comes down to it. He wraps his grip around the neck of the jug and waits. Lying on his bunk, a smile has creased Obediah's strong face. He stands very slowly. Lionel shifts his weight uneasily. "I don't see why we got to bed down with this mongrelized heathen, anyways," he mutters.

Obediah rolls his neck from side to side. "'When I was a child,'" he says, quoting his Corinthians as he calmly removes his shirt so as not to stain it with blood, "'I spake as a child, I understood as a child, I thought as a child: but when I became a man, I put away childish things.'" Suddenly everything about him hardens into stone, his breadth of shoulder, his dense rib-sheath and iron forearms. "I got heathen in me, Lionel Jeffers, true enough. But make no mistake: I bear the righteousness of the Lord in my fists."

"A dangerous combination, to be sure," concedes Carlson. "Which is why I'm going to ask you, Obediah, to forgive Lionel for his stupidity. And Lionel, if you can't see how foolish you're being, then you've not got the sense God gave a jackass."

"All right now," says Hank, coming to his brother's aid with a finger to Carlson's sternum. "That'll be enough of *that*, John Lee."

"Hands off the professor, Hank," warns Abrams. "I ain't foolin'." He redoubles his grip on the whiskey jug.

Everyone in the room is standing. Abrams has taken the course of the fight and knows that after shoving Carlson out of harm's way, he will crumple Hank's left knee with the first swing of the jug. A fluid, back-handed blow up into his nose and Hank will go down for the night. From the killing look in Obediah's eyes, Abrams is not concerned about Lionel in the least. As if on cue, Lionel takes a step forward. Obediah's head drops as he chuckles softly to himself. Thumbing his nose, he, too, takes a step forward. He is built in the manner of most Creek men—a strapping six-footer, lithe in every movement. He and Lionel are roughly the same size, though Obediah has the advantage: not only is he sober and a practiced fighter, but he believes with equal piety in his Christly support and the warrior blood flowing through him. He has endured in-sult from far better men than Lionel Jeffers and beaten them pitilessly many times over because of it. He debates now as to the extent of dam-age he will allow himself to inflict.

"Is that alcohol?" The sharp voice is their captain's, and it forces the men to stand down at once. In the barracks' doorway, Jean-Baptiste peeks from behind the figure of Charles A. Bruslé. When Bruslé receives no reply, he repeats himself. "I asked if that was alcohol."

"Yessir," admits Abrams after a pause. "And if someone needs blamin', it'd be me."

"Where'd you get it?"

"Had it with me all along," Abrams lies, "from Camp Jackson. Figured tonight'd be worth celebratin', is all."

Bruslé juts his chin and sets a fist on each hip. "And is it, do you find? Worth celebrating?"

"Havin' a roof atop us? Beds below? Four walls and a wood-burner in the corner? Yessir, I'd say that's worth something."

"Uh-huh. And how much did you pay for it?"

"Sir?"

"For the bottle. How much?"

"Ten dollars."

The men avoid their captain's stare. Save for Obediah Todd, abstinent from the abuses seen among his mother's people and the teetotalism among his father's, they have transgressed and they know it. Hank investigates a fingernail. Carlson is stroking his beard nervously, wondering how he will explain to his wife and father the disgrace of time spent in the stockade, locked there by a family friend. Lionel, little more than a boy shocked by the arrival of some greater agency, has grown immediately ashamed. His face has fallen, the rising tide of guilt precluding him from meeting the other men's eyes. Obediah Todd remains impassive, his head held high. Abrams, caught red-handed, has decided he will accept whatever punishment he is given.

"Ten dollars, huh?"

"Yessir."

A hard moment passes. Bruslé sniffs. He holds out his hand. "Jean-Baptiste, please." The boy appears from behind him and passes his master a half-gallon bottle of commissary. "Then soldier, damned if you didn't get yourself robbed." Bruslé steps closer, uncorking the bottle with his teeth. Holding each stare in the room, he takes a deep swig. He offers it next to Obediah Todd.

"Appreciate it, sir," says Obediah proudly. "But no."

The bottle remains outstretched in Bruslé's hand. From his posture, he will not accept refusal.

Obediah Todd understands. He takes the bottle from his captain. He closes his eyes and drinks. He hands it back over to Bruslé, who then turns to Lionel Jeffers. "Now you," he demands. "And if I catch you wiping any spittle from that bottle lip, Corporal, I'll have you clapped in irons faster than you can spell 'bigot.' Do not test me in this. Drink."

Abashed, Lionel Jeffers looks down at the floor, which he kicks. He takes the bottle. He drinks.

"There," says Bruslé easily, "like whelps from the same litter, nursing from the same teat, how nice." He steps away from them. He looks over his men. His blue eyes are unrelenting. "I'll say this once, gentlemen, and once only." The tone of his voice is severe. "If you've hate enough in your hearts to accommodate any more enemies than those already threatening the Army of the Confederate States of America, then truly you are wretches of a most miserable sort and variety."

21

The next day at dawn, the men are terrifically hungover. An hour has passed in the saddle and their heads droop low, chins bouncing just above their pommels. Lionel has vomited more than once from atop his horse, spooking the animal and staining its haunches with bile. All faces, except for Obediah Todd's, Bruslé's, and Jean-Baptiste's, are ashen, their mouths as though shoveled full of shit and sawdust, their heads thundering with what Carlson refers to as "the steady discharge of cranial 12-pounders."

The night before, upon Bruslé's departure from the barracks with Jean-Baptiste in tow, the men were left standing in sheepish silence. After a half-minute of unease, with shuffling feet, Lionel at last offered an apology. Obediah, convinced that there is no honor in defeating a child, flopped onto his bunk and returned to his Corinthians without another thought on the matter. Then, for lack of a better option, the others coughed into their fists, sat with creaking knees, and began passing cards between them. The first tentative joke was told five minutes later. A half-hour and countless belts of whiskey to follow, and beyond that garrison barracks could be heard the whoops, howls, and backslapping of men in the midst of a marvelous time. Soldiers understand that petty grudges are of little use in war; it is the larger ones that sustain them. That is why these men of the Third Louisiana, even though they will kill with every ounce of their cunning and strength, will never, deep in their hearts, hold an individual enemy soldier in true contempt. They may think him an alien species of man and despise him for it. They may curse his Yankee mother and perform acts of barbarism they would have thought incompatible with their rearing. At their core, however, beneath the bluster and claims of hatred, they will never disrespect the man who acquits himself with the same desire they suffer themselves.

Already a full hour had passed when, after the tenth hand of five-card stud, Abrams, winner of four of the previous five pots, staggered out into the night to urinate. Ever one for company, regardless of the enterprise, Carlson decided to join him.

Together they leaned their palms onto the barracks' walls and, warmed by their shares of whiskey, applauded Bruslé's handling of the situation. "He's one of 'em bastards who can still you with a look, you know? Think of the jailhouse stint we could've got, he wanted to give it. But naw, gives us a bottle of corn instead." Abrams whistled in admiration. "That's a gentleman, there."

They praised the strength of Obediah's beliefs and shook their heads at Lionel's foolishness. They talked of missed straight flushes and Hank's poor card play. With the stars of the Indian Territory bright above them, they moaned with pleasure at their emptying bladders and the marvelous sense of inebriation in a world that had grown far too sober for Elias Abrams' liking.

"For the first time in ages, John Lee, I'm tellin' you, I'm just about feelin' fine," he confessed, now fully drunk. He turned to give his friend a hard, intoxicated stare. "You mind, I ask you something personal?"

Drunk in his own right, swaying on his feet, Carlson said he would be honored to field any such question.

"How d'you know it, anyway?" Abrams tilted his head hesitantly. "That you was in love, I mean."

At this, Carlson broke into an enormous grin, for nothing gave him greater joy than to be reminded of what first drew him to his wife. He closed his eyes so that he might focus more clearly on her image. He inhaled deeply. "There I am," he began, his hands spread wide like a visionary, "standing on that Nayades Street steam car, coming up from Tivoli Place, when what do I see but this slip of a girl sitting wedged between two brutes, sleeping soundly as can be." Carlson opened his eyes and exhaled. "My God, Abrams, what a sight she was. Golden strands of hair loose from her bonnet like veritable beams of sunlight, her eyelashes thick, her nose no bigger than a button. So peaceful, her face, just so delicate, like an angel's, you know? But it was the parting of her ruby red lips, and the long thread of sleeper's drool that emanated from between them—well, that was it for me. I was done for." He pauses. "Now it wasn't the drool, per se, that spelled my ruin—I may be idiosyncratic, but I'm no fetishist—so much as her reaction to it. Because when she bucked awake, she didn't look away ashamed as most women would've, but rather she held my gaze, only to then burst into such voluble laughter that—oh, Elias, if you could've been there—just to watch her throw her head back and laugh and laugh, at herself, at that ridiculous string of drool, you would've fallen in love with her, too, no two ways about it, any man in his right mind would've. *That* was Cupid's well-aimed arrow to my heart, that right there. Such abandon, such lack of concern for other's judgments, such an absolute *joie de vivre*." Carlson sighed with longing. "So there you have it," he said, righting his Panama and straightening his blouse, "my Imo, my love." He cleared his throat. "Seems this Nora Bloom's quite affected you, too, I'd say."

"Well, them letters you've been puttin' me up to've been doin' some strange things to my mind, I got to admit." Abrams rubbed an ear. "See, I've been studyin' on it for a while now, and it's like this. My momma had this gardenin' book she was fond of, had me read it to her over'n over again. All the time, seemed like. She loved this one passage in particular, 'bout how foreign plants can do just fine here in the States, long as they're given time enough to prosper first. How all they need's a little tenderness and patience." He spat. "Reason I'm tellin' you this is 'cause I ain't never understood the feelin' she got from it, that passage there, till I started readin' and writin' down a few notions of my own to this Bloom gal. They got some power in 'em, words do, you use 'em correct."

Carlson chuckled at this observation, the same he had dedicated his life to, but then, recognizing the poignancy of Abrams' story of his mother, grew quickly serious. Rather than speak of the living women in their lives, a topic Carlson knew they might explore at some later date, he decided to take the opportunity to delve into Abrams' past, now that his young friend had broached it. "Speaking of your upbringing," he said cagily, "sounds like you might've had a rough go of it. Redemptioner's background and all."

"Naw, c'mon." Abrams stomped his heel in the dirt. "I'll tell you what ain't been easy, though. What ain't been easy is these here last months. No sir, stuck with your gabby ass all day long, forced to fight other feller's battles, tradin' fists with them scummy sons-of-bitches. My damned scruples never leavin' me be, not even for a minute. Runnin' off from New Orleans for a crime I didn't aim to take part of in the first place—well, I did, true, but in the end, got more out of hand than I wanted it to, so it don't count, my bein' part of how bloody it got." He spat again. "Anyway, that *there*'s been the rough go of it."

Carlson asked him, delicately, what that crime could have been.

Until recently, Elias Abrams had spent his life erecting a levee within him meant to stem the flood of all effusion, ensuring with sod and stone that no needless sentiment overflowed into his daily affairs. Trained toward self-governance, he had long grown accustomed to it. After a great deal of whiskey, however, after drafting letters of admission to a woman he had not yet met, after the months of easing restraint on all that he might say, feel, and trust, he was at last able to stand back to watch the levee within him begin to give way. And in its breaching, he was once more surprised to discover a beautiful sense of release. He sighed. "Let's just say I've been runnin' wild with a group of fellers for years now, and a few months ago, together we pulled ourselves a burgle I had a good part in plannin.'"

"I see."

"Only I didn't like the way it come out in the end," he added quickly, "not by a long shot, and I told 'em so."

Carlson lifted his Panama and ran a hand through his hair. "Care to spare any details?"

"Believe me, John Lee, nothing'd make me happier, gettin' this here load off my chest, but while I may be drunk, I ain't a spilled bucket quite yet. So for your safety more'n anything, I ain't givin' you no more of that crime's particulars'n what I already done. Honest, you're better off for the not knowin'. That don't mean I can't fix you a bit of a sampler plate, though. Reckon you deserve at least that much."

And so, as the night grew more and more chill, with coyotes yammering in the distance and the autumn moon shining brilliantly in the night sky, rather than return to the warmth of the barracks, Abrams began to speak earnestly of his past. As with Lieutenant Colonel Hyams over a month before, he soon thawed to the idea of divulgence altogether, stories beginning to stream out of him without reservation. Quietly, the air frosting his words, Abrams spoke of his history with Silas Wolfe and their recent clash, though he offered few specifics other than, "Overheard one of the boys tellin' him he was sure I'd go turncoat, what with how raw I took things that night. And seein' as Sy ain't one to brook turncoats lightly, didn't figure to give him the chance. Enlisted the next morning." Abrams breathed heavily. "He ain't much for democracy, see. Toleratin' a difference of opinion ain't among his long suits."

Abrams next mentioned the warrant he believed to be outstanding for his arrest: "Now I ain't sure, but I'd wager a hundred-to-one the Cypress Stumps ain't the only folks after me. Must be, Sy somehow convinced them cocksucker police I'm the one who done the dirt alone, goddamnit. Only explanation I can figure on why I ain't been nabbed yet is either 'cause I'm wrong, meanin' they don't know about me, they're too busy slappin' hands in New Orleans to send someone up to fetch me, they're too stupid to check the company roster if they *are* lookin', or 'cause—if they *do* know where I'm at—they're just too goddamned lazy to steamship it up here to get the job done right. More rigged to their own convenience 'n a one-roostered cockfight, them police of ours. Even so, I'm lookin' forward to a caged homecomin', I ain't careful."

Abrams went on to explain to Carlson his misguided fears about a possible collusion between the Cypress Stumps and the cousins from Algiers: "See," he concluded, "I was wrong about that there, I ain't too proud to admit. Jumped in feet first only to find hard stone beneath the surface." He quieted at this, scratching the back of his head. "Now I ain't one to express gratitude easily, John Lee, but I ain't no ingrate, neither, I know when it's warranted. So for all you done that night in helpin' me face them cocksuckers down, and everything since"—here he gestured at Fort Smith around them, a place they would not be were it not for Carlson's initiative—"I'm here to say thanks, once and for all. You'll like to make me regret all this sentimental claptrap come morning, I don't doubt it, but for right here and now, I got to tell you, professor, I'm damned pleased to've made your acquaintance."

The drunken embrace to follow was awkward and masculine, each clapping the other's shoulders, hard. Its sincerity caught them both off guard. They had not expected it. They returned to the barracks in silence.

That next morning at dawn, however, Abrams is pleased by very little. Neither of them is. They are not embarrassed by the night before, for at the moment, they are too pained to feel embarrassment about anything at all. It has been months since they have drunk so much whiskey, and they, like the Jeffers brothers, are now paying dearly for it. Abrams bounces loosely on Small Bill's back, eyes rolling in his head. His mouth tastes of dead mouse. Carlson winces, his memory of Abram's tale dim at best, and groans wherever he looks, bilious belches rising in fumes from his unsettled stomach. Hank has gone from ashen to green. Lionel vomits for the fifth time in as many miles.

"Hope y'all had a good one last night," states Bruslé. He looks dashing atop Gaston, and lords this fine condition over his men with dignified glee. "'Cause y'all sure look like shit today."

The day is overcast. The air has grown bitingly cold. The only sound the men hear is that of several crows hectoring a large, great horned owl above. The owl's wingspan is broad, its mottled color that of slate and snow; its feathered tufts are devilish in aspect. The crows cartwheel violently around it. The owl dodges them, attempting to find refuge from the oncoming light of day, silent save for the hushed flapping of its massive wings. The crows are raucous, enraged, like death. It is an aerial battle such as the men have rarely seen. "Well, I'll be," says Hank Jeffers in awe. "Would y'all look at that."

Obediah Todd is disturbed by what they have just witnessed. He tells no one. He repositions himself in his saddle. The day ahead, he fears, will see change.

22

Miles later, on the road beyond Scullyville, they pass an increasing number of farms, the cabins on them crudely constructed of log and mortar. At one, owned by Mr. T. Enos Highwater, full-blooded Choctaw, and his wife, a massive squaw, they stop to water their horses. The couple is cordial, their home tidily furnished, their family of slaves quartered comfortably behind it. One member of that family, a tall, rail-thin Negro girl in a faded red gingham overshirt, attends to the mounts while the men, ill as they are, gulp down mouthfuls of foul water from a shared, dented tin cup. They ignore the water's oily surface, its whiff of carrion and the parasites within, seeking to slake the punitive thirst that so often follows such nights of abuse.

Smoking his pipe in the morning air, Captain Bruslé offers to pay his host for his hospitality. The offer is dismissed. "Y'all just shed some Yankee blood, first chance y'all get," says Highwater. "That'll be payment 'nuff for me." His rheumy old eyes harden at the thought of a Union victory in this war. He is a dedicated Southern patriot; perhaps no group so loathes the U.S. government as that of which he is a part. Marched halfway across the continent from their native lands in the east, dying in droves along the way, with each staggering pace the Cherokee, Chickasaw, Choctaw, Creek, and Seminole tribes' hatred for those Union officials who forced them afoot has set into a singular quest for revenge. By the time they reached their westerly destination, despite the squabbling and bloodshed they would experience between them, theirs was one, true enemy. "Yanks been runnin' wild in these parts for weeks now," Highwater continues, "small bands actin' like rabbits on the fly after the whippings y'all gave 'em at Manassas and Oak Hills. So mind y'allselves. 'Cause rabbits got teeth, too, they care to use them."

It is noon, and the men pass more homesteads. Some plots are well-kept, others spare and fallen into disrepair. Some are worked by slaves, some not, but all are owned by people with a degree of Indian blood. Children squall on porches. Proud men approach Bruslé to ask where they might enlist. They are tall and bear the appearance of men who do not suffer fools. Nothing would give them greater pleasure than to tear the hearts from the chests of those who have robbed their people of their land and dignity. That, or to die in the attempt, for little frightens an Indian man more than the idea of dying in his bed, a woman holding his quivering hand and wiping his shit-stained backside.

From atop Gaston, Bruslé provides them the necessary information. "Go to Captain Pike, at North Fork," he says. "That's where we'll be mustering." He offers his hand and welcomes them aboard.

The landscape shifts to rolling prairie and spreads grandly for miles in each direction. Wherever Bruslé's men train their bloodshot eyes, they see lush green grasses framed by the vaporous blue walls of surrounding mountain ranges far off in the distance. It is scenery unsurpassed in its natural beauty, yet Abrams scarcely notices. Though he is a man with a steadfast love of the land, try as he might, he simply cannot shake how poorly he feels.

Bruslé reins up besides him. "Private," he barks, slapping Abrams jovially on the back. "I'd like you to ride up ahead with Private Todd, scout out the country."

Abrams turns to his captain with a lamentable look in his eyes: "Sir?"

"A small price to pay for a ten-dollar bottle of contraband, don't you think? Go on now, get."

Left no choice, Abrams spurs Small Bill to catch up with Obediah Todd, already a diminishing speck on the horizon. The others shake their heads with pity but offer no words of condolence. They are too concerned with the holding down what modest breakfast they have been able to manage.

Abrams has endured worse hangovers, though never a worse circumstance in which to have one. Riding hard to meet Obediah, he is concentrating on steadying his breaths and quieting the percussion in his head. He achieves this by focusing instead on his confession to Carlson of the night before, listing all that he remembers having said. He recalls the exchange. He thinks of possible regrets. To his pleasant surprise, despite the rising nausea, he quickly discovers that he has none. With the land sprawling before him in ways exceeding even his most vivid imaginings, he realizes that although he revealed himself to another, a day later, he has no reason to fear it.

Soon he and Obediah Todd are plodding along silently. The afternoon sets into a bone-numbing cold. They pass a canteen of tepid coffee between them. As protection against the fallen temperatures, each trades hands on his reins, alternating between exposing clenched fists to the elements and cramming them down into the warmth of their filmy and stinking crotches.

Almost an hour later, Obediah breaks the silence. "You was forced to put a man in the ground, how'd you do it?"

"Sorry?"

"Gun? Knife? How?"

Abrams thinks on this. "I ain't particular," he says after a pause. "Long as he ain't breathin' come sundown, guess."

Obediah Todd grunts his approval. They ride on.

Twenty minutes later, he breaks the silence once more. "You been saved?"

Abrams has been asked this question before. Once, following his reply to the whore who asked him while in the midst of coitus, he watched her face fall into a crushing sympathy. She had stopped abruptly, pushing his shoulders up and away to catch a better view of the pagan she was fucking. "You mean to say y'all don't accept Jesus Christ as your Lord'n Savior?"

"No ma'am, not as such. But if you do, naked and hard as I am at the moment, believe I ain't above convincin'."

That frigid day southwest of Scullyville, Abrams tells Obediah Todd of the faith into which he was conceived. "Born a Jew," he answers simply. "Raised a man."

Obediah mulls this over. Although he is convinced that flames will lick and char this person with whom he rides for an eternity to come, he further reflects on Bruslé's parting words of the previous night. He will be no wretch, he decides, nor treat Abrams as one. He shrugs. "Least we got something tribal between us," he allows.

"Least we do."

They ride on.

Before long, they are on the return trail to Bruslé. They have scouted out the land a mile in advance and found the terrain to be rolling, framed on each side by dense forest, occupied by little save skittish white-tailed deer and rabbits. With dusk settling atop them, they dismount at a stream to water their horses a scant half-mile ahead of their brothers-in-arms. They do not speak. They pass a few minutes munching on cold venison steak, sitting Indian-style, when Obediah Todd suddenly cranes his neck erect. He jumps to his feet. Sharply, he turns an ear to a line of trees to their right.

"What you got, Obediah?" asks Abrams.

"Hush."

Obediah Todd crouches. He places his hand to the earth and assumes a look of great absorption. As he does, fear ripples down Abrams' spine. He does not like to see men so intent. When they are, he knows something grave is to follow. "On your horse!" he is instantly ordered. "Now!"

Following Obediah's lead, Abrams swiftly mounts Small Bill, whips him around, and kicks his heels into the beast's belly. The horse, unaccustomed to such authority from Abrams, pitches its ears backward before rearing up and darting in the direction from which they first originated over an hour ago. At once Obediah Todd and Abrams are riding with all the haste their steeds are capable of marshaling. His long black hair dancing, Obediah turns to see if they are being followed, by whom, Abrams does not yet know. From the alarm he sees in Obediah's eyes, this does not matter. The point now is to simply hang onto his reins and ride harder than he has ever ridden before. The sudden flush of fear coursing through him has dispelled whatever remnant of a hangover he may have had. Their horses' hoofs are pounding the earth, each exhalation rhythmic and harsh in the crisp air. The animals' manes flap in the wind, saliva frothing madly from behind their bits. It is only when Abrams spots Obediah Todd turning a third time, and notices in his eyes a widening before he prods his horse further, that Abrams himself finally looks.

What he witnesses forces his stomach to buckle in horror. "Yah!" he screams, redoubling his heels into his horse's belly—"Yah! Yah!"—for bearing down hard upon them, not four hundred yards away, rides a squadron of Union skirmishers in a furious and mortal pursuit.

The first shot goes off-target, the rifle crack arriving well after the bullet has sailed wayward. Obediah Todd and Abrams urge their mounts for all their worth. If they can make Bruslé's crew now a quarter-mile hence, they will have a chance. The current odds of five-to-two, though he is a brave man, Obediah Todd understands to be overwhelming. A second rifle shot. This one, too, misses its mark.

In the robberies and small violences of his past, Abrams has been the target of numerous gunsights. He has dodged each bullet, stormed forward with his sap raised high when he sensed failing nerves, but never has the goal of his death been such a concentrated effort by so many men of training. Not among the Cypress Stumps, not even at the Battle of Oak Hills, have this many weapons been pointed at him at once.

Small Bill is slowing. He is a methodical horse, one of endurance, but no long-range sprinter. The distance between him and Obediah Todd begins to lengthen as a result, the rump of the half-breed's horse pulling ahead. Abrams turns again. A lump wells in his throat. There is no question: the Federals are gaining.

Small Bill stumbles but quickly regains his footing.

Abrams' life does not pass before his eyes. He does not think of his mother or his father, of Miss Nora Bloom, or all he has done wrong. He does not think of the War Between the States or his best cardplay or the Cypress Stump Boys. Rather, his mind possesses a determined focus geared singly toward survival. And the way to best achieve that survival, he has decided, is to reach the crew of which he has become a part. He sets his jaw. His knuckles whiten on the reins. In numbers, he will be returned unto strength.

A fourth, fifth, and sixth shot ring out. The soldiers behind him continue to close. Abrams can goad his animal no harder. Already, Small Bill's tongue is lolling, his head beginning to fall. Again, he stumbles. Abrams holds on for dear life, nearly slipping from his saddle each time his mount lurches. The prairie over which they fly is a blur. The bitter air in more peaceful times would freeze him with the piercing quality of daggers, only now, in their flight, Abrams feels nothing. "C'mon, Billy boy!" he urges. "Yah! Yah!"

He hears Obediah yell something, but with the rush of wind in his ears, can make out no words. The scout shouts once more. This time, Abrams discerns what he has been told: "Look yonder!" he hears, watching Obediah Todd hitch his head forward. "Bruslé!"

Abrams looks up. The men with whom he has ridden over the past week are pitching forward into the fray, the Jeffers brothers, two gifted marksmen, high in their seats with the butts of their carbines lodged between their brawny shoulders and strong chins. Abrams spots Carlson with his pistol raised in aim, Bruslé's too. Little puffs of smoke are followed by little cracks of thunder, bullets sallying by him from each direction. Abrams balks for an instant, going straight-backed in his saddle before ducking tightly behind Small Bill's lathering neck, aware that he and Obediah Todd are now caught as fulcrum in the crossfire of two advancing forces. The Confederates ahead are making tremendous ground. Abrams must reach them. Once there, he will halt, turn abruptly and charge back into precisely the same direction from which he has just ridden. He has faith in the men of the crew. They are skilled. He need only enter their ranks.

Obediah is a hundred yards from Bruslé and the others, Abrams perhaps one hundred and fifty. *Ain't done yet,* thinks Abrams doggedly. *Nossir, not hardly.* But as he is about to slow Small Bill so that he might then whip around to face his pursuers, something truly strange occurs. He does not hear the rifle shot. He does not feel any specific sense of pain. He does feel, however, a wrenching sense of torque so powerful it can only be likened to having been struck from behind by a very succinct tornado. Hurling violently forward up and out of his saddle, he is baffled that Small Bill is now moving toward him. He understands neither why he has thudded to the earth nor why his horse's hooves are striking him mercilessly in the knee, groin, and ribcage. At the moment, Elias Abrams understands nothing at all.

Bleeding and broken on the ground as the two warring parties advance on him, his mouth filled with dirt, Abrams searches dazedly to his left, eyes blinking, and sees only the augmenting glow of the grasslands around him. He strains his neck to study the cracked sky, the light of dusk above burning oddly brighter. He coughs and sputters. Indeed, very little makes sense.

He shakes his head groggily to clear it, yet amid the grassland's burning brightness, Abrams is suddenly at the mercy of a welling unlike anything, ever. It is massive, a wall. Stone mountains begin to crumble within him, trees are blown from their roots and roofs from their homes, all of it awash in a remarkably blinding light. It is a pure feeling, this one flooding Elias Abrams, yet bewildering in its scope as it forces him to hold resistant to the onslaught until, at once, when the light in his eyes beams too dazzlingly, he issues a gasp so mighty that he is as frightened by it as his broken body is racked by it. Instantly he is an infant loosed upon a dangerous world, gasping at the ache now settling into his back, crushed ribs, and busted knee. He gasps and gasps until his hands ball tight and thump the sides of his thighs to the driven beat of this fresh and descending agony.

He can think of nothing solid, nothing substantial, not of anybody or anything, but gasps only at the arrival of an impossibly searing pain that has spread through his soul like the slow seeping of boiled tar over a baby's pinkest flesh. All around him light scalds his sight and in this gasping, less air gets through, less oxygen, no plea, nothing but the onset of a death to which Abrams has borne proximity on scores of occasions but never with such a deep and abiding intimacy.

The last thing he acknowledges before darkness settles on him is how—his tongue still muddied with earth—that great expanse of prairie on which he feasts provides him with the most thoroughly galling meal he has ever tasted.

23

"Where's momma?" the Smile asks him. "Where's she, where's momma?"

"Right there," he says. And there she is. She has hoisted herself onto the dancehall stage and stands shyly before the darkened audience. Only she looks nothing like the woman he recognizes as his mother. She is large and bears a full set of teeth and possesses no limp. She is naked in the candle-light. He has seen her somewhere before, but never like this.

"Hoorah!" cheer the Cypress Stump Boys, and they lunge, single-file, onto the stage. "In we go!" they shout, and his mother smiles weakly as each dives into her maw, hands clapped above their heads in prayer. They squeal like joyfully choked piglets slipping down a sow's gullet, swallowed whole. Soon, they are gone, engulfed in his mother's distended belly. From within, he hears the voice of Silas Wolfe, as if bellowed from inside an enormous drum: "There's so much room!" he shouts. "Goddamnit all, there's just so much room!"

"Where's pa?" asks the boy, terrified. "Any of y'all seen my pa?"

Receiving no answer, he turns toward the audience, who are no longer people but wolves, and their snarling applause leaves him, a small child, petrified. Before he can move or speak, from burlap sacks each pulls fistfuls of meat, which they then bolt down, rent and swallowed with indifference to chewing. Saliva flies in improbable arcs, teeth clash sharply. This bestial

160

banquet lasts only seconds, but in that ferocity, he sees one more ravenous than the next. Hands clutch and claw, eyes narrow, the room goes loud with jealousy over who has more and how to get more. When there is no more, each is forced to obey his hunger by turning on another's jugular to feast, flesh sustaining flesh.

When he finally thinks it is over, his legs weak with fear, his stomach turned, he spots a man of slight build, a thin, gray-haired man with a hawk's nose, sunken cheeks, and sharp jaw behind hoary old sideburns, from whom laughter booms loudest. Gold-rimmed bifocals perch at the tip of that nose, fronting an intense pair of eyes. It takes a moment for the boy to realize that it is his father. "Get accustomed to it, Elias, my child!" his father roars above the din. "This is how it's going to be!"

Abrams gasps and bolts up from the stinking canvas stretcher on which he has been raving, his eyes wild and body drenched with sweat.

"Hold tight, son," says Carlson tenderly, pushing his friend back down. He pats Abrams' forehead with a damp cloth. "You just hold tight."

Abrams blinks. No recognition registers in his eyes. He is panicked, his gaze darting throughout the simple, candlelit room. Surrounding him is disarray, all manner of surgical instrument, bone-handled and blunted. Here, a half-empty brown bottle of ether. There, a chipped enamel basin filthy with soiled rags. Hatchet-edged surgery mallets, amputation knives, bone cutters, scalpels, and bullet probes. Though it is already the first week of November, flies remain thick in this room. The room itself bears a heavy, decaying scent, one more suitable to an old butchery than that of any human dwelling. Abrams comprehends none of this, nor the squat, jowly man examining him, his apron stained and splattered, his shirtsleeves rolled up to his elbows, his forearms crusted with stale blood. An imperious-looking soldier with a thick mustache and worried aspect looms over the squat man's shoulder. Beside the captain, two strong lads and a half-breed Indian of equal concern. A Negro youth peers fearfully from the corner of the room. Abrams nearly identifies the man in the Panama hat who attempts to dab his forehead over the squat fellow's ministrations, but in the end cannot. Again, he falls unconscious.

"*It's your own doing, anyway," says his father. "So stand tall and take some responsibility for your actions, damnit! Where'd you learn to be such a milksop, I wonder?*"

"*You ain't need to take that from the likes of him, Elias," says the Smile. "That there's the man who done you and yours wrong." The Smile stands with his arms folded. Above, on the dancehall stage, the boy's mother has vomited out each of the Cypress Stumps, who now recede softly into the darkness of the theater's outer wings. She descends the stairs. She approaches. She hugs her child in silence, for a very long time, and then abandons him forever. "This here was your idea," the Smile goes on. "You planned it. Time you finished it.*"

The boy chokes with embarrassment. "I can't."

The Smile grins. "'Course you can." He hands the boy a cudgel. "First, you've got to clout him on his head real good."

Timidly, the boy accepts the Smile's offer. With all his might, he then smites his father at the base of his skull. With a small groan, the older man slumps to the fine parlor Oriental.

"*Good," says the Smile proudly. "Now, finish him off." He has withdrawn from a sheath a knife with a long, thin blade. "There," he says, pointing. "Between the ribs.*"

Again, the boy accepts the Smile's offer. Tentatively, he kneels beside his father. "Aw honey, hush," he whispers. "Everything's fine, just as fine as can be. You'll see." And then, with all his boyish strength, he pierces his father's back, killing him instantly with a deflating wheeze. Yet when he looks up for approval, rather than gazing upon the Smile beaming down, he realizes instead it is Elias Abrams himself standing above. The Abrams he observes is stunned. Wolfe is now the one crouching on the floor atop that fine parlor Oriental, gently petting the dead man's head. "Hush now," he whispers up into Abrams' horrified stare, his smile wicked. "You just go on and hush."

John Lee Carlson, the last remaining attendant for the night, leaps to his feet from his dozing, startled by the screams erupting from the young man, his friend, prostrate before him. On and on Abrams screams, his eyes wide and maniacal, his brow perspiring, every muscle taut, as Carlson frantically tries to relieve him of the fever that has ravaged his body. These screams, the professor quickly recognizes, are in fact howls of grief, suggestive of the deepest lamentation he has ever heard a man's soul muster. They resound well beyond the jagged walls of Fort Smith, far out into the cold of the Arkansas night. But even more chilling than the autumn frost into which these screams echo is the anguished apology possessed therein. For now, despite his every effort to sequester his involvement in his father's murder away from the rest of the world, Elias Abrams, only bastard son of I. J. Lieber, Esq., recently deceased, has made his great secret known.

TWO

24

Two tortuous days pass. Abrams' fever continues to rage unabated. His lips crack and whiten, and the wound in his back, just below his left shoulder blade, has begun to fester. The skin around the hole has grown necrotic and fills the rooms with the ripened scent of putrefying meat. He has suffered two fractured ribs and a severely bruised knee. The jowly man in the blood-splattered apron, a surgeon named Riggs, believes Abrams is free of internal bleeding, though he has likewise asked whether a praying man exists among them. Obediah Todd stands proudly forward, Bible in hand. "Done all I can," sighs the surgeon, avoiding eye contact with those who seek it. "Got the slug out, anyway. Cloth from his blouse, too." His own odor is strongly etherized, his hands trembling, his hair madly disheveled, but his heart, Carlson decides, is earnest. If Abrams dies, it will not be due to the surgeon's lack of sincerity. The professor does not know that until two months prior, this same Riggs was the town of Jasper, Arkansas' lone barber. "I'll keep scrapin' out the hole, swabbin' it with whiskey," says Riggs, "but I won't make no promises. Them purplin' flakes can't be a good sign. That stink neither."

The morning of the third day arrives and only once, during the dawn, has Abrams come to. In that short span of wakefulness, Carlson hurriedly explained to him the situation, avoiding all mention of the preceding nights' confession. A drained Abrams motioned for his friend to come closer still. His voice scarcely above a whisper, he instructed Carlson as to his own convalescence. "For my fever," he whispered, licking his dry lips, "boil up some thoroughwort, serve it to me hot, hot. Should break it 'fore long."

"The fever's not the real concern, Elias," answered Carlson gently, "so much as the way your wound's taken to infection."

Abrams paused. "He maggot me?"

"Come again?"

"Dead flesh, ate up clean by maggots. Ain't pretty, but it's saved more'n one man. So, what then, the doc maggot me?"

"No."

"Well, least tell me I got burned."

"Burned?"

Abrams rolled his eyes. "Some damned fool's got to cauterize me, John Lee. My blood'll poison if it ain't already, less y'all act but quick." He began to fade at this point but struggled to stay alert for an instant longer, his eyes flashing wide. Then, just as he had awakened, Abrams once again fell unconscious.

Minutes later, Jean-Baptiste was scouring the Arkansas countryside for thoroughwort, while Doc Riggs, cursing his ether-addled mind for having forgotten a practice as simple as cauterization, stomped swiftly back from the smithy, a red-hot soup ladle in his swaddled hand. Along the way he pined for simpler times, when all a man needed to call himself content was a pair of sharp cutting shears, a full head of hair before him, and a set of customer's ears to pour his lies into.

"Flip 'im over," he demanded. "Stand back. No, wait, you fellers there, hold 'im down. He's fixin' to jump like spit on a skillet."

The smoke that next billowed from Abrams' rotting back filled the room with a scent so sickening that both the Jeffers brothers and Charles A. Bruslé were sent reeling into the light of day, hands clapped over their mouths. "God willin'," said an exhausted Riggs, his job completed, "that should do 'er."

Another day passes. In that time, Abrams has been provided several mugs of thoroughwort tea. His fever has indeed broken. His back is blistered and blackened but has begun to heal with surprising speed. His ribs, though ferociously painful, are on the mend. He sleeps without night terrors for the first time in seventy-two hours.

"John Lee," says Bruslé softly at Abrams' bedside. "We've got our orders."

Carlson nods. Standing over his friend, he does not wish to leave.

"That kid's tougher than alligator hide," Bruslé continues. "He'll be fine."

"I'd sure like to be here when he wakes. Most particularly, to thank him for saving his own goddamned life."

Bruslé grunts. "Friendship's important, no doubt. But our mission's more so. We've already lost four days. Procedure on the prisoners might work as an excuse for a day or two, but I'll be busted back to private, McIntosh finds out about the delay." He shifts his weight. "Come. The others are waiting."

Carlson sighs. He places a hand on Abrams' shoulder. He lets it linger. "Ten minutes more, Charles. That's all I ask."

Bruslé pinches his bottom lip and nods toward the plankwood floor. "I'll have Jean-Baptiste pack up your kit in the meantime."

———

Dear Elias,

If you are cognizant enough to read this, only then can I be assured that you have survived the most terrifying ordeal to which I have ever borne witness. Please forgive my hasty scrawl, but I have little time to impart to you a near tome's worth of information. Bruslé and the others currently await my company, though his generous spirit has granted me this moment to enlighten you as to the circumstances in which you are now entangled.

We rode hard upon those who unseated you, they us. As you lay earthbound, one of the Jeffers brothers—they argue about it still—repaid our enemy doubly in kind, sending two of their hapless kin to the ground with a greater sense of finality than they did you. These cold two now lay beside each other, partnered for eternity to respire no more. Of the remaining three, grown fearful at the fates befallen their brethren, each dropped his rifle and reins to thrust his cowardly arms upward to the heavens in surrender. Truly, God stayed our hands that day.

The Union soldiers soon detained, Obediah dismounted to tend to your broken form, macerating some prairie weed to help stanch the bleeding. Quickly then we whisked you upon a litter, he and I, and rode as hard as your condition would allow us the twenty-mile return to Fort Smith. Desperate were those miles, I must declare it. This, while Bruslé and the Jeffers boys marched those craven miscreants here to arrive but three hours later. Thus incarcerated, I pray they will trouble devoted members of the Cause no more.

But as to your state. It has been precarious, though from the ease with which you now sleep, I trust that you will gain full recovery of both limb and wit. Such peace as your slumbering face now conveys, I would wish upon mankind forever.

Alas, Bruslé calls. My departure is nigh. I leave you with a few sentiments more. The first, my young friend, is my desire for your complete restoration. The convalescent furlough you have been issued should serve you well, as New Orleans has curative powers admired by even the least Hippocratic among us. Thirty days should be time enough to regain your strength, for when you return, I fear you will need it. In your brief homecoming to our beloved Crescent City, I am enclosing a letter I would be deeply appreciative if you delivered to my wife. Tell her of our acquaintanceship and of my fortitude. Be not sparing of detail, for I know she will cling to your every word. Secondly, although it is perhaps beyond my place to do so, I implore you to introduce yourself to Miss Nora Bloom of Hercules Street. I have every faith that her delicate touch will aid in your recuperation with far greater efficacy than any apothecary's poultice ever could. Lastly, I would ask that you be extremely discriminating as to whom else you contact while home. This Silas Wolfe bears the mark of the beast, there is no question. His soul, from what little I have heard of it, appears to be more cunning than kind. I know this, dear Elias, beyond your conscious admission of it, because in the midst of your febrile descent you spoke at length on matters most disturbing. I do not know who wielded the deadly blade to which your ravings alluded, nor do I possess the divine right within me to bear judgment of it. Indeed, I do not know whether you have the vaguest notion of the subject to which I am now referring, or for that matter, whether this killing occurred at all. I only know that if you are acquainted with such a deed, be it perpetrated by your hand or another's, atonement must be made. Find a way to mend your spirit, Elias. Like Odysseus' son, the clear-headed Telemachus, seeking to set right the wrongs visited upon his father's kingdom, whatever you must do, for the mercy of your encumbered soul, you too must set right this wrong.

Yours in sincerest fidelity,
John Lee Carlson

25

Abrams spends the next six days on the water. Shipped out from Fort Smith, a garrison embanked on the Arkansas River, he transfers from his military flatbottom to a bulky civilian steamboat moored at the Arkansas' confluence with the Mississippi twenty miles southeast of Fort Hindman, two days downstream. The sights and smells of such a familiar leeward expanse remind him instantly of home. The new terrain glimpsed since enlisting has proven wondrous, but the idea of sailing upon the dear Mississippi, from which he pulled countless shoepick and gaspargou for food and fertilizer in his youth, forces Abrams to inhale a deep, agonizing breath of pleasure. Bound in a soiled linen dressing, his ribs are fragile. His knee is still swollen but gaining in flexibility each day. The wound in his back, while tender to the touch, he keeps smeared with a sweet myrrh unguent, meant not only to help heal and disinfect but also to keep Abrams from reeking of death. He smokes his pipe for hours at a stretch on a deck-side chaise lounge, wrapped in a clean woolen blanket as the chill of the sharp river air nips at his face and fingers. He checks his pocket watch. Noon, it says, then two and three, though from the unrelenting gray above, there is no way for Abrams to endorse the watch's claim. He winces whenever he repositions himself too quickly. In his frozen grip, he clutches the letters. He rereads Nora Bloom's and now, John Lee Carlson's, tokens of caution and affection, over and over again. He declines his fellow travelers' offers of conversation and card games. He sleeps often. He eats much.

The *Galatea* makes good time, the morning fogs thus far kept at bay, a strong wind astern. With water levels more than ample, the steamboat captain has decided to sail through the night. During the days, Abrams watches each vessel in the Mississippi's flatboat fleet do its part to clog the waterway, frantically hauling goods and timber. He eavesdrops on the bickering and bragging of those sailors working the smaller boats on the river below. They grunt with each tug of their crafts' thick, hempen ropes. They roar with laughter while performing a thousand menial tasks. They swear furiously, sing with the impiety of fallen angels. The crews—strapping men in iron-studded brogans and linsey-woolsey trousers—sleep under the stars, share their meat from a single, massive pot, fight like the world's toughest sons-of-bitches, and drink such vast quantities of Monongahela rye whiskey as to make the thirstiest landlocked tipplers toast their glasses in admiration. Their lives possess a freedom that Abrams has long admired but, in their landlessness, has never wished for himself.

Still, there is rumor of imminent Union control of the river. Fear has floated northward from New Orleans, a city in the midst of asphyxiation from its Gulf-side blockade, choking each Confederate bastion above it with a skulking sense of dread. Abrams' home, if the rumors are to be believed, is slowly being strangled to death.

He tries to appreciate the brief peace he has been offered nonetheless. Only a week before, the issuance of a sanctioned furlough would have caused him to ball his fists in joy. Now, however, granted his wish, rather than feel such joy, he is instead overcome with fury by his delirium's betrayal. Over the past months he has been learning the value of speech, but what disturbs him most is the way those few remaining words within him so successfully earned their release. He spits in disgust at his mouth's great treachery. He surveys the stark autumn world that passes him by.

"Shit," he mutters, "from how I must've rambled on, I'd bet old John Lee can keep my own goddamned secrets better'n me."

Grown uneasy by the thought of this kind of accidental honesty, Abrams shifts his position too abruptly. In this quick movement, he detonates a pain so explosive that his face twists in agony, his body contorting into an instant stillness. He awaits his pain's passing with two very wide eyes. Once gently settled, he returns to his musings, unable to escape the clash raging within him. For despite the anger he has been directing at himself, he realizes, too, that since mentioning aloud his part in his father's murder, with every passing minute its reality becomes more and more certain. And in his growing acceptance of this certainty, sickened though he may be by it, he begins to feel the very sense of unburdening of which he has been in such desperate need. This is the frustration from which Abrams suffers following his unwitting confession to Carlson—one healing and cruel—now that he has let slip his deepest secret.

Ain't that a kick in the gut, he thinks disdainfully, *what happens, you get what you aim for? All day long, there you are, bellyachin' to yourself 'bout what you done, then, once you finally get that load off your chest, can't believe your own goddamned ears.* Abrams shakes his head. *Studied on that son-of-a-bitch's death for years, you did, couldn't stop thinkin' 'bout it for a fuckin' minute. But lo and behold, old Silas gives you just what you been aimin' at all this time, and look what that gets you. Poor bastard, deader'n hell, and you in it up to your goddamned eyeballs.* Abrams sighs. He takes a long, baleful pull on his pipe. He stares off miserably into the afternoon sky. No birds fly. Clouds do not move across the grayness. He draws his blanket tighter over his shoulders. The world has grown too cold.

But he is not done. He thinks beyond the unwitting confession, to what such an admission actually means now that it has been revealed. He thinks of how resigned his father looked on the night of his murder, how vain, how proud, of his last words, of their twinge of apology. Abrams reflects upon all that made these words necessary, wonders whether the motives behind them were true, and then thinks, of course, of his own grave offenses committed as a result. He contemplates forgiveness, debating which outweighs the other, the sins of the father balanced against the sins of the son. Life has taught him that men desire most to know only themselves. So, too, is he discovering that few ever arrive at such knowledge, though they continue to awaken at dawn, every dawn, to attempt and fail at precisely the same lesson.

This is not the brutish beating of the pimp Blackwell. This is murder, and the man, his father. True, he had every reason to hate I. J. Lieber, Esq. His ways were vile, his actions indefensible. But these reasons, Abrams has come to conclude, are not justification enough.

In the end, who truly knows his own begetting?

A child appears out of nowhere to ask Abrams what ails him. "I'm from Gaines Landing," says the boy. "I'm Virgil, but you can call me Braxton." He wears a fine blue woolen shortcoat. His hair is snow white and arches from his forehead in a large, curved cowlick. A decade ago, as a child himself, Abrams often bloodied boys such as this. Awaiting his question's reply, young Virgil jams a stubby finger into one of his crusted nostrils.

Abrams sniffs. He wipes his eyes. "What ails me?"

The boy nods. He is vigorously screwing his finger now.

"Well, for starters, the sight of you rootin' for grubs in that goddamned snot-nose of yours ain't doin' me a world of good, I can tell you that much."

The boy's face falls horror-stricken. He turns and runs off squalling in search of his mother. His slapping, flat-footed paces echo the length of the otherwise silent steamboat deck. He does not know that rather than sympathize with his sense of indignity, his mother will instead call him "a filthy little piglet" and scour from beneath his nose with a coarse handkerchief a full layer of his most tender facial flesh.

Later that night, after nabbing a string of blood sausages, two loaves of rye, a crock of country mustard, and a couple bottles of claret from the ship's galley simply because they were left untended and, thus, fair game, then stowing it all in his cabin, Abrams draws on his pipe in sober reflection of Carlson's advice. Prior to any clash with the Cypress Stump Boys, he will meet this Nora Bloom. He must discover the truth of his human heart. It troubles him beyond his guilt, not as a result of any wound or weaponry, but from the fact that over the past months, from the very instant it opened in union with Nora's first envelope, it has perhaps since been fashioning him into a liar. The fondness he feels for her may indeed be falsely born. And so, with every mile that the *Galatea* bears him southward, with every second he gains in proximity to her, the weight of his heart fluctuates between that of love's most feathery kiss and that of an anvil.

In considering the full extent of Carlson's counsel, he grows unsure whether challenging the Smile is wise after all. Even at his strongest, Abrams is a poor match for Silas Wolfe. His punishing hand speed would easily dispatch Wolfe in a battle of fists, but Silas Wolfe, he knows, will allow no such contest. Abrams is not deluded. He understands that when he at last confronts his old friend, theirs will be an exchange of metal. Sailing southward, he gnaws on his lip, uncertain what to do.

Abrams' thoughts roll on.

Mindful of all he owes Carlson, he soon asks a passing deckhand for some writing supplies, a request promptly honored. He considers drafting a note to Miss Nora Bloom as well, but then quickly decides against it, supposing that their next expression should be in person. Besides, John Lee Carlson, he believes, at least for the time being, deserves his sole attention:

Dear John Lee,

I am writin now to say Thank you for everthing you and the Boys done for me back at Fort Smith I think I would be a goner if it was not for you all thats a sure fact My wounds are heeling fine but I will tell you I do feel the odd acke in the morning I will give your Imogene the leter you gave to Me and I will give your gurls each a kiss on the cheeke and say they are from you direct. I will meet this Miss Nora Bloom to and if it goes nice, I will marry her just to prove your a dam fool I am now reading this and am afeared my leters are in beter shap when you are there to help with them I trust you will keepe your mouth shut to about everthing I sayed when I was asleep John Lee Do not make Me regrette all the time you and me done shared.

Your frend,
Elias

His letter mailed at Vicksburg, with New Orleans still days away, aside from tending to his wounds and fending off a deep melancholy, aware that for the moment he can do nothing, Abrams spends the remainder of his time bundled in his chaise lounge, absently flipping through a deck of cards. He counts and recounts his billfold's ninety-four dollars in graybacks. He speaks to no one. He notes the jowls of fat civilians, imagines the dimpled elbows of their fat wives. He hears them grunt and strain, thighs chafing against their own girth, feet tender and swollen with gout. He would like to see them all starve.

It is after breakfast following their brief stop in St. Francisville, but a day's journey home, when Abrams spots a fresh and absolute peril, his heart thundering at the sight of it. As quickly and calmly as possible, he thus clatters out of his chair and limps with furious restraint indoors toward his cabin. Once there, collapsed onto his berth, panting hard from such unexpected exertion, he runs a hand delicately over his eyes. "That motherfucker," he whispers in the dark. "Got more bloodhound in him than—aw, just, goddamnit all already." He sighs.

Behind his locked cabin door, in his pain and frustration Abrams is envisioning John McClelland, the New Orleans chief of police, the whalebone baton he is well-known for, and the bucktoothed yokel-of-a-special-officer named Dalrymple he evidently deployed to patrol Louisiana's waterways, whether to search for Abrams or for other fugitives, Abrams himself does not know. This same deputized yokel now stamps over the upper deck of the *Galatea* in thick-heeled boots, weighted down by his pistols and sense of righteousness as he suspects, with eyes like slits, each passenger of his own particular strain of sin. Dalrymple is stocky and young and fractious, ready to prove to whomever dare challenge him that maintaining order in New Orleans is "a helluva lot tougher'n anything Old Lincoln, that Sucker State cunt-licker," could ever throw his way. Abrams has heard tales of Dalrymple and knows by sight and reputation the special officer to be little different from Gallatin Street's most venal brutes and rogues. That these two have never met is testament to Abrams' elusiveness alone. This fact does not now embolden him. He realizes that Dalrymple will happily bash a head in reply to an insolent look, then rifle through the wallet of the dazed offender. He will whore and ejaculate on dresses and cackle through his rotting buckteeth all the while, yet never once pay for his leisure. He will steal fruit from honest vendors and break arms and splinter bones and, if pushed, will shoot without qualm squarely into the backs of fellows before him, be they already clapped in irons or no. As with all officers of the law, Dalrymple's only arguable merit is his belief that when he acts, he acts justly. Yet nothing, Abrams knows, is more dangerous in a man.

Aware that he is now confined to his cabin for the remainder of the journey, thankful for having retained enough of his former self to swipe the provisions when the occasion presented itself, an embittered Abrams tries to settle into his berth as comfortably as he can. He carefully inclines his wounded back with a pillow. He drapes his feet over the edge of the bunk, dropping them hard onto the floor. Growing ever frustrated with the soreness in his ribs, he shifts his hips. Try as he might, however, for his every attempt to fall upon a posture that might ease his pain, Elias Abrams, alleged patricide and universally marked man, can simply find no relief.

26

New Orleans is not as he remembers it. The blend of Mediterranean hues and architecture, the two- and three-stories of masonry and stucco, the stone arches and loggias and delicate wrought-iron gallery grillwork, all seem to possess a quaint peculiarity now, as though Abrams has arrived to foreign shores. The scores of French-speaking *Orléonois* strolling on the boulevards further add to the city's steamy exoticism, and with them, the notion that such exoticism inevitably fails in the face of sterner, domestic truths. Live oak limbs along the levees now give the impression of sagging more despondently toward earth, the bales of cotton that once clotted the docks seemingly too spare in number. Where is the balm of memory, the soothing familiarity of past life and love? There, at the corner of Old Levee and Dumaine, where Abrams once held Angeline's hand in his and kissed her knuckles gently, for free, because she had asked him to. "Like you was my beau," she had said, suddenly shy. "Like we was groomed to be good, you'n me." Or there, before the St. Louis Cathedral, where General Jackson has sat warlike for the past five years astride his charger, a bronze reminder that battles over New Orleans may be lost. Fleeting are Abrams' memories of his many monte victories earned along the lengths of that Quarter square. At the moment, he can gain no traction in them.

He witnesses, too, in the faces of those shoppers who bustle by, his mother's market from which they have just fled now grown bare, the kind of worry that demands a determined pace, as if some degree of advance might compensate for other, more inert, failures. In truth, in his limping walk through the Vieux Carré, his sack of belongings slung over his good shoulder, Abrams finds little welcoming in these streets. They provide a route for those who would hurt him. They ring with no music, no laughter or joy. Gloom exists throughout. The Federal naval blockade is taking its toll; the war has come home. Abrams has no question; this is not the city of his youth. And yet, it is not capitulation he senses in New Orleans either, nor resignation. Indeed, the rich air in his lungs, long capable of fueling his every imagined bawd and festivity, continues to flow, only somehow in far thinner supply.

He blows into a fist. The cold has trailed him downriver.

He arrives at John Lee Carlson's home a touch before nine o'clock. Among the last to disembark the *Galatea*, with Special Officer Dalrymple already an hour gone, Abrams decided that before tending to his own affairs—a scalding hot bath, a good tooth polishing, a close shave, a new uniform and set of brogans fitted from the New Orleans commissary, a bowler from LeDoux's, all followed by a much-anticipated visit to Hercules Street—he will promptly hand over the missive he has been called upon to deliver.

From the immobility of his days on the river, rather than take a trolley, despite the risk of encountering a member of the law or a Cypress Stump, he has chosen to walk through the stiffness of his knee, hoping to gently ease it back into usage. His wound continues to pain him, his ribs remain delicate, his left arm snug to his side in a sling, but in the steady healing of the past week, he feels stronger than he has in quite some time. He takes a deep, nearly uninterrupted breath even as his eyes sweep the thoroughfares, nervously searching each alley for some newly fashioned threat. He hoists his britches. This day has much in store for him.

Located on Urania Street between Magazine and St. Charles, Carlson's upriver home is but a mile from where Abrams was reared, though geography, Abrams quickly learns, is the only proximity these two neighborhoods share. Whereas the Lafayette City tenement of his youth was little more than a single, interconnected hovel, a snaking, wooden tinderbox of slanted, loose-planked floors and dark, lopsided rooms, John Lee Carlson's house stands self-sovereign, immaculate. It is not especially large, but the shrubs of hydrangea, heliotrope, and oleander in the yard before it are all conscientiously sheared, its stone steps well-swept. Stark white and strong-columned, it was homes such as this that as a child Elias Abrams railed so enviously against.

He sniffs and then knocks.

When Imogene Carlson answers, her morning perusal of the *New Orleans Bee* over a cup of chicory disrupted, her first fanciful impression of the young man standing kinked in her doorway is that he is, by profession, a harbinger of Death. Instantly she gasps in dismay, her hand quick to her mouth, her eyes at once fearful and uncertain. He is a grotesquery, this boy, an ideal corruption of the human form. She has never beheld such a beleaguered presence, one so wounded and rank.

Abrams sees her reaction to him, and so drops the sack from his shoulder to drag the bowler from his head. Kneading its tattered brim, he looks down to the deplorable state of his shoes. They are little more than shreds of leather at this point, stained black with shit and piss, the waste of a thousand male beasts. He covers the exposed toe of one shoe with the other, shyly. He is ashamed, not because he finds Imogene Carlson striking in ways unexpected from a professor's wife, but because he has not spoken to a woman of such evident quality in recent memory. Standing before him, curiously awaiting his announcement now that she has recovered herself, Imogene Carlson presents an elegance that intimidates the young Abrams, though hers is not a traditional beauty. In her emerald green morning dress, with its closed sleeves and fitted front, she appears thin, her hips more angular than the rolling swell his tastes prefer. Her hair is more frayed jute than the veritable beams of sunlight of Carlson's description. Her right cheek is blemished by a small, maroon birthmark that the petty folk of her life have clucked spitefully behind screens and doors as too similar in aspect to blackberry-stained bird shit. Her blue eyes are small, her nose, somehow smaller. Taken as a whole, however, Abrams finds her grace disarming.

"May I help you?" she asks.

Bowing awkwardly, Abrams coughs into his fist and gives a hasty explanation. He withdraws the letter from his breast pocket, at which Imogene Carlson, once she grasps what he is proffering, simply blinks in disbelief.

Quickly then, she ushers him indoors.

Moments later, in the well-appointed parlor, she has all but torn her husband's letter open and begun reading through it. She offers Abrams neither a seat nor any refreshment, but he recognizes that this is no time for etiquette. The room is silent. It possesses many books.

"Oh dear," she soon whispers, wilting onto a brass-studded leather ottoman, her knees weakened beneath her. Her face has fallen into despair. She looks up to Abrams and holds the letter aloft for his inspection. "It's *Hamlet*," she says plaintively. "*Hamlet*. Already."

Seeing that Abrams does not understand, she quietly explains. In their relationship, Professor John Lee Carlson, a man of love and letters, delights in crafting scenes unwritten by canonical authors themselves, completing existing soliloquies, placing words into the mouths of famed dramatic heroes and heroines so that he might articulate his love for Imogene in ways he believes to be the most perfectly expressive. Mostly, his letters convey pure joy. Other times, such as this day, his method of tender surrogacy conveys instead a perfect sadness.

Staring at the floor, she shakes her head and then looks up once more, her eyes rimmed with tears. "Would you mind?" She is holding the letter out to him.

"Ma'am?"

The letter remains outstretched.

Abrams accepts the page and sits, his unslung sack of belongings crumpling against his foot. Although he is uncomfortable with such intimacies and would prefer not to soil her furniture with the refuse of war, from the anguish reflected in Imogene Carlson's face, he realizes that he has little choice in the matter. Abrams is unsure what she needs from him precisely, only that she needs from him a kindness:

UPON OPHELIA'S DEATH: V.I.

Ham: What, gone? Then I am myself alone,
   Entombed with entombed Ophelia.
   Alas, though my grief be not numbered in the stars,
   Constellations now do feign their brilliance,
   Whilst below on this diseased spit of stone
   Once so proudly proclaimed Denmark,
   Milchcows 'twixt herbéd lips low
   No sound more departing
   Than these night-ripened notes of sadness,
   Struck by such a love lost.
   In fell meadows will I ever walk,
   Astern my sisters burthened,
   Whispering to their tails, my own.
   I, a fool in manner, a fool in mark, left now forever
   To a coffin's pall and mine thus imposed.
   Truly this is a sorrow more beckoned than brash,
   A field of despair grown toward expanse
   In the measure of a breath diminishéd.
   Sweet, sweet Ophelia, as honest and fair
   As the tenor of her constancy, and I,
   Constant only in my honest and fair fraud.
   For this, the stars above shall prove
   My dreams a cold stone dish,
   From which I'll an eternal silence feast.

I dare not express to you at such a distance, my dear Imo, how fervently I long to be by your side.

Your faithful husband
John Lee

Abrams pinches his bottom lip in thought. After a moment, he whistles and returns the letter to its proper owner, saying, "Now I ain't entirely sure what's all goin' on in there, Miss Imogene, I ain't got the mind for it. I ain't sure why you're wantin' me to read it so, neither. But one thing's for certain—it's a world of *something*, ain't it?"

"I wasn't expecting *Hamlet* for another six months," she laments. She places a palm gently to her cheek and begins to sob. "Not for six months at *least*."

—

Abrams is soon limping back through the chilly air toward the Vieux Carré, come from an exhausting spell of consolation. In that time, after waving off Imogene's apology for having little more to feed him than a couple stale croissants and a cup of weak chicory, results of the blockade, Abrams held his friend's wife in his one free arm, assuring her as she dampened his shoulder with her tears that John Lee Carlson was a fine man, a brave man, a man who loved her with vehemence and grit. He talked about his friend's intelligence and the quality of his heart. "Your man's done me a world of good," he confessed honestly. "'Course, takes him twice as many words to do that good as it would a sane feller, but still, he's rock solid, that John Lee."

At the mention of her husband's chatting ways, Imogene Carlson laughed through her tears. She pulled away from Abrams' shoulder and wiped her eyes. She expressed deep embarrassment. He did the same, but for the odor he presented her. He asked, gently, whether he might meet the twins. They were visiting their grandparents out in St. Tammany Parish, she told him, though they would return by Sunday evening.

"Shame, that," Abrams answered. "Promised I'd give them a kiss for him."

Imogene's brow went quizzical. "Well, surely you'll come back." Her eyes widened. "For a visit? Before you return to the front?" When after a pause he still offered no response, she added breathlessly, "Oh, Mr. Abrams, you simply *must*." Then, to his great surprise, she leaned back into him, placing her cheek delicately to his breast. His spine stiffened. She nestled her head beneath his chin. He eased. She sighed. Warily, he drew his good arm around her. Blood rushed to his genitals, but he did not think of how he might angle her toward the couch. Instead he held her, she him, their hearts beating stoutly, each holding the other as though clutching a stump against the wind of some improbably fierce gale. Silently, they lingered like this. They stood alone, together. At last, Imogene Carlson turned away.

He promised to return.

Now, two hours later, Abrams pushes through the swinging doors of a flophouse on Dauphine Street, not far from where he last lodged on Customhouse. Before enlisting, he had come to live an unsettled life, tossing his hat onto the backs of spindly chairs in a dozen cheap hotels in as many months. This itinerancy, because Cypress Stumps did not live together, a policy dictated by Wolfe. He would have no man know his every secret, he told them. Some things, Wolfe demanded, were nobody's business but his. Thus, in his rented room on Customhouse, his last before fleeing the city, Abrams left behind little worth remembering.

He has not missed any of it, the roaches and rats, the smoking wick of an oil lamp he was prohibited from burning after ten o' clock, the cloying stink of other men's semen worn for years into the wooden floor, the stale pungency of their pisspots. He has not missed sharing pillows with past syphilitics, their faces slowly rotting into coarse fabric as they slumber their noses away, nor sharing walls with consumptives and their chronic, death-rattling coughs. He has not missed sheets so foul that their rare washing does little but make further threadbare an already near-translucence. He has not missed paying cretinous men for the right to sleep. When asked what the idea of home means to Abrams, his face sours at the thought.

At least in places such as this flophouse on Dauphine, he feels safe from lawmen and the Smile's spies. And so, as it approaches noon on the day of his return, on his feet he now wears a new pair of stiff-leathered boots, bought for almost twice their peacetime worth. Tucked under his free arm he cradles a brown paper package, bound tightly with twine. In that package, a new uniform, for after much debate, he opted against a civilian outfit, though that is what his tastes would have preferred. He decided this because Miss Nora Bloom, he concluded, would much rather be presented with a man in the gray denim frock of the Third Louisiana, with its ten polished brass buttons down the breast and two at waist-level in the back, than in the finely tailored sack coats of the cowardly or aged who have thus far escaped their duty. Only in uniform, believes Abrams, will he present her the full force of his charm.

He will visit LeDoux the haberdasher next, braced for the exorbitance he now expects to pay. But first he must scour the grime that has bonded to his flesh over the past eleven days with the tenacity of horse-hoof glue. His wound's dressing must be changed; already, despite the sweet myrrh unguent, it has begun to taint. He will purchase the establishment's best linen sheet from the flophouse hôtelier whatever the price, pay for it to be boiled clean and torn into strips, and then, providing all goes well, in but a few hours' time request that Miss Bloom change his dressing for him. He will be half-naked and injured and this will prove irresistible. Abrams is vaguely aware of the manipulation he conceives, an act from which he hopes to elicit an uncontestable flush of sex and nurturance, but he does not care. Mere hours from their meeting, he feels to be jumping out of his skin.

As he descends the stairs to the washroom, a tattered towel and brick of lye soap in hand, his new uniform beneath his arm, the parlor pimp asks from below whether he wants "a world-class cock cleanin'. 'Cause old

Bernice here'll scrape the cheese from yer sack, then draw out every ounce of jism you can buck, sure as the Lord made a cunt snug'n proper."

The proposition stops Abrams in his tracks. He scratches his bristly jaw. Though powerfully tempted by the offer, he decides at last that he would rather meet Nora Bloom with hungry eyes, wishing her to measure the sexual animal in him as much as she does the mind of man. Any orgasm now, he fears, will dull his edge.

The bath is a miracle. Its surface steams. The water is fresh and hot and perfumed with Arabic oils, all perks for which he paid an additional two dollars. Slipping gingerly into the freshly scrubbed tub, Abrams closes his eyes and groans. His aching knee eases in the heat of the water. Sighing, his thoughts dance from the poetry of his friend's yearning, to Imogene Carlson's saddened response to it, to the image of the Nora Bloom his mind has so thoroughly constructed. For the time being, contented as he is, he has no time for thoughts of guilt or Silas Wolfe or war. Instead, deciding as he has to maintain those fiery deposits of sperm within him, idly polishing his teeth with a dash of Thurston's powder and a new boar-bristled toothbrush, Elias Abrams works hardest, not to distract himself from the remorse that has so tormented him over the past months, but to discipline himself against lingering too long between his legs.

Soon, standing in the tub naked and wet, suds dripping down the length of his lean body into water now the color of muddy wagon ruts, he runs a blade at his throat, the room's silence broken by the scraping sound of metal on lather and hair. After a moment, he quits shaving to study his reflection in the looking-glass, noticing that his face, being shorn of its whiskers, is quickly regaining its youth and angles. He splashes the straight razor into the water at his knees. He shakes his head and smiles to himself.

This day has much in store for him indeed.

27

Girded within by a fine calfskin sweatband, Abrams' new morefelt bowler fits his head as though Monsieur LeDoux designed it for him alone, his new boots quickly conforming all the more comfortably to his feet thanks to the layer of soft chamois leather cut and inserted into them by the Frenchman, free of charge. Along one of his boots' inseams, just above his right ankle, Abrams further requested LeDoux stitch in a sheath for the stag-handled dirk, bought earlier that day, he has vowed to keep hidden on him at all times. Now, save for his shoulder sling and hunched posture, in his crisp new uniform Abrams looks the very standard of Confederate soldiery. After a quick nap, he feels refreshed. At Mc-Gloin's a half-hour before, in a dark corner away from the prying eyes of others, he consumed a dozen raw oysters, a heaping bowl of chicken-and-andouille gumbo, and three beers, each gold and foamed like buttermilk.

It is approaching mid-afternoon, and on his way up to Hercules Street amid the wintry air, hothouse peonies in his grip, Abrams notices that the struggling businesses have begun to close early. He learns from a passerby there is soon to be a review of the city's soldiers on Canal Street. Abrams nods his appreciation and then picks up his pace. Knowing the mind of Nora Bloom as he does, he is sure she will attend the review, and so he feels compelled to catch her before the marching rows of fresh-faced recruits, their chins still high, their midriffs still solid with home-cooked meals, their ideals and uniforms as yet unsullied by the filthy truths of war, have the chance to rob him of her attention.

Using her letter's return address, Abrams arrives at a residence much like John Lee Carlson's, though it is far, far larger. He looses a long, slow whistle of admiration. It, too, is white and fronted by stately columns. But unlike the professor's, in the Blooms' tidy front yard stands an audience of Roman statuettes awaiting in perpetuity, like some punishment of old, their owners' daily entrances and exits. Abrams exhales sharply. He lifts the gate's iron latch. At the door, he rings the bell. A Negro girl answers.

"Miss Nora in?" he asks, his voice cracking. "Is Miss Nora in?" he repeats, firmer.

"No suh, she to synagogue." She is a pretty, thick-lipped girl named Violet, dressed in the oversized, hand-me-down garb of a white woman. She offers Abrams nothing more.

Promptly stating his purpose, he asks, politely, if he might wait for Miss Nora's return indoors. Abrams stomps a heel for warmth, and winces in pain for it, hoping to emphasize to Violet the discomfort he feels.

Skepticism settles over her face. She folds her arms. No true gentleman comes calling upon a lady without first sending ahead a visiting card to request a meeting. And yet, thinks Violet, he certainly appears earnest enough in his uniform, this young soldier. Such dainty flowers, such soulful eyes. *He fine-lookin', too,* she adds to herself, *even if he scrawny and got a bit too much of the broke down in 'im.* A moment passes before, as if acting against her natural inclination, she begrudgingly steps aside and allows Abrams to enter Nora Bloom's life for real.

Alone in the parlor, warming while Violet prepares him tea, Elias Abrams falls to studying the room around him. Its furnishings and decor, he quickly realizes, are startlingly similar to his father's, and at that, he shifts his weight uneasily. The mustard-hued latticework wallpaper, the breakfront full of crystal cut back in Salzburg, the fine Oriental rug beneath the small oaken table on which rests a recent issue of *Godey's Lady's Book,* the oil paintings of faraway cityscapes like those found in

Charleston and Rome. In one corner, a bamboo birdcage inhabited by a stuffed red macaw, given to the Bloom family by a Brazilian *empresário* several years before. On the mahogany bookshelves, tomes on entrepreneurship and Talmudic study. Beside them, a silver *menorah* and engraved *kiddush* cup. It is a Jewish room, there is little doubt.

From the antique rapier above the mantel to the Georgian longcase grandfather clock that now seems with each swing of its brass pendulum a metronomic notching of his own great failures, Abrams finds the parlor's resemblance to his father's uncanny. He is growing increasingly ill-at-ease. He tugs at his collar. His eyes dart around him. He expects the ghost of I. J. Lieber to drift through the door at any given moment.

He looks down abashedly to his new boots, unable to quell the image arisen of his father in a pool of black blood, his ribs parted by Wolfe's long, thin blade. He fidgets on the leather sofa. He coughs into his fist. Looking for a distraction from the memories that now surge brutally through him, he withdraws from his billfold those sprigs of parsley and mint he plucked from a neighbor's herb garden along the way there. Ruminating upon the killing he helped commit in all but the same room as the one in which he now waits, he begins to chew most soberly. His breath may be clean upon Nora's arrival, but this is an inauspicious beginning. The minutes that follow are eternal.

Violet returns with tea and a few old ginger biscuits. Quietly, he thanks her. She leaves with a grunt.

Not five minutes more pass when, to the great clattering of Abrams' heart and swimming of his mind, he succumbs at last to the oppressive familiarity of the room, its walls closing in, its heat grown infernal. Nearly overturning his cup and saucer, he thus bolts to his feet and bustles out of that parlor, bumping into Violet in the doorway as she arrives to check on the sound of clanging porcelain.

"Reckon I'll be off then," he mumbles, unable to meet her eyes. "Them flowers on the table, they're yours, you want 'em." He tips his bowler and flees the house as though it were afire.

Only twenty minutes later does Abrams come to realize the path he has just wandered. He has passed by the Dispersed of Judah on Carondelet a dozen times, its first location on Canal a dozen more, in each instance to case it for wealthy congregants on their way home from the sort of religious service he has forever dodged and disdained. Once, on Canal, he stopped to read the engraved plaque sealed into the portal. Below a Hebrew inscription that looked to Abrams like some idiot child's scrawl, in English he read, *This building was first erected and used as a place of worship for non Israelites; but through the liberality of Judah Touro (a son of Israel) it was purchased and donated to the "Hebrew Congregation of the Dispersed of Judah" as a place of prayer to the Most Holy God, the sole Lord and Creator to whom be praises everlastingly. In testimony of which this stone is solemnly deposited beneath the portal through which the faithful are to enter to praise the Lord.*

Abrams chose never to enter that building.

Instead, when not working his scams with Jules Bouchard the monte man, he would affect a wretched air on its stone steps, begging alms from the departing Hebrews with one hand while filching wallets and watches with the other. In truth, during his youth, Abrams had thought himself a master of the Jews' stupidity. Counting out his spoils, he would chuckle cynically afterward, these congregants' willingness to trust so blindly in the misery of others. More pathetic still was their willingness to pay in hopes of easing that misery, as though philanthropy might purchase a way into the arms of a society that did not want them, nor ever truly would. At least, as a new orphan, Abrams felt he was beginning to understand the coldness of the Christian world, having learned through months of indifference that no amount of bribery would ever gain him warmth from it. And this was his developing opinion of humanity before he met Silas Wolfe. Oftentimes, though, Abrams' thieving proved to be unnecessary, for he received so many coins of condolence he ultimately decided it was not worth the risk of capture. That he was eventually captured, and that capture led to his introduction to the orphanage and thus to Wolfe, he would for years dismiss as a mere hazard of his trade. He heard words like *mitzvah* and *shanda* as the money rained down into his cupped hands, but he had no use for these words' meaning. He wanted only as much from these people as might enrich him.

At present, however, standing in front of the enormous Greek Revivalist building on Carondelet, its thick white columns like those Carlson once described of the great Parthenon in Athens, its size comparable, Abrams wants from this temple something else entirely. *Nefutzoh Yehuda*, or Dispersed of Judah, looms before him, its spear-tipped outer iron gates protecting his darling Nora Bloom within from the unruly gentile streets. Its doors, twenty feet high apiece, hewn of stout oak, welcome only those powerful enough to open them. Although he admired the rugged terrain of Arkansas and Missouri, believing the land there to be ineffably divine, Abrams now concedes that places of worship such as this might accommodate gods of their own after all.

The idea scares him to no end. It scares him because he has heard over the years from pious, wide-eyed men of God's wrath, how the Lord delights in showering fire and brimstone with impossible accuracy upon those who transgress. There is no escape, they say. The Lord is King. He judges all and, in this, is without mercy. Now, standing before the synagogue, Abrams does not know how literally this God punishes, whether by lightning bolt or some more insidious method, but in terms of transgression, he can no longer deny the sins he has committed.

Still, he enters. It is the first time he has ever crossed a synagogue's threshold. His Adam's apple bobs with each tentative step forward; his palms perspire like a penitent's. An outsider in an outsider's community, a man without kin or shared creed, without a sense of belonging even to a culture that itself does not belong, Abrams has never felt more alienated. Inside are *his* God, *his* people, and yet, he knows nothing of them.

Inside, too, might be absolution. Inside is Miss Nora Bloom. He is driven onward.

Beyond the vestibule, the large oaken doors closed gently behind him, the small foyer blossoms quickly into a cavernous room of prayer. It is awe-inspiring, easily two hundred feet deep by eighty feet tall, the domed ceiling buttressed from within by another set of huge pillars. Stars of David adorn that ceiling, their intersecting triangles in gold, their recessed, half-spherical backdrops in royal blue. Six windows of intricately laid stained glass frame Abrams on either side, luminous in their reds and yellows from the autumn sunlight streaming through. Together, they signify the twelve tribes of Israel, though there is no way for Abrams to know this. Instead, he looks at the small penned-in area to his left, where an assembly of well-dressed house slaves sits patiently corralled, silently biding their time until their masters' prayers are done.

But it is the sea of Hebrews in the oaken pews ahead of him that overwhelms Abrams most. He has never seen so many members of his faith in one place. He is a stranger among them, he knows this, a hypocrite, a traitor to their beliefs, but then, he has come here of his own choosing.

Only he is more uneasy than he could have imagined. He fears he has made a terrible mistake.

Ashamed, feeling grossly out of place for knowing so little about these people whose blood he shares, Abrams is stricken immobile. Of that scarecrow Jew he erected years before, he knew nothing of its construction other than what his mother had suggested, Gerta herself stretching the limits of her knowledge of their faith. He now feels sheepish for this ignorance, and quickly snatches his bowler off his head to offer one of the few tokens of respect the Christian world has successfully bred into him. Abrams' blush quickly deepens as his confusion grows, however, for in observing the congregation more closely, he sees that the heads of the men—those few who remain, the war having already thinned their ranks—are all covered, as are the outnumbering women's by scarves and bonnets. Some sport small skullcaps, along with the prayer shawls draped over their shoulders, while others wear their daily stovepipes and toppers, but every male head bears a hat. Unsure what to do, Abrams thus puts his bowler back on and ducks into a pew in the last row.

To his surprise, he meets the dark eyes of an elderly Jewess beside him. They are intelligent, those eyes, possessing an air of wealth and dignified assurance that Abrams cannot help but admire. She is immaculately dressed in black, her hoopskirt's girth eager for bench length, the coral cameo at her throat of fine craftsmanship, her Bavolet bonnet of the best French lace. She is inspecting him with interest, searching his own eyes for an answer to a question he has not yet been asked. Then, after appearing to find what she is looking for, she grins and pats his knee twice. Abrams smiles in reply.

It takes another few seconds to realize he is surrounded by women alone.

The congregation is segregated by gender. He does not know that the wooden-railed partition is called a *mechitza* or that women are positioned toward the rear to keep male thoughts pure and focused on their worship ahead. Abrams knows simply that he has committed—yet again—some sort of insult, and so stands awkwardly to leave, only to be gently pulled back down by the elderly Jewess at his side. Her smile tells him that he need fear nothing. Her hand is warm on his; he breathes easier for it. Slowly, he returns to his seat.

"Whatever the cause or the result of the present agitation may be," intones Reverend Gutheim before them, his voice a deep baritone, "every good citizen ought, with moderation and wisdom, to espouse the cause of right and justice, be ready for all sacrifices, and, discarding all prejudice and self-interest, exhibit a true and pure patriotism." He stops to allow his words their significance. "Actuated by such a spirit, we may at all times assuredly count on the protection of Providence, and look with a cheerful countenance into the immediate future."

Reverend Gutheim halts here once more, his hands gripping each side of the pulpit, his kind yet penetrating gaze scanning his worshippers for those who would not believe in Providence or the merits of moderation and wisdom. He is a distinguished-looking gentleman, his silvered beard and hair well-shorn, his black suit impeccably contoured to his trim body, his *tallith* of white silk, the *kippa* on his head elaborately woven with the finest golden thread. A native of Menne, Westphalia, James Koppel Gutheim was once a student at the Teachers' Seminary in Muenster, where he earned a diploma in Hebrew proficiency but not rabbinical ordination. Following brief stints in New York, Cincinnati, and across town in New Orleans at the Gates of Mercy, he finally settled at the Dispersed of Judah synagogue in 1853.

Later, in April of the oncoming year, five and a half months after that November day when Abrams first enters the temple where he now sits among the wrong sex, after Federal Admiral David Glasgow Farragut finally charges up the Mississippi from the Gulf to conquer New Orleans once and for all, rather than take an oath of allegiance to the Union, Gutheim will leave New Orleans altogether, preferring exile from the city he loves over capitulation to a government he so despises. On that day in November, however, Gutheim knows none of this. He does not know that he will soon be splitting his time between congregations in Montgomery, Alabama, and Columbus, Georgia, or that in 1868 he will return to New York, the heart of his enemy, where he will stay a short time until he is recalled to New Orleans to be named rabbi of the new Temple Sinai. He does not know that he will remain at that temple until his death in 1886, a man at peace with his place in the world. Nor does he know that the newest member of his congregation, the wounded soldier now sitting in error beside a mother who lost two sons at Manassas, feels to owe him a debt of gratitude beyond expression, beyond measure. Or that this same soldier is, at the moment, seeking his own inner peace, wishing above all to atone for past crimes for which he seems unable to find forgiveness. This, as that same soldier scrutinizes the pews for the face of a young woman he has neither seen nor met but one day hopes to marry.

Indeed, standing before his flock of believers, Reverend Gutheim is assured of two facts, and two facts alone: that the Confederate States of America deserve the fullness of the Almighty's love and attention, and that humankind, for all its flaws and failures, must strive however unfeasibly toward its own salvation.

28

The service ends shortly thereafter.

When Abrams is offered a warm, guttural greeting in a language he does not understand from the elderly woman to his right, a demure smile from another in the pew ahead, he merely nods and mutters. He avoids their gazes by hastily exiting the building.

Once outside, at the base of the great steps where those slaves, once sequestered within, now prepare their owners' carriages, Abrams watches the worshippers leave for home. Overhearing the banter they share, their quips and compliments, he is surprised to find that in spite of their education and breeding and attempted assimilation, he no longer holds these Hebrews in contempt for the lives they have chosen. Some may be fools, others cheats and scoundrels, but it dawns on him that possessing such traits has nothing to do with their faith. He is delighted by the sense of pardon he feels for them.

Young women of all shapes and sizes, though of similarly dark complexion, tease one another and skip down the synagogue's stone steps, chattering on about next season's dress patterns from *Graham's Illustrated Magazine*, about men, about which Brontë sister they prefer, about the Canal Street soldiers' parade soon to begin. Their hoopskirts sway like great, cumbersome bells with each step descended, the fringes of their paletots' capes rippling across each dainty back. Abrams sees their joy, their childish femininity, and is likewise shocked to discover that though these girls know nothing of brutality, he now hopes that they never will. Whereas months before he would have happily introduced them to his world of disease and degeneracy, Abrams is suddenly content to allow them to go the remainder of their delicate lives without the knowledge that such a world exists. He envies their ignorance, true, but he no longer blames them for it.

Abrams considers skulking ahead to where Melpomene meets Hercules, to loiter on the corner he knows Miss Nora Bloom must soon pass, but then decides there is no nobility in setting such a crude trap. He will return to her home instead, as quickly as his wounded form will take him, hoping that Violet will again allow him entrance. He admits little difference in these two plans other than that in the comfort of her own surroundings, he expects Nora to view him more as a respectable soldier granted welcome by a trusted servant than as some lurking vagabond.

Abrams understands that his brief time attending the service has not changed him. His soul is not cleansed. And yet, that he entered the temple at all, that he dared to embrace an experience he had for years scorned, he feels within him a burgeoning maturity that, were he to foster it tenderly, might give rise to a newfound sense of hope he had no idea he had been so wanting.

—

Minutes after Abrams enters the Bloom household a second time, Violet chuckling as she leaves him, two girls burst into the parlor where he waits amid an enormous bustle of crinoline. They are giggling, their freed, thick sable hair cascading over their breasts and backs, their entrance filling the room with the familiar scents of rosehips and lavender talc. In their blue Sabbath dresses, with small hands covering their tittering mouths, they are undoubtedly related. "And that lieutenant in the third pew," one is saying, "have you *ever*—oh my." She gasps, interrupted by the presence of a strange man standing awkwardly before them.

His hat in one hand, the reclaimed peonies in the other, Abrams struggles to compose himself. At last he is presented with Miss Nora Bloom, her hair showing darker than pitch, but hers, he believes with a gulp, is a divine pollution. Outside, people are racing toward Canal Street, hoping to find a vantage from which to watch the soldiers' procession, set to begin in just a few minutes time. Violet is nowhere to be found. The parlor is silent. "Miss Nora," he says at last, offering a stiff bow. He is looking at the wrong girl.

Nora Bloom steps forward. She is the less comely of the two.

He turns his attention to her. He licks his lips. "Miss Nora," he repeats. "I'm Abrams." He thrusts the flowers at her, his elbow locking rigidly.

Nora's face puzzles in reply, her mind attempting to find purchase in his name's meaning. Finally, just as Abrams is about to sputter forth an explanation, upon a dawning recognition, her face blooms into the most voluminous joy he has ever witnessed. It is marvelous, her reaction, her entire face illuminating with delight. She squeals. She claps her hands once. She bounces, her eyes almost closing in their happiness, as though, unable to compete with the enormity of her smile, her other facial features have gladly surrendered to the elation registered best by her mouth alone. Other than this eruptive grin, however, she is unremarkable in aspect. Her breasts are still developing. Her nose has a high, broad bridge. Acne dots her forehead in small, dainty clusters. But that smile. *Goddamn,* thinks Abrams to himself, inhaling with pleasure. *I'll be a son-of-a-bitch if that face didn't just break into a million pieces of smile.*

The next few hours will prove to be the best he has ever known.

As the three of them sit in the parlor, the circumference of the girls' skirts taking up half the room, Nora's large brown eyes are alight as she immediately begins to pepper Abrams with question after question. About the front, about the morale of the men, about the manner in which he suffered his wounds. "You poor man," she declares. "Does it hurt much? Is there anything I can do?"

Abrams smiles wryly. In the end, he decided against requesting that she wrap him in a fresh dressing. Back in his room on Dauphine while drying himself off from his bath, he came to decide—only just—that bullying the Nora Blooms of the world into love, even if it exists as an appeal to their goodness, is not a just method of courtship. He will rely on the honesty and strength of his person or nothing at all. "I'm fine," he responds at length. "But thank you kindly."

She is relieved, she says. She can scarcely sit still. She spills the tea she pours him and giggles in shame for it. Violet returns with a crystal vase in which Josephine, Nora's older, prettier sister, carefully arranges the peonies. "They're glorious," says Nora with an admiring sigh. "Simply glorious."

"I'm glad for it," says Abrams, nodding into his teacup.

Their mother, Nora explains, parted with the girls after services to visit with a family friend over hands of whist and cups of black-market pekoe. Their father is serving as a sutler in the Virginia campaign. As she tells him this, of their family and friends, Nora knows she will be rebuked should her mother learn that a gentleman has come calling unannounced, and that his stock will be questioned because of it. But she does not mind. Rather, she likens the delicious abruptness of the events now unfolding before her to the most melodramatically rendered *Beadle's Dime Novel*, for Nora Bloom, like all unripened romantics, still prefers to lend those few perfect moments of her life to fiction.

She mentions his letters. "I received your second only last week. But were you to ask anyone in this house, Mr. Abrams, they'll assure you I've done nothing but speak glowingly of you time and again throughout these past months. Tell him, Josie."

"Indeed she has," laughs Josephine, her eyes rolling in agreement. "She's positively been a mynah, this one."

Of his letters, Abrams demurs, claiming that he is no poet. He admits to the help he received in their drafting. He falls silent. He then leans forward and places his cup deliberately in its saucer. He furrows his brow, frustrated in his search for the correct words. "Miss Nora," he manages at last, his tone excruciatingly earnest, "see, it's *you* who done the miracle here, not me."

She laughs at his sincerity, a sudden, surprising laughter that calls to mind gusts of springtime wind blown through a clutch of dangling sweetmilk bottles. Then, to the skipping of Abrams' heart, she touches his knee with the tips of her fingers in appreciation of his comments. He studies the delicacy of her hand, finding it no bigger than a child's. How desperately he wishes to clasp it to his breast, to awaken beside her to the sound of rain on a tin roof, warmed by the embrace of each other's arms, their legs entwined in clean linen sheets. How he wishes to see her alongside him gardening in the years to come, to see them dancing together to string music finer than he has ever heard, to be in love with her, she with him, for the rest of their lives. Blood thunders in his ears so passionately he can hardly hear himself think, all because a young woman he barely knows has touched him in a place scores of women have previously touched him, but never before to such a thrill. There is nothing overtly sexual in the gesture, he realizes this. It is misguided innocence, nothing more. Still, he swallows. "It's a damned fool thing to say, I know it," he wishes to tell her, "it ain't my style in the least, but plain and simple, it's you, Miss Nora. You."

He is embarrassed. He can find no words. Instead, he simply bores nakedly into her eyes with his own.

She stops laughing. She removes her hand from his knee as though scalded by it. Her face flushes. She has never been looked at so.

Although his grammar is poor, his diction clearly born into streets far muddier than those she usually strolls, she finds the figure and depth this young soldier presents her to be indisputably magnetic. She is fascinated by his earthen upbringing. She likes the looks of him. His profile is Semitic and strong, his mind evidently quick. She is charmed by his halting manner. The timbre of his voice is masculine and soothing, his lack of facial hair she finds pleasantly boyish. His brooding hazel eyes, despite their fierceness, when gazed into bear a sorrow that makes her heart throb. The scar above his lip, she has decided, she hopes to one day stroke with her finger.

Josephine is raptly attentive, too, but as acting chaperone to her younger sister's first official suitor, she concedes that her presence is no longer warranted despite the etiquette demanding it. As such, she places her China cup into its saucer and stands to excuse herself. To the tinkling of his own cup, Abrams stands beside her. "Miss Josie," he nods, but his focus is on Nora alone.

"Mr. Abrams," says Josephine with a curtsy, then leaves the room.

He returns to his seat beside Nora, silence now falling heavily between them. They are young and full of turbulent emotion. They do not know how to express the longing they share. Their hearts rage in their throats, their stomachs are hollow, yet together, theirs is a perfect silence. It is an artist's use of vacancy, the lack of something implying a whole.

Soon, the ache in her chest booming in ways for which her most fervent imaginings could not have prepared her, Nora is forced to turn away. "Shall we play some Beggar-My-Neighbor then?" Already, she is reaching for a deck of cards.

Abrams clears his throat and clumsily consults the pocket watch he stole from the battlefield back at Oak Hills. "That review's fixin' to get started any minute," he says, carefully stretching his side. "Figure you'd be wantin' to scout it out." He holds his breath before adding, "'Course, if you cared for an escort, I'd be happy to lend an elbow, broke though it may be."

Her eyes are large and honest and devastate him where he sits. "Providing it's all the same to you, Mr. Abrams," she says in a voice little more than a whisper, "I do believe I'm reviewing the only soldier I care to see."

29

It is after midnight and Abrams is by now staggeringly drunk. Experiencing a capacity for jubilation he did not know he possessed, after leaving the Bloom home and securing Nora's gift of a Burmese silk scarf around his neck as sling, after devouring almost a pound of *boudin* sausage from its links of intestinal casing and retrieving his LeMat revolver from his room on Dauphine, Abrams' first celebratory act of the night was to head off for a fresh bottle and a moderately expensive fuck.

He found both at D'Artagnan's, an upscale brothel on Ursulines known for its stable of imported Parisian whores and its fine collection of port. There, a quarter bottle of rye hastily dispatched, he marched up the stairs following the firm buttocks of Mireille, his good hand in hers, his sling-bound hand clenching the whiskey to his hip. With each stair he climbed, he chuckled at the memory of his playing Beggar-My-Neighbor with the girl he fully expects to one day call his wife. This, while an entire battalion of eligible soldiers of nobler birth and superior education paraded but six blocks away. *Goddamn if she didn't choose to spend her time with me, though,* he marveled to himself. *Private Elias Abrams, redemptioner's child, backroom card-flipper, how d'you do?* At the brothel, halfway up the stairs to a forthcoming orgasm, Abrams shook his head in smiling disbelief. That he could have easily cheated Nora at cards, and did not, he believes attests to his devotion.

Throughout his time at D'Artagnan's, during which he ejaculated twice and polished off much of his bottle, he rarely stopped talking about his visit to Hercules Street. With Mireille straddled gently atop him due to his wounded condition, her feet flat on the mattress, her knees bent toward him to provide leverage and spring, Abrams discoursed upward and at length on Nora's wit and smile, on her delicate touch and generosity of soul. He spoke of her refinement and the language that she used, of her enchanting scent of rosehips and lavender talc. He spoke of the names he planned to give their male children and of the resolutions to the arguments they will never have.

Mireille, ever the professional, in her broken English asked whether he would prefer to call her Miss Nora instead. "Many, many mens," she said, "zey do zis."

Abrams stopped her fucking in mid-stroke. "No offense, now," he replied, "but my Miss Nora don't belong between no red satin sheets."

A half-hour later, standing above her as he buckled his belt, Abrams kissed the top of Mireille's head at precisely the spot where her greasy hair parted. Sitting slumped on the mattress, she cupped his cock delicately in return.

"Iz not fair, *toi*," she said desolately, "to give such a geeft as you have to one girl alone. Zis Nora had better be happy for eet."

Abrams laughed at the lie. As much as anyone he knows, he has long admired a good swindle. For her attempted guile, he awarded Mireille another dollar.

Not long after, his new undergarments fresh between his legs, his pants hitched high, Elias Abrams, drunk and well-fucked, is whistling his way toward Gallatin Street. He struts with a bravado best known among young men in love and those who have never once experienced it. Along the way, he stops dead in his tracks. He thinks of Nora Bloom's eruptive smile, of the following day's promised visit, of Mireille's gifted mouth on him, of his mouth on her, of the whiskey distilling in his gut, of the sounds of night in the city of his birth. He sighs. He has never been so content.

Abrams inhales the raw air into his lungs, his nostrils wide as he breathes in the faint odors of mold and horseshit and fecund Mississippi riverbank earth. He detects notes of deep-fried meats and rank perfumes. Surrounding him, crickets chirp their last of the year, the freeze advancing on New Orleans this night poised to silence them all for winter. He hears the cacophony of several Gallatin Street concert saloons ahead, pianos tinkling within them, their patrons roaring and banging tables as they strain to catch sight of, if for a split-second, the swollen, scabrous crotches of those long-legged *clodoche* dancers they will gladly pay between acts to fuck in broom closets. The most debauched barrelhouses and gin mills destroy their patrons' livers for five cents an evening. Gas lamps flicker, failing to light the nooks of the French Quarter night in which a whole host of devilry lurks. Suddenly, a scampering rat forces Abrams, in a joy bred of inebriation and new love, to whip the LeMat clumsily from his belt. Weaving unsteadily on his feet and breathing windily through his nose, the large pistol bobbing in his attempt to level it, with a squinted eye Abrams struggles to focus on tracking the rat with his gunsights. His revolver hand sweeping poorly in pursuit, he then pops his wrist and whispers a soft "pichew!" to echo the sound of a shot disrupting the night. But he does not fire. Instead, as the rat scurries safely away, Abrams eases into a grin and stands tall, lazily jamming the LeMat back into his belt. "I'd of got you, Silas Wolfe," he proclaims with a hiccuping nod. "I sure as shit would've."

At the moment, he fears nothing, for he is not only emboldened by his love for Miss Nora Bloom, but the whiskey in his blood shields Abrams against whatever might do him harm. And in the invincibility he feels, he has decided with a declaratory pat to the LeMat that it is time, once and for all, to attend to those most dangerous and pressing of affairs. Indeed, in the words of Professor John Lee Carlson, for the mercy of his encumbered soul, he must set right this wrong.

It is at Truett's Saloon, the scene of the pimp Blackwell's thrashing years before, that Abrams finally tracks down the Cypress Stump Boys.

The room has changed since he last burst drunkenly through its swinging doors. Where once a visitor entered a dark, iniquitous den comprised of a few rickety tables and chairs and dastardly men who stole and stabbed, Abrams now finds a surprisingly opulent court of sorts. On the walls, in place of the longhorns, with a sobering shudder he spots his father's oil paintings. On the floor, the bloody parlor Oriental, well-scrubbed. The plankwood bar itself has been torn down and erected true. Built of iron studs and cypress timber—the namesake wood of those who demanded its restoration—its brass rails gleam in the lamplight. Abrams does not know that since his enlistment, the Cypress Stump Boys have claimed the saloon as their own, slaying two members of a rival gang feared for its use of smithy bellows in blasting arsenic cloud-bombs into its victims' faces, in the fierce effort to stake their territory.

Truett Jones, the establishment's thick-set owner, wears a cravat knotted at his throat above his oilskin apron as he wipes down the bar with a rag. Garters gird his silken sleeves, his Derby boots he keeps spit-shined. His beaver bell crown top hat is brushed to perfection. He has little say in the matter. Successful as they have become now that many of their competitors have been vanquished or are off fighting, the Cypress Stump Boys have outgrown a squalid image of themselves and thus require those with whom they interact to dress accordingly.

Abrams is stunned by the saloon's transformation, but the back of the room presents the most head-clearing surprise. For there, lounging on the floor among Moroccan cushions, whores, and a variety of jugs, laze the Cypress Stump Boys. And in the midst of them, enthroned in a large, claw-footed chair behind what was once I. J. Lieber, Esq.'s, own large, claw-footed desk of the same design, sits the terrifically bored, kingly presence of Silas Wolfe himself.

Abrams takes a deep breath. He plants his feet solidly apart. In the span of seconds he has gone from slaphappy to stone serious, jolted by the sight of his father's furnishings and the fact that Silas Wolfe, once prone to sprawling among his brethren with unmatched abandon, seems now to have detached himself from such pursuits in the aloof manner of the most despotic of men. The LeMat, only minutes before flailing cockily in the night air, feels suddenly moored to Abrams' belly. "Silas," he says warily. "Boys."

Wolfe looks up from his thin cigar, his gray eyes narrowing. Then, as has been his custom for as long as Abrams has known him, his mouth creeps into that seductive smile. It is more than charming. It is like barely hugging yourself warm from a chill, like catching a second's worth of yourself in a street-side windowpane. And in that second's reflection, without looking very hard, you fail to spot all those things that no one teaches you to look for when facing yourself on gray days in November. You do not see the series of small, bifurcating wrinkles around your eyes, wrinkles that were not there but moments before. You do not notice the steady northward recession of your thinning hair or the beginnings of your first double chin. In the breadth of that smile, you do not take the time to see how bloated your eyes have become, your cheeks, rounder than they once were, or your skin, gray like winter. You look at Wolfe's lips and teeth and you do not know that they are slowly devouring you. You may feel it vaguely, tragically, deep in your bones, that you are being aged by the Devil's very presence, but you do not know it for certain. Such is Silas Wolfe's smile. It bears the power to wilt.

"Elias Abrams," he whispers, clapping his hands in delight, "my, oh my. Boys!" he then shouts, slapping the desk hard, "looky here!"

Goliath Mueller, his blond hair longer than Abrams has ever seen it, throws aside his whore and quickly leaps to his feet. Tasker Gundy, propped on an elbow, spits out a persimmon slice to laugh from his supine position, his head tossed back in glee. Jimmy Byrne draws on his pipe and offers Abrams a slightly approving smile. Placide Arceneaux, the quiet killer, has in the meantime gone silently for his blade. It is this man, Abrams knows, who must be most closely watched. But for the strictures of his Creole code, Arceneaux would surely be the deadliest of them all.

Wolfe's eyes fall in sympathy at the sight of Abrams' sling. "Aw, no," he clucks, "seems our little birdie here's broken a wing."

Abrams looks down at his arm. He lifts it. "Ain't nothin'," he says.

"Well, of course it is, honey. Of course it is." Wolfe gently places his cigar in a marble ashtray, then stands and stretches his back. He is taller than Abrams, but just as lean. His jaw is angular and clean-shaven, his nose strong. His mane of thick, black hair, slicked back with a twice-weekly application of scented pomade, has also lengthened, and now curls behind his ears. He slaps the whore who had been sitting on the arm of his chair lightly across the cheek, but hard enough to garner her full attention. "Our little broken-winged birdie's in need of some re-freshment," he says. "Go fetch the twelve-year-old."

Abrams hardly recognizes her. Yet there stands Angeline, his first fuck who through patience and puppy dog affection eventually matured into his first love. She has since withered under Wolfe's nurturance, and though her eyes flit toward Abrams, he can detect no life there. She offers him only a flash of acknowledgment before her gaze once more goes lifeless. Whatever Gaelic beauty she may have possessed has faded, her lustrous red-auburn hair now thin and oily, her freckled cheeks gone sallow. She carries herself with the portage of an oft-whipped dog, her shoulders hunched.

"Say there," says Wolfe, noticing this exchange between them, his eyes wet with gloating, "y'all two was friends once, huh? Intimates even?"

Abrams tries to ignore Wolfe's gambit, knowing perfectly well why Angeline has been chosen as his most recent target of cruelty. He smiles apologetically at her for it.

She, in turn, takes a timid step toward the saloon doors and then flinches, her fingers brought tentatively to her lips. "About that twelve-year-old," she asks Wolfe, holding her breath. "Girl or boy?"

"*Whiskey*, you dumb cunt," laughs Wolfe. "Go fetch the twelve-year-old *whiskey*." She scurries over to the barkeep. Wolfe returns his interest to Abrams. "Women," he says, rolling his eyes, his smile immaculate.

"Got three holes in 'em already, you count the mouth 'longside the cunt and bung, but Lord knows, sometimes I wish I could give 'em all a fourth—right between the fuckin' eyes, I say."

The Cypress Stump Boys laugh wickedly. Abrams remains silent.

Wolfe strolls from behind the large desk. His charcoal evening suit is woven of the finest Lincolnshire woolens, the lapels of its fitted frock-coat extending sharply toward his shoulders, a waistcoat snug to his chest beneath them. All the men, in fact, appear to be dressed in clothing of high refinement. From the saloon's renovations to their ivory-tipped canes and new habiliments, it is evident that in Abrams' absence, the Cypress Stump Boys have done quite well indeed. With the first Confederate military draft still months away, clearly these young men are content to forge ahead with their lots in life. "Now would y'all just look at our soldier boy here?" says Wolfe admiringly. "Why, 'cept for that crippled little wing, some might say you make a damned scrumptious sight, Private Abrams. You kill anyone yet?"

"Silas," says Abrams again. It is all he can muster. Drunk as he was on his way down from Ursulines, Abrams had practiced the mumbling speech he planned to give upon their meeting. He had imagined he would stand defiantly before his old friend to inform him that he has had enough of this game, that he holds no grudges but demands to know Wolfe's intentions. Then, once granted a satisfactory answer, Abrams had expected to declare that he has moved beyond their path, that he has seen death on a scale too massive to recount and been exposed to kindnesses of which he previously did not believe possible. Abrams wished to explain that he must atone for the sins he has committed. And the way to atone for such sins, he had envisioned himself telling Wolfe, was to first understand those who shared in them.

Now, however, standing in front of the Cypress Stump Boys—men with whom he had laughed and loved and loafed for years, men he supposed might even come to his defense once he explained himself—Abrams finds he can voice none of it. Standing before them, much as he did following his botched affair with Cobb and Petitgout, he realizes that there is no sanctity in this kind of forthright confrontation. *It's a fuckin' lark,* he thinks bitterly, *a fuckin' sham. Men'll rape children in this godforsaken world, they'll kill a gal after plowin' her in the ass, they'll beat kittens with shovelheads till there ain't nothin' left but blood and pulp, yet here I am, tryin' to act all noble?* He spits. *Goddamn if you ain't one greenhorn fuck, Elias Abrams. Goddamn if you ain't.* Though he is young, he has lived in this world. He should know better. He remembers how close he came to death that night with the cousins from Algiers, and his knees nearly buckle for it.

"Honey?" prods Wolfe. He is leaning against a corner of the desk, his arms folded across his chest. His smile is enormous. "Believe I asked if you killed anyone yet."

"We got air between us, Silas," states Abrams finally. "And I'm here to clear it."

"Ah, so then the answer's no." Wolfe retrieves his cigar from the ashtray and takes a long, deliberate drag. He nods once, emphatically. "Clear air's fine," he says, exhaling. "I'm fond of clear air. Placide, how 'bout you? You fond of clear air?"

Placide admits that he is.

"Tasker, you?"

"Fuckin' love it."

"Goliath?"

"Naw." Mueller spits. "Not me."

"Aw, Goliath," fusses Wolfe, "you ain't got cause to hate your lungs so, strappin' feller such as yourself." The cigar clenched in his teeth, he then walks over and glides his hands over the brute's massive shoulders, sliding them tenderly down over his side to cup his ribcage. "You gotta love them lungs, Goliath," he whispers into Mueller's ear, hugging the man tightly to him. "Love 'em." He stands straight and returns his attention to Abrams. "Please Elias, do sit."

"I'm awright where I'm at."

209

The smile vanishes from Wolfe's face, his eyes deadening at Abrams' disobedience. "Goliath," he demands, "move some of them pillows, get our soldier boy here a seat." His tone says he is not to be trifled with.

Mueller does as he is bidden, the other men moving to accommodate the chair in which Abrams quickly sits. Returned to his place behind the claw-footed desk, Wolfe bridges his fingers into a steeple of airy contemplation. Angeline in the meantime, with a stealth born of abuse, has left a bottle of twelve-year-old Islay single malt and two crystal tumblers on the desk's blotter, and then retreated quietly into the shadows. "Angie," says Wolfe, his eyes leveled evenly at Abrams. "Pour."

She darts forward from the recesses of the room to obey him. Once done, again she recedes into the dark.

"Drink?"

Abrams knows better than to refuse. The crystal, he quickly recognizes, is from his father's set.

Wolfe studies his glass. He sniffs. "Speakin' of clear air," he says absently, "heard tell air up in old Missouri's purer'n hell. Not like this New Orleans swill we're forced to snort every goddamned day. That true?"

Abrams is aware that he must keep himself in check. He detests Wolfe's antic innocence, yet he knows he has thoughtlessly placed himself, once again, in grave danger. His ears are hot with self-recrimination for it. To make a mistake once, he knows, is forgivable. But twice? His saliva has turned to gall in his mouth. If he lives through the night, he swears he will never again act so recklessly. Considering the peril in which he again finds himself, however, he is doubtful he will ever get the chance to learn from these mistakes. "Pure enough, guess."

"Well then, if it's clear air you're seekin', you best head back on up to where it's at." Wolfe leans forward with a devilish wink. "Seems to me you made yourself a commitment, Elias, once you went ahead'n enlisted."

"Reckon so." Abrams coughs into his fist. "Soon's you and me get a couple things settled, I'll gladly be on my way."

Wolfe's eyes go flat. His mind quickly traces the course of prospective events, moving beyond plot and intrigue toward points of hard conclusion. He considers the revolver he spotted jutting out of Abrams' belt. He purses his lips judiciously. With narrowed eyes, he takes a meditative drag on his cigar. Finally, just as Abrams is about to explain himself further, Wolfe reaches into the desk to withdraw a soiled envelope, which he flaps lazily in the air for Abrams' inspection. He holds it to his nose, his eyebrows arching, impressed by the faint scents of rosehips and lavender talc.

Abrams' bottom lip quivers once.

"Some chickenfuck or other," yawns Wolfe, "just sent this on down from Missouri, home to all that good, clear air." He tosses the letter onto the desktop.

Abrams drops his forehead into his good hand. No poker face exists for this type of surprise. He stares at the floor but sees nothing. His mind has gone blank. His mouth flushes anew with the taste of something bilious. Out of necessity, he had grown to believe, dangerously, it is now evident, that Carlson was correct: providing he had gotten his hands on it at all, Petitgout would never use the letter to advantage. Had Abrams let himself think otherwise, he would have been unable to sleep since noticing its loss.

Clearly, he could not have been more wrong.

"You come here," says Wolfe, "broke down like some old mule in need of a bullet to the brain, all ready to make demands? You, of us? Without a killin' to your name even?" He laughs. "No."

"Silas, wait—"

Wolfe holds up his hand. "Now you skedaddled after that little to-do on Toulouse Street, fine. You had your reasons, thought you might be in a pinch. Believe I can accept that, even though I took some offense to it, truth be told. Hurt me, honey. Hurt me bad. Like I'd do anything to harm you, all the years we've known each other. Please."

Abrams knows better than to believe what he is being told. Had he stayed behind, he is certain he would be long dead.

"But see, honey," says Wolfe, "you *did* leave, you *did* hurt me—not so much as a quick 'adieu' even—and for it, don't know if I can forgive you quite yet. And them I can't forgive don't get a whole lot of second chances, you know that. Still, that don't mean I ain't above considerin' the circumstances that sent you packin' in the first place. Fact is, can't say I much blame you for it."

Mueller growls at where he finds this conversation going, but Wolfe silences him with a stare.

"So believe it or not, Elias, I'll be lettin' you walk outta here tonight, you darlin' bastard son-of-a-corpse, 'cause we got a love, you and me, a love I doubt you even figure on. And since we got us this love, I'm sendin' you on back up to the front, where, more'n learnin' to fulfill them commitments, you're gonna prove you got a big old pair of gorgeous balls between them legs after all." Wolfe stops speaking. He snaps his fingers. Angeline rushes from the dark to pour him another round. He punches her in the ass, hard. She limps in retreat. He takes a sip. "And just how're you gonna prove you got them big old gorgeous balls, you're wonderin'? Well, just this, honey: any chickenfuck I ain't never met who'd turn tattle on my dear, sweet Elias, all to get on my good side? Well, frankly, that chickenfuck don't deserve to scratch the earth a day fuckin' longer, I find. Imagine, scum like that, thinkin' he can best my best man?" He shakes his head mournfully. "Sad state, world's coming to."

Abrams says nothing. His face betrays nothing. He is on the verge of vomiting.

"So's after you're back up there, aside from soldierin' on straight and true, for your own goddamned sake—for *your* own goddamned sake now—you got the bonus chore of slaughterin' this here chickenfuck for the dirt he aimed to do you."

Abrams has no reaction to this. Absolutely none at all.

"Gracious as I'm feelin' tonight," allows Wolfe, "I'll even tell you why. See, Elias, I figure it's high time you did your own killin'. And I don't mean shootin' blind at some fuckin' Lincolnite from across no hayfield, neither. I'm talkin' up close and personal, like lovers and haters. 'Cause Lord knows, this cold world of ours won't truck with them who can't." He takes another contemplative pull on his cigar. "I'm talkin' 'bout something important here, 'bout commitment and justice and such, 'bout learnin' how to fend for your dignity whenever that kind of fending's called for. For your own good, I'm sayin'. And this Petitgout fuck— shit, to my mind, he's as proper a hornbook to start with as anyone. More, even." He shrugs. "'Course, you got a problem with this, we can all of us take a visit over to that little gal's house. Fact is, Goliath here was sayin' the other day how he ain't never tasted no Jew peach. Ain't that so, Goliath?"

"It is."

"Then maybe this one here's got a bit of fuzz you'd like to give a nibble to, huh?"

Abrams bolts to his feet.

"Now, now, Private," says Wolfe with a grin, "you do your chore successful, you outlive your service, you heal up that crippled wing all good and strong, *then* you come back up in here and we'll have a nice long chat, 'bout whatever you want." Wolfe daintily taps his cigar into the ashtray. "And don't you worry that pretty little head neither. Ain't none of us touchin' that Hebrew cunt in the meantime, I swear it." He giggles. "Silly boy."

30

Worn and weary, Abrams arrives at the docks the next morning, escorted by the hulking presence of Goliath Mueller. "Can't for the life of me figure on why Sy's lettin' you scamper," grumbles the large man, his thick forearms folded across his chest. "You was my ward, I'd skin yer hide alive, leave yer goddamned bones to the curs'n buzzards." He shrugs, and runs a hand through his long, golden locks. "Yessir, it's a regular queerness, way that feller's taken with you."

Abrams wants nothing more than to bash this brute's head in. Violence laces his tongue like a turned vintage. He imagines the slow destruction of Mueller's health, the broken limbs and battered features and blood flowing through holes God did not intend mankind. But in his wounded condition, and now, with Nora Bloom's life at stake, Abrams begrudgingly accepts that he must not act.

The night before, the task of slaughtering Petitgout already assigned him, Abrams was promptly held captive by the Cypress Stump Boys until dawn, where they demanded he regale them for hours with stories of the battlefield. Whenever he tried to angle the conversation toward his father's murder, Wolfe calmly brought a finger to his lips and shook his head slowly.

His LeMat yanked from his belt by Mueller at Wolfe's command, made to knock back shot after shot, Abrams soon loosened despite the hatred he felt for his company. Grown sloppily drunk from the fifth of sloshing in his gut, he went on to dourly recount the hardships endured since he last drank among them: the Battle of Oak Hills, the starvation, the privation, the inclement weather, the enemy lead in his back. Only once did he show his frustration. "Well goddamn!" he slurred at one point, jumping to his feet, "y'all want to know what war's like, go on'n join up your own damned selves. I ain't no grinder monkey!"

The boys hushed and looked to Silas Wolfe, who merely smiled and inclined his head to the envelope on his desk.

Abrams wilted into his seat. Grumbling to himself, he knocked back another shot.

On his staggering way out of Truett's Saloon as daylight broke, his eyes drowsily closing with each stumbling pace, arm-in-arm with Wolfe, Mueller a few paces behind, Abrams was bucked awake by a last warning. "Oh, and by the by," Wolfe had whispered into his ear, "if you're thinkin' of sneakin' me by another man's hand, maybe payin' off old Backyard Bobby or that crazy bastard, Fontenot, or one of them other fool assassins, and somethin', shall we say, regretful, befalls me or any of the other boys here, rest assured, honey, whoever's left among us, I can guarantee they'll be headin' on over to that Jew peach's house, munch on her all night long." Here Wolfe snatched Abrams by the chin to offer direct notice. "You gettin' me?"

And so, on his return trip up the Mississippi, Abrams slumbers much of the time, exhausted as he is by a dark and besieging melancholy. When awake, he dwells somberly on the mistakes he has made. He looks about him, helpless. He clamps his eyes shut, grinds his teeth. The past months have seen a steady progression of personal resentments, but never has he been so violently contemptuous of himself. Aboard the steamship he sits alone and pinches his bottom lip, pondering his many sins as he stares at the countryside that passes him by. In truth, he sees very little of the land. *Can't fuckin' feature it,* he thinks to himself, disbelieving. *Honest to God, like some goddamned scourge born to the world.*

Of his father's murder, nothing has been resolved. Of the murder since assigned him, he spits in disgust. Of Nora, while his heart has been proved just in its affections, he cannot stop mulling over the danger in which he has placed her. *Goddamnit all,* he thinks furiously on. *Why's it everyone I care for—poor Angeline, even—they spend a little time with me, get their lives all caught up toward ruination? Answer me that, would you, you goddamned fool.* He pauses before responding to his own rhetoric. *'Cause you're a dim-witted and dangerous fuck, that's why. How 'bout that, Elias? Them reasons enough for you?*

Deprived of the chance to leave an explanation behind, while steaming northward to join his regiment that first morning, Abrams hastily drafts apologies to both Nora and Imogene. In them, he is forced to lie, claiming that his furlough was necessarily revoked for reasons he may not explain. He regrets any inconvenience he might have caused but hopes they will forgive him the duty he has been called upon to fulfill.

After a raging internal debate, he decides at last not to inform Nora of the threat that his enemies now pose her. To sound the alarm, he knows, will do no good. Should Wolfe want her, he will get her; that is irrefutable. Thus, already sick with apology and longing, in misery he concludes, *so while I am gone please try to be viglint against all sorts of badnes out there Keep your eyes wide Miss Nora cause I would find a cliff and jump straight off, I was to learn you were payned in this life by the Evil it owns up to Please be carful out there.*

See, we may be apart for a goodly spell now but you can be sure that meetin you was better then all the holidays of the werld rolled into won I caint say it no plainer then that. You are my selabration of the Spirit.

Fact is my hearts been a stone mostly but with you there to help me bear it up it feels to be as lite as them gentel breaths we shared between us just yesterday. Honest to goodness I do not know how I would ever pick it up agin, my heart, if something poor happened to you So agin please be viglint.

Now I know we are from diffrent worlds and that I dont have the lernin or refinment that you must be used to in all your life. That is trew. But heres

this. I understand that to love something you have to overcome its obstakuls.
So from this day forth I will not think of you as Miss Nora Bloom no more
but I will think of you as my darling Nora, my darling darling Nora. I hope
you aint mad for it I humbley ask that you do not be.

Eternaly yours forever,
Pt. Elias Abrams

Ten days later, mired in the deepest despair of his life, Abrams steps
ashore in Arkansas.

Since his departure for the Creek Agency, since his wounding and
subsequent furlough, the Third Louisiana has moved from Camp Mc-
Culloch, in Missouri, to Cross Hollows, Arkansas, where they are
presently establishing winter quarters.

A scant two miles from the White River, Cross Hollows is located in
a valley running east-west, hemmed in by sheer walls of rock to the
north and south. The terrain around it is a sequence of lofty, stony hills
and confining mountain passes. Encased on all sides by crags and
hillocks, their camp provides shelter from the winds of the angrily advancing season, yet feels to some of the men like a prison from which
they will never escape.

Abrams reports to his captain's quarters. He takes a deep breath before knocking. With a salute, he informs Captain W. W. Brezeale that he
believes his convalescence would be best concluded among the men. He
is lauded for the lie. He is asked about his wounds and to speak of home.
"It's fine," says Abrams. "It's New Orleans." He has returned to his army
by a mere hour, though the battle raging within him has known no
truce.

He tracks down Carlson a short while later, finding him among
scores of other Pelican Rangers in Bunkhouse 8, affectionately dubbed
"The Manse." From across the great room, he spots Carlson making up
his berth. The sight of his friend sparks a brief flash of happiness, which
dims just as quickly. "John Lee," he says tonelessly.

Turning to the call of his name, Carlson drops the tattered shirt he is folding and, dashing across the barracks, nearly assaults Abrams with affection. They hug, separate, and take a moment at arm's length to appraise each other warmly before Carlson, beaming, looses a barrage of questions: "Dear God, son, what're you doing back so soon? "How's your wound?" "You're healing well?" "Please, how's my Imogene?" "How'd she take to the letter?" "Isn't she beautiful?" "She received you well, I trust?" "And the girls?" "They're lovely, aren't they?" "Was I lying?" "What of New Orleans?" "How direly has the blockade taken its toll?" "Oh, and what of your intended, this Nora Bloom?" "Did y'all meet?" "Is she as sweet as she sounded?" "Christ, listen to me prattle on—it's just so damned good to see you on your feet, Elias. But tell me now sincerely, why're you back so early?"

Abrams answers in both lies and truth. He will not divulge to his friend the new predicament in which he has become embroiled. He is too ashamed, especially since it is another danger of his own creation. Carlson has been a miracle teacher, but this trouble, Abrams knows, he must deal with alone. Without further elaboration, he pulls from his canvas sack a pair of Jefferson boots, two sets of thick, woolen socks, and a heavy felt slouch hat.

"Here," says Abrams unceremoniously. "Compliments of K. Judson Mercantile, of Little Rock, bought on my way upriver."

Carlson's face puzzles.

"Take 'em. Ain't gettin' no warmer out there, and that idiot Panama's lookin' more like a crow's nest every goddamned day, all that cane busted through and frayin'." When Carlson still makes no sound or movement, Abrams begins to grow impatient. "Go on, John Lee, take 'em already."

With great reverence, Carlson accepts the gifts. Quietly and dearly, he thanks his young friend.

From Carlson in return, Abrams learns where to recover those possessions he left behind before heading out to the Creek Agency. He also discovers that Bruslé's crew reentered camp only a few days prior, to great fanfare. According to the professor, Bruslé proved himself so capable that he was granted but one day's respite before receiving further orders to lead his Company A, along with Viglini's Company K, ahead to Fayetteville, to act as provost-guard.

"So hold on now," interrupts Abrams. "Company K, them Pelican Rifles? You're sayin' they're off to Fayetteville? They ain't here?"

"Can you believe it?" answers Carlson cheerily, clapping Abrams on his good shoulder. Already he has placed the heavy, broad-brimmed hat atop his head and is angling it to his fashion. "Yes sir, those rapscallion sons-of-bitches, gone from camp until Lord knows when, by the grace of our most accommodating God."

Unexpected as it is, this news stumps Abrams. He grunts and shifts his weight. That Cobb and Petitgout have been stationed miles away alternately relieves and terrifies him greatly.

Hours later, after he has bedded down for the night with a lap desk across his sore knees, Abrams once again puts nib to paper: *Silas,* he writes bluntly, *that gent you got in mind for me aint here cause his companys done moved on He is with Company K, I am with G, look in the papers if you need it for proofe So I am sayin' it will take time fore I can get at him. Somthing big will probly have to happen to get all us together but you will know it from the papers so read and follow along and you will know when it comes to pass. Dont worry none I will take care of what is mine to take care of like I swore I would do Till then if I lern something bad happened to her, given the choise, you would be luckyer to take on the whole goddam Dutch army stead of havin me as your lone and fearsome enemy I aint braggin on myself neither I am just tellin' you the trewth is all.*

Elias

"You've really taken to the epistle, I see." It is Carlson, who is peeking over the side of the bunk above.

"It's awright." Abrams folds the note and stores it in his breast pocket to post the following day.

Carlson props himself onto an elbow. "And *you*, Elias? *You* all right?" His voice has no cheer in it. "Because surely you don't expect me to believe you've returned here of your own accord."

Abrams offers no reply. Instead, he turns toward the wall and sighs. "John Lee," he says after a minute.

"Yes?"

"D'you think killin' makes you more of a man?"

Carlson bursts into laughter at the absurdity of the question but then bites his tongue once he realizes its sincerity; sometimes he forgets Abrams' youth. He frowns. Understanding that the question put to him is one of the most delicate he will ever field, the professor quickly decides to choose his words wisely. Ever the Athenian aesthete, he will certainly make sure to avoid mentioning the ferocious Spartan custom of the *Krypteia*, or the "period of concealment," in which boys just turned twenty, precisely Abrams' age, crept from their countryside hideouts at night to stalk and kill Helot serfs on the plains below as a test of their manhood. "No, Elias," states Carlson matter-of-factly, "I do not think killing makes you more of a man."

"Huh." Abrams is asleep in seconds. Though he will slumber uninterrupted through the night, his dreams will prove horrific.

31

A frigid winter sets in. The men of the Third Louisiana have never endured such cold. Beyond their nestled encampment, icy driven winds seem to go uninterrupted for years, all attempts at civilization blown away, where the Midwest's eternal spread of land bears relentless gusts, grassroots scarcely holding fast to dry, packed earth. During the preceding months the men had heard accounts of northern winters, of toes blackened stiff and broken off, of skin as white and hard as bone, of lungs iced through from a single inhalation, all tales so terrific they went disbelieved. Before their enlistment the previous spring, sweating from the heat of the Louisiana noon, they laughed at the ominous idea of a harsh fourth season, warmed as they were by their incendiary love for the Cause.

Only now December's ashen dawns have arrived, and with them, the most brutalizing frosts these soldiers will ever know.

The piercing cold that settles atop them is a cold, Carlson mutters bitterly one mid-December eve, that should be numbing a language not their own but one further to the north, the tongue of men who know ice enough to embrace it as an ally, as both weapon and shelter. His oaths fall like frozen stones to earth. The wind shrieks mercilessly beyond the valley. Everywhere the ground breaks brittle at their footfalls. Smoke leaves chimneys, thinning, upward and away from the freeze. Bailey Boy, one of the camp's several Catahoula hounds, often barks once and then falls immediately quiet, afraid.

Abrams is as frozen as the others yet will admit to no man but Carlson the numbness in his feet or the chill that has lodged itself in his spine. Nor will he admit to those questions that plague him as he shivers wide-eyed in the dark or to those earnest and pagan prayers he offers the sun come the following morn. All day, each day, he stares at the bleakness of the sky and listens to the complaints of his company beside him. Then, one moonless night, viciously whipping aside his thin blanket, he finds that he can take it no more; it is time for another letter.

Dear Cheif McClelland,

My name is Elias Abrams and I am a solder in the Third Louisiana and Im writin to aks if you wood look in on Miss Nora Bloom of Herkulaes Street because I am afrayed that Silas Wolfe and the Cypress Stump Boys will be after her for reesons I don nt want to disguss at the moment. If you or your Dalrymple feller are now lookin for the likes of me then I will give my Self over to you when I am put at Liberty from my servise in the Army here. If you do not no who I am then that is fine to because it does not matter who I am or what happens to me as long as Miss Nora Bloom is held safe from these men I have just menshioned to you. I will hold you acountible now if something should go wrong becauze of the thret I am informin you of is the gods honest trewth. Protect her Cheif please.

Pt. Elias Abrams, Company G, Pelican Rangers

The letter folded and sealed, Abrams dispatches it to the chief of police's office, hoping fervently that it lands before willing eyes. Afterward, he exhales and, for the first time in weeks, sleeps soundly through the night.

Huddled indoors by their hearths, the remaining men of the Third Louisiana smoke what little tobacco is left. They swap the same stories, trade what they know of the war's progress. "Whupped 'em good at Round Mountain and Caving Banks both," says one proudly. "The bastards."

"Maybe so," says the group pessimist, "but they got theirs at Belmont, Mizzou-way, and word tell, just the other day at Dranesville, over in Virginny."

A third, an arbiter by nature, stands between them. "Shit y'all, *both* sides laid claim to the scrap at Alleghany Mountain, so let's call it a draw, call it a day, and get back to our goddamned meals, huh?"

They laugh, but find nothing funny. They are starved. For many, dreams of a sizzling goose have replaced the Lord as the subject of reverence, cornbread-and-oyster dressing, its divine adjutant. Bowls of steaming hot gumbo chunked with smoked tasso, piping hot buns and sweet yams thick with melted butter and cane syrup. Eggnog and whiskey and ale by the gallon. The men, nearly frozen through and famished, construct these imaginary meals with the piety of a thousand grieving penitents. The very notion of Christmas pudding forces more than one soldier to weep openly. The birth of their savior merely reminds them of what they do not have.

The cold is taking its toll. Coughs and muted curses disrupt the quiet of the camp, echoing wetly down the length of the valley. Medical attention is scarce, and as a result, much of the fallen snow becomes additionally mottled with the diseased, yellow phlegm of countless expectorant soldiers.

On New Year's Eve, Abrams receives a terse reply from Wolfe. It tells Abrams to take all the time he needs. It closes with "XOXO."

Abrams burns the note.

January comes and goes. He hears no response from the chief of police. He requires all his restraint to keep from obsessing over whether he has made a mistake in this, too.

During that period, Nora has sent him three more letters, and he has written as many in return. In them, despite his daily agonizing, their courtship blooms beyond the page. *How concerned I was,* she writes in the first, *when you failed to show for Monday's supper, but the arrival of your explanation quickly proved a comfort. In it you beseech me toward caution, and for your worry, I thank you. I shall be on guard, fear not.*

You also request my forgiveness, though surely it is I who should be pleading for your mercy. That you could think me capable of anything but support for your every endeavor favors the view of my misrepresenting myself. Please, rather than think me a petty little thing, jealous of that which might deprive me of such delights as your company, trust instead that I am ever for your worth and goodness. Oh dear Elias, despite our disparate upbringings, you are so, so right as to overcoming love's obstacles. In your wisdom, I sense in you someone soulful and loving and deeply tethered to my own tender importances. If truth be told, presumptuous though it may be to profess, I would therefore have you know that from this point forth, I deem myself ever yours alone, in life, in love, in loyalty.

Love,

Your darling Nora

Abrams reads and rereads these letters. He holds them to his nose and inhales to the fullest extent of his lungs' scope. He closes his eyes so that he may see her more clearly. He nibbles the pages' corners and swallows them down.

Nevertheless, much to Carlson's dismay, over these passing months Abrams has retreated into himself. He haunts the bunkhouse like a wraith, silent and mean. At night he plays Solitaire for hours on end, winning hand after hand, and yet each time he is through, he snatches up the cards resentfully, as though, while he is no loser, he has forgotten that a man might know victory against himself. If his physical injuries have healed, it is evident that those wounds bred of some emotional assault have not. Carlson blames it on the patricide to which Abrams alluded while febrile but will not now discuss, despite the professor's repeated offers to do just that. True, they trade friendly words. At the ruthless cold, they chatter their teeth and stomp their feet beside fires with the same winking conspiracy. Abrams answers whatever simple questions are asked of him. But while they are sociable, Carlson cannot avoid noticing the guarded veil once again fallen over Abrams' eyes or his steady regression into the mistrustful boy first met a half-year before.

Still, while Abrams may have returned to his sullen ways, Carlson believes that if his young friend were stripped bare but for the white silk scarf he has taken to knotting around his throat, the one Nora gave him to act as sling, were he reading one of her letters, Abrams would feel no cold at all. It is only when reading her letters that he seems to thaw in the face of that frozen black debt owed within him. In these moments, his cheeks flush with the very fever of love. Indeed, her words are the fuel to heat Abrams' soul.

The professor does not know, however, that while Abrams has come to adore this girl with his every waking hour, with his every steaming breath, her letters are, too, a bittersweet reminder of his most outstanding failure as a man. Thus, when he catches Abrams sighing, Carlson supposes them to be sighs born of a lover's ache alone, and not, as he would be shocked to discover, long steeped in an air of dread and self-slaughter.

32

One late February morning Abrams is awakened by a brusque prodding of his shoulder. It is a hard jab Abrams feels, forcing his subconscious to go swiftly for the stag-handled dirk in his boot. His vision clearing, the blade in hand, Abrams discerns Adjutant Holcomb, Hyams' personal amanuensis and one-time beneficiary of Abrams' angry fists, standing over him. The adjutant's prim Vandyke has flourished into a full-grown beard, and his once tidy uniform is now a pieced assembly of patches. "The lieutenant colonel wants you," states Holcomb coldly. "Now."

Minutes later, Abrams again enters his commander's quarters, this time a wooden bunkhouse. He takes a quick glimpse around him and finds the room nearly identical in decor to the tent those months before. The same camp table and folding chair, the same rolled maps of the Western campaign, the same tintype of that severe-looking matriarch atop the same large, leather-hinged pinewood chest overflowing with Hyams' belongings. At present, however, Abrams is not interested in studying his commander's sense of domesticity. He does not know why he has been summoned, but in the past has learned that when authority beckons you thus unexpectedly, accusations are not long to follow.

Hyams, like those hundreds he oversees, is but a third of the man he once was. The burden of leadership, the ever-constant struggle to keep his soldiers well-fed, well-shod, and decently sheltered, has taken its toll on the gentleman an editorial in the *Picayune* once proclaimed "almost indecently charming whilst inarguably competent." Now, months of fatigue and worry have etched their mark into his face. He has begun to sigh out of habit. He does not offer Abrams a tin cup of coffee dosed liberally with a fine Kentucky mash as he did upon their first visit. He has lost all patience for such pleasantry.

"Abrams," he begins, scarcely waiting for the private to come to attention, "apparently, you're on more familiar terms with the New Orleans police chief than most law-abiding men tend to be."

Abrams is stunned by these words. His nostrils flare wide at them, his Adam's apple quivers. He senses at once where this is heading and feels the noose slowly tightening around his neck for it. But before his surprise can betray him, he shifts his feet and stands upright, his chin reasserted toward the plank ceiling above.

"Yes, well, that's fine, too," says Hyams with a wave of his hand. He sits heavily onto the folding army chair and begins to shuffle through his papers on the table. He finds the page he is looking for and, looping his wire-rimmed spectacles over his ears, skims through it, his manner aloof as he mumbles while he reads. "Personally, I've met the man several times, McClelland," he says at last, looking up and removing his spectacles. "I myself find him to be, as the Ashkenazim might say, a bit of a shyster. But then, we're to respect the powers that be, the lot of us, don't you think?"

"Reckon his boots're big enough, yessir," concedes Abrams through very guarded lips.

Hyams stands with a groan, tossing the letter and spectacles onto the table. "So then, you sent him some sort of note a couple months back?"

Abrams nods cautiously.

"Care to tell me its gist?" He folds his arms in wait.

Abrams sniffs but does not speak.

"I see." Hyams paces away from Abrams, and then returns to him slowly. "Well, seeing as I've got a grasp of its contents from his reply anyway, doesn't make much of a difference whether you care to enlighten me as to its specifics or not."

Again, Abrams responds with silence. He is too busy feverishly concocting an escape route from the bunkhouse, from the encampment, from the Confederate army as a whole. In roughly twenty minutes he figures he can be scrambling out of the valley, eventually over the snow-capped mountain peaks, then to descend toward the flat expanse below where he will be forced, however reluctantly, to embark forever on the life of a fugitive.

But Hyams is not done. "Now for whatever reason, seems Chief McClelland thought it meet to send me a letter that, as far as I'm concerned, should've more appropriately gone to you, its rightful recipient. Guess he decided to stick me as middle man, a place that, as anyone who knows me well enough will assure you, I absolutely abhor. That being said, Abrams, I've a question or two that I'd like to ask you, but perhaps with a greater sense of prompting this time: his letter there mentions a fear you may have about Miss Bloom's safety. Why?"

"Wanted to see she's well-tended to, is all," says Abrams vaguely. "Girl like that deserves it."

"I take it you've met her then? During your convalescence?"

"Yessir." Abrams does not elaborate.

Hyams grunts. "McClelland's letter also suggests an affiliation you may have once had—or may currently have, he's unsure—with a rather tough band of Gallatin Street ruffians called, I believe, the Cypress Stump Boys. Is this true?"

Abrams grits his teeth and nods.

"A band, he claims, likely responsible for the murder of one I. J. Lieber." Hyams' eyes fall serious. "Or, as coincidence would have it, your father."

"I didn't kill him, sir," says Abrams defiantly. "I'll swear to it on any book you got handy."

Hyams purses his lips and begins to pace anew. He is again in his element, for he is of a judicial turn of mind, one that accords him great respect from his acquaintances and great concern from those he does not trust. "Calm yourself, Private, I never said you did. Nor for that matter, does our good Chief McClelland."

Abrams cocks an eyebrow at this: "Sir?"

"On the contrary. He requests instead that as your commanding officer, I demand something of you—I gather that's why he sent this letter to me, so that you're assured to receive its message. Seems he wants me to furlough you back to New Orleans immediately, wherein you're to somehow help him ensnare these Cypress Stump Boys, the very same fellows who, or so he writes, appear to be running amok these days as the woolliest Java men ever did."

Abrams' tone grows wary. "Help him how?"

"Well, due to the relationship to which you've just so reticently admitted, he'll likely just sit you down and ply you with questions about their ways and means. As things stand, from what I can infer from his letter, they've proven a bit too elusive for his current resources. Either that, or too formidable. Whatever the case, they've been pawning your father's goods with a fairly reckless abandon all throughout the Vieux Carré."

Abrams wants to spit but does not.

"Alas," sighs Hyams, "your deputization will have to wait, Private, their involvement in your father's appalling death notwithstanding. With Curtis' forces amassing near Bentonville, I've not a man to spare. Truth is, General Van Dorn's just ordered me to desist from issuing additional furloughs of any kind. Of course, when you do eventually arrive home—sooner rather than later, let's hope, as should we all, God willing—you're hereby instructed to stop by the station house at first chance, provide them the interview they're asking for. Agreed?"

Abrams claims that he will. He does not necessarily mean it.

"Good," approves Hyams, clapping his hands with an air of finality. "Now, as it wasn't addressed to you, I won't be giving you McClelland's letter after all. But trust me when I say I've just granted you the kind of gist you only minutes ago so willfully denied me." He pauses. "Oh, and Private? One more thing."

"Yessir?"

"I'm afraid there's the none-too-small matter of your father's outstanding patrimony to reconcile as well."

The meaning of these last words is beyond Abrams. He does not grasp them.

"Your patrimony, son. Your inheritance." Hyams' eyes are twinkling now. "Plantation out in Napoleonville, Toulouse Street, your father's varying business interests, all of it. Should be quite a substantial sum, everything considered. McClelland's got the will secured in his possession. Meant to lure you in for your help, I'd wager. He says it's all yours—you've only got to make claim on it."

Abrams is speechless. He cannot move.

Hyams grins at his man's stupefaction. "In doing so, though, I should warn you, you'll likely be forcibly conscripted into helping him lock these murderous bastards up, whether you want to or not. It's a tad extortionist, I'll admit, but evidently he's desperate for aid." Hyams' smile grows. "At any rate, let me be the first to congratulate you on your newly acquired wealth, tragically earned though it may be. Least now you've got the chance to do right by your father, whatever past y'all might've shared." He sighs again, clasping Abrams' shoulder. "Indeed, we should all be so lucky."

33

After a winter of polar frosts and vicious winds, hunger and deficiency and petty skirmishes with Union forces, Major General Earl Van Dorn's Confederate Army of the West, in which McCulloch's Third Louisiana Infantry has been subsumed, is once again on the verge of battle. Forced to tramp twenty miles in heavy snowfall over the course of twenty-four hours, near-starved by their daily ration of a single, stone-hard biscuit, weary from another sleepless night spent shivering on the frozen earth, the men of the Confederacy look ahead to the dawn, and with it, Brigadier General Samuel R. Curtis' Federal Army of the Southwest lying in wait.

At Pea Ridge, thirty miles north of Fayetteville, Abrams and his brothers-in-arms have at last been given the order to fall in. The cold has thinned their ranks. Scores of men have lost their lives to it. Assembled, they are a band of miscreants, wild-eyed and madly bearded, their stomachs shrunken to the size of fists, their teeth scummy and loose from scurvy. They are haggard in ways that the Bible accounts no man, their shredded uniforms reeking pungently of their common descent into a bestial past. They no longer think of home. They do not suffer delusions of any existence but the one to which they have been damned. In truth, many find warmth in this brand of resignation, for those who persist in begrudging their fates totter on the brink of lunacy, forced to admit that theirs is a realm where hardship has become the sole precept by which life itself is now governed.

Private Elias Abrams, like all members of Van Dorn's army, is aware of the Yankee army, over 10,000 strong, on the move from Bentonville. It had been set for days, horses by the thousands feeding on frozen Arkansas grasses, Union tents pocking the countryside in a plague of trespass. He is therefore startled but not surprised by the eruptive booming of the Union artillery that awakens him at daybreak on March 7, 1862. It is a democratic thunder, quickly belonging equally to all, possession felt in the feet and knees and teeth, causing sinners to kneel with matched faith beside the saintly. No church ever housed such devotion.

Minutes later, these prayers are further lost to the absolutely deafening departure of the Confederate cavalry. Soldiered in part by those paint-faced volunteers recruited by Bruslé, with shrill war whoops and murderous rage McIntosh's cavalry sweeps like a killing scythe upon the Federal battery before it, an apocalypse of Horsemen not four, but four hundred strong.

This is how the Confederate cavalry first engages the Union ranks at the Battle of Elkhorn Tavern, hooves kicked to flinty stone, air rent by metal, bullets sent thudding into hearts and lungs, the shrieks of men and pleas for mercy and the scalps of Union heads scraped bloodily free of their skulls by the blades of a warrior race the U.S. government had been working so methodically to destroy. By the time the battle is done, in their lust for revenge, in the very intensity of their hatred, half-breeds and full-bloods each will have collected a multitude of gory human pates for their belts, the odd Confederate scalp taken unapologetically among them.

So, too, in the days preceding the battle, could Elias Abrams be found plotting a vengeance of his own, Cobb and Petitgout's company having returned from Fayetteville's defense upon Van Dorn's demand. Aware of their arrival in camp, Abrams as a result took to scouring the stark winter landscape between drills, kicking over rotting logs for any sign of a

Destroying Angel, a white-capped, white-gilled mushroom so venomous that even his mother had spoken about it in low tones. "One cap," Gerta had warned him as a child, "just one little cap now, and that poison'll rake at them liver and kidneys you got like a rusty razor, lead you to Mister Reaper's doorstep quicker'n you can say, 'That ain't no chanterelle at all!'" Here she pinched her son's nose, wrinkled her own, but in the iron warning of her words, young Elias understood he was to interpret no mirth.

Thus, contriving the deaths of Cobb and Petitgout as artfully as any antique Roman, Abrams' plan was simple: after drying and grinding whatever deadly fungus he could find, he meant to funnel the spore-rich powder into their canteens of stale coffee as they slept. Minutes after they drank off the dregs, foam sputtering from their mouths, their hands would claw at their throats as they staggered and bashed into trees, retching and gagging and falling over themselves. It would prove an excruciating death. The actual end would arrive hours later, but not before bouts of fitful paroxysms convulsed their bodies like gasping fish thrown sadistically ashore.

Certainly, Abrams realized this was no gallant act he proposed. Over the course of the past half-year, however, he has had his fill of gallantry. He has decided to offer these disgusting men neither quarter nor last reasoning as to what has brought them to such a foul conclusion. They will die; he will be their killer. He owes them nothing more. Because while he may find the underhanded scheme he has planned distasteful, he also knows that only once it is completed will his life have a chance to regain its footing.

Among his many preoccupations, Abrams must now likewise grapple with the notion that he may be inheriting more land than he could have ever foreseen for himself. Since hearing this news from Hyams, he has thus been wavering between doubt and guarded optimism, understanding the need within most men to compensate those they have offended in the hopes of clearing their names of past misdeed. *Could be, he was just buyin' off his own damned conscience, the cocksucker. It's possible.*

I mean, could be. 'Sides, seemed sorry enough, night Sy done him in. But wait, that means he wrote me into his will—well hell, no tellin' how long ago. Question is, providin' it's bona fide, do you take what it's offerin'? Lord, after the part you played that night, you think you're even deservin'? 'Course, we're talkin' about bringin' down the Stumps first, and that there's a whole other kettle of fish. Sure as shit's worth thinkin' about, though, ain't it? 'Cause, if that son-of-a-bitch's land's for the takin' after all, I tell you what, Nora, I'll give some good, goddamned thought to us walkin' that parcel like we was king and queen, you and me.

Along this line of reasoning, Abrams trusts that for the time being, Wolfe will honor his word and stay all acts against her, as well as free him of his obligations once the cousins' murder is done. He has no reason to think this way other than what his gut tells him. Yet he knows, too, that this moratorium will not last forever.

And so Abrams concentrates foremost on the task he has been assigned. Only when the cousins have been killed will Nora be safe. For his sanity's sake, he needs to believe this. He cannot rely on the police to protect her. He must take these men's lives himself. Already accepting of this hard fact, he therefore lowered his head and plodded deeper into the Arkansas woods, his eyes trained on the land, searching for the mycological weapons he meant for them.

Now, however, the Battle of Elkhorn Tavern has fallen brutally upon him and, with it, a most grave distraction.

All along the hills and valleys on that violent March morning, cannons continue to boom ceaselessly. One howitzer in particular, set deep into a mountain hollow, remains a phantom. The most eagle-eyed men in the South curse as they trade binoculars between them, unable to locate it. This, as the howitzer drops pound after pound of lead among their ranks with the accuracy of a giggling child dripping water atop a stream of ants, creatures so naturally determined that instinct prevents them from any deviation of course. Only Elias Abrams does not share their formic resolve. His brow is creased with fear, his eyes dart quickly about him, while his rifle, perched against his shoulder, poised toward the heavens, appears aimed at God alone. John Lee Carlson is no calmer than he. While the professor holds his bladder tight this time, his knees seem to have lost their purpose. He nearly slips upon the call to march. He readjusts his glasses and steps hesitantly forward. "This is it," he tells Abrams with a bolstering breath.

"Reckon so."

The countryside around them is thick with underbrush and heavy timber, enclosed on all sides by the sheer hills of northwestern Arkansas. Abrams has for months believed these snow-capped mountains to be stunning, admired their gentle swells, for although his mood has soured, he has not been purged of the joy he finds in the terrain about him. It has been his one salve against himself. He has been cold and hungry, weary and glum, but the land, taken in by quick and furtive glances, has continued to thrill him despite his every self-abusing attempt to the contrary.

He has no time now for such wonderment. The cornfield through which now-General McIntosh's cavalry just swooped to success stands trampled before them; at present, Abrams' company has been ordered to skirt its easterly edge to secure the captured artillery ahead.

Among the hundreds of starved and sleep-deprived, he trudges in formation, John Lee Carlson by his side. They have much to say but few words to say it. Faint from fatigue and hunger, the men weave on their feet, occasionally lurching into the backs of their comrades columned in front of them. Abrams, himself exhausted and hungry beyond measure, has difficulty staying focused on the danger awaiting him. His head bobs, his eyes roll white. His thoughts wend headily between consciousness and dream as he slips and staggers, his feet shuffling aimlessly through the muddied track. Try as he might, he cannot fix his mind, his attention easing from the morning in which he falters to thoughts of his darling Nora. He grins dumbly, his eyes closed. He would gladly give his life, he decides, were he granted but one warm hour to spend beside her. His smile grows. He continues to reflect on what Hyams told him those ten days before, still vacillating by the moment between suspicion and hope. Suspicion of not only agreeing to a possible collaboration with the law, but also that his father might have bequeathed him such a fortune after so many years of neglect. That his father might have chosen to reach out to his bastard son at all, even in death, Abrams has found suspect. And yet a small part of him has been hopeful, too, for what that same inheritance, should it actually exist, might mean toward a future with Miss Nora Bloom. It could mean everything. Now, as he stumbles toward the enemy in wait, imagining the patrimony long since collected, he envisions the roaring fire of his inherited Napoleonville plantation home, the thousands of acres behind it, and how wonderful it will be to share all that with Nora forever. He sees them together, their quilt kicked aside from the heat they are kindling, a stone hearth in the background home to a blaze. He smacks his cracked lips, tastes the burn of a fine whiskey. He feels his cock afire within her, his face glows like a smoldering ember at the very thought of it, and, sighing from the fever of love with which each roasts the other, tramping through the ice and mud into the second great battle of his life, Elias Abrams basks in the incendiary fury of their fucking—

"Elias!"

Abrams snaps to, his eyes blinking.

"Head up, son," warns Carlson. "Up yonder, Curtis's recruited at least ten thousand ways to kill you, meaning you now have ten thousand different deaths to dodge. So pay some heed."

The heat of Abrams' reverie quickly freezes stiff. He blinks to clear his head, slaps his own face, and with a dogged look and steeled jaw, plods onward.

It is mid-morning, and cannons from both armies detonate without end, reminding the men of Oak Hills. Whereas in August it was the blistering sun and thirst that nearly vanquished them, this day it is the frost and hunger. The muddy road does not surrender to their feet gladly. Already heavy with sulfur, the air smells of brimstone to those of a Biblical turn, and with such a scent they fear an eternal familiarity, one born of the sins they failed to confess before setting off to battle that morning. In the distance Abrams sees puffs of cannonade, hears their screaming shot approaching, and cringes as their lead comes crashing into the earth, the clods of ice and stone raining down hard upon him.

Despite having just cautioned Abrams against the dangers of day-dreaming, Carlson, too, as light-headed as any man in the Confederacy, feels himself slipping amid the clamor of the morning fight, sliding easily into the comfort of past texts, swaddling in their pages, enveloping warmly in their prose. He conjures up places where only his mind has been. With each mighty crack of the cannons about him, he dreams of northern seas and great shards of glaciers splintering free of their moorings, grinding under the weight of their own magnitude into the churning water below. Yet as he marches in that Arkansas cold toward wherever his feet take him, he cannot sidestep the cruel and corollary knowledge that Sir John Franklin, author of the account that introduced him to these collapsing walls of ice, perished at the pitiless hands of cold himself, but not before he and those with whom he was trapped—desperate, freezing, and starving—were forced to resort to eating companionable flesh in a vain attempt at survival. More terrifying still, unlike the revulsion he felt years before when first learning of it, Professor John Lee Carlson, tender husband and doting father, dear friend and devoted instructor of humanity's most civilized works, now understands with perfect clarity, with near-envy even, just how a man might sink his teeth into another.

On they march, into the grayness.

Tramping toward the lone captured battery, his stomach whining, his feet and knees frozen and hurting beyond belief, Abrams soon spies a thicket off to his left. Something about it catches his attention, nearly stopping him in his tracks. He cannot put his finger on it, though this particular thicket is different from the rest of the land around him, of that he is certain. *Where's the snow on them brambles?* he wonders in pacing toward it. *Save for that stretch there, every goddamn length of the world's covered in it. Not there, though. Huh. Queer, that.*

At once, it dawns on him. His stomach turns to water.

"Sweet Jesus!" he screams at the top of his lungs, shoving Carlson to the ground, "they got us in their—"

But Abrams' warning is lost to the ferocious clamor of Federal rifle fire exploding from the thicket.

The Confederates are instantly thrown into a panic, ducking and clamping hats to heads as they bolt to escape the furious volleys pouring into their ranks. The smoke of the rifle discharge quickly settles upon the men in a hazy, funeral shroud, forcing them to crash into one another blindly. Atop his terrified horse, a young lieutenant named Washburn works to rally the men toward organization, but his words hardly escape his mouth before his head explodes into a fine, red mist. As though emancipated from the laws of gravity now that he no longer has a mind to construe them, Washburn's uncapped torso wheels from the saddle slowly, almost petulantly, plumes of crimson spraying into the early morning air along its sweeping path. In the midst of the commotion, his body lands with a thud to leak itself dry onto the iced and impermeable earth. It will take hours to identify his corpse.

All around Abrams his comrades are falling, wails and rifle reports and shouts for advance or retreat fill his ears, while cannons continue to blast eruptions of soil and rock. For the men of the Third Louisiana, a great confusion has snapped many of their minds. One private, a young cobbler from Terrebone Parish, has thrown his weapon aside and torn his chest free of whatever threadbare rags remained of his uniform. His white flesh bound to his ribs, he is skeletal, yet his blue eyes flash maniacally, his bony arms raised high to the sky in the suggestion of some personal triumph. He is braying like an ass, he is gobbling like a jake, he is hopping askance like a rabid dog, for in the very madness of the moment, the world as he knows it has become a pure mockery of itself. And in the mockery he senses, a comforting insanity has compelled him to act equally absurd.

Together through the tumult of resounding artillery and whistling Minié balls, through the riotous morning air rich with sulfurous smoke and agonized screams, Abrams and Carlson are zigzagging their way over the edge of the cornfield, coming up hard upon a ditch beyond the range of even the most decorated Yankee sharpshooters. "There!" cries Abrams. "Quick now!"

They run as unenlightened men, less thrilled by the progressive aspect of travel than by its absolutes, departure point and destination. That they have not yet been killed despite the amount of metal in the air they would, in quieter times, have deemed miraculous. They are not now thinking in terms of miracles at all, for in the interminable violence of that morning, they have no time to spend on such nutritious beliefs.

On their flight toward the ditch, they leap and bound over dying men, men who implore them with their eyes for a merciful bullet in the brain, men who grab at them, begging for water or a whisper of companionship. Men who, later, after they have at last been frozen to the land, will need to be pried free by iron rods from their places of final rest. "C'mon, goddamnit!" shouts Abrams. "Just ahead!"

Carlson is hard on Abrams' heels. His twins Ella and Marguerite have begun to sing sweetly in his ears, they jump rope and skip through green grass, they beg to be tickled and call him *papa phile*, "my dear Papa," in the Homeric Greek he once taught them. He envisions Imogene standing in that dirty ditch ahead, his salvation. Her arms are wide, her eyes beseeching. "Come to me, my love," she is whispering. "Come to me as though our very lives were at stake."

"I'm coming, Imo," mutters Carlson, almost losing his footing to an explosion in the earth fallen before him. His lungs are near to bursting, his legs weak from the course over which he has been running, the nine pounds of rifle in his hands have multiplied their weight a hundredfold, but he will not fail her.

At last, he and Abrams make the ditch. Once they crest its lip and dive towards its trough, they discover a mass of men squirming there like maggots in the belly of some day-dead mongrel. They collapse at once among the others who have likewise sought harbor in the small, earthen depression, burrowing their bodies into the frost and mud. "No messenger at Marathon ever made such a dash," gasps Carlson, clutching his friend's wrist in relief. "Hermes even, a regular snail by comparison."

Abrams is breathing hard. He is not impressed. "Plenty of gauntlet yet to be run," he says grimly. "I'd keep your steam, I was you."

"To be sure," agrees Carlson. "I'm merely suggesting that—"

But Abrams is no longer listening. Instead, to the great knotting of his guts, he discerns a lone scream of cannon shot arcing above them that, if he is not mistaken, rides the one path he knows should be feared most. As it approaches, he gulps to realize he has never heard such a pitch. It is the Devil's very whinny, a shrieking crescendo of some pain impending and profound. He looks up at the smoke-filled sky, searching for the trajectory of the time-fused shot heading toward them, when, to the widening of his eyes, he spots the missile plummeting directly toward their position. "John Lee!" he cries, leaping to cover his friend's body with his own. "Get your head dow—"

The explosion that next arrives sends those ditch-bound men it does not immediately demolish into seeds of bloody meat and bone aloft into the morning air, like pennies flipped leisurely toward heaven by childish thumbs. They are pinwheels in the breeze, these men, crudely cut paper-jacks tossed high, blowing wherever the morning wind fancies. And as Abrams, too, soars over the land he so loves, looking down with perplexity upon it, he can only conclude in his daze before he again thumps broken and bent-jointed to earth, that God, in his unremitting need to steal every delight from the world he claims to have wrought, is nothing short of a fucking larcenist.

34

"You're deservin' of this, old man. Can't say for a second you ain't."
"Oh no, don't get me wrong, I am, I know I am, most certainly. But you must understand, I'm asking your forgiveness here. The fact is, I'm begging for it."

"'Cause you got a cloudbank 'bout to burst over your head, that's why."

"Perhaps. But of the many lessons I now regret never having taught you, Elias, you should know that when a man asks your forgiveness, even when you're in a position to question his sincerity, you've got to at least consider the prospect of its truth."

"Only thing I got to consider is how the boys'n me are gonna haul all this here loot out your front door."

"I see. You've evidently made up your mind then, and for that at least, I applaud you. Having said that, knowing just how mule-headed Lieber blood can make a man, you may by all means do your worst—"

Abrams awakens with a gasp, though he promptly wishes he had not. His head feels glutinous, as if clotted with tar and lead and cotton, his ears echoing mutely all he hears. Painfully, he looks about him. He brings his fingertips to his concussed brow and touches it gently. Dimly, he recalls something of an explosion.

Abrams cranes his neck and sees he is among hundreds of other men. The disquiet provoked by the nightmarish memory quickly fades and is replaced instead by one born of a hard-set reality. He is in an open meadow under the cold night sky, trapped in a pen girded on all sides by a smooth-wired fence. It is late, the air is frigid, and the moon is bright above him. He shivers, his breath steams. His trousers, up to his knees, are frozen stiff like rawhide. Men around him mutter and weep. Abrams is beginning to understand his predicament. To the soldier beside him, he asks where they are.

"The belly of the fuckin' beast, that's where."

"Captured?"

"Too goddamned right."

Abrams closes his eyes and groans.

"Maybe they'll feed us," says the soldier wistfully. "Lord knows, I might could be convinced of old Abe's stock after all, these boys feed us right."

Abrams has no interest in talk of politics. He is working to clear his head. "You seen an owl-eyed feller anywheres 'round? Runs by the name of Carlson?"

The young man ignores this question, already surrendering himself to the treason he will gladly commit in return for three hot square meals a day. He will swear an oath of subservience to the blackest nigger alive, he decides with a prudent nod, just as long as he gets fed for it.

Abrams labors to his feet. He totters for a moment, palms flat out to catch him if he falls, before he begins a sore trek to find Carlson through the mass of shivering and defeated captives, his fellow Confederates. It is a hastily composed prison pen, he soon discovers, impromptu in construct, makeshift in its every aspect, and yet its purpose bespeaks the million-year permanence of man's bitter war on himself.

In the darkness of the night, in the defeat they endured earlier, those Southerners still awake struggle to hold their chins high below their trembling lips. They grumble and speak of second chances. Deep in thought, they stoke the few fires they have been allowed. In their small quorums, they have already begun to fight future battles. Many lose their composure, however, when, like a swift and deadly corruption, word spreads of the deaths of generals McCulloch and McIntosh, each slain late that morning at Pea Ridge. They learn in solemn whispers how McCulloch had ridden ahead to scout out the enemy position when he reined up directly, tragically, into an entire Federal company's aim. Among the swarming shots, a marksman's took him in the heart, out of his saddle, and with him, all hope for a Confederate victory. To add to the disaster, his second in command, General James McIntosh, fearless leader of that first cavalry attack, then charged ahead to recover his commander's body, only to be shot dead himself mere minutes later.

Deprived of two of its most brilliant military minds, the Confederate forces were quickly thrown into a state of disarray from which they never recovered. In the end, the Battle of Elkhorn Tavern was lost, and lost mightily.

To this appalling news, scores of soldiers have begun to tear at their breasts and wail like washerwomen. Others have fallen into silence, their eyes slowly closing, wishing to see nothing more of the day that has bred so much despair. Their father in warfare, the venerable Benjamin McCulloch, hero of the Texas Revolution, proud Texas Ranger, U.S. marshal and brigadier general, most esteemed champion of men, has left them forever, and in the orphaning now foisted upon them, they must bear the pain of an abandonment few had dared to consider possible.

Abrams plods steadily onward. He has deeper griefs to negotiate. "You best not be dead, you son-of-a-bitch," he mumbles as he steps over those sleepers who have relinquished themselves to their exhaustion. "I won't brook it, John Lee, nossir. Already had my goddamned fill."

From the ground level, in the throng of men milling about, he cannot get a true sense of the size of the field in which they are being held. Eight acres perhaps, maybe ten. All along the perimeter, beyond the wire fence, Union guardsmen have been placed, their weapons loaded, their bayonets fixed. They are nervous young boys of the lowest possible rank and greenest service, and their feet shuffle and fingers twitch at the slightest movement in the pen behind them. They lick their lips and breathe quickly. Their eyes flash with worry. In truth, they are unnerved by their proximity to those they have conquered. They fear such failure as one fears a contagion.

In his quest to find Carlson, in the middle of the pasture and thus away from the gaze of his Union captors, Abrams discerns a skirmish among the men that surprises him in its intensity. He hears muffled shouts and oaths, thuds of punches, and onlookers who have seized the brief opportunity to cheer. Abrams rubs the back of his neck, exhaling in disgust. After the unrelenting violence of the day, that these people might still possess any lingering aggression he finds astonishing. He is only now coming to terms with the fact that, in the crude method of men, even those bound by loss will turn on one another. They will spit into night fires at the thought of those they no longer trust, condemning their comrades' foibles, their leaders' mistakes. They will plot. They will betray and themselves endure betrayal. "Who says we ain't kin to the beasts after all?" sighs Abrams. "Worse off, most like."

Still, he heads over to investigate.

Once there, what he discovers forces him abruptly to a halt, his mouth to drop half-open. Shaking his head, he chuckles acidly at the ground, then slouches and sighs again, for it is none other than Cobb and Petitgout who are the focus of the trouble. "Christ, if that ain't about right," he laughs bleakly. "If that ain't about too fuckin' right."

He ducks behind another spectating soldier, understanding that he must take a moment before acting this time. He has spent countless nights fantasizing about the ruin he has meant to rain down upon these men. In his mind, Abrams has envisioned fists thrown and dodged, deaths delivered, his darling Nora saved and swooning with thanks. He has imagined himself heroic, a credit to his very kind, though as time passed, as days eased into weeks into months, he had begun to hope—to pray even—that he would never see them again. A Union bullet, maybe cholera or the cold or the dueling pistol of some offended Fayetteville gent, would dispatch them more efficiently than he ever could. This was not cowardice Abrams embraced, but merely the patience of a cardsharp who prefers to let his opponents bleed each other dry before ultimately stepping in to sweep the pot toward him. Anything but his own two hands.

Only now, following the most tragic day of the war thus far, he detects in this chance encounter an incontestable example of *bashert*, a notion first introduced to him many years before at the orphanage. There, Mrs. Estelle Gorowitz, that frumpy old matron with eyes set deep into her biscuit-dough face, with a mole like a desiccated fig on her neck, had informed him as she scrubbed his ears how young Abrams' failed attempt to pick her husband's pocket on the temple steps that morning had been *bashert*. "It means 'destined,' my child," she had explained kindly, running a wisp of steely hair from her forehead with the back of her wrist and burst of air from her mouth, "'fated,' if you will, something that's meant to be." She went on to explain that had Elias not been caught picking her husband's pocket, he never would have been brought to the orphanage. And had he never been brought to the orphanage, he would never have had the chance to embark on the sweet and wholesome life she had in store for him.

Young Abrams, his face raw from the scrubbing, eyes stinging with the suds of lilac soap, decided not to disabuse Mrs. Estelle Gorowitz of her belief in the providence of their intertwining paths. He did not tell her that he had been trolling those same holy grounds for months to far greater success. Or that he could have easily broken free of her husband's ear-pinching march toward her guidance. He certainly did not tell her how he had, in fact, relished the paternal lock on him, how in spite of his toughness, he had docilely allowed himself to be led.

Rather, he simply thanked her, ate whatever bread and turtle soup she offered, and lit out the next day for those same gutters from which she wished to see him saved. Because he would return to the orphanage of his own accord and eventually meet Silas Wolfe there, Abrams would, however, be forced to grant some concession to the idea of *bashert* as Mrs. Estelle Gorowitz had originally meant him to take it.

Over the course of his life, he has been learning that such fortuitous events occur every day, all the time. Old friends met on the street after years apart, bearing news of some strange pertinence. Information garnered from the least likely of sources. Love, as he is so thrilled to be gathering, found through the least likely of means. There is no use denying them, the serendipitous affairs of the world, so men of experience know that there is no use trying. Still too young to fully grasp this, Abrams is only now beginning to realize that in the instance of *bashert* at hand, he alone must interpret how to best govern it.

For the moment, the cousins from Algiers are too preoccupied with kicking their victim in his ribs and face and shins, pummeling whatever space he grants them, to pay Abrams any heed. "We'll just be takin' all yer goddamned jerky then," Petitgout is declaring, "'cause no man'll hoard his stock, not when my guts're barrener'n an old mawmaw's womb, he won't! Go on, Cobb, kick that cocksucker! Go on'n kick 'im good!"

Cobb obeys with a giggle, a gargantuan child performing a task it loves at the request of an authority it loves all the more. He grunts in his effort. Even after the man at his feet has quit defending himself, Cobb kicks. "Ribs is goin' mushy, boss," he tells Petitgout.

"Well shit, son, kick 'em."

Men in the crowd have begun to grow concerned. "Hey now," says a soldier without much conviction, "that's enough, there." It is one thing to watch a man take a beating to distract your mind from the one you just suffered yourself, but it is something else entirely to witness that man's murder.

"Y'all just quit," says another.

"Yeah," echoes a third, "leave 'im be already."

Petitgout whips his snarling attention toward them. "Who's gonna stop us, I'd like to know? I seen y'all out there on that field today, all of y'all." He scans the men before him through narrow eyes, his tone recriminatory. "Ain't none of you got the fightin' sense God gave a Quakerite, I say! So head on out, find y'all's sisters, go on'n play dollies with 'em, you yellow bastards!"

A sheepish silence follows. More than one fellow toes the dirt.

"Y'all gonna let that son-of-a-bitch there call y'all cowards?" It is Elias Abrams, standing aside from his place of hiding. Blood is galloping in his neck, but since he has initiated his attack, he knows he must follow it through to whatever gory conclusion lay in wait. "Can't hardly believe it," he says, "y'all lettin' him get away with that."

"Well, I'll be," murmurs Petitgout, a smile creasing filthily across his face. It is an abomination to see. "If it ain't our very own lover man."

Earl Cobb stops his kicking and, exhausted from the exertion, peers up at his cousin's words. His mouth falls open at the sight of Abrams, his bottom lip glistening like a bloated slug in the moonlight.

Petitgout is grinning wickedly, his hands gone to his hips in disbelief. "Lazarus hisself, must be."

But Abrams has no time. His plan requires him to strike immediately, while his enemies have drawn the ire of those about them. "Y'all spent all blessed day out there on that field," he informs the men, "fightin' and dyin' for a cause that's bigger'n all of y'all combined, and you're gonna let that bastard there claim y'all ain't worth spit?" He takes a stern step forward. "Ain't right."

"Lord, please," chuckles Petitgout, "you think these skunks here'll listen to you? Shit."

"Skunks ain't nothin' but stink-ass weasels, boys," says Abrams, his eyes leveled at Petitgout alone. "Is that what y'all are, then? Stink-ass weasels?"

"Naw," says one.

"Hell no," says another, firmer.

Petitgout quits smiling. His eyes glance around him. He is beginning to see Abrams' words settle into their audience.

"McCulloch, dead," Abrams goes on, his voice growing strong as he pulls on a thumb to elucidate his point. "McIntosh, dead. Y'all sayin' *they* were stink-ass weasels?"

"No, sir!" cries a voice.

Abrams' eyes are alight, his heart thumping in his chest, but he has made his decision. "We're men of the Third fuckin' Louisiana!" he is now shouting, "and I'm tellin' y'all, don't much matter what this bastard says, 'cause we're made of steel, we're made of stone, we don't give a goddamned inch in this world, don't much matter if we're locked up in this field or not!" The rage erupting from Abrams as he rouses these men toward action shocks him in its clarity and opens his eyes in ways for which he was unprepared. It is an extraordinary feeling, this sudden welling in his lungs, like moonlight squeezed through a windowpane, a bubble through a square. Abrams has been suppressing himself for months, been frustrated into an utter and infuriating silence. Since first enlisting the year before, he has been helplessly swallowing back his spirit in the hopes of appeasing powers more formidable than his own. Traditionally a man of confrontation, he has thus been suffering a long, slow suicide. Such beautiful wrath is too often overdue. "And yet!" he roars, "this feller's standin' here, tellin' y'all you ain't got no pluck?" He lets his reasoning sink in. "No," he concludes icily, boring down into Petitgout's frightened eyes. "Nossir."

He stands forward. The men hush. The blow he then lands is so mighty, it breaks Petitgout's jaw in two places. Abrams has never felt such a satisfying crunch.

In an instant, he has wheeled away from Cobb's advance, praying that the men of the crowd, those brothers-in-arms he has attempted to rile, will now join him in the fray. He spins to one knee, the dirk flashing in the night, as the dam holding the resentment of the men back, that logjam of loss and embittering defeat, suddenly gives way to the torrent of their fury. It is a swift mass of bodies that moves on those cousins from Algiers, clenched fists and hard feet and groping hands all seeking to tear asunder the symbols of such enemies in their midst. In the name of McCulloch and McIntosh they strike their blows, in the name of their abandoned wives and threatened homes, in the name of their beloved God and country they lash out at Cobb and Petitgout, two bullies who, in the span of mere seconds, have diminished into cowering and quivering children as they endure fist after fist, kick after kick, oath after bloody oath.

Abrams is braced. He is not thinking about the moral consequences of the actions he is about to commit, but rather the knife grip he must use to most effectively accomplish them. He lowers his head, the blade gleaming. It has all come down to this. He exhales a long breath, and then steps ahead, one pace, then another—

A pistol shot shatters the night. The dozen or so men who have joined in the assault quickly cease their violence, instantly turning their heads to the sound of the blast. Time has stopped, though for Cobb and Petitgout, whimpering on the ground, covering their greasy heads with their broken hands, it has not stopped soon enough.

A Yankee sergeant struts forward, flanked on each side by worried teens bearing Springfield rifles. The sergeant, a crushed blue kepi squat atop his flaming red hair, his belly rounder than any the Confederates have seen in months, is drunker than sin. Immediately Abrams senses the menace in him. As a result, he stealthily slips the dirk back into his boot. He knows a man seeking an excuse to harm.

"What seems to be the problem here?" The Yankee's accent is unlike any Abrams has ever heard, where percussive consonants and flat vowels meet a slightly Slavonic lilt. A member of the Thirty-Seventh Illinois Infantry, Sergeant Cyryl Schwientek, native-born to Silesian Pole pig folk, Catholic as a bishop, drunk to the core, and disdainful of everything that he is not, raises his bushy red eyebrows as he awaits an answer. When he gets none, he takes a small, deliberate step forward. "I asked what the problem was." He pushes his kepi to the back of his head, and belches.

"Them cunts, there," moans Petitgout from the ground, cradling his jaw, "they fell on us for no reason but we was mindin' our own." He spits blood. "That feller, 'specially. I'd shoot 'im dead, I was you. He ain't no good."

"Is that right?" Schwientek is weaving on his feet. He flails his Colt dramatically in the air. "That's what you'd do then, eh? You'd shoot him?"

"Oh, I'd shoot him awright."

Schwientek turns to Abrams. His eyes have a difficult time focusing. "You started this?"

"Finishin' it, more like."

"Ha, good," says Schwientek. But he is not amused. His jawline is lost amid a billowing of red muttonchops, his lips full. They do not now smile. His eyes shine with inebriation and an undercurrent of something intensely mean.

"Go on, shoot 'im, bluebird," urges Petitgout from his seat. "If y'all are such a goddamned force to reckon with, why don't you go on'n prove it?"

"You got rags, Petitgout," warns Abrams. "You're drawin' dead."

The other men are in the meantime slowly receding into the night, dragging the first victim away with them, giving Abrams, the cousins from Algiers, and now Sergeant Cyryl Schwientek and his two young guards a very wide berth.

"C'mon, blue," goads Petitgout, "plug 'im full."

"Love to," replies Schwientek. Here he cracks a thin, hiccupping smile. "But I've got conditions against it."

"Conditions is irascible things."

Schwientek agrees. Conditions are indeed irascible things.

Petitgout's eyes glint in the moonlight. His jaw has begun to throb, but he has too much venom in him to be rendered mute. "So go on then," he whispers seductively, "grab that bull by them bollocks, shoot this'un here. Show us what you made of."

Schwientek hitches his stance and cocks his head, for he is having a difficult time believing the gall of the repugnant little man on the ground before him.

Petitgout struggles to his feet. "Just *shoot* 'im already, goddamnit," he pleads nastily, "go 'head, show us yokel Rebs just who we dealin' with."

"Uh, Skip," says Cobb under his breath. "Maybe you best shelf yer mouth awhile, huh?"

"And maybe y'all," hisses Petitgout, accusing the mob around him, "maybe ALL of y'all, best go on'n fuck y'all's mommas right up their crusty old cunts." Though his jaw is fractured, he feels no pain. He is suddenly beyond rage, beyond all wisdom, blinded as he is by a black, passionate loathing for a world that has kicked and battered him since birth. He can see no reason whatsoever, his words taking him to places of which he has no preconception. A coonhound on the hunt will run for miles without any idea as to where it is running next, its path dictated only by its nose and an instinctive need to kill. When it eventually achieves its objective, more often than not, the result is some degree of bloodshed. Such is the path on which Petitgout now so dangerously treads.

"That's about what I thought," he sneers of Schwientek, "ain't nothin' but a goddamned pederast." He turns scornfully back to the retreated crowd. "Ain't that something, y'all? Today we done got whipped by nothin' but a bunch of no good, nigger-lovin' *pederasts*." He spits again in bloody contempt and then turns to walk away. "Shit, my jaw's achin' so, I ain't got time for all y'all's foolis—"

A second shot rings out in the night, hard and metallic.

The .44-caliber bullet that pierces Petitgout's head comes clear through the other side of his skull, splattering steaming fragments of blood, brain, and bone throughout the cold, dark pasture. Skip Petitgout, inveterate whoremonger and rat-faced sadist from Algiers, crumples to the ground without as much as a sigh. A small man, he makes little impact.

Frozen for an instant by the sight of his dear cousin's death, Cobb quickly snaps beyond reason himself, and despite the recklessness of his efforts, despite the death warrant he has just willfully signed, lunges for Schwientek's throat with a howl. With a surprisingly steady hand considering the amount of celebratory whiskey in his system, Schwientek in turn demolishes the brute's face with a third shot of his Colt. Cobb hits the earth with a more substantial thud than did his cousin. His left leg quivers before going still.

Sergeant Cyryl Schwientek looks lazily back to Abrams and then sniffs once. His eyes are heavy-lidded. He holsters his weapon and straightens his uniform by tugging on the bottom hem of his blue blouse. He tucks his kepi under his left armpit so that he might run a pocket comb through his brilliant red hair in calm, measured swipes. All is silent, except for the rasping of those swipes. Soon, his hat repositioned jauntily on his head, Schwientek sighs in mild disappointment, his mood dimmed by having met yet another goddamned fool incapable of keeping the breath in his lungs.

"You there," he orders Abrams at last. "Come with me."

35

Abrams is soon stripped naked in the early March night, his hands tied behind his back around the base of a tall Arkansas pine. He feels the scrape of bark on his shoulders and buttocks, the soles of his feet quickly gone tender from the frosted ground beneath them. He hops on one leg, then the other, and leans toward the earth, chafing against his bonds and chopping his breaths in the vain attempt to keep warm amid temperatures that hover just below freezing. The holding pen is off in the distance, far from the tree line where they now stand. Abrams is alone with Schwientek and the two armed youths, neither of whom has spoken a word.

That he was told to strip bare scares but does not surprise Abrams. When Schwientek sees his prisoner's circumcised penis, however, and infers the faith into which he was born, Abrams knows the danger is real. The Yankee's eyes flicker for a second and then dull. "My, my," he says flatly.

Abrams lifts his nose to the sky, but says nothing.

"Our own little chosen one, eh?"

Abrams offers no reply. He knows what is coming but does not know the precise manner in which this punishment will arrive. Abrams has begun to shudder uncontrollably, his lips turning blue, his teeth chattering violently. His testicles hike desperately upward, seeking refuge in the warmth of his abdomen.

Schwientek's Colt is back out. He traces it languidly from the notch in Abrams' throat, down over his clavicle to the pale leanness of his chest and stomach, over that same warm abdomen, into Abrams' thick mass of pubic hair, then tucks it under his shrunken scrotal sack. The cold of gun barrel metal is almost impossible to bear. "Private Jankauskas?" demands Schwientek quietly.

One of the youths stands forward at attention.

"You wearing socks?" Schwientek's sinister eyes are locked on Abrams', his breath befouling the air between them with the ripened scent of pork and whiskey. "Socks," repeats Schwientek. "You wearing?"

Private Jankauskas shifts his weight uneasily, and then looks over at his fellow youth, Private Grayson, who shrugs. "I am, Sergeant."

"Good. Take one off."

"Sergeant?"

Schwientek turns to Private Jankauskas and with a look of consummate boredom, raises his pistol from Abrams' genitals to aim it directly between the youth's eyes. He cocks the hammer back. Calmly he says, "A sock, Private. Now."

Private Jankauskas is on the ground, quickly removing a shoe. In seconds, he is standing with one foot notched awkwardly beside the other knee as he proffers Schwientek the requested item. It is the foulest sock imaginable, rigid with the rank foot sweat of a thousand miles marched. It was once knit of quality Manchester woolens, but now, after so much time and absorbed filth, has taken on the clotted properties of the most fetid bogs and swamps. Schwientek nods his admiration, removes his aim from the young man's head, but makes no move to accept what has been offered him. "Now," he demands, "pull it apart at the toes, just a bit. Should tear easily enough."

Private Jankauskas obeys without resistance.

"Good boy," says Schwientek. "One last step." He looks back to Abrams and sets his jaw hard, his gaze among the most malevolent Elias Abrams will ever hold. "Slip it over him, calf-end up," he tells Jankauskas, "down there." The contempt in his voice is absolute. "It's about time he learned what a real Christian prick's supposed to look like, this half-dick Christ-killer."

—

Over two hours later, Abrams' breathing has slowed, and the words he has been mumbling to himself have slurred. He is being overtaken by a lethargy that, were he more cognizant, he would have known is a sign of terrible things to come. His eyes blink slowly, and his muscles are beyond exhaustion from the shivering they have performed in the effort to heat him from within. He stands alone, the soiled, open-toed sock tied with bailing twice over his penis and scrotum, his only attire. From above, his penis looks like an infant's woolen-clad limb stemming from beneath his gut, dangling dejectedly toward the earth.

In truth, he had been expecting worse, a suffering born of honed metal or hard wood, but over the past hours has come to grasp the true genius of the humiliation he has been forced to endure. He can see his boots, bowler, and clothes a mere dozen feet away; Sergeant Cyryl Schwientek, in a last act of calculated malice, had ordered Private Grayson to fold and stack the clothing into a neat little launderer's package. And so, as Abrams shivers himself to death, he is granted a full, if maddening, view of that which might save him. Beside his stacked uniform remain the charred flakes of Nora's and John Lee's letters, those he had kept in his breast pocket, close to his heart, burned now to cinders by Union flint and fire. Few Greek gods, Carlson would have claimed, were ever capable of such an inspired sense of torment.

Over and over as he shudders, bound to that pine, Abrams replays in his mind the murder of the cousins from Algiers, watching each time the blood and bone of their heads splatter gruesomely into the night. He recalls their slumping bodies, the steam from their gaping skulls wafting into the frigid air. Cobb's quivering left leg, and then its stillness. He sees Schwientek turning back to him, the look of something so demented in his eyes that it approximates something exhaustively sane, as though, were he not to have killed these men in cold blood, he would have been acting irresponsibly.

Abrams' head nods. His eyes roll in their sockets. He has not eaten in thirty-two hours. He is beginning to cease shivering. The constant yawning taxes his jaw muscles.

His thoughts wend groggily between, as they inevitably do, his darling Nora Bloom and his dead father, all that he has never told them, all that he still wishes to say. He mumbles of love and guilt, of the failures he has perpetrated in their names, of the future triumphs he had hoped to win by her side. He sees Nora's inner beauty and smells her scent of roseships and lavender talc, hears her giddy laughter, and feels the gentility of her touch. He thinks of his father, dead and possibly, inexplicably, charitable. And in such thoughts, begins to curse Lieber's name, to rail against him for the brutality of his past crimes, to call him a "cunt" and a "scoundrel," claiming "no feller's more deservin' of his fate, goddamnit." But then, in a sudden shift born of cold and lunacy, Abrams begins blubbering with apology, weeping like a shamefaced scourge. The tears streaming down his face are so hot they do not freeze until many minutes later, well after hitting the ice-block earth.

He grasps everything and nothing, and in the cold, dark night, these crushing truths prove too much. Stranded, abandoned on the Ozark Plateau, Abrams, in a last, wailing clutch at awareness before being overwhelmed by the heat of an impending unconsciousness, wants urgently to grab each side of his pale ribcage to wrench himself apart, to crack himself wide open, wherein the world might find the passionate beating of a heart once incapable of such a furious rhythm.

Instead, his chin falls to his chest as his eyes ease shut, and in spite of the cold, Abrams feels as if, from his toes to his crown, he is being slowly baptized in the warmest water he has ever known—

It's you I thought of today, and not my feet—

Struggling, his head bobs once, and then slips slowly toward his shoulder.

They was bad for a time, my feet, all yellow and hard from them many years—

His eyelids flutter.

People who sat in them soft-pillowed chairs laughed and said I shuffled, so I laughed too, but it wasn't for real. Today wasn't the same, though, 'cause I thought of you, like I do every second, of every day—

With an enormous sigh of relief, Abrams finally surrenders to the night.

A man, a Mister, came to my cart once. He wasn't a man to admire like I expect you'll one day grow to be, and I think if he didn't have no teeth, he'd of been ashamed to smile even for his children. But he was a man who paid easily enough, and now I wished I'd of set aside that sum for you, so my grandchildren would've been happy at my name.

This feller was wearin' a fine coat, only it was plenty ripe with the smell of fish, for that's what he told me his job was. Swear to the Lord, he smelled of your little hands after you'd come home from catfishin' with the boys, smelled of your rough cloth shirt and neck on them days, when you held and spoke to me as your momma.

I remember your face when I first said I was leavin', in that awful time of the fever. "No more," I said. "Won't be livin' among that little boy fish smell no more, I'm afraid." I remember my love and your silence and your back. I remember the look you gave me 'stead of debate. I explained though you didn't ask me to, of this Heaven where I'd meet you, how I wished for you to eat beef every day and talk good English and honor this world. I wished that you wouldn't never be afraid to share plates with a man in more silk than you got neither, or concern yourself with the alleys of the night or the blank appetites of foolish men. For you, I wished strength and earth alone—

"Slap him," orders a captain. "Harder. Here, pour some of this whiskey down his—careful now, Private! You, Jankauskas, take that revolting appendage off him this very instant, rub him down, get his blood running, drape that blanket over his shoulders. Quickly now, all of you. We've not a moment to lose."

Maybe I shouldn't have lost myself to sadness. I grew old and less handsome than even when you was born to me, though I loved you every day like wildfire. Eleven years we worked on our knees side by side, growin' the food of others, and one morning, like sadness, the fever came for me. Now I'm gone, and you're left to seed the land helped only by the strength I meant to give you, though seems to me you ain't growin' nothin' these days but misery.

I left you a goodly spell ago, in the time 'fore you was ward to streets, but I'm back now. And I'm here to say I know what you done, how you've tried to defend my name respectable, but the way you done it ain't set right with me. So for a while now, truth be told, I've been ragin' at you, hellfire-ragin', the way you went ahead to find your peace. But no longer, nossir. I'm all raged out, wishin' only for a basin of warm saltwater. I'm wishin' for a day when I might sit and rest my feet in a basin of warm saltwater, imaginin' it's the saltwater we worked so hard to keep out of the land of our home. And together, our feet soft and pink and all prune-like, you and me'll laugh at the idea of fish—

"To the infirmary, posthaste!" The captain snatches Jankauskas by the arm. "As though this man were your brother, Private. As though his very soul were your own."

36

Swaddled in a warm, woolen blanket, his raw fingers and toes bound in linen, by midnight Abrams has come to at last. Though blood pounds in his temples, his digits sting, and he is still terribly chilled, he has warmed enough to be freed of jeopardy. Lying on a cot, he groans as he props himself up onto an elbow to take in his surroundings. The makeshift hospital is composed of two conjoined canvas tents, forty feet long apiece, so arranged as to permit a central passage to run their length. Several oil lamps illuminate the blood-splattered nuns who scurry to and fro, frantically ministering to the injured. A few patients moan and others writhe, but apart from these occasional outbursts and mumbling conferences between surgeons, the infirmary is silent. Beside Abrams is a small folding table, on which someone has left cooling mugs of horse chestnut tea and shadow soup. Quickly, before he has another waking thought, he snatches up both and, famished as he has been over the past days, drains each mug with the hunger of a man grown too familiar with his body's shrill dependencies. Sighing with the desire for more, Abrams carefully rims the bottom of the soup mug with a gauze-clad finger, and then sucks on it like a child does a wound, as though, like a child, nourishment might still be found in injury.

Abrams groans again. His boots, bowler, and clothes he sees are tucked primly beneath the cot; unsurprisingly, the stag-handled dirk is no longer sheathed within. He rises fully to a seat, his legs dropped over the bedside. Gently, he clenches his right hand into a loose fist. "Whooo," he mutters, touching the tip of his nose. "Goddamn."

He looks to the right, where in the next cot over, Abrams spots the slumbering victim of Cobb and Petitgout's initial assault, his ribs bandaged. He appears to be as cadaverous as Abrams feels himself becoming with each rousing breath.

To his left, in the earthen aisle between the rows of occupied beds, he watches one of Schwientek's privates march swiftly toward him, rifle in hand. The notches on that rifle butt indicate the number of lives he has taken in battle—four, thus far—as demanded of all of Sergeant Cyryl Schwientek's men, though it feels to the young Union private a perverse use of the *Ars Mathematica* that his father, a DuPage County schoolmaster, so assiduously beat into him as a child. "Thank Christ," he gasps upon arrival, a note of the miraculous in his voice. "You're alive."

Abrams squints in pain as he carefully stretches his spine. "So's a gutter rat, reckon," he grunts, "but doubt you'd wanna be one."

"Well, whatever you are, stay that way. I'll be back."

While the private is gone, Abrams tries to stand, though the stinging pain in his feet forces him to return to his seat, hard. He winces at the effort and blows his frustration to the canvas ceiling. His extremities are afire, even as the flesh of his torso remains cold and clammy to the touch.

"Might I help you?" A nun looms above him. Her face is pale and Germanic, almost perfectly round with two large, blue eyes set a hint too far apart. But the perfection of her smile, the honesty of her inquiry, takes Abrams aback. Kindnesses, for him, have grown remarkably rare of late.

"Just lookin' for a friend, is all. Honestly, don't even know if he's here."

Her lily white hands are clasped ceremoniously together. She asks for a description of the man he seeks.

"Name of John Lee Carlson. Spectacles, hair like a summer hayfield, red-bearded, 'bout yeah-tall, real bookish type. Given to ramblin' on 'bout old-timey Greeks'n such."

The nun's face darkens for an instant, a betrayal that proves her innocent of the art of the bluff, before quickly regaining its composure. She smoothes her hands down the front of her habit, flattening what little Abrams can discern of her breasts beneath. Adjusting the large wooden crucifix that dangles around her neck, she exhales while Abrams braces for the worst. "Providing you're able," she says, "please follow me."

He does, though it is a hobbling path he takes.

She leads him toward a cot at the other end of the infirmary where, although the patient's eyes are wrapped in bandages, Abrams has no question as to the identity of the man who wears them. The nun then sets Abrams into a chair, rests her hand on his shoulder, and departs, but not before asking whether he needs anything else. Although he is still starving, slumped mournfully where he sits, Abrams shakes his head and sighs. He is unprepared for this. Before him on the canvas military cot, beneath those bandages, lies his friend and mentor, his brother and father, all of them, now maimed. Indeed, something within Abrams breaks. "John Lee," he whispers, "it's me, Elias."

The body on the cot stirs. The head shoots up from the pillow, twisting this way and that to isolate the direction from which the sound has come.

"John Lee," repeats Abrams tenderly. "It's me."

The mouth cracks an enormous grin, and then its head eases back down onto the pillow. "Telemachus, my boy," says Carlson weakly, "how good to see you again."

Abrams' mouth screws a smile, but he does not laugh.

"My spectacles," explains the professor, once he realizes that Abrams is capable of offering nothing more. "Blast seems to have shattered the lenses directly into my eyes. The surgeon, God bless his tactless soul, told me they resembled pickled quail eggs upon my admittance, dashed most gelatinously by innumerable shards of glass. Blinded for life, I'm afraid."

Abrams is at a loss. Carlson chuckles, though there is no humor in it. Silence falls heavily between them.

"At least it isn't very painful," adds Carlson. "Not yet, anyway. Wonderful stuff, that laudanum, my *word*."

Sitting beside his dear Carlson, Abrams feels within him a rusty-hinged vault slowly creaking open, and from within that vault, all the misery that has nothing to do with his own personal affairs now attempts to escape. It is a pure and generous anguish from which Abrams suffers, one that affects him only inasmuch as it affects this man he has so grown to love. Having lived since his mother's death almost entirely for himself, such compassionate concern is new to Abrams, and therefore, utterly awkward to grasp. He swallows down the lump in his throat, his eyes welling with tears. Scarcely able to contain his grief, he grips his friend's arm and then guides his fingers toward Carlson's bristled cheek, where he lets them linger for a moment. "Come to find," he manages at last, "world ain't much to look at these days, no how. You'll be awright, John Lee."

"*Tut, tut*, none of that now. Of course I'll be all right." Carlson grins at a vision that has little to do with sight. "Yes sir, from here on in, it's the home front for me. Nothing but my dear Imo and twins, my chindangler and my porch rocker, my face raised to the warmth of that delicious vernal sun." He inhales deeply, his nostrils flaring. "You know, I dare say I can smell those honeysuckle blossoms from here. And trust me, my young chum, they do smell fine."

"I wish my men were half as brave as you, sir," interjects a deep voice. "Truly."

"Who's there?" snaps Carlson, his reverie dispelled by the arrival of a Union captain standing above them, the private there upon Abrams' awakening at his elbow.

"Captain Henry Newton Frisbie," replies the officer, "Thirty-Seventh Illinois Infantry, Company G, mustered in Chicago, born in Oswego, New York, at your service." Frisbie is thirty-three years old, a dark-haired, full-bearded man of moderate height and build who, in the years to come, after arriving in New Orleans eighteen months hence, will eventually lead the Corps d'Afrique's Ninety-Second Infantry, U.S. Colored Troops, at the Battle of Yellow Bayou, Louisiana, and thus help salvage the Union's otherwise failed Red River Campaign. In time, he will achieve the rank of brigadier general and, ironically, settle in New Orleans forever, where, after marrying a woman forty years his junior, he will die a proud member of the community he had once fought so valiantly to defeat. But for now, standing benevolently above these two wounded Confederates born to the city where he will one day be buried, Frisbie offers nothing but peace. "I want you to know," he says to Abrams, "I've initiated court-marshal proceedings against Sergeant Schwientek for his most egregious breach of our military Code of Conduct. I should add that his current incarceration is being flavored by an especially piquant touch: I've made sure that his gag is the offending article of clothing in question." Frisbie leans over and speaks earnestly into Abrams' ear. "So tell me, Private, how're you feeling? Have you warmed?"

"What's going on here, Elias? 'Warmed?' Who *is* this man?" Carlson's tone has gained a frantic edge, as if, for the first time, he is beginning to understand the limitations of a life sensed by sound alone.

"I'll explain later, John Lee."

Begging the men's pardon, a nun returns with a cup in which she added pulverized opium to whiskey, concocting the laudanum whose properties Carlson so admires. She then lifts his chin to pour it down, for which he thanks her, Frisbie and Abrams waiting in embarrassed silence beside him. It takes almost a full minute for Carlson to begin to rub his nose and fade, but before he drifts off, he fumbles for Abrams' hand, pats it twice, and offers a dreamy, "G'bye, son."

With Carlson now asleep, Abrams turns to assess the enemy officer lording above him.

"I'm terribly sorry about your friend," says Frisbie.

Abrams grunts his appreciation. He looks hard into Frisbie's eyes, where he spots the kind of sympathy native to only the best of men and most accomplished of liars. He has listened to the split tongues of Gallatin Street for a decade now, watched the eyes of Silas Wolfe in action, even been forced to master the art himself. This man, Abrams quickly decides, is no liar. And so, for the time being, he chooses to set aside his own stores of anger to respond as graciously as he realizes this captain deserves. "I appreciate y'all savin' me. I ain't fibbin' when I say I'm much obliged for it. Name's Abrams."

"Nor am I fibbing, Private Abrams," answers Frisbie, "when I ask that you please accept my sincerest apologies for any maltreatment you may have suffered at the hands of the United States Army." He grabs a folding chair by its back. "May I?"

Wrapped tightly in his blanket, Abrams shivers and shrugs. "It's your party," he says.

Pleased by the invitation, the captain pulls up the chair beside Carlson's cot, orders Private Jankauskas to fetch them a bottle of something Irish and a bowl of hot cinnamon oats for Abrams, leans forward, and proceeds to tell all that he knows of what transpired after Schwientek abandoned Abrams at the base of that Arkansas pine. Jankauskas, Frisbie informs him, after dashing back to his barracks to replace the sock then doubling as foreskin, soon began to suffer pangs of conscience he had never before experienced. The fact that two corpses lay freezing stiff in that field nauseated him, but the prospect of a third man dying as a result of his active involvement proved too much. So, after Schwientek finally passed out sometime later, in spite of the wrath he anticipated upon the sergeant's awakening, Jankauskas took it upon himself to alert Frisbie to the misdeeds of the night.

Frisbie concludes his tale through tight, apologetic lips. "On my honor," he declares to Abrams, "Sergeant Schwientek's being dealt with in the harshest of all possible manners, I assure you."

"That man's plenty used to harshness."

"Indeed." Frisbie coughs into his fist. "Those men he killed tonight, they were friends of yours?"

"No." Abrams spits. He has nothing more to say on the matter.

Frisbie pinches his bottom lip. Understanding that the precise nature of Abrams' relationship to the slain Confederates makes little difference now that it has been violently ended by a man under his command, he decides to change the subject. "I'm assuming you're aware this is a parole camp, then?"

"Heard tell of such, but can't say I'm kin to the particulars."

"*Parole d'honneur*, comes from French, 'word of honor.'" Frisbie creaks in his chair. "In essence, should you sign an oath claiming that you'll not take up arms against the Union until there's an official prisoner-of-war exchange, I'll see to it that you're released on your own recognizance. It's quite common."

Abrams goes straight-backed in his seat and then narrows his eyes suspiciously. "You're sayin' I sign some paper, I can just get right up'n walk on out of here, head on home if I want to?" There is skepticism in his voice. "Simple as that?"

"*Voilà*, parole camp. Surely you don't think we're capable of any long-term internment here. We've been capturing so many of your kind recently, my goodness, we've nowhere to put you all." Frisbie slaps a haunch. "As long as you agree to stay yourself from all belligerent acts against the United States of America, you may go wherever you please, Private Abrams. You'll even have documentation to guarantee safe passage. What's more, in certain instances—say, I don't know, like *yours* for example—that kind of swap could take quite some time to transact. Why, I'm ashamed to admit that on occasion, paperwork such as yours even gets misplaced entirely." Here Frisbie's eyes show his captive their deeper meaning before they flit away toward his knee, which he dusts off distractedly.

Abrams' mouth falls slightly open. His heart begins to skip rapidly in his chest, for suddenly he is overcome with visions of his two inherited homes and their acres, of his darling Nora, of a life free of Wolfe now that the cousins from Algiers have been dispatched and his military service fulfilled. And yet, as if reacting to the wrong card flipped on the poker table before him, he cuts short his dreams just as quickly. Abrams has been so aching for words like these that, once heard, they are simply too suspect. He thinks of the dodgy proposals he has received throughout his lifetime, the false temptations, the inevitable failures of promise. His mother and Silas Wolfe, loves now dead to him. His father, a love never known. His darling Nora Bloom, a love he still fears at times he has been forced to invent. He thinks of Chief McClelland's suggested partnership, and of the patrimony Abrams might have coming to him in return for it, an idea he is on the verge of letting himself believe in but to which he cannot wholly commit. He ponders all these things and is sure about none of them. He has been a pawn too much in life. There must be an angle here, he decides. Nothing comes without a price. His jaw stiffens.

In returning his gaze to Carlson beside him, however, he softens. Men, he has been learning from this kindly professor, are as capable of nobility as they are of misconduct. It is the *choice* Abrams must now make, actually daring to distinguish between a person worth believing and one who must be doubted, that is humanity's greatest gift and its greatest damnation. To neither hate nor love exclusively, but to take responsibility in choosing the occasion of each—such is the burdensome trust we place in ourselves. "Just so's you know," he advises Frisbie at last, "I ain't goin' nowheres, 'less it's with this feller here. That's a deal breaker."

"Well, considering his current state of health," says the captain, "considering both your states in fact, I wouldn't have it any other way."

37

The river flows beneath them. Along the way home, Abrams' near-frostbite subsides and Carlson, when not succumbing to the merits of his laudanum, appears in good spirits. His eyes sting and throb, but both men are surprised by how well he can function. They have eaten more in the past week than in the past three. At first, their constitutions rebel against the heft of their meals, but soon, to their great delight, each man once again finds his stomach. On deck, wrapped in Union-issue blankets, they smoke and chat about the lives they have in store for them.

"Call me Tiresias," nods Carlson one afternoon, taking a judicious pull on his pipe. "Struck blind by the gods, that old Theban was, but eventually came to be seer of all seers." He chooses not to mention the prophet's insight into Oedipus' murder of his own father. "Not a bad skill to have," he adds, "a bit of the oracular."

"Couldn't hurt at cards none." Abrams decides to play along. "What you got in mind for me, then?"

Carlson purses his lips in contemplation. Were he still possessed of sight, to a bystander he would have appeared to be staring far off into the distance, a man in the midst of studying the dimensions of something deep and wide. "For you, Mr. Abrams," he begins in earnest, "I foresee a life richly woven, one filled with love and famine, tenderness and pain, victory and defeat. I see wisdom and age, joy and folly. I see children, a home. I see fields of your own planting. I see a lovely wom—"

"Awright, awright," laughs Abrams, "let's not go on and hoodoo it then, neither."

"What's so funny?" Carlson's tone has grown serious. "You asked, and I'm telling. Yours, my good sir, will be a well-lived life after all. In the words of dear, blinded Gloucester, but one of Shakespeare's many repentant fathers, 'I see it feelingly.'"

Abrams, still amused, expresses his thanks for the prophecy bestowed upon him, though in truth is more concerned that Carlson has shown no grief at his new condition. "And them eyes?" he asks carefully. "What kind of life you see for yourself without 'em?"

"Pish-tosh, a fine one. I may have lost my sight, but I'm alive. Lord, we both are. And after the months of suffering we've endured, what're the odds of that? You're the gambler, you tell me."

Abrams grunts at his friend's point.

Carlson strokes his beard. "Perhaps I'll turn to composition. If both Homer and Didymus of Alexandria could do it, why not John Lee Carlson, I wonder? Old Milton was blind as a beetle toward the end, and there's a fellow who dared to challenge the notion of Paradise itself." Carlson stops to consider the implication of his words. "He failed at it, of course, horrifically in fact, but you've got to admire his gumption." Almost as an afterthought, as if addressed to no one but his own literary tastes, he adds with a shudder, "Puritanical poetry, good *Lord*."

"But readin' all them books, John Lee," Abrams presses further, "you won't miss it?" He is only dimly aware of his insensitivity, that it might be too early to delve into his friend's loss like this, but as they steam southward toward his future with Nora, Abrams simply must know what it is like to look forward to a life deprived of that which you value most. Because while he is hopeful about the prospects Carlson has foreseen for him, he is no fool.

Carlson snorts. "Days ago, I would've claimed books feel emotion as profoundly as any man, but I'm through with metaphor. War's done me in on that, whether I begin writing them myself or not. At least I'll now be able to inhabit the world into which I've actually been born." He pauses. "Honestly, Elias, I walk through that front door, I expect to feel the embrace of my family as if for the first time, I just know it. Shoot, were there a bottle to be had, I'd drink in celebration of my condition, not to its wretchedness."

Later that night, however, Abrams is awakened in the cabin by the quiet sobbing of John Lee Carlson. The weeping Abrams hears before punching his own pillow and turning over for the night is that of a man in love with letters who has been forced, through tragedy and circumstance, to rewrite the very definition of his life's purpose.

—

They arrive in New Orleans four days later, eleven after the Battle of Elkhorn Tavern. During the rest of that time, Abrams avoided all talk of his friend's disability and in turn, explained in detail Schwientek's killing of the cousins from Algiers, then of his own humiliation at those same hands.

"But does it mean nothing to you," Carlson had asked in dismay afterward, "this Judaeophobia of his? Lord, you were nearly killed, for what?"

Abrams shrugged. "I ain't sayin' I enjoyed it now, but if the streets have taught me nothin', I've learned bein' different's only as hard as the man who's viewin' it as such. And that Schwientek feller, well I can tell you, he's got a pair of eyes on him that sees only meanness."

"So you're immune to the judgment of others, are you?" Carlson folded his arms doubtfully.

"Hold on now, John Lee, I ain't poured out the whole goddamned bucket yet." Abrams paused to get his thoughts in order. He knew that he was risking hypocrisy, for in his past he had been quick to fight anyone who mentioned his faith with the least perceptible slight. On that riverboat beside his friend, however, after a second's reflection, Abrams was surprised to discover that he was not talking tough for the sake of appearances alone. Rather, this was what he had come to truly believe. "See," he continued, "it wasn't so much my bein' Hebrew that stuck in his craw, I'd say. It didn't help, 'course, don't get me wrong, but could've been a clubfoot down below, what-have-you—wouldn't have mattered none. Man wanted me dead, plain and simple. Fact of my bein' Hebrew just gave him the route."

"But that's just my point, Elias. It *was* your being Hebrew. Now granted, I'll credit you with an admirably sophisticated outlook on things—Christ, when I was your age, I could hardly wipe my own back-side—but to be such an apologist for this man's behavior, I don't care how stern a headmaster the streets of your youth were, you must admit is perhaps too forgiving, no?"

"Bah," scoffed Abrams, dismissing his friend with a wave that Carlson did not see. "It's that way with all manner of hatred."

Of his mother's ghostly words out on the Ozark Plateau, Abrams will say nothing to anyone, ever. He remembers it only vaguely, anyway, though the presence he felt, be it death's approach or his mother's actual arrival, he will never forget. The sense of calming it has since granted him in the odd times of the night Abrams attributes solely to the warm memories of Gerta's love. Some conversations, he realizes, are not meant for company.

Instead, he expressed to Carlson an honest desire to see his part in his father's murder reconciled with what he now believes to be right. They spoke of it only once, tersely over supper, but in such a way that the professor never asked Abrams about it again. Abrams in that time alluded to Chief McClelland's letter and the prospect that were he to help jail the Cypress Stumps, he might come into his father's inheritance as a result. Yet Abrams wondered whether Carlson believed such an inheritance was likely at all, considering his father's long absence. "Seems awful fishy to me," he confessed. "Just can't wrap my head 'round the reasonin' as to why he'd do it, you know?"

To this, Carlson beamed beneath his bandages, saying that according to his own experience as a father, there was simply no telling what a parent might do. "You were his *son*, Elias," urged the professor, "you've got to remember that, and no amount of distance on his part was ever going to change that fact. Remember, too, that man's a notoriously sentimental beast, disposed to bouts of fierce regret and nostalgia, particularly as he ascends into the twilight of his years. So I can absolutely see him leaving you what's rightfully yours. Primogeniture demands it."

"But after what I done," said Abrams, his voice suddenly shameful, "I mean, you think I'm even worthy?"

"Was the Prodigal Son worthy of *his* father's inheritance?" replied Carlson. "The Gospel of Luke apparently thinks so, but that's only because the boy's repentance upon his return home was in earnest, as yours must be. *Ergo*, helping to imprison the Cypress Stumps won't only act to vanquish your nemesis there, but if your father did actually make you sole heir and beneficiary, it'll also enrich you immeasurably in terms of birthright, thereby adding to the Bloom family's estimation of you. Wonderful. But more importantly, Elias, I've no doubt that, if you allow it to, it'll help you resolve some of your complicity in his death indeed. Three birds with one stone, if you will. So again, in answer to your question, yes, I do think you're worthy of this inheritance, as much as any man I've ever met. Of course, before you collect a dime of it, you must first address this Wolfe character."

"Hell, I know what I gotta do, John Lee," was Abrams' only response. "And far as I'm concerned, that's all there is to it."

And so, coming ashore at the riverboat docks on the morning of March 18, 1862, John Lee Carlson clutches Abrams' left elbow and, with his other hand, prods his way through the world with a brass-tipped cane, a gift from Captain Henry Newton Frisbie of the Thirty-Seventh Illinois Infantry. Abrams slings their canvas sacks over a shoulder, each filled with what possessions they have accumulated since their internment.

The weather in New Orleans has been fickle of late, alternating between thunderous downpour and unexpected chill, but this day it has warmed. For the first time in months, these paroled Confederate soldiers squint at the brightness of an oncoming sun. "We two, Elias," murmurs Carlson, "like blinded Orion led by the youth Cedalion, in search of Helios' first light."

Together, they walk onward.

Though it is a city under martial law, decreed by Confederate Major General Mansfield Lovell but three days prior, though its port flirts with an enemy drifting closely ashore and its streets brace for the invasion of foreign heels, New Orleans remains proud. Whatever may come, whatever calamities it may face, and whatever challenges lie ahead, its inhabitants have come to accept that everything about New Orleans is so incongruent with the rest of America's ideals that there cannot possibly exist anything beneath it all but great scandal. Yet it is the jubilation with which they deal with that scandal that gives it such charm. The people of New Orleans possess the exact amount of *joie de vivre* each New Yorker or Bostonian is forced to surrender when living in a place where outward action exceeds the importance of inward freedom. For this reason alone, Abrams could not be happier to be home, regardless of the threat his city is facing. Nora's Burmese scarf knotted loosely at his throat, his companion by his side, he inhales gloriously the scents of tea olive and river mud, feels the balm of a breeze gently escorting him from behind as he strolls his city streets like an old-time familiar. He hitches the sacks over his shoulder. At his elbow, John Lee Carlson urges him to pick up the pace.

On the Nayades Street steam car, chugging toward Carlson's upriver neighborhood, Abrams tries to ignore the clucks of the female passengers aimed at his blinded friend beside him, the civilian male nods of sympathy and support. For John Lee Carlson, the subject of their concern, none of it matters: he is so looking forward to returning to his family that he is oblivious to such things. Eagerly rocking back and forth in his seat in anticipation of his wife's first kiss, he has no time now to suffer the pity of strangers.

They arrive at Urania Street before long. Striding quickly over from their trolley stop on St. Charles, Carlson halts once to remove his slouch hat, run a hand through his hair, and take a deep, cleansing breath. "Most men," he says, licking his lips nervously, "well, they'd be concerned about arriving home like this. About their wives' reaction, I mean, about how having a husband maimed as I am, they might be overwhelmed by the eventual infantilism of it all." He sniffs and then holds his head up high. "But I've no such worries, Elias. Not with my Imo."

He then grabs Abrams by his elbow and spurs him ahead.

Minutes later, they are standing before the columns of Carlson's home. Abrams turns to his friend. "Daffodils beginnin' their bloom, John Lee. Crepe myrtles not long to follow. You sure you're ready for this?"

Carlson takes another deep breath and smiles. "Like nothing before in my life," he says proudly. "Lead on."

—

The screams of delight that will erupt from that home in the oncoming hours would have caused complaint from his neighbors under almost any other circumstance, had those neighbors, too, not soon appeared and joined in their elicitation. The twins will bounce gleefully on their father's knees and pull at his bandages. They will squeal as he pokes blindly at their bellies. At dusk, they will fall asleep in the crook of each arm. Imogene Carlson will speak little as she watches this, and though she will be anguished by her husband's sightlessness, the purity of the joy registered on her face will exhaust her cheeks for days to come. Elias Abrams, a most welcomed young uncle, who when not pulling cards from behind the girls' tiny ears or holding Imogene around her shoulders or tugging on John Lee's hairy chin, will take a series of moments to lean against a wall and study a family happier than any he had thought possible. And in such a wonderful sight, while he will leave his belongings behind at the Carlson household, a place he has been invited to stay for as long as he wishes, Abrams will know precisely whom he must visit before the day is done.

"Elias, Elias, Elias," Carlson will sigh cheerily as they feast on what beefsteak Imogene is able to muster, "for as many defining moments as you'll be entitled throughout your life, you'll have an equal number of chances to forget exactly who you are, where you came from, and what you know to be true. More, perhaps. With such platitudinous words in mind, dear friend, unsolicited though it may be, my final counsel for the night is this: don't you dare forget any of it. That being said, the door'll be unlocked upon your return. Use it." Carlson concludes his lesson by pounding the table festively. "Now then, how about one of you sighted wonders pours me a dollop of that gravy there, huh?"

38

Abrams reaches the station house a few minutes after sunset. Located on the first floor of the Cabildo in Jackson Square, a jail situated behind it, over the years those headquarters have housed as much malfeasance and cruelty as the most reprobate Gallatin Street hideout ever has. Surprisingly, Abrams has only been inside once before, when he was nabbed as a youth for single-handedly thrashing three wealthy merchants' boys, the reasons long since forgotten. Cuffed about the head, ears pulled raw, and rump kicked repeatedly by laughing policemen, with a stern oath Abrams swore as he was tossed out onto the slate steps that he would never again enter those headquarters if he could help it. He realized, too, that he got off lightly. Hundreds have entered, never to be seen again.

Abrams walks in now nonetheless. After witnessing the joy on the faces of his friend's family, after basking in the comfort of the furnishings their moderate wealth has been able to afford them, Abrams knows that if he is to have any real chance with Nora Bloom, he must present her with more than mere desire. He must present her with prospect. He will therefore collect on whatever legacy he has coming to him, whether justifiably owed or not. If Wolfe's ruin is to be part of the bargain, so much the better. Still, crossing that station's threshold sends a coldness down his spine.

Perched at a desk just beyond the foyer sits a stubborn-looking policeman scrutinizing a ledger, his brows knotted with confusion. He looks up. His face is a withered fist.

Abrams takes a deep breath. "I'm here to see Chief McClelland," he announces a bit too loudly, "he ain't gone home already. Name of Abrams."

"Well, la *ti*." The old sergeant then stands with a mutter and disappears into an office behind him. Abrams looks around the room. A handful of lawmen sit at their desks, Special Officer Dalrymple among them. He looks blankly at Abrams, a toothpick jutting just beyond his obscenely bucked teeth. His expression could not reflect greater stupidity as he huffs at their new guest and closes his eyes, his folded arms wriggling comfortably into his chest. Within seconds, he is snoring. Some doze with their dirty boots kicked up, others slumber on forearms crossed over their ink blotters. Those few who are awake pay him no heed. Villains do not enter this place of their own accord.

Abrams exhales apprehensively, though his feet remain firmly planted. *It's 'bout you and Nora and the inheritance and all that goddamned land,* he thinks, steeling himself. *It's 'bout movin' on with your life already, so just be strong, goddamnit.* There is too much at stake for him to leave now.

The sergeant returns a minute later trailing Chief John McClelland, a dapperly dressed man of indeterminate age. Clad entirely in civilian black, his single-breasted frock coat of European import, McClelland is neither tall nor short, his eyes gray and granular, as if etched in chips of rock salt. They are determined, like the various margins of his face. Beneath his finely crafted bell crown topper, his hair might have the odd streak of gray in it, too, though Abrams is unsure. His dark mustachios are well-pruned but otherwise indistinguishable from the thousands that sweep down New Orleans' city streets each day. In a lineup of the accused, John McClelland would escape detection every time. It is this vagueness of aspect that makes him such a talented law officer; he is less a vessel of his own personal experience than one of something far more archetypal. Other than his eyes, his only discernible feature is the whalebone baton he keeps sheathed in his belt. With it, he has broken many men.

From beyond the wooden railing that divides the station house, McClelland smiles politely at the sight of Abrams. Then, without introduction, he holds the swing gate open, suggesting that his young guest walk through. Abrams does so, silently.

Back in McClelland's office, a room as difficult to qualify as the man who occupies it, Abrams is instructed to please sit down. "How old're you, son?" the chief begins as he, too, sits.

"Twenty."

"Bet you never imagined you'd voluntarily walk into a place like this."

Abrams defies his nerves with a shrug of indifference. "Lately, there's lots of places I been I never featured I'd enter."

"I don't doubt it. Glass of water? Whiskey?"

"Nossir, I'm fine." Abrams shifts in his chair. He will waste no time. "You look in on that Bloom family like I asked?"

Chief McClelland lies with ease, as gracefully as any child, assuring Abrams that he has put his very best men on it, though he has done nothing of the sort. He is too busy taking in the soldier before him to be concerned with such meager truths. During his tenure as lawman, McClelland has confronted rowdies and garrotters and brawlers by the thousands, men far viler in nature than any this Abrams could ever conceive. Baby fuckers, corpse fuckers, horse fuckers, rustlers, thieves, outlaws, arsonists, rapists, voodooists, sodomites, butchers, bashers, duelers, drunks, murderers, madams, whores, pimps, pocket-pickers, opiumheads, grave-robbers, road agents, renegades, firebrands, embezzlers, usurers, counterfeiters, cutthroat niggers, and once, a cannibal named Blanchet who, while awaiting incarceration, his wrists fettered tightly behind him, had gazed upon the staff of gawking policemen with a look of preternatural longing. Abrams thus presents him with nothing new, though the chief finds he is somewhat impressed by the coolness of the private's demeanor, the obvious intelligence in his eyes. He will be no rube, of this the policeman is sure. "I've got something here I want to read to you before we start," he says, withdrawing a yellowed trail of newsprint from a drawer in his desk. "Sort of an hors d'oeuvre to the meat of the meal, as it were."

Abrams yawns. It is a false yawn, triggered by the anxiety of where he now sits.

"The *Bee*," reads McClelland aloud, "March 22, 1854, and I quote: 'The police in New Orleans have become a source of universal and well-founded complaint, a mighty and odious despotism now foisted upon the community. They are, in this reporter's eyes, little more than a powerful, well-disciplined and unscrupulous balloteering machine, employed by skillful and reckless management to influence doubtful elections.'"

Abrams crosses his legs and sniffs. He will not contest such a claim.

McClelland has more, and from the drawer pulls a second clipping. "This one here's the *Delta*, January '55: 'A thousand murders might be committed in New Orleans, and if the murderers are not found on the spot, our authorities never afterward make any efforts to have them punished.'" McClelland tosses the clippings aside. "Now, any idea why I might have such antiquated articles in my possession?"

Abrams yawns again, more aggressively. He cannot help himself.

McClelland sighs and pulls the whalebone baton from his belt, placing it ominously on the desktop beside the clippings. "They're in my possession, Mr. Abrams, so they might act as reminders of what I must do in the fulfillment of my job's responsibilities. They are proven reminders of our department's past failures." He carefully arranges the papers on his desk. "Of course, they were written during Crossman's and Lewis' terms, not Monroe's, I understand that. But as I was asked by our new mayor to clean up these streets, especially now that martial law's just been declared, I'm going to do my damnedest to make that happen. Do you understand?"

"Reckon my English is fine, yessir."

McClelland clenches his jaw and stares at the young man, wondering whether it would be prudent to cave in his skull at this stage of negotiations. After a long minute, he decides against it. "That's not all," he says. "Here." He takes out a third newspaper clipping from the desk and hands it over for Abrams to read. It is the *New Orleans Daily Picayune*, dated January 1, 1862, published but two and a half months before the conversation they are now having:

WANTED

Good able bodied men to join the McClelland Guards, Company "B" to form the 5th Louisiana Battalion into a Regiment, now stationed at Columbus, Kentucky. Pay to commence immediately, on signing the roll, and liberal bounty paid. Uniforms, arms and equipments furnished. Apply at once.

Abrams hands the notice back over. "Mighty gallant of you, Chief, but come to find death don't need no seekin'."

"Be that as it may," replies McClelland, "I've some fight left in me that no amount of civic duty can satisfy. I was up in Kentucky and Tennessee back in October of last year, looking in on our boys. Suffice it to say that it inspired me, their dedication. But before I leave, I've got matters to tie up locally. The truth is, Abrams—and I've already leaked this out into the streets to stoke the coals a bit, so tell whomever you'd like for all I care—I've initiated a sweep on a scale heretofore unseen in New Orleans law enforcement. Bill Swan, Bison Murrel, the whole of the St. Thomas Street Willies, that mad harpy Lizzie Collins and her crew, what's left of *Les Diables Jeunes*, the Claffeys, the Laheys, the Hash Brothers, and the list goes on and on—they're all about to get a mighty rude awakening but soon, I can promise you that." The chief goes quiet and then adds by way of explanation, "There's a colonelship waiting for me, you see."

"Congratulations."

"Fuck your congratulations." McClelland is done humoring the boy. He bears down on Abrams, his right grip now white-knuckling the baton. At the moment, he is unaware that in only a month's time, as colonel, he will act as Mayor Monroe's emissary to Federal Admiral Farragut in surrendering the city of New Orleans. Neither does he know that he will eventually be jailed himself by Union forces for services so nobly rendered to the Confederate cause. At the moment, McClelland has but a single, governing concern: "I also happen to want those goddamned Cypress Stumps."

Abrams slowly removes his bowler and runs a hand through his hair.

"They were recently spotted as far uptown as Upperline, where, or so one of my informers tells me, they brutally robbed several of our wealthier citizens, bruising far more than their egos. One of the unfortunate gentlemen—a dear fellow and family friend—remains comatose, his outlook bleak." McClelland releases the baton and pushes away from the desk. "So you see, Abrams, I don't care how you do it, just get it done. You once belonged to them, if you don't still—you'll decide on which way's best. Dead, alive, doesn't make a difference to me. Hell, I'll take that shit-heel Wolfe alone, if he's all you can manage. The others will scatter like a house of cards in a hurricane, we get him behind bars."

"Believe that's so," sighs Abrams in agreement. He props forward in honest inquiry, his elbows to his knees. "You don't mind my askin', why can't y'all just round them up y'allselves, you want 'em so bad? They're down to five lone men, last I heard."

"I've got policemen enough for the job, true," concedes McClelland. "Problem is, we can't ever seem to catch them off Gallatin, when they're most vulnerable. Of course, there's always the prospect of confronting them there directly."

"Oh nossir, I wouldn't counsel that."

"Fine, so then you know we can't take a step onto that street before the alarm's sounded on us. Rogues there just vanish, like ghosts. And even if we did somehow drag them from their hole, aside from the fight they'd put up themselves, we'd have a hell of a time making it off the street alive, you know that, doesn't matter how many men I bring. Too many windows and doors with too much anonymous lead flying from them."

"How d'you plan to wrangle up them other mobs then," Abrams wonders aloud, "even if I was to hand over Wolfe like you're askin'?"

"I've my ways," says McClelland blandly. "By which I mean, of course, that's none of your business. What is your business is the current topic of conversation. And the fact that I'm running out of time. And patience." McClelland's tone drops again; its tenor shows that he is not fooling. "Only if you can't give your assistance, if you find that your loyalties prove a little difficult to realign. I'll then be forced to consider you still among those Stumps after all. And if that's the case, I'll have no choice but to very quickly yet very thoroughly make you see the error of your ways."

Abrams gnaws on his bottom lip. He must ask. "You ain't curious 'bout my part in all this? What they're accused of?"

McClelland opens his palms as if warding off disease, his back going stiff as he stands straight. "Son, I never met your father. They tell me he wasn't much for the politicking circuit. Fine. But that doesn't mean I'm not responsible for seeing to it that someone answers for his death. Now, whatever part you may have had in it, I'll just leave that between you and your preacher. I don't know. And frankly, Abrams, I don't *want* to know. I *do* know, though, that in all my years no murderer's ever contacted me first, never once, as you did with your letter. Not particularly social types with the law, most killers. I'd therefore put my money down that somebody else gripped the hilt that night." McClelland arches his eyebrows. "But see, that's not all I know. I also happen to know that war heroes such as yourself are a tough sell at the judge's bench these days, and growing tougher by the day. So as far as I'm concerned, you get me Wolfe, we're square. Whether you're square with the Lord or not—well now, that's up to you."

Abrams brushes his mouth grimly with his foreknuckles.

"Just to prove I'm not all intimidation," adds McClelland, relaxing into his chair, "I've got your father's will right here in this drawer." He pats his desk affectionately. "You do this right, you do your best to get me what I want, and everything he owned is yours, simple as pie. You do it wrong, though, and I've got to tell you, Abrams—Christ, to be perfectly frank, it won't much matter in the end *what* I tell you. Wolfe'll have his say in that." He stares hard. "Are we clear on this?"

Abrams stands. "As juniper gin, sir."

39

Throughout his walk over to Hercules Street, his pace a brisk clip, Abrams feels his lungs expanding with a giddiness that forces him to stop on more than one occasion and shake his head with laughter. He is buoyant with the confidence born of a youth just having dealt with authority and been treated by it as an asset. McClelland's implied threats do not faze Abrams; life has taught him that such positions of power invariably demand the use of iron words. They are no more ominous to him now than the daily discourses of his past. More important still, he knows that the upshot of all this is too great for him to dare refuse the chief's request. *Relax*, Abrams thinks to himself. *Ease your mind now, Elias, you'll take care of Wolfe in time, ain't nothin' to worry about there. No reason to be scared of him no more, all the war you've seen. You ain't breakin' no law of Gallatin Street Wolfe ain't broken first. 'Sides, McClelland's only askin' for what you've been wantin' to do for yourself now anyway. He knows you ain't killed your daddy, told you so himself. Didn't give you no due date on when it needs gettin' done, neither. Unlike the drunken fool you was last go-round, you just take your time, plan it out real good, step-by-step, and everything'll fall in line, guaranteed. 'Cause once you get that wrapped up, you'll be earnin' outright what the old man left behind for you, free and clear, with Nora sure to follow."* Abrams stops en route and smiles, his hands going to his hips. *"Goddamn if this ain't what you've been aimin' at all along."*

In receiving McClelland's pledge that his father's land is indeed his for the taking, Abrams thus walks even livelier toward the Bloom home. Now that he has no choice but to confront the boys—a sentence he finds somehow relieving—and for it receive more than the redemption he has been seeking since his father's murder, Abrams decides for the interim to clear his head of all thoughts but those dedicated to Nora. That he has practiced for days what he will first say to her, that he has debated whether to take her up into his arms with a mighty whirl and dare to kiss her lips forthrightly, he now finds irrelevant. "I'm back, darlin'," he has decided to say, "and I don't expect to leave you again."

Sitting lovingly beside her, his hand cupped in hers, Abrams imagines he will then speak to Nora of *amores bichos*, love bugs, those swarming insects from the tropics he had once heard described to him by a Costa Rican whore in the huffing midst of their congress. He will explain the poetry of how, once coupled at their abdomens, they become the very meaning of visceral attachment. A grafting, like ice to ice. He will mention how, bumbling in one direction and then another, they pull themselves taut and back, a concertina wheeze, mindless and flying and never questioning who or why and never pining for a single moment of solitude. How their motives go unquestioned, always. An "I love you," never withheld because of who said it last. They simply become one because.

Abrams plans to pass on all these lover's proofs to Nora, and more. He will tell her of everything he has endured since their last meeting, of the pain and the misery, of the wounds and the starvation, but he will not exploit these hardships. He will only inform her of them so that she might understand how her love made his life worthwhile in times when it could have meant so little. He will tell her of the land and inheritance he has coming to him and of his desire to share them with her forever.

Abrams arrives at her home just before eight o'clock. With his bowler clutched in hand, he looks up to the evening sky, mumbles a quick prayer, and then raps on the Blooms' great maple door. Awaiting an answer, musing on the friendly chidings he received from the Carlsons that afternoon for not sending ahead a visiting card this time either, he is bouncing on the balls of his feet, whistling a tune he does not know, and working hard to stifle the pounding of his heart. His anxiety is different from one born of combat, but as with combat—the racing pulse, the shallow breaths, the beaded brow—Abrams' nerves are beyond his own control, and he thus feels love and combat each to be drawn from a very similar deck.

The door creaks open. He holds his breath. It is Violet, whose eyes flash wide at the sight of him and then look imperceptibly away.

"Evenin', Violet," he says with a broad smile. "Appears I've come a-callin'."

Violet picks at a speck on the doorframe. She cannot meet his gaze. After an uncomfortable pause, she says, "Don't believe she be wantin' to see you, suh."

"Oh?" Abrams raises an eyebrow and then hitches his stance. "And why's that, d'you think?"

"No suh, ain't for me to say."

"Well then," he says, "how 'bout we find us someone who can?"

"No suh, don't believe." Shaking her head, Violet gums back her tears and begins to close the door on him.

"Wait now!" he cries, throwing a palm hard against the door, "just hold it right there, nigger girl. Somebody's got to explain to me what the hell's goin' on here. Please, I'm askin'."

"That don't mean nothin' to me, you askin'." She looks at him frankly. "Only person you *should* be askin' is the Lord Almighty, and that's fo' His forgiveness."

The door slams in his face. As surprised as he is by it, Abrams does not notice the *mezuzah* affixed to the upper third of the doorpost on the right side, or its upper slant inward. Nor does he know that, among the Bloom women, his first visit to their home has already been likened to the Angel of Death's.

He has been struck in the midriff many times throughout his life, but never has the wind been taken from him so swiftly, so completely, by such an odd combatant. He has been kicked in the balls by bullies, bashed on the head by apes, and left for dead on three distinct occasions. Never, though, has a moment without violence left him feeling so hollow. He stares about him, dumbstruck. He replaces his bowler atop his head. He looks down the street, to the palatial homes of Nora's neighbors, and does not think of the women within, of their breasts and hips and mouths, of their warm embraces and the manner in which they might sugar his beignets in the morning. Abrams does not think of the satisfaction they might bring him at night. Instead, he thinks only of the dreadful pit in his stomach. Offering a lingering look at the Bloom house, he spots his darling Nora peeking from behind their lace curtains. He waves at her, anemically. She lets the curtain go.

Suddenly, he sets his jaw, for it dawns on him that he has traveled thousands of miles since receiving her first letter to arrive at the site where he now stands. He has fought in pitched battles, been shot, starved, wet and frozen and filthy like a February puddle, humiliated until near-dead, told like a dog to fetch the lives of his enemies, and borne the unceasing guilt of a patricide he had ultimately decided against committing. It is enough; something in him snaps. *Not like this, not after what I've went through, nossir!* He thus starts banging on the door with all his strength, first one hand and then the other, a relentless bid for entry, and although he does not call Nora's name aloud, his desire to be near her resounds throughout Hercules Street. Seconds pass, and his fingers sting with each thump on the door, but he has decided to see this day through to its end.

An older woman he can only assume is Nora's mother answers. She is wrapped in a dark fishu, her Garibaldi dress beneath, an even deeper shade of mourning. The jeweled cameo at her throat and onyx earrings dangling from her lobes are her only suggestions of vanity. Her face is wooden, her eyes impassive. She possesses her daughter's broad-bridged nose and thick black hair, here fisted up into a severe bun, but something in her aspect betrays a sadness of which he hopes Nora will never be capable.

"Ma'am," says Abrams, removing his bowler with a quick bow. "I'm Elias Abrams, soldier friend of Nora's. Sorry 'bout the rumpus, but afraid I'm needin' to see your daughter."

Rosa Bloom's face falls from saddened to sickened. Her lips begin to tremble, her hands begin to shake, and, an instant before losing her composure altogether, she lifts her nose haughtily aloft. "I thank you, sir," she manages, fighting back her rage, "though we've had quite enough association with you, I should think."

"But that's just it," rejoins Abrams, his voice shriller than he wishes, "if you could tell me exactly *what* I done, I could easier wrap my head 'round how to undo it."

"The only thing I would have you *undo*, Mr. Abrams, is your ever having met my daugh—" Rosa Bloom's tirade is interrupted by the hasty steps of someone approaching the other side of the door, which then opens wider as that person arrives. It is his darling Nora, her day dress a deep indigo, her face much anguished. And in her grief, in the vulnerability it bequeaths her, she has never looked more beautiful.

Abrams' heart breaks at the very sight of her: "Aw, Nora," he says softly.

Dr. Chester Rayburn Killick, the aged neighbor next door, has in the meantime hobbled onto his porch to investigate the disturbance. He says nothing, but through his thick spectacles studies the scene with passing interest. When he quickly realizes that the heretics on the porch beside him will in no way further infect his evening, he nods at Rosa Bloom once, politely, and then returns indoors where, alone as he has been for decades, he will finish off his reserve of amontillado.

Nora offers no reply to Abrams' tender acknowledgment. Like Violet, she, too, avoids his eyes. The three of them stand in silence. The distance between them is immense.

"I'm askin' y'all, *please,*" begs Abrams, his frustration growing from heated to hopeless, "won't nobody just tell me what I done already? An explanation ain't too much to ask, is it?"

Nora's mother sees the earnest inquiry in Abrams, and it startles her. She knows men who lie, for while she has long been aware of her husband's affair with Selene Giroux, a beautiful quadroon the color and languid pacing of bayous on whom he lavishes jewels and affection, a nineteen-year-old he has situated in a part of town to which Rosa has never been, Solomon Bloom will confess to nothing. She sees no such untruth in the young man now before her. Indeed, in a world rife with deception, it takes little skill to detect the brand of honesty Abrams proposes. The perplexity in his eyes, the appeal in his voice, the obvious depth of his concern: she knows that no true sinner arrives at the home of the transgressed against thusly equipped. It is for these reasons she has not threatened Abrams with the police or requested Dr. Killick call them when earlier given the chance. And yet, in the tragedy befallen her daughter at what she has been told is the fault of this same young man, she forgives him not an inch. "You may say goodbye to him, Nora. But that is all." She folds her arms, refusing to move. A chaperone has never been more necessary.

The intensity of that porch's silence is matched only by Abrams' desire to snatch Nora up into his arms. He has so much to tell her. Of the plans he has laid for them, of the great house in Napoleonville he is set to inherit and the children they will raise there, of the proud agriculturalist he will become and the joy he will afford her. He wants to catalogue every seed they will sow in the garden plot behind that great home, every leaf they will nurture, every bounty they will reap. Over the passing months, he has constructed hours of such fantasies and wants now to explain them to her in meticulous detail, as though speaking them aloud will give further credence to their likelihood. His emotions roiling turbulently within him, he can stand it no longer. He takes a step toward her.

She takes a step back. She has begun to cry.

"Goddamnit all!" he shouts, stomping his foot, "why won't nobody *answer* me?"

"Young man!" spits Rosa Bloom, "such language will hardly benefit your cause!"

Yet the urgency of Abrams' tone forces Nora's eyes and nostrils to flare wide, causing her to consider him as if for the first time. Though he has been associated with the worst of crimes, she, too, sees in him an honesty that, in its unyielding manner, has begun to erode her resolve. She desperately wants to believe him, for she is young and above all else wishes to adhere to the forgiving properties of love. "Truly now," she says skeptically, "you're saying you don't know?"

"Lord, girl, I can't say it no plainer."

"If you're manipulating us here, Elias," her voice still mistrustful, "God have mercy on your soul."

"We live in a sinful world, I know it. But please, just start with the tellin'. That's all I ask."

She looks to crumble where she stands. "Only last week. It happened only then." She turns to her mother, who has herself begun to cry. "Oh, Elias, it's just too terrible." Her eyes rimmed in tears, Nora stops to nibble apprehensively on a finger, as though what she might next say will inflict wounds from which her tongue shall never heal. "*Ravished*," she whispers at last, her eyes wide, her voice quivering with grief, "ravished by a great beast of a man."

Already at these words, his gaze gone hard as stone, his teeth clamped furiously together, Abrams begins to calculate how many men must die. "Describe him."

"A great beast of a man with long, golden hair," continues Nora, "who claimed that *you're* to blame, that it's *your* doing, Elias, all of it!"

With closed eyes, his breath easing from him, Abrams sees the precise method with which he will kill Goliath Mueller. He will bronze that long, golden hair with blood. He will make an art of it. It will be a masterpiece.

Nora has begun to weep piteously into her hands, her mother weeping behind her. "Poor, poor puss," she moans, "our poor, poor Josie."

Abrams eyes flicker open: "Josie?"

When Nora nods her miserable assent, Abrams' knees nearly buckle with relief as he moves toward her, Rosa Bloom stepping frostily between them. "If you had nothing to do with it," whimpers Nora, "why would he say it's your fault? How would he even know your name?"

Before she can press him on this, Abrams moves a full pace forward, gently. "Listen to me, Nora," he murmurs over Rosa Bloom's protective shoulder, "both of y'all, please listen. If you don't never hear another word I say, I need y'all to hear me right now—I ain't had nothin' to do with that." He regards Nora at an arm's length. "I'm awful, awful sorry for what happened, and trust me, I know more 'bout such things than you'll ever care to believe, way it can affect a woman and her kin both. And don't y'all worry, neither, I'm gonna find that son-of-a-bitch what done it to Josephine, too, and make him pay long'n painful." His stare moves from Nora to her mother and back again. "But it wasn't me."

"Swear, Elias." Nora's eyes are large and pleading. Her mother's are closed. "Swear you had nothing to do with this."

"I done plenty wrong in my life, Nora, I won't deny it, but what you're talkin' about here just ain't among 'em."

"Swear."

Elias Abrams, his eyes unbroken from hers, gets deftly down onto his knees and braids his fingers into a solemn act of beseeching before these two women. Though his next words will be honest, in his past familiarity with the Cypress Stump Boys, in the tangential sense of blame he will later assume for Mueller's crime against Josephine, for his not having warned the Blooms more explicitly when given the chance, Abrams will in fact need years to fully forgive himself, just as he will never forgive McClelland for his lie about their protection. But for now, all prospect of future joy hanging in the balance, Abrams' sole concern is persuading his darling Nora Bloom and her mother of his innocence. "*I swear,*" he whispers, "on a stack of all that's holy, I didn't have nothin' to do with it. Fact is, Nora, I ain't done nothin' these months but love you."

Mother and daughter study Abrams through discriminating eyes, this young man who has taken to his knees in the attempt to convince them of what Nora prays to be true. Neither woman knows the extent of Abrams' intimacy with the culprit, and even if they did, they would find it difficult to blame him for the immoral acts of another. Nora herself draws no parallel between his earlier words of warning and this consequent crime. Indeed, standing pigeon-toed before him, her arms falling limply to her sides, she trusts in Abrams' innocence, for like her mother, in the cynicism of their times, Nora has grown astute at distinguishing looks of falsehood from truth. And yet, to her own deep and abiding dismay, she knows, too, that she is left but one thing to say. "Oh, what does it matter?" she laments, "what does it really?" She turns away from him. "Such mawkish fools we've been, we two."

Quietly, she follows her mother into the house. Then, with the deliberation of one whose cruelty is not intended but whole, she closes the door on Elias Abrams, locking it tightly behind her.

40

Abrams does not know how the Colt has come to be in his hand. He has acted without awareness before, in the midst of the Third Louisiana's two great battles, the reliance on instinct to navigate him through danger. Here again, he acts solely on reflex. His march toward Gallatin Street is unyielding, his paces mechanical. His head does not turn. His eyes remain fixed. He seethes the whole way.

So this is what it is like to drown.

Once arrived at Truett's Saloon, he parts the whores and drunkards who clutter the first half of the bar, the cardsharps and dandies and country oafs with dirty slits for mouths, on his storming path toward the back where the Cypress Stump Boys reign. Little grog monkeys, a job Abrams himself once held at age seven or eight, flit underfoot, distributing whiskey and newspaper-lined baskets of boiled shrimp and raw oysters while dodging the goose-pinches of the lechers whom they are paid to serve. At the back of the bar, Abrams finds the Moroccan cushions empty, as is I. J. Lieber's desk and chair. He whips his head each way in fury and frustration, seeking some release for the killing inside him. All forbearance, all concern and caution, have been replaced in him by a need for reprisal. He has lost everything he had ever dreamed of now that Nora is gone, and someone must pay, even if it means his own life. The inheritance without her to share it has no worth. The land will reap only embittering reminders of her absence. If he has learned nothing over these past months, Abrams has learned that the best of men—the ennobled and the wicked alike—will die for what they believe. The meaning of life is thus to find a reason why you might then willfully end it. And even though the South was not a cause for which Abrams would gladly sacrifice everything, he will defend the honor of Miss Nora Bloom's family until his very last breath. Of that he is without doubt.

In his youth, however, he has failed to grasp a last relevance: no man kills for honor alone. To kill, there must be an appeal to wrath. And it is this appeal to which Abrams has this night so graciously yielded. He bolts from the saloon, unsatisfied.

Unfit to return to the Carlsons' home, he spends the remainder of the evening back at that flophouse on Dauphine, a bottle in hand. He drinks in the room he has rented, muttering endlessly to the floor. He contemplates his gun. He drinks more. He does not consort with any of the parlor whores. He does not bathe or touch himself. He simply stares at his boots, drinks grimly from the bottle, and heaves such sobs of grief that his walls soon thunder from the fists of a disturbed neighbor beside him. When Abrams in turn crashes into that neighbor's room with the Colt in hand and a tragic fierceness in his soul, the man, quickly construing the menace before him, offers his sincerest apologies.

"You go ahead'n squall all you want now," the man says warily, his blanket drawn up to his eyes. "Sometimes a feller's just got to get it out, them demons what ail him."

A palm to his tear-swollen eyes, Abrams leaves without word and staggers downstairs to demand from the hôtelier a set of writing supplies. Back at the crude table beside his bed moments later, sobbing with regret and simmering with rage, Abrams drafts the last love letter he will ever write Nora Bloom.

—

When he revisits Truett's Saloon the following evening, he is still furious, though his impetuosity of the night before has been tempered, lost to an anger more thoroughly considered. It has gained heft.

The Moroccan cushions remain empty, but I. J. Lieber's chair and desk are not, for there sits Silas Wolfe in all his resplendence. Crystal tumbler in hand, he is attentively studying the blueprint of a mansion filched from the city archives, a gift from a disgruntled clerk looking to join the gang. Over the months, Wolfe has demanded that the boys leave him be when planning a crime. Less contribution from others means less power deferred.

Abrams plants himself before Wolfe, his knees locked, his feet shoulder-length apart. He cocks the hammer back and aims. "Mueller," he demands by way of stern greeting. "Where's he at?"

His eyebrows arching at a point beyond Abrams' left shoulder, his nose and chin lifted to it as well, Wolfe then settles back in the chair and takes a nonchalant sip of his Scotch. "Don't be silly," he chuckles. "Put that thing away. You're among relations."

"Silas, you can either tell me direct, buy yourself some breathin' room, or die here'n now. Don't much matter to me. He'll turn up eventually, I'll find him, I ain't scared of that."

And then comes that radiant smile. It creeps to Wolfe's lips and eases across his face like a plague across a nation, slow and relentlessly spreading. "Naw," says Wolfe, snickering into his glass, "now *that* ain't a bet worth takin'."

Abrams shifts his weight, readjusting his aim.

"I told him," begins Wolfe, "you want her, you got to bury her afterward. But the man went all fool on me, talkin' about how he ain't never expected to bear him a son of refinement, how that girl, well, she was such that he was hopin' she might help him plant his seed into high society." Wolfe leans intimately forward and winks. "Squirted off inside her, you see. Thrice, seems."

Abrams breathes hard.

Wolfe's face lights with pleasure in his torture. He toasts himself and smacks his lips. "Least I kept my word, though, didn't I? Can't say I didn't, 'cause it wasn't *your* Jew he poked now. And trust me, wasn't easy to keep him off her, neither. Lord, you should of heard that son-of-a-bitch complain. Day and night, 'Lemme at her, lemme at her.' Had to do *something*, didn't I? Man's got to throw the occasional bone, don't he? So I give him the next best thing." He leans forward, his index finger stabbing the air. "'Awright, Goliath,' I says, 'you can have the sister, but she can't be 'round afterward, havin' her go all runnin' to the law now, hear?' Only the jackass couldn't riverbed her like I told him to." He takes another sip. "Hell, it's one thing to rape a whore, but this girl's got links. Sooner or later, somebody'd come knockin'. Least with your pa, weren't no witnesses to rascal us out—except for you, 'course."

Abrams makes no mention of his meeting with McClelland.

"So," Wolfe groans with a stretch, "Caesar's got to do right by Rome, and Mueller, God fuckin' bless him, had to pay the price for his stubbornness. We'll miss his muscle, true enough, but these days, seems there's a line of fellers lookin' to join up, all shapes and sizes." His smile has grown impossibly smug.

"And I suppose the boys just let you do it, too, huh? Just like that, one of their own?"

"Naw, well," shrugs Wolfe, "they've been a bit punky about it, sure, but then, they ain't the ones wearin' the fuckin' crown, now are they?"

"You're a goddamned liar, Silas."

"About many, many things," concedes Wolfe. "But not this."

"Then I thank you."

This is not the response Wolfe was expecting. His smile dims. He looks up at Abrams and peers into his eyes, only to be surprised by something peculiar within. He cannot explain it—a dullness, a meanness, a vacant quality perhaps—but something is not right. "Say now," he dares, shifting a bit uncomfortably in his chair, "the fuck're you doin' back here, anyhow? Ain't you got a war to fight?"

"It's fought."

"Oh, I see." Wolfe giggles. His hands begin to patter against the desk-top. "Then what, you take care of that chickenfuck I meant for you? Because that girl of yours still ain't safe 'less you done it, you know."

Abrams nods, once. "Done," he whispers.

Again, Wolfe looks deeply into Abrams, and although he is unfamiliar with what he sees, he knows he is being told the truth. As a result, he next toasts Abrams, polishing off the remainder of his Scotch. "Can't say I'm not impressed, Elias."

"You should be," replies Abrams flatly. "Prepared me for you."

Wolfe places the tumbler down in an act of great deliberation. He then leans back once more, and, his hands knitted behind his head, after a moment of intense scrutiny of the man before him—the question as to the rigidity of his spine, the willingness to do what a killer must—his face suddenly blossoms at the sight of something arriving behind Abrams. "Why hello there, boys," greets Wolfe merrily, rocking forward and slapping both hands onto the desk, one after the other. "Y'all remember Elias."

Abrams turns. Earlier, upon his entry, one of the grog monkeys behind him had received Wolfe's dancing eyebrows to mean precisely what he had intended them to: *go fetch the boys*. And so, the youth had fled the saloon in search of the others with a pounding heart, knowing that the ensuing tip would be enormous, but the cache earned with the Smile would be more impressive still. He quickly found them halfway down Gallatin Street, in an alley behind Agatha's Fat House, rolling some upstart Cajun pimp from the hinterlands for the night's gross, and beseeched them to follow him.

Yet unlike his last encounter with the Cypress Stump Boys, this night Abrams has words in him. Politely, he gives Byrne and Gundy each a silent nod. They are without visible weapons, but their stances show they are ready for action, their right hands at the lower lapels of their coats, set to flip them aside to access whatever lies hidden beneath. They nod in reply but say nothing. It is to Placide Arceneaux that Abrams gives his full focus. "Placide," he says quietly, "been a while, I know it. You mind, I ask you something?"

Arceneaux nods.

"You're a man of honor, huh? Y'all Creoles trade in it?"

"We do."

Abrams lowers his pistol from Wolfe and turns to Arceneaux completely. The honesty on his face is disarming. "Then you, of all people, should know I ain't here without cause."

Arceneaux carefully straightens himself.

"Believe your kin would be in agreement, too, they was privy to the details."

Arceneaux's eyes are emotionless at these words. The hand hovering above his sheathed blade drops slightly.

"Now I was to tell you," adds Abrams, "you, Gundy, and Byrne here, y'all ain't have no part of this, that I ain't grudgin' y'all nothin' for what happened before, that y'all are free and clear of everything far as I'm concerned, you'd trust that I was tellin' you true, wouldn't you?"

Arceneaux takes a moment to consider this. "Believe I would, Abrams. Yes."

"Elias, please," scoffs Wolfe from his seat, "we're bound by kindred flesh, you and me, but this keeps up, you won't leave me no choice but to kill you outright." He runs a hand over his slick-pomaded hair, exhaling once to concentrate on the plans before him. "Now, if y'all will kindly excuse me, I got plannin' to do, y'all have whores to fuck, whiskey to drink, and the goddamned money I *made* for y'all to spend." He looks back up at Abrams. "And as for you, out of the goodness of my heart, 'cause we kindred flesh and all, I'm forgivin' you the hornet's nest you're tryin' to stir up tonight. You might have grounds, I ain't denyin' it, but we're done here." He returns his attention to his blueprints in a gesture of dismissal. "Go on now," he concludes with a wave, "leave me be."

But the remaining Cypress Stump Boys do not move. Abrams, so long awaiting these words of reprieve, is unaffected by them.

"And if I was to remind you," Abrams says to Arceneaux, "that this feller here killed your boy Mueller—what, just the other day, must've been—how'd that sit with you?"

Arceneaux's lids fall to half-staff. "Poorly."

Wolfe sighs in exasperation. "Placide, you fuckin' mongrel, you know as well as me that Muell—"

"Can't be in cold blood, Elias," declares Arceneaux firmly. "Not with him unarmed. Got to be dueled out, that's all there is to it."

Something inside Abrams quails at these words, but he does not flinch. "Boys," he says, turning to Byrne and Gundy. "You awright with this?"

"Can't say I wouldn't find it entertaining then," Byrne admits through his brogue, his arms folded across his chest. "As long as I'm clear of those past peccadilloes you're just now mentioning."

"*Free* and clear," replies Abrams.

"Then duel on, m'laddy boys, duel on."

"Tasker?"

"By all means," says Gundy. "I ain't no man's second, though."

"They'll be no seconds," states Arceneaux. "Just these two here."

Wolfe looks from man to man, his eyes placidly taking in the scene. Although he is brilliantly shrewd, he has not yet learned that in the vein of the world's most charismatic tyrants—the same vein he has been so thoroughly mining in the past year—his men may fear him, but they do not love him. They do not love his distaste for them. They do not love his foppish manners or the way he dotes on his own concerns. They do not love the way he leers at the world or fancies himself their god. They fear him only, because like a god, he kills too easily, even for their liking. And yet, as with any god, any man so feared may be destroyed without regret. It takes only one brazen enough to stand tall among the kneeling thousands and say, "No more."

"'Course, we got to ask Silas whether he's game," adds Arceneaux, his deference thinly veiling the scorn he has been masking since Mueller's death.

Wolfe purses his lips. He knows he is being challenged here. He has studied the dogs of the streets, seen the petty insurrections risen from within their packs, the fanged and punishing responses from the dominant males, and understands that such occasional mutinies are necessary to any healthy gang: for once they are crushed, the subservience of those who remain is as absolute as the slaughter of the individuals who instigated them. Thus, weighing the danger of displaying weakness now against the danger of anything Abrams might embody, Wolfe quickly comes to a decision. He will rebuild the gang once this night is over. Abrams and Arceneaux will die; the other two he will grant pardon. With a snap of his fingers, he will recruit many men. The Cypress Stump Boys will be larger and more imposing than ever, its new members to be slave-loyal, Wolfe's grip on its leadership unyielding. And so, sitting across from what he has just decided is left of a suddenly former institution, he settles into an air of casual confidence. "I've had enough of him, anyway, "the fuckin' ingrate. Boy don't know the first thing about affection. Let's have it then, Placide, you cunt. What'll it be?"

"Got an old Creole cardman's gambit in mind for y'all." He turns to Abrams. "First off, the gun."

Abrams balks at the idea of handing over his weapon in a room full of countless others and tells Arceneaux so.

"You don't, that's fine," Arceneaux shrugs, "but you'll be dead and one of us'll have to head back on over that girl's house for a visit. Choice is yours."

Abrams hands it over.

Arceneaux quickly hits the cylinder release, breaking the pistol barrel forward, and in a deft motion dumps the six .44 caliber slugs into his left hand, pocketing all but one. "Now," he says, "how much money you got on you?"

Abrams skims through his billfold. "Twenty-eight."

Arceneaux nods and looks to Wolfe. "Silas, take out the same. Tasker, get us a second chair, set it up on the other side of the desk there." Both men obey, each equally intrigued by the proceedings. Wolfe, though initially unsettled by the subtle change in Abrams, has regained his swagger. Because although his boys may be humoring Abrams with this obscene duel they have proposed, Wolfe is simply too brash to fear death at the hands of a man like Elias Abrams. For now, he will enjoy the game as it unfolds. "There," he says, laying down his bills on the desktop. "Twenty-eight."

Abrams is placed in a chair across from Wolfe. His heart is racing, but he, too, like Wolfe, is blanketed by a calm that belies the peril of the moment. It is not that he has grown indifferent to whether he lives or dies. Rather, he feels that something about these circumstances is absolutely right, that sitting before Wolfe, dueling for the highest of all possible stakes, is the culmination of what is meant to be, and suggests to him an instance of *bashert* like never before. An instance, Abrams knows perfectly well, from which he cannot flee. He takes a deep breath.

Wolfe licks his lips long and languorously. His smile is grotesque.

"Awright now," explains Arceneaux, "here's the rules. That gun, it's empty, I'm placin' on the table between y'all. Beside it, a lone bullet. Only—and here's the punch—that bullet there costs exactly fifty-six dollars, not a penny more or less. Duel's this, then: with this deck of cards I'm holdin', y'all will play for the pot. Whoever wins the other's stack entire, down to the very last coin, wins himself that fifty-six dollars. He wins himself that fifty-six dollars, he can buy himself that lone bullet, let him do with it as he pleases."

41

———

The money, the bullet, the very lives at stake—Elias Abrams grasps in an instant that they must be stripped of all meaning. They must become grains of corn, no more. Chaff. Worthless. The troubles that have plagued him over the course of these months, someone else's problem. The devil in jest before him? He must not recognize. John Lee Carlson? Blinded, in possession of a family he wishes for himself? No recollection. His father's inheritance? No such thing. His darling Nora Bloom? Abrams has never heard of her. He must put all these things away from him. He must win, that is all. He must become impenetrable, his will impossible to read. Everything he has ever gleaned from his poker-playing life, every lesson he has ever learned, every instinct acted upon, every pain detached—it has come down to this.

He closes his eyes to focus on the idea of breathing.

—

Twenty minutes later, he and Wolfe have traded a series of small pots between them, neither prepared to play too aggressively the hands they have been dealt. The game is five-card draw, no limit, awkward to play with just two contestants, but then, theirs is no ordinary sport. Arceneaux, acting as dealer, has said little except that "any man caught cheating'll immediately forfeit his stack to the other, guaranteed."

Leaning over the desk, shuffling a deck he swears is true, he possesses a proficiency that impresses even Abrams. Arceneaux has evidently practiced since they last sat together. In the iron-fisted power Wolfe has assumed over the past year, the boys have been left to idler pursuits. In another time, under different circumstances, Abrams would have allowed Arceneaux a compliment, but this moment is not one for pleasantry.

Wolfe smiles. Since those first days at the orphanage, he has played poker against Abrams for hours on end. For years, they have swapped small fortunes and dirty looks and loving jibes, and even if he is aware that Abrams is a slightly better player, he is convinced that no man alive exceeds his ability to gamble. And this night, he knows, playing for such stakes as they are, will be a night of very real gambling indeed.

Wolfe plays those first hands right into his opponent's eyes. He mocks Abrams openly, his face a japer's. His concern is affectionate. His threats are real. His words are tender. Knowing Abrams as he does, it is this inconsistency, this badgering followed by devotion, that will rattle him most. His tactic seems to be working; already by the end of those first twenty minutes, Wolfe is up by six dollars.

"Been quite a few months, huh, Elias?" says Wolfe, absently rearranging his hand. "I mean, Lord, get yourself all shot up, tangled with that chickenfuck fool, fall for a gal who, from the looks of things, ain't gonna let you bung her out anytime soon. Then, to top it all off, you're stuck here playin' cards, bidin' your time till I win that goddamned bullet to shoot you with. Yessir, quite a few months."

Abrams lips go thin. "Your bet," he says.

Wolfe trickles three coins into the pile. "Oh, and I plumb near forgot." His smile grows. "The year you killed your own daddy."

"You killed him, Silas. Not me." Abrams mutters this reply into a pair of eights, not to take Wolfe's bait but to keep these words from gaining too much ground within him. His father's death, he realizes, is the one subject he must avoid if he is to maintain his poise.

"Well hell, Elias, I may have bled him some, but you did the killin'. Your idea."

"Play your goddamned hand."

Wolfe puts his cards down. He knows he has Abrams on the verge of tilt and so goes in for the kill. "Honey, please," he laughs, "here you got a man who didn't never want you a day in your life, nor give you a dime of his money for it. Now if that ain't enough to hate someone to death, I don't know what is. But after what that old cunt of a washerwoman told us about him, *surely* that's grounds for a killin', ain't it? I mean, shit, Elias, ain't you even remembered what she said?"

But Abrams is already gone. Despite his every precaution, despite his every attempt to keep his mind clear and soul in check, he is lost to the story that refreshed his hatred for his father, the one that decided for him the need for vengeance in the form of the Toulouse Street murder he would later plan.

Drunk one early morning back in July, Abrams and Wolfe had staggered arm-in-arm upriver toward Lafayette City. Abrams had wanted to show his friend the neighborhood of his youth, and Wolfe, in his desire to know his companion as intimately as any man might know another, gladly agreed. "I tell you, Silas," Abrams had slurred, "my momma's house wasn't much, but goddamned if that woman couldn't grow a root."

Wolfe, drunk as he was, merely hugged Abrams to his breast. They marched on.

After scrounging around the weeds of the garden plot behind his abandoned home, knocking at the Jewish scarecrow's crossbones on which Wolfe jokingly crucified himself, Abrams was struck by the notion that Brona Kincade, the old Irish neighbor with whom he had lived for a while after his mother's death, who had long before given Gerta the mother-of-pearl-handled straight razor meant as protection against the advances of men, might have a jug of mash stored somewhere inside her home. Just as they were attempting her latch, though, she whisked the door open on them, fully aware of their intentions. "Look at ye," she had said to Abrams in disdain. "Just look at what's happened to ye. Your mother, God rest her soul, she'd think ye a disgrace, Elias, she would."

The boys kicked the earth in shame. Even Wolfe, typically inured to such abuses, looked at his feet.

Brona Kincade clucked her tongue, her hands on her hips. She had aged, her hair thinned into gray wisps. Her nose curved downward over an old crone's mouth, but the sharpness of her eyes was as piercing as ever. "Such a sweet child ye were, too, Elias. Yet here ye are, drunk as a shite heap, running with all breed of foolishness. Poor Gerta, as if her life wasn't pained enough."

Abrams apologized, claming that he just wanted to show his friend where he grew up.

"Well, from the looks of tings, haven't grown up much then, have ye?"

His response was silence.

"Jaysus," she sighed, "come on in already. Ye want your friend to know how you grew up, 'tis time you learned it then, too. Maybe if ye hear what your poor ma actually went trew, you'll learn that this is no life to be wasted on drinks and louts."

So she brewed coffee for her two young guests and, with a loving heart despite her harsh words, told Abrams for the first time of the tragedy that had truly befallen his mother. She told both young men these things, and watched their faces grimace for it.

With the Abrams' family passage from Alsace shouldered by the company that shipped them over, once arrived in New Orleans in '28, their redemptive labor was then sold to a private third party. That private third party, Brona Kincade informed her two guests, was none other than I. J. Lieber, Esq., sugar magnate of Toulouse Street and Napoleonville.

Upon receiving this news, Abrams just stared at her, hard. He knew none of this. Wolfe placed his hand on his friend's shoulder.

Gerta had instead told her son that she had served out her time working for a family whose name seemed to change each time he

questioned her about them. When as a youth Elias asked her how he
had come to be, Gerta had added tersely that she and his father had
been a mistake, that is all, but that young Elias himself, she assured
him, was not.

Lieber had purchased the Abrams' family labor not out of an act of
magnanimity, it would turn out, but because the cost of their redemption, temporary though their work might be, was far less expensive than
that of four new auction-block niggers. He had little chance to get his
money's worth, however, for not long after arriving, the Abrams parents
died of typhus, leaving Gerta and her sister Beatrice to fend for themselves. When Beatrice died soon thereafter, Gerta was left all alone. As a
five-year-old redemptioner, her parents and only sibling dead, she was
thus required by law to fulfill her indentured servitude until her eighteenth birthday.

"Surprised the son-of-a-bitch didn't just pack her off to the orphanage," spat Abrams in disgust.

Lieber, it seems, simply did not care enough about her to do so. By
the time he realized that he was ward to a five-year-old immigrant, his
concerns had long moved elsewhere. As a result, Gerta was raised by a
series of slave women, each of whom taught her the ways of herbs and
gardens, and once weekly by a white schoolmistress whom Lieber had
contracted before his indifference to her became the norm.

He and Gerta seldom spoke during her formative years. They had almost no direct contact. He would watch her kneel in the garden and
seed the earth, but they were passing, blank looks. She became a
bleached member of his increasingly large staff. Indeed, Lieber was so
busy with his various affairs that Gerta Abrams made little impression
on him at all. Until the eve of her eighteenth birthday, that is.

In his dedication to his interests, Lieber was oblivious to the fact that
his teenage charge, lacking an accepted avenue of release for her flour-
ishing hormones, had developed a crush on him. Her eyes fluttered to
no avail as he passed her on the garden paths. When she sighed near

him, he heard nothing. He was, in truth, so ignorant of her flirting that it was not until she bent over her valise as she packed to leave him, letting her rump linger long and quavering in the air, that he finally grasped what she was proffering.

By the time Gerta realized that her game had grown too serious, her smile vanishing as her small hands struggled in vain to push him away, it was already too late. Ever a man to see a deal through to its completion, as with all attuned entrepreneurs when presented a desirable commodity for free, Lieber was by then committed to getting what he had come for. Violently.

Gerta never mentioned any of her young coquetry to Brona Kincade. She preferred instead to damn herself to silence about it for the remainder of her days, assuming a burdensome guilt for encouraging the kind of behavior she could not have believed mankind to possess but would since learn is all too common in life. She would take only a handful of lovers in the years to come, some for whom she felt affection, kindly men Elias would call "uncle" as they tousled his hair until they stopped visiting, others for whom she felt nothing but their hardening bodies. These relationships were so fleeting because in spite of the occasional marriage proposal, after the night of her eighteenth birthday, Gerta Abrams would never again trust her heart to anyone but her son. When her Irish neighbor asked, she thus chose to tell a different story.

"One day more," Brona Kincade went on that morning to the boys, "and your ma, bless her sweet heart, would've been free of his service forever. Told me how on that eve, packing up as she was, he just walked into her room, the pig. When she struggled, your da showed no mercy. For a wee slip of a ruthless devil, he had some power in those fists. Broke her jaw, he did, cracked her teeth from her head. And her pelvis, oh sweet Jaysus, Elias, it never did heal correctly." She stopped. "I tell ye this, not to make your blood boil, but to let ye know the injustices she suffered. And to see ye now, drunk, prying into my home with this codfish here—well, I just want ye to know, it'd break her heart." Her judgment was brutalizing. "Now ye can come back for a visit," she concluded, dusting her hands clean, "but only when you've grown some. Until then, get out."

———

"You're the bastard son of a rapist, Elias," sneers Wolfe over those dueling cards, "and *still*, you couldn't kill him? The fuck kind of man're you, anyway?"

Abrams looks up from his hand. "You know, Silas, for all your goin' on about what it means to be a man, seems kind of peculiar, don't it, how you won't lay public claim to the murder you done that night? Reckon a real man wouldn't go hidin' behind no lie. Reckon a real man would be proud of what he done, go shoutin' it all through the goddamned streets. Then again, that's just me." Still expressionless, he looks back down at his cards.

Wolfe's eyes twinkle with delight at Abrams' attempt to lure him into an outright confession. "Nice," he admits. "But nossir."

42

It is well after midnight. Money has been traded between them, but neither player has been privileged to a hand worthy of pushing all in. Abrams levels his stare across the desk at Wolfe, who, cocksure and lethal, has found himself on a punishing run. He has stolen three pots in a row. He is up by eleven dollars.

The revelers in the saloon, that contemptible crew of scoundrels and whores, have moved toward the back of the room to spectate. They jostle one another with quiet murmurs and long, slow pulls on their pipes and whiskeys, failing to understand the full extent of the game's stakes, but not its significance.

Wolfe antes. Abrams does the same.

Arceneaux, an admirable dealer, passes them their five cards in sequence, flipping from one player to the other. Wolfe is rambling on about how he intends to name the bullet after Abrams' mother. "No wait," he says, "Nora. I'll name it Nora, and then kiss it right on the tip before plantin' it between your gorgeous, fuckin' eyes."

"Don't believe that's gonna happen, Silas."

"Well, sorry to say, when it *does* happen, you should know that after you're dead, I might just have to pick up where you left off. With the girl, I mean. Rake that I am and all." Wolfe leans wickedly forward. "Once I've wooed and then ruined her, once her name's as soiled as her sister's, I'll decide that maybe we're not such a fine match after all. I'll decide that maybe I'm better off without that kind of whore in my life."

Abrams fumes but says nothing. *You got a place inside you,* he thinks calmly to himself, *a place no other feller's allowed. All you got to do now is to keep it locked up tight.* He breathes to settle himself down before looking to the cards he has just been dealt. His heart leaps at the sight of them. Over the past hour, they have been cold, so he has had to bluff his way through several rounds to keep from being bullied out of the game. This hand, however, has promise. He bets half his stack before the draw.

Wolfe giggles excitedly as he calls Abrams' bet. "That's it, you magnificent bastard," he says. "It's about fuckin' time."

Abrams, his face made of stone, his heart raging, goes against every tenet of his training and thinks of Nora Bloom, to ask for her blessing. "I'll take one," he says softly to Arceneaux, slipping his discard over the desktop to the dealer.

"One," repeats Arceneaux. He burns a card from the deck stub, and then passes Abrams a single card.

"Works for me," grins Wolfe, and he, too, slips a single discard over to Arceneaux.

"One," nods Arceneaux, and after again burning a card from the deck stub, obliges Wolfe's request.

Abrams peeks at what he has been dealt. Over the course of the night, he has attempted to dull his eyes as much as possible, his mouth he has kept slightly ajar so that it will reveal neither dismay nor pleasure. He sniffs. It is not the card he was hoping for, but it is strong nonetheless. The king of clubs. With this hand, with Wolfe having already gained much of his pile, it is time for Abrams to make his move. "All in," he states coolly, bridging his fingers together.

Wolfe erupts from his chair. "Whoo-eee, can't y'all just feel it in y'all's cocks!" he bellows, slamming the desktop with the flat of his palm, and then grabbing a handful of his crotch. "Like to make a man hard, this game, goddamn! I'll call, Elias, I'll call you good!"

"Let's see 'em then," declares Arceneaux.

The moment of truth is upon them. The tavern is as still as a mortuary at midnight.

His pulse driving madly, Abrams stands, though his knees are weak beneath him. Slowly, to the great gasping of the spectators, he flips his cards to show two pair: jacks and queens, with a king-high kicker. He had been hoping for either a third jack or queen to make his full house, but he believes that the way Wolfe reacted after first being dealt, he has little to worry about. Although Wolfe's tells have been difficult to unmask, something about the timbre of his voice at that moment felt to Abrams a betrayal of weakness. But two pair, while staunch, he realizes may not have been the hand on which to bet everything after all. Mathematically, there are simply too many remaining permutations that can beat it. Straights, flushes, full houses, three, four of a kind even. Abrams is confident, yet not wholly so.

"Silas," says Arceneaux.

Wolfe, too, stands. He is quieter than he has been in hours. Mournfully, he flips one card. A jack. Then, a second jack. The third card, a queen. The fourth, a second queen. They have the same hand. They have precisely the same hand.

Abrams is about to faint. Blood thunders in his neck like never before, his stomach is queasy, he can scarcely keep his composure. This, while Arceneaux swears under his breath, promising that he shuffled the cards without bias, that he does not know how such an improbable deal could have happened. "On my momma's eyes, y'all," he vows, his hands held up in defense, "I dealt 'em clean."

Abrams does not mind. He knows that he has all but won an enormous pot here, for a king-high kicker is essentially unbeatable. It is possible, though unlikely, that he and Wolfe might chop the pot between them, but considering the cards left in the deck, Abrams knows he very nearly has the nuts, and his palms sweat for it. *Dear Lord,* he thinks as the bar fills with the hoots and hollering of those who have taken their position as onlookers, *I got that king you sent me. Let his kicker be anything but.*

Abrams' wish is granted. It is no king. It is instead the ace of diamonds.

A tremendous roar bursts forth from the crowd, hats and arms sent skyward, as Abrams collapses heavily into his chair. His knees have at last given out beneath him, his stomach buckling in horror. He has lost. He has lost everything. This hand, his life. If he has been cheated—which his gut tells him is not the case—he has played enough foul poker of his own to know that being gullied is as valid a loss as any upright defeat. His death has therefore never been so assured. His eyes wide, staring at the floor, he brings a few fingers to his brow to grapple with just what this fact means. He can come to no conclusion.

Wolfe is silent and smiling amid the applause. For the moment, the world exists exclusively for him. "We're the same," Wolfe is mouthing. "Only see, I'm better'n you."

The bullet, the gun, his enemy, his death—they all loom before Abrams, who slumps in his chair.

"We're the same," Wolfe is saying. "But I'm better."

The men and whores of the bar still shouting raucously, Truett Jones receives a nod from Arceneaux to empty the room. "Everybody out, y'all sons-of-bitches!" Jones yells over the cries of the masses. "You load of sorry cunts, come back tomorrow!"

Abrams hears none of it.

The dozens grumble and moan, but ultimately obey, shuffling out of the saloon dejectedly like children forced to their beds before supper. Within moments, save for Abrams, his fellow Cypress Stump Boys, and the proprietor, the tavern is empty.

Abrams has little strength left in him. His thoughts are few. "Do what you got to, Silas. Just don't you fuckin' miss."

"I don't aim to." Wolfe has already paid Arceneaux his fifty-six dollars in winnings and is loading the pistol.

"The girl," adds Abrams. "You can leave her out of this."

"Naw." Wolfe aims the barrel between Abrams' eyes. He thumbs the hammer back. "Y'all out, too," he tells the others. "This here's between Elias and me."

Eager to heed their leader's command, the remaining Cypress Stump Boys and Truett Jones trail one another out of the saloon in silence. Not one of them acknowledges Abrams in their departure, for they are too busy working now on how to best repair their relationship with Wolfe. They will kowtow, they decide as they push through the swing doors out onto Gallatin Street, and show him overwhelming new levels of respect. They will offer him such sacrifices of gold and young flesh as one presents a vengeful god.

Abrams has closed his eyes. Facing his death, he wishes above all to focus his last moments on matters of consequence. He wants his life to flash meaningfully before his eyes. Gnawing on his lips, he wants to think of the dead Union soldier he may have killed those months before at the Battle of Oak Hills, and what that death now means to him. He wishes to reflect upon his father's death as well, of their respective apologies, of their guilt and forgiveness, and the legacy he would have earned because of it. His brow goes damp as he searches earnestly for the image of his mother in her grace and wisdom. Yet nothing comes. Where, too, are the thoughts of John Lee Carlson or of darling Nora Bloom, with her first loving letter and final parting sigh? To his growing alarm, Abrams realizes that he can latch onto none of it. He cannot even manage fleeting images of the land or of all that he will never now experience. Rather, in his consumed wish to think these thoughts, he is damned to learn in those final seconds that he can muster nothing but that wish itself.

Just at that instant, an explosion cracks across his left temple like the blinding flash of lightning across an expansive southern sky. The blow is so unexpected, so violent, that he is knocked from his seat and sent sprawling onto the plankwood floor. He groans as he dabs at the head wound, his eyes blinking dumbly. When he tries to prop himself up onto his elbow, he slips from its buttress and falls awkwardly back to the floor.

Dazed, he looks up to Wolfe, who, with a soft thud, has placed the un-fired gun onto the desktop. Slowly, Abrams begins to grasp what has just occurred: he has been pistol-whipped but not shot dead. "Sorry, honey," he hears Wolfe say. "But I'm needin' your attention for a minute. Figure that's the only kinda buss that'd fully get it."

Abrams squints and coughs. From the shock to his head, he is having a difficult time focusing. Blood leaks everywhere.

"I know you," Wolfe continues matter-of-factly. "Shit, I know you better'n you know your own damned self."

Abrams shakes his head to clear it. He tries, but fails once more, to stand.

"You ain't got a killin' bone in your body," Wolfe is saying. "You might have some fight in you, I don't deny it. You might've even taken care of that chickenfuck, though more I think about it, I'm tending to doubt on that, too. But thing is, you ain't got the *man* in you, son, the kind you was talkin' about earlier. You just ain't. Here, I'll prove it." Wolfe pauses to confirm the logic of what he is about to do. He thinks of all the frailties Abrams has shown over the course of their lifetime together, of the series of infuriating disappointments he has felt in his friend as a re-sult. Yet Wolfe thinks, too, of the particular fondness he has for Abrams, a fondness that if gone unchecked over the years can twist a man's mouth in his skull, making him mean. Mad-dog mean. Unable to quell the rumors breeding within him for nearly a decade now, Wolfe resolves to channel these feelings at last into a permanently destructive act, and thus an act, at least, his own. He stomps a heel resolutely. He will endure the frustration no more. It is not enough to kill Abrams; he must be crushed in spirit *before* he is killed in life. And the only, the best, way to truly crush his spirit first, Wolfe decides, is to give Abrams this opportu-nity here and have him fail at it. "You take that bullet now," Wolfe de-mands. "My gift to you."

Abrams is stunned into awareness. He does not move.

"Go on. Pick up the goddamned gun."

"You got the chance to use that thing," warns Abrams, "reckon I'd use it, I were you."

Wolfe ignores these words. He is too preoccupied with his thoughts as they are unspooling within him to pay heed to anyone else's. Abrams has seen this look before, the kind of earnest didacticism Wolfe assumes whenever he finds it necessary to explain to the world the depth he claims to feel for it. He starts to pace behind the desk in slow, plodding steps. "See now," Wolfe begins, his eyebrows knitted gravely as he walks toward the wall, "someone had to show you how to stand tall in a world that'd just as soon slit your throat as look at you. Personally, I done what I could." He stops and spins toward Abrams. "But when you couldn't kill your pa after all the shit he'd shoveled at you—well, that like to have about killed *me* instead. That's why I aimed that chickenfuck for you in the first place, why I'm offerin' up that bullet as we speak. Not that you got the brass to use it, 'course. I'm talkin' life lessons, honey, tendered out of love and affectio—" Yet here, to Silas Wolfe's gasping astonishment, his speech is interrupted by the cool, steel accuracy of a man wishing to purge himself of his life's violence forever, and has therefore been forced to act hastily, without thought, before the stores of violence inside ever again have a chance to find their renewal.

Elias Abrams, in the midst of the lecture, had simply picked up the pistol and shot Wolfe once directly in the heart, killing him where he stood.

43

Abrams awakens the next morning, unsure where he is. Blinking, delicately testing the dried wound at his temple with his thumb, he discovers that he is in his mother's small garden plot, in the upriver faubourg of Lafayette City. It is early, and the only sound he hears is that of birds. He rolls to a seat. He runs a hand through his hair, pulls a weed from his mouth. He spits. It is herbaceous still, the flavor of his mother's land, rich and strong. He groans. He is not drunk but, from the fog in his head, feels as though he might be. Why he had felt the need to sleep on this plot is beyond him.

The night before, after dispatching Wolfe, he marched back to the Cabildo to demand that the sergeant on duty go fetch McClelland from his bed. Then, once McClelland arrived, his disheveled dress appropriate to the lateness of the hour, Abrams followed the chief into his office to state plainly the murder he had just committed and the recompense he demanded in return. Although still incensed by it, Abrams mentioned nothing of McClelland's lie about the protection the Blooms were to have been receiving; in exposing the rape, he knew he would have been hastening Josephine's already inevitable ruin. It was for this reason that Chief McClelland had not heard of the incident. Rosa Bloom, as aggrieved as she was, chose to keep such tragedy close to the family that suffered it most dearly. Her daughter was disgraced for life and would never now have a decent proposal for marriage, regardless of how diligently they worked to keep her outrage a se-cret. As a mother, she knew the embittering truth that strangers and friends alike seek to unearth the misfortunes of other people's children like feral hogs rooting for acorns in the forest. Back in the station house that night, Abrams thus chose not to speak of Josephine at all. "But I do need it known," he added, "out loud-like, that I planned my daddy's murder. And while I didn't do the genuine killin', while I didn't even want him dead by the time he got stuck, he'd still be alive if it weren't for me. So you want to slap them cuffs on me, Chief, reckon I'm deservin' of it."

"Your confession's duly noted," replied McClelland with a dismissive frown, "but that won't be necessary." From behind his desk, he leaned forward onto his knuckles. "Now you're sure Wolfe's been taken care of?"

"Yessir, I'm sure."

"And the others?"

"Down to three. Doubt they'll be rufflin' too many feathers anytime soon."

McClelland smiled broadly at the news. "A fine job then, Abrams. You've done your city a great service."

"My land, Chief."

"Your what?"

Abrams inclined his head toward the desk drawer where his father's will lay. "My land," he repeated. "You say I'm free and clear of my daddy's death, and for it, I'm more grateful'n you'll ever know. Been heavy on my heart and mind like a pig-iron anvil, I can promise. But you asked for Wolfe, I got you Wolfe. Now I want what's comin' to me."

"Considering the circumstances you just admitted to, Mr. Abrams, I should think exculpation would be reward enough, don't you?"

"I might, if I knew what you meant by it."

"What I mean by it is that I'm sorry," explained McClelland, a sour smile creasing across his face, "but seems your father wasn't quite as gen-erous as I may have made him out to be."

Abrams narrowed his eyes. "And just how niggardly we talkin'?"

"Well, I don't have the will here, per se, but I did give it a perusal prior to his attorney filing it with whomever he would've filed it. Wanted to see if it might've provided any motive behind the murder. But were I to have it here, you'd see that your father left his entire estate, not to you, but onanistically enough, to his own enterprises, every last penny of it, with some pretty strict stipulations that while his next-in-command might access its funds, absolutely none of it was to go toward personal usage. Toward keeping the plantation and his varying other business interests alive, as it were." McClelland cleared his throat. "You were awarded nothing, I'm afraid."

Abrams bolted to his feet, fuming, his chair screeching behind him.

"Yes, yes, I know, I should probably now admit to having taken some liberties with the will's actual content." McClelland exhaled a mildly apologetic breath. "But let's be frank: I wanted the Cypress Stumps, and thanks to your efforts, my dubiously offered carrot aside, I got them. All in the name of justice, you see."

Abrams simply spat on the floor and left.

Now, the following morning, he looks up to see the crossbones of the old scarecrow looming above him. He sees no caricature there anymore, no nigger, no Jew. He sees no exterior at all, of any kind. All that remains after the years of wind and rain and sun is the bare wooden skeleton beneath, weather-beaten but standing. Abrams sighs. His anger has cooled since learning his father's estate will go uncollected, realizing as dawn approached that at root men do not change. For his father, McClelland, Schwientek, Wolfe, and a million others like them, there is no legacy to be claimed but what personal justice they are able to entitle themselves. In the crossbeam shadow of the scarecrow above, the bare essence of man, Abrams is thus coming to terms with the sense of justice his own life has cultivated for him.

In this, he suffers no regret for his killing of Silas Wolfe. He saw in Wolfe's dead face the night before their shared history, a once-true friend, a hero, a mastermind, a brother and father, a tragedy, a crime, a love, his very worst enemy. He saw an uncommon relation there, each a Hebrew in a world of gentiles, each born to a redemptioner mother from the old country, each poor, each orphaned, each an eventual journeyman of the streets. He saw in Wolfe a mirror, a distortion. The same man, only different. And yet, from his mother's gardening book, Abrams thinks back to a passage that has echoed in his mind for months: *The method that I propose to destroy the coco vine may appear erroneous to many people who think it indestructible. Some of them, in fact, will pretend to have used the procedure that I recommend without success; but if they had persisted and applied all the care that I recommend, I am persuaded that their land would be purged. Let everyone be persuaded then that what is necessary is work at the opportune time and the perseverance to make this noxious plant disappear.*

Silas Wolfe was that noxious plant. Still, the night before, his appraisal complete, Abrams gently shrouded Wolfe in his father's parlor Oriental, the same rug Wolfe himself once stained black with another man's blood. Now, Abrams' first obligation of the day is to return to the saloon and await the mortician's arrival. He has buried his father at last. His friend and enemy will be properly interred as well.

Abrams pats his breast pockets. In each, he finds folded leafs of paper. In his left, Nora Bloom's only remaining letter, the one Petitgout sent down from Missouri, recovered from the claw-footed desk after the deed was done. In his right, two pages that require a moment to identify. The first is his stamped parole slip, the provost marshal's traveling paper pass folded within it. The second is the apology he wrote to Nora two nights prior, back in his flophouse room on Dauphine. Crouched in the dirt where his life began, he rereads these words to her:

Dear Nora,

For years I have herd folks tell of love. I did not hold no stock in it thouh untill there was you May be it wont do no good now but you came to me at seventeen and took the words I gave you as a sign of my Faithe Im sorry for what has happened. Honest to god I am. I loved you for a littel whyle and for that time you loved me to and I wished we could have one day been maried But it dont matter now cause on nights like tonite the sky wins over them kind of wishes On nights like tonite darkness is all we got.

My stomack aint mine no more Nora. My knees aint as I have come to relie on them nether. I dont know if your silence will never break about us or if even once in the years to come you will tell that man you will marry about us, and the idea of not knowin will break my own heart cause I will always wunder. I guess Ill wunder about what brought me to your door at all.

I use to beleve in Evil and how man grows it like a feild of cane I got to confess my beliefs aint changed much, for theres nothing trewer in this world than that we men are just a bunch of boy monsters grown mad.

But I wish you could know how I feel in my soul I wish I could see you agin and may be tell you. I wish you could find a place inside you to know what Im tellin you is trew and that you would want to see me again for it. May be you would love me for it to May be this does not matter but I love you. What ever else is false in this world, my love surely aint among them

Goodbye,
Elias

He stands and dusts himself off. The earth smells to him of his mother, and now, having slept on it overnight, so does he. Brona Kincade creaks open her back door and awaits a sign. He tips his bowler and walks away. She smiles in return.

He is walking back toward the city proper. Along the way to Truett's Saloon, he decides he will ask John Lee Carlson to ask his father, the wealthy Levee Street merchant, whether there is a position to be had in his business for an earnest young man. Abrams is confident that Carlson, despite his distaste for nepotism, will honor him this request. Then, in a couple years, after he has stowed away enough money, Abrams will outgrow textiles and return to the land that feeds him so. Heading down a long, bare stretch of road toward the Quarter, he nods to himself, envisioning it all, certain that this will be his fate.

Abrams knows, too, that he will never post this last letter to Nora but will soon return to the Bloom household nevertheless, after he has secured employment with Carlson's father. He will send ahead a visiting card this time, but it will be Josephine's audience he seeks, not Nora's. If she does not respond, he will send another, and another. Because although he will love Nora deeply and eternally for the letters she sent him when he needed them most, for the affection she gave him when he did not know that he had any within him to give in return, he understands that requesting Josephine's hand in marriage is what he must do. She may not accept his proposal at first, but Abrams will dedicate his life to convincing her of his sincerity, of his capacity for tenderness and contrition. He will attend synagogue if she asks him to, he will even earn his *bar mitzvah*, though at the moment, walking back toward Gallatin Street for what he presumes to be the last time, he makes no promise to love God well, only her. He will care for Josephine Bloom just as he hopes she will one day care for him. He expects that theirs, in time, will be an enviable love.

The sky is streaked with morning. He has never seen such a horizon. The land surrounds him for miles, while beyond the walls of the Vieux Carré where his mother once sold her greens, the sweating backs of the field, the hard-bitten mules and the chickens bathed in dust, the Louisiana heat will in the months to come warp his vision of those plantation homes, his heart's desire, in the distance. The whole of Creation, now girded by the horizon before him. Only he is no longer afraid of the sky. A decade after his first visit to the land, he walks easily, looking above the soil his mother once taught him to admire, for even though the land throughout his life has forever grounded him, the crops Elias Abrams will one day reap from it mean little without those heavens toward which to aspire.

ACKNOWLEDGMENTS

Of the many people to whom I'm grateful, I would like to begin with my parents, David and Susan Melman. Their support has been unflagging over the years, their love a constant. Add Libby Charles to the mix, along with Liz and David Petrillo and their children Tess and Zach, and I'm truly blessed. A son and brother could ask for nothing more.

For those who read the manuscript in its varying stages or offered advice along the way, for the kindness you've shown me, I cannot thank you enough. All my gratitude therefore goes to Erin Cartwright-Niumata, Matthew Dube, Richard Fulco, Jeff Hephner, Greg Hutton, Stephen Kunken, Christie Lowrance, David Lowrance, Camille March, Anya and Edward Rubin, Jeff Talbott, and Ken Wheaton. A special note of appreciation to Kelley Anderson, for the many pages read over the many the years of a marvelous friendship. For your eyes and ears and patience, I thank you. You're generous souls, the lot of you.

I would also like to thank the faculties of the University of Louisiana at Lafayette's Creative Writing Program and Hunter College High School; your encouragement, both personal and professional, has been invaluable. To the staffs at Barnes and Noble in Lafayette, The Elliott Bay Book Company in Seattle, and BookCourt in Brooklyn, all at which I worked, if poorly, I offer you my heartfelt thanks as well.

For their aid in my research, additional gratitude goes to Pamela D. Arceneaux, The Historic New Orleans Collection/Williams Research

Center; Ruth P. Asher, City of New Orleans Police Department; Rabbi Andrew Busch, the Touro Synagogue in New Orleans; Steven P. Darwin, Department of Ecology and Evolutionary Biology, Tulane University; Douglas Harper, compiler of etymonline.com; Laura D. Kelly, History Department, Tulane University; Michael Mizell-Nelson, Assistant Professor of History, University of New Orleans; William J. Platt, Professor of Plant Biology at Louisiana State University; Michael Wex, Yiddish scholar; and James D. Wilson, Jr., Center for Louisiana Studies, University of Louisiana at Lafayette. Though we've never met, I thank you all.

Among the many texts I consulted in attempting to make this work as historically accurate as possible, I am particularly indebted to Herbert Asbury's *The French Quarter*; Elliott Ashkenazi's *The Business of Jews in Louisiana, 1840–1875* and *The Civil War Diaries of Clara Solomon*; Edward C. Bearss' and Willie H. Tunnard's *A Southern Record: The Story of the Third Louisiana Infantry, C.S.A.*; John Bailey's *The Lost German Slave Girl*; Bertram W. Korn's *American Jewry and the Civil War*; Irwin Lachoff's and Catherine C. Kahn's *The Jewish Community of New Orleans*; Francis Peyre Porcher's *Resources of the Southern Fields and Forests, Medical, Economical, and Agricultural*; Sally Kittredge Reeves' translation of Jacques-Felix Lelièvre's *Nouveau Jardinier de la Louisiane* (*New Louisiana Gardener*); Robert N. Rosen's *The Jewish Confederates*; John Stravinsky's compilation, *Read 'Em and Weep: A Bedside Poker Companion;* Louis Voss' "The System of Redemption in the State of Louisiana," *Louisiana Historical Quarterly*; Alan Wellikoff's *The Civil War Supply Catalogue*; and Bell Irvin Wiley's *The Life of Johnny Reb: The Common Soldier of the Confederacy*.

In Lucy Childs, my agent at the Aaron M. Priest Agency, I have a remarkable confidante and cornerman. The laughter, the wisdom, the resolve: every writer should be so fortunate. In Amy Scheibe, my editor at Counterpoint, I have been privileged with great insight and intelligence, a voice willing to foster my own for the benefit of collaborative effort. I owe Carol Smith, my project editor, and Beth Partin, my copy editor, thanks for their efforts as well. To David Steinberger, Jo Ann Miller, and John Sherer of the Perseus Books Group, I appreciate the opportunity you've granted me. You all have my sincere gratitude.

To the city of New Orleans, your resilience is historic. I thank and love you for it.

And finally, to Elena, my friend, my lover, my wife, for all the early mornings. It wasn't the necklace that caught my eye, dear, it was you.